120 Days

ROSE RICHARDS

120 Days

A Caged Soul. A Shackled Heart.
And an Hourglass.

Copyright © 2023 by Rose Richards

All rights reserved. No part of this publication may be reproduced, stored or transmitted in any form or by any means, electronic, mechanical, photocopying, recording, scanning, or otherwise without written permission from the publisher. It is illegal to copy this book, post it to a website, or distribute it by any other means without permission.
This novel is entirely a work of fiction. The names, characters and incidents portrayed in it are the work of the author's imagination. Any resemblance to actual persons, living or dead, events or localities is entirely coincidental. All brand names and product names used in this book and on its cover are trade names, service marks, trademarks, and registered trademarks of their respective owners. The publishers and the book are not associated with any product or vendor mentioned in this book. None of the companies referenced within the book have endorsed the book.

Line Edit: My Brother's Editor
Copy Edit: Andrew Ingles (A Taylor(ed) Edit)
Proofreading: My Brother's Editor
Formatting: My Brother's Editor
Cover Design: Murphy Rae

*For the twenty-year-old me whose imagination created this society.
We're finally sharing our world with others.*

"Once in your life, I truly believe, you find someone who can completely turn your world around." —Bob Marley

Prologue

SKYE

I remember the bliss of being in love, but the oblivion is why I steer clear. The power that four-letter word had over my life. My every decision altered to cater to its needs.

It is a drug that, once dosed, takes rehab to overcome.

I recollect the sentiment all too well, so instead, I remain focused on the love that keeps me striving—the love for my son, my family. Although that isn't parallel to the passion associated with intimacy, someday it *may* happen—just not yet. And if never, I'm not opposed to that either. I take pleasure in being in complete control of my life, moving per *my* terms.

As arrogant as that may sound, I'm content to live that way.

CHAPTER 1

Skye

Beep! Beep! Beep!

The piercing sound of my alarm rings through my ears, disturbing my peaceful sleep.

Beep! Beep! Beep!

Screw the office today. I'm not getting up. I bury my head deeper into the cloud comfort of my pillow and blindly stretch my arm to my nightstand and palm around for my phone, to no avail.

Beep! Beep! Beep!

Ugh, where is it? Now I'm forced to lift my head—it's on the farthest end, connected to the barely three-foot-long charger. I make a mental note to buy a longer cord. My first thought is to hit snooze, but with one look at the time, I think better of it. It's five a.m.

That's right. I'm not working today. Julias and my flight to Georgia is at eight.

The stupor that nearly held me captive quells and excitement brews. Suddenly, in a better mood to get moving, I rub the grogginess from my eyes and shoot up in bed.

I ready myself in record time but leave the mirror while wrapping my incredibly long curls in a bun and follow the delightful scent of coffee filling the air of my home. I hum at the first sip, and after downing the last drop, I'm grateful for the energy.

It's time to wake the dinosaur.

I head to Julias's room, mustering patience for the worst. There are not many things my four-year-old dislikes. However, the playful cub during the peak of the day becomes a raging T-Rex when their sleep is interrupted. I nudge him once, twice—after the third time, there's a hint of movement. "Juji, baby, it's time to wake up."

"Mm," he groans.

"Come on, little dinosaur, time to see Mawmaw and Pawpaw." I nudge him a bit harder, and he begins to whimper. *My poor Juji, he's so sleepy.* I attempt to lift him and fail when he curls his body, squealing. Taking a deep breath, I try again.

"No, Mommy, no!" he whines. His eyes are squeezed shut, *but he's awake,* and that's all the confirmation I need.

"Okay, well, bye-bye. I'm going to see Maw and Paw without you," I bait.

"Nooo!" he cries but hasn't moved.

"Okay, well, let's get ready, Juji. We're going to have so much fun."

And with that, he slowly rises. I prepare my adorable, frown-faced preschooler for our trip.

Tightening my grip on the luggage handle, I lead Julias in front, but then I catch a glimpse of my laptop bag and pause for a beat. *No. No work. Vacation with Grandma and Grandpa this week.* Without another thought, we head through the door.

Snow peppers the lawn, white fluff blankets my windshield; when the crisp air comes into contact with my skin, I move with urgency to get Juji strapped into the warmth of my car. Gray skies over a winter wonderland during the month of May are no unusual occurrence in Rochester, but where we're off to, balmy spells began two months ago.

With Julias secured in his car seat, I loaded our luggage in the trunk, but as I proceeded to the driver door of my white four-door Lexus ES, the thought that took no longer than a beat to push down pricks once again.

As if the device was calling my name from inside my home, demanding to vacation with me, I give in.

I run inside and grab the narrow pink bag with my career tucked inside, cursing its power over me. *You can come too, inconsiderate nuisance. You take up enough of my life as it is; vacation with me too, why don't you?*

After thirty minutes of driving, we arrived at the nearly empty airport. Juji grips the toy train he can never part with. And with my free hand, I hold his little fingers while we shuffle through security.

As we wait at our gate, Julias, already not very good at staying still, gets irritable—he hasn't eaten. And though I know Grandma's got something delicious waiting, the baby dinosaur can't wait.

I spot a Dunkin' a few feet away and grab him a quick meal, and by the time he's gobbled it up, we're being called to board.

We settle in our seats—Juji has the window—and at takeoff, when they announce we can connect to Wi-Fi, I pull out my phone, plug in my headphones, and start up episode 734 of *One Piece*.

Glued to my favorite anime, I don't know how much time has passed, but after the midpoint of another episode, I hear a barely audible announcement and glance at my watch to see an hour and twenty minutes have passed.

We must be preparing to land.

I take a deep breath and nudge a sleeping Juji. He's getting ready to fuss until he opens his eyes, glances around, and remembers we aren't home.

"Time to get off the plane, baby," I softly voice. When he lifts his head, I chuckle at the frown that's the spitting image of my older brother, Kumar.

His skin is as yellow as his father, but his features mirror his uncle. Whenever we're in public together, Julias gets mistaken for my brother's son instead of mine—and boy, does Kumar take pride in his nephew looking just like him.

I find it astounding, because while my brother has shared features between our parents, I am a carbon copy of my mother. And though he's always been overprotective, his teasing words—that I was adopted—were brutal for me when we were kids.

Love Atlanta. Hate their airport.

I grip Julias's hand, and we finally exit the congested Harts-field-Jackson, dodging people and their luggage on the way out. I immediately spot my grandfather's '12 Corolla.

"Hey!" he greets us as we approach.

"Pawpaw!" Julias takes off running in the direction of his great-grandfather. "*Yook* at my *twain*." He shows his toy train.

"Hey, Grandpa." I greet him with a hug as he pecks me on the cheek.

He takes the luggage to load in the trunk while I strap Julias in the car seat I had shipped down specifically for when we visit. After shutting the child-lock door, as I approach the passenger side, my peripheral vision catches a green sweater falling to the ground.

I glance in that direction; the man whose suitcase it fell from doesn't notice and is walking away.

"Hey, sir!" I call and lift the thin material. "You dropped this."

"*'Preciate you*, ma'am." He looks up and takes the sweater.

"No problem. And I'm not that old. I'm not a ma'am," I jest, aware ma'am is a common Southern term, and he's simply being polite.

"Oh. Sorry, ma'... uh."

I laugh. "It's okay. Have a good day."

He smiles before taking off.

"What was that about?" my grandfather asks when I settle into my seat.

"A guy dropped his sweater," I say. "You know, I've been visiting for years—every summer since you and Grandma moved here, and I'm still not accustomed to that *'preciate you* lingo. Seriously, what's wrong with simply saying *'thank you'* or *'I appreciate you?'* Just say it right."

He laughs. "Typical New Yorker. Bothered by everything that is *not* New York."

"Not true. *'Preciate you* is just cringe."

"Yes, ma'am."

"That too!" I declare, shooting up my index finger.

"See what I mean?"

Rolling my eyes, I chuckle. I've missed my grandpa.

"Mawmaw!" Julias charges toward my grandmother when she opens the front door. Grandpa and I unload the luggage before making our way down the flowery-line entryway of their ranch-style home in a peaceful neighborhood in Griffin, Georgia.

"Hi, Grandma." I stretch my free arm for a hug.

"My Starry! How are you?" She joyously addresses me by my childhood nickname.

"I'm good. Glad to be back. How are you?"

"Blessed, darling. Have you two eaten?"

No matter the time of day, once Grandma knows we're visiting, cooked food is prepared—*and we better be hungry*. That woman lives *in* the kitchen and *for* the kitchen.

"Julias has, but I am *starving*," I exaggerate. Though I'm not a breakfast person, I'm sure to be this week. Refusing any of my grandmother's authentic Guyanese cooking is criminal.

A gladdened smile stretches at her lips, and we move inside the home where I once spent every summer break since I was twelve until my high school graduation. Reminiscent of a time when life was simpler, those summers were the most memorable.

While forking a dumpling, my phone vibrates, and I roll my eyes at the sight of my boss's name.

Ignore it.

Excusing myself from the table, I proceed out the front door. Her call reminds me that my laptop still sits in the trunk of my grandfather's car. *Let it burn in there.*

"Hello, Cathy," I answer.

"Skye, where are you?" she asks with more authority than I appreciate. Of course, she somehow misses nothing on her calendar except my vacation.

"In Georgia, why?" I'm sure she notices my aloofness and willful ignorance, but she'll ignore it—business as usual.

"What do you mean, *why?* Did you inform me?" *You knew, Cathy. Now, what do you want?*

"Cathy, it's been on your calendar for six months."

"I need the Friday report." She diverts, not acknowledging my reminder.

"I'm on vacation. Amanda is handling the reports. We had a meeting about this."

"Well, she hasn't, and I need it. Do you have your laptop?" *Yep, saw this coming. Fine, you win, Cathy.*

"Give me ten minutes."

"Awesome, thanks!"

I proactively stayed in the office later than usual Thursday to complete the Friday report after sensing that this might happen. But Amanda didn't *fail* to send it. The workday has just begun, and Cathy is impatient. Her expectations are partly my doing. Promptness is my custom. I could have fibbed and told her I don't have my laptop, have her wait for Amanda, but I'm in no mood for contention. Ten minutes won't ruin the week.

I open my laptop, connect it to my mobile hotspot, and skim through the numbers one last time, double-checking whether the report needs updating. I compose a new email, attach the file, and send it to Cathy. The *sent* confirmation appears, and I shut the device. *Done.*

Another ring from work. I'm ignoring it. *Don't kid yourself. No, you won't.*

Before heading back inside, I lean on my grandfather's vehicle for a bit and take in the benign weather, basking in the warm air while the soft, refreshing breeze sways the scent of freshly cut grass. Only an hour and twenty minutes travel in the sky, and the climate differs drastically.

My attention shifts to the sound of an oncoming motor. Rounding the corner is a delivery truck. It halts in front of my grandparents' yard.

A man in a blue uniform descends from the vehicle holding a small package.

"Sarju residence?" I ask.

"Yes." He hands me the box, then pulls a small electronic device resembling a phone from his back pocket. "Just need you to sign right here."

"*'Preciate you, ma'am,*" he says after I sign.

My "welcome" is a slight upturn of my lips before turning around and retreating into the home.

I am seriously never going to get used to that.

CHAPTER 2

Skye

"Call on line one," Amanda informs me.

After a rejuvenating vacation, it's back to business.

"This is Skye," I answer the call on hold.

"Skye?" *You have got to be kidding me.* Why the hell is he calling my work?

"Jason, I'm at work. What do you want?" I ask discourteously.

"C'mon, why are you ignoring me? I've tried your phone over and over."

Then stop trying, idiot.

"I took Julias to see his great-grandparents. Ignoring you was part of the vacation. Again, what do you want?" Growing impatient with every passing second on the phone with him, I make it a point to express annoyance.

"I want to talk to you about the other night. Look, I'm sorry."

"I don't care, as long as it doesn't happen again." And if so, I'll call the police to escort his wasted ass off my property.

"Are you ever going to forgive me, Skye? I'm not the same man I was back then. At least try with me." *Try what? Dude, go drop in a ditch.*

"Jason, I'm at work. I have to go." I attempt to end this conversation.

"Now that you've got your golden career, you think you're high and mighty. Well, I don't care. I want to see my son!" he barks.

"Are you drunk?"

"No." But he is. That's the only time he seems to remember he has a son.

"Don't call my work anymore." I tighten my grip on the phone before hanging up on the biggest mistake of my life.

A toxic narcissist with an alcohol problem, my son's biological father, Jason Pagan, has never actually cared to spend time with him and instead uses him to summon my presence.

Once, yielding to his manipulation, I let him spend a day with Julias, only to arrive at his apartment to see my son being watched by a piss-drunk Jason.

As if that situation never happened, he continues to pester me about *us* when he's sober, but my suggesting he become a better man for his son, then it's crickets for weeks—followed by random drunk phone calls protesting to see the son who has no clue he's his father.

Whose fault is that? Certainly not mine.

"I need the profits and loss statement for the Rockwell account by eight a.m. tomorrow," Cathy mentions in passing, as if her demand were a simple task.

"Eight a.m.?" I gripe, needing her to reconsider the request. "Cathy, it's already four; there's not enough time. There's no way I could ask my team to do that." *Is she serious?*

"Excuses are for amateurs, Skye." She leaves my office in cold confidence.

Unease swirls in my stomach at the thought of piling this on the tasks I've already assigned my team.

It's unethical.

Pushing down the fermented feelings, I decide I'll do what I do best: make it work. I pick up the phone to call my mother.

"Hello," she answers.

"Hey, Ma, can you keep Julias tonight? I'll pick him up in the morning."

"Yes, of course. Is everything okay?" Concern in her voice.

"Yes. I had a last-minute project come up at work."

"Okay, well, make sure you get some rest. Julias will be fine."

"Thanks, Mom." With that, I prepare to work an extra seven hours at the office to meet tomorrow morning's deadline.

"I knew you'd make it happen! Thank you," Cathy praises me. "Why do you think I made you head of the department?"

I barely slept, but the job's done. Though I appreciate Cathy's acknowledgment, my exhaustion begs to differ.

My morning regime is to take Julias to daycare, go for a morning run, and marinate in a cup of coffee. In this order, I mentally prepare myself to take on the day. While I don't appreciate being thrown off my routine, I push the resentment down by reminding myself this is my career, the field I've excelled in. At twenty-eight, I'm the head of the finance department. I strived for this position. Reproof subsides after I consider my every reason to be proud. A few late nights won't change that. When Friday rolls around, I put in a half day to start my weekend early. It's a perk I have enjoyed since my promotion: working as needed, on my own schedule, from either the walls of my office or the comfort of my home—as long as I remain disciplined.

And I always am.

Less than a ten-minute drive further past my neighborhood is my parents' home. It was never purposeful that I moved near them. I was born in Rochester and grew up in the small town of Webster just outside the city, and I never wanted to leave.

Some might say I never actually left the nest, unlike my

brother, who moved six hours away. And speaking of the devil, parked in the driveway is his dark blue, souped-up Subaru WRX —Kumar's pride and joy that he named *Thunder*. And it's clear as day where all his money goes.

Notorious for surprise visits, I can never plan for his arrival. However, his visits never fail to lighten my mood. As I move through the brick-lined path leading to the front door, I can only hope I've missed the lecture about saving money.

"Kumar, you better be saving," my mother says every. Single. Time. And though it's directed at him, somehow I always end up involved.

An electrician downstate with our uncle at NYC Transit, Kumar also educated himself in trade and investing, which he utilized as another income stream. Now, he resides in a lavish condo in a Manhattan high-rise, and though responsible as an adult, his adolescent years sparked worry.

As a teen running with the wrong crowd, our father received at least one phone call a week that Kumar skipped school or got into an altercation. My poor mother, for the life of her, could not ascertain the cause of his acting out. As far as I know, we're born of the most loving household on the planet.

But I assume that was the actual problem.

My father, as fun-loving as he is, is as tough as nails, dishing out the discipline fair and square; his word was law. However, our mother can be smothering. We're aware it's simply how she shows her affection, but my theory is Kumar rebelled against the smothering and, upon introspection, considered himself weak for actually *liking* it.

Nonetheless, the troublesome teen grew into a man who has made his parents feel honored and proud.

Besides running off at the Rochester Lilac Festival one year— worrying my mother half to death—the worst I've ever done was steal a doll. My father drove me back to apologize to the store's manager, and the next day, my doting parents arrived home with the same doll.

"The money walks through the door!" Kumar greets me when I enter.

"Kumar! I've missed you." I reach for a hug, and when he wraps his arm around me, I almost feel swallowed. Taking a step back, I scrutinize him. "You've been working out?"

"Oh yeah, been hitting the gym lately," he brags, flexing his arms. He's four years my senior and a shade darker than me, with corkscrew curls kept in a low ponytail. The once tall and slender, Kumar is now athletically built with defined biceps. *Who does he think he is?*

"Relax, you still look like a beaver." I roll my eyes, refusing to indulge his ever-growing ego.

"So, if x equals ten to the fifth power and the equation is..."

"Shut up," I cut him off.

"And you're still an accounting major that can't do math," he quips.

He's convinced I should be able to do full algebraic equations in my head because of my degree. *God, he's annoying.*

I hear Julias in the back yard playing the role of a train conductor as his grandfather gratifies him by acting as a passenger, and I take the opportunity to plop down on the brown embroidered living room sofa and kick up my feet.

"So, how's the concrete jungle treating you?" I ask.

"Life's good. What's it like being the boss?"

"Ugh. Nothing special." I throw my head back. "Just a bigger boss to answer to."

He smirks. "It pays, but it slays, sis. Come on, let's take a ride."

I don't refuse, I never do. When we shout from the living room that we'll be back in a few, our mother's voice echoes from upstairs: "Kumar, no speeding!" We chuckle as we head through the door.

As I take my seat, the leather cools my skin. When the ignition fires up, his swift takeoff makes the turbo spool, and inertia pushes my back flush to the seat. *I feel a rush.* The kick-up speed makes the engine roar; I'm sure the entire neighborhood knows when Kumar's in town. This is one of my favorite parts about his visits, joyrides across town in Thunder, his dark blue monster.

After a long week, a night on the town with my big brother is well-needed.

CHAPTER 3

Skye

"Is the finance statement prepared for the merger?" Cathy steps into my office. *Why doesn't she ever knock?*

"I need another day to finish that." My eyes never leave my current task.

"Another day?" she questions as if I'm asking the impossible. "I gave you two weeks to work on that."

My attention breaks from the computer, and my eyes dart to where she stands in my doorway. "It's not due for two days. My team has already completed it, but I will not get a moment to review it until tomorrow."

She places a hand on her hip. "You and your excuses, Skye." *Is she serious right now?*

"Excuses? You've given me four last-minute projects in one week. I have a life, you know." I reality-check her.

"Is this position too much for you? If so, I understand. We can consider other options. Last-minute projects come with the territory. I was once in your shoes—and it's no easier in mine."

I'm not falling for that. She knows how serious I am regarding my career. It's damn shameful that she had the audacity to hold it over my head.

"Cathy, just give me a day. I'll have it for you by tomorrow morning." I find no point in arguing. If I spend the extra hours finishing it tonight, there will be one less thing on my plate tomorrow.

"Eight a.m. sharp," she stipulates and leaves my office. I can visualize the swish of her hips and the sway of her arms with each click of her heel as she struts down the hall.

Cathy has admirable confidence, but I wonder if her cold sophistication derives from her lack of compassion. She smiles, but it lacks sincerity. I know nothing of her personal affairs, but I'm curious to know if she lives a loveless life.

I spend an extra hour at the office, only breaking away to pick up Julias and care for his needs, then work from home for another six hours before I finally shut my laptop.

I was unwilling to ask my mother to keep Julias, so I brought work home tonight. She'd begin to concern herself with my working extra hours, and then I'd have to listen to lectures about stress and mental health. To avoid such a conversation, I kept the same routine she knows.

I gaze at my precious boy while he peacefully sleeps. Warmth washes over me, and I smile in endearment. Some days are more complex than others, but it doesn't stunt the feelings of pleasure when I remind myself of the life I've been able to provide for him —and myself.

A future of stability, for which the reward will be far greater.

I recall praying for all I have now—a *homeowner before the age of thirty.*

My support system crosses my mind. My family, born into poverty, strived to provide a different life for their children, and to their gratification, we've grown to make them proud.

"Yeah, we may be exhausted today, and there may be more

exhausted days to come, but to achieve fulfillment and be surrounded by love—life is good," I whisper my thoughts before cuddling my Juji and drifting into slumber.

CHAPTER 4

Skye

"Remember when you dropped your bracelet and ended up lost trying to find it?" My mother recalls. A memory that I couldn't forget if I wanted, because she'll never allow it. She asks if I remember this incident every year we visit the Rochester Lilac Festival.

"Mom, how could I forget?" I ask drearily. "The only thing I can't remember is the face of the woman you claim is the *angel* that helped me."

"She was! God had his hands on you that day. He placed her right in your path. People kidnap children, especially little girls. The woman separated from her family, unwilling to leave your side, until we were reunited. God bless her."

"I'll hand her my soul if I ever see her again, Mom," I say with bleak sarcasm. "That's if I even recognize her."

My mother can be sizably dramatic. I mean, I get it—it was a scary day for her. I was eight years old; my memory of that day is vague, but I'm empathetic from a maternal standpoint.

"Don't be ridiculous," she protests. "I'm surprised to see you wearing the bracelet again. Where did you find it?"

"My old jewelry box," I recall. "I had forgotten about it, but at first sight, I remembered why I stopped wearing it."

Funny how that works. Irretrievable memories are sparked by a sudden sight or scent, then the forgotten flow in vividly as if they never faded.

Looking down at the pink butterfly bracelet Grandma made for me when I was eight years old, I was in love with this thing and fought the urge to continue wearing it in fear of losing it.

"I put it away because it kept slipping off my wrist at the time. I remember telling myself I wouldn't wear it until I got older. Now, I can't seem to part with it." I chuckle at the sentiment of my twenty-eight-year-old self, fulfilling the wishes of an eight-year-old me.

"Well, I know Mom was happy to see you wearing it." She's referring to my grandmother.

The sight of shrubs, clear of people, catches my attention. "Mom, let's go take pictures over there," I suggest.

She nods, and we motion through the grass, phones in hand, prepared to take photos near the flowers, which added radiant colors to the otherwise monochromatic greenery throughout Highland Park. When the colorful shrubs sprout after spring showers, they're beautiful. And today, with sunny and clear skies, it's a pleasant afternoon to spend outdoors with my mother during our favorite time of year—when the lilacs blossom.

CHAPTER 5

Skye

This is the sort of smooth week I appreciate most, with no last-minute projects or analytics. However, even when things seem overbearing, I've got my weekends ahead.

Most weekends I simply stay in, read, watch anime, or live vicariously through online travel bloggers. This is part of my rejuvenation. I'll stay in unless required to go out or something of interest surfaces.

Some might say I've become introverted, but that's not true. The friends I frequently spent time with still exist, but I've shelved outings and pivoted my life around my studies and then my career.

My priorities changed, and the decision to decline invitations proved well worth it.

Speaking of friends, my best friend Chrissy's name lights up my screen as the vibration of my phone shakes the pens on my desk.

"Hey, lady," I say, bringing a wireless earbud to my ear.

"Skye, where have you been?"

"Working. I went to the Lilac Festival last weekend. Have you gone yet?"

"No, it was my plan to go this weekend. I called to ask if you'd like to come, but never mind since I never got an invite."

"Relax, I went with my mom. Y'know, *like I do every year,*" I remind her.

"Oh right, your only friend is your mom now."

"Shut up. You forgot about my brother," I add to her sarcasm.

"Is Kumar in town?" she asks casually. However, from her mouth, it's anything but casual. She's been practically in love with him for the last twelve years, but when she hinted at her feelings to him five years ago, he wasn't interested. To this day, as we're nearing thirty, she believes there's still a chance, and there may be, but I want no part in it. So I lie. "No."

"Liar!" *I'm a terrible liar.* "You're a cockblocker."

"Um, ew." It wouldn't be so 'ew,' if the *cockblocking* she was referring to wasn't regarding my brother.

"He rejected me once anyway; I won't give him the opportunity to do it again." *Good.* "And when was the last time you dated? Do you even get out and meet people?"

"I was in Georgia two weeks ago."

"And what? Hung out with Gram and Gramps?" she taunts.

"Oh hush, they're fun. I've missed them."

"No, you need a man. Have you *ever* dated since Jason?"

"Yes. Well, no, but it's for good reason. A relationship doesn't exactly fit into my life." *Wait, did she just say I need a man?* The feminist in me wants to challenge that claim, but I decide to ignore it.

"Nothing fits into your life, Skye," she sighs, and her comment stings. She isn't talking about a man; she's referring to us. Chrissy and I once did everything together, but that changed when I decided to buckle down.

The problem is, I'm still buckled down. I unintentionally transformed it into a lifestyle.

"Let's go out this weekend," she offers.

I consider it. "How about the following one? My last few weekends have been quite eventful, I need this one to be in."

"You do that every weekend!" she retorts.

"Except for the last four."

"Fine," she acquiesces. "But I'm not taking no for an answer, so don't try backing out."

"Fine," I agree, and the call ends.

I truly enjoy solitude, and after the last few weekends, I long for my tranquility.

"Skye, see you Monday. Remember the meeting on Monday at nine. We're taking on a new account. We need to show them they need us," Cathy reminds me as she glides past my office on her way out.

"Haven't forgotten," I assure her. *I totally forgot.*

"Hey, Amanda," I call. "What do we know about this new account?"

"That they have too many accounts," she murmurs, clearly displeased that we're attempting to do business with them.

"Send me all the information you have. I'll put something together this weekend," I request.

She acknowledges. I am gathering my belongings and preparing to leave for the day when I realize what I just proclaimed.

Did I just mindlessly decide to do work this weekend?

Pushing down any second thoughts, I prioritize what's needed. In Cathy's defense, she *did* mention it to me weeks prior. I've just been preoccupied. *With what? Just more work, idiot.* No, it's my time management. I'll pull it together.

Meeting successful. Though I'm pleased we won the business, I couldn't be happier that it's over. The insight I offered the marketing team aligned with the new company's goals and managed to persuade them, and a delighted Cathy treated me to lunch after our success. I always dread the extra work I require myself to put forth, but evermore am I proven that my efforts never go unrewarded.

Thursday rolls around, and as I look forward to enjoying two days of unbothered peace, my phone vibrates with Chrissy's name lit on the screen.

Damn, that slipped from my mind in the worst way.

"Hey, Chrissy," I answer with nervous excitement.

"You're about to cancel, aren't you?" *Make me feel like a terrible individual, why don't you?*

"Why would you think that?" I ask, hoping I've hidden my guilt well.

"Because of the way you answered. How long have I known you, Skye?" *Damn.*

"Okay, listen," I plead my case. "I ended up having to catch up on some work last weekend. Plus, I had Julias..."

"Skye, make Jason step up to the plate," she interrupts. "You work and be a mom while he gets the privilege of doing what he wants. That's unfair."

Her mention of Jason makes me cringe. "I don't give a damn what Jason does. I don't need him, nor does Julias."

"That's still his father. You shouldn't be the bearer of all burdens," she cautiously advises. And although I understand what *she's saying*, I don't think she's grasping what *I'm telling her*.

"Look, I'm not. Where Jason lacks, Julias's grandparents have sufficed. My father is more of a dad to Juji than Jason has ever been. Why do you think I haven't filed for child support? I can support Julias without him, *as I have been*. He might as well give up his rights. He's proven himself unfit; it's evident he gives not one damn about his son."

"That's too far, Skye. He can still change."

"Well, I'm not holding my breath."

"Okay, girl," she sighs, ending this topic, which I appreciate. "You've got this. You're established. I understand. I was only concerned about your well-being."

"Girl, I am *more* than good," I sass.

"Tap your crown, queen." She feeds my ego.

"Let me adjust it. Chatters of peasants may have caused it to tilt."

She laughs, and the tension dissipates. As much as I'd like to stay home this weekend, I virtually promised I'd spend time with her. The sound of disappointment in her tone when she assumed correctly weighed in my chest, so I alter my decision and tell her, "I'll come out with you this weekend, Chrissy."

"Really?"

"Yep."

We set the day for Saturday at noon before ending the call. After another hour at the office, I gather my things, jump in my car, and head to Twelve Corners. My stomach is asking for something other than my usual cobb salads.

"One slice of cheese, please," I order.

"Right up, miss," the employee behind the counter assures me.

I thank him, move to an open seat, and wait. Slightly turning my head, I glimpse a couple holding hands, and my mind recalls Chrissy mentioning I hadn't dated since Jason.

I remember the bliss of being in love, but the oblivion is why I steer clear. The power that four-letter word had over my life. My every decision altered to cater to its needs.

It is a drug that, once dosed, takes rehab to overcome.

I recollect the sentiment all too well, so instead, I remain focused on the love that keeps me striving—the love for my son, my family. Although that isn't parallel to the passion associated with intimacy, someday it *may* happen—just not yet. And if never, I'm not opposed to that either. I take pleasure in being in complete control of my life, moving per *my* terms.

As arrogant as that may sound, I'm content to live that way.

"I'll see you all Monday," I tell my team and prepare to leave the office. Caught up on all work-related matters, I've decided to leave at 2 p.m. It's Friday, and I couldn't be happier to begin my weekend. With Julias in my mother's care this evening, I'm not rushing to fetch him. So, as I push through my front door, I don't hesitate to change into something comfortable before pouring a glass of wine.

The first sip of sweet red livens my taste buds, and I exhale in relief as the week's tension loosens its grip on me. Connecting my phone to the charger, I set the alarm to pick up Julias by six before laying atop my pink satin comforter and sinking into its solace. I grab hold of the remote and power on my mounted fifty-inch television to find the current anime, which serves as my mental escape.

Relaxation washes over me, the week's stress takes its toll, and I grow weary. *One Piece* continues, and I become lost in the show, admiring Luffy, the protagonist. *I wish I could be like you, Luffy, and explore the world.*

I'm tranquil as my thoughts transform into a lucid daydream, commencing a fantasy of being careless and free. I'm *here* in the comfort of my bed, but I'm *not* here—I am somewhere else, *somewhere far*—somewhere where I'm *ultimately liberated.*

Closing my eyes, I dive into the abyss, allowing the serenity to consume me. The salted smell of the sea, the cool breeze on my skin, a place different from anywhere I've ever known—and I'm calm.

The echoes of *One Piece* in the background grow distant as I sink deeper into my world. I slowly part my droopy eyelids, and the colors flash on the screen, however, my being has traveled to another realm. My eyes become hooded, growing heavy under the languid feelings engulfing me. I plan to remain here until my alarm sounds. No longer seeing what's in my room, I gaze at where my mind has traveled. Clear skies, calm seas, open land in the distance, and *I'm free*. My eyes finally close, and I shed forms to a *new me*. I fall into the depths of my fantasy as it lulls me to snooze and follows me into my dreams.

CHAPTER 6

Skye

I am awoken from my nap, but not by my alarm. I'm being gently rocked, and the rigid surface under my skin isn't my bed. Fighting the sleep that begs me to return, my weak limbs evoke exertion past my physical limit. Slowly blinking, everything is a blur. I have no sense of what's ahead, but wherever I am, *it's not my home*.

That scent. Sea water. *That sound.* Wood creaking. *Am I dreaming?* If so, it feels more real than any dream I've ever had. I blink rapidly, determined to clear my vision—I need to see where I am.

A white flag sways above—no, it's a sail. *I'm on a boat?*

A full moon and dots of stars spread across the darkened heavens. The wooden surface, enclosed at the sides, rocks as it moves forward, and I sit upright to peer overboard at the sight of the blackened sea under gloomy skies. I notice I am wearing the same attire I changed into after work, and trepidation creeps in at the thought that this isn't a dream.

Relying on the wooden edge of the small sailboat for support, I drag myself to stand and make my way ahead, hoping to find someone. A salt-and-pepper-haired man wearing a white uniform is steering the boat. I call out, "Hello?" No response, not even a flinch. I move closer to the strange man's presence, fighting the angst threatening to send me into panic. My heart races as I draw near. I walk along the edge until I'm as close as my wits will allow and call again in question. "Hello?"

"Oh," he says, startled. "Hello. My name is Sylvester. We will arrive at your destination shortly." Greeting me with a cheeky smile, he looks to be harmless, but my apprehension does not waver.

"Is this a dream?" I ask.

"Oh, no. This is very real," Sylvester replies. "Please make yourself comfortable."

What does he mean, "This is very real?"

My chest heaves and panic takes hold of me. Uncertain of what's happening, I'm scared with nowhere to run. *Have I been kidnapped?*

"No! I have to go home!" I shout. "Where am I?"

His smile disappears, replaced with an expression of sympathy, but I don't care.

"Who are you?" I yell.

Instead of responding, he turns his head forward, and I follow his line of sight to see we're nearing land. "Our destination is near, Lady Skye, please be patient," he instructs me. "You are aboard my transport, and my name is Sylvester."

He knows my name?

I can barely pinpoint where we are. My vision isn't doing well, and I feel depleted. Sylvester exits the boat, gesturing for me to follow, but I refuse.

"You will not be able to remain aboard my transport," he says.

"Well, I'm not going anywhere until you tell me where we are!" I snap.

"Those of this world call this Land Sandemia."

He aligns his posture, and a smile plays on his lips. *Why the hell is he smiling? And what does he mean, "This world?"* This is sick.

"*Trust him,*" something, or *someone,* whispers. Startled, I look around to see no one. However, *that voice* sounded *familiar.*

As if he heard the whisper, he says, "Please, listen. Trust me."

And instantly, my feet become wet. I glance down at my socks, and the boat dissolves into the air where I stand. However, the vessel *isn't* dissolving—*I'm sinking through it.* I break for the shore.

"What was that?" I ask.

"You are unable to stay aboard the transport," he reiterates. "Please follow me. You do not have much time." He begins to walk, and with no other choice, I follow.

"Have much time? Time for what?"

"You have exerted much energy, Lady Skye. If you continue, you will deplete where you stand."

I stop and glance back at the boat, reading the letters spelled at the front with green and blue stripes: *Livity.* I sob where I stand, unable to take any of this much longer. I'm more exhausted than I've ever felt in my entire life. Angst consumes me. "Please, tell me something," I beg.

"Please do not weep," he says sympathetically. "I am only here to fulfill my duty. Please come along."

He continues moving forward, and I can no longer resist the urge to follow. He's right, I'm physically weakening by the minute. My legs cry out in agony; walking much further entails their death sentence. A small home surrounded by neatly-shaved grass awaits our entry, and identical homes line both sides of the dark road.

"Please make this one your home," he encourages and opens the door.

I step inside. There's not a shred of light in sight. I'm fear-stricken, but my body refuses to produce the adrenaline needed to take flight. I turn back to Sylvester, who nods in my direction. His hand is curled over the doorknob, preparing to retreat.

"Wait," I softly urge. It's all the energy I have left. "What did you mean when you said to fulfill *your* duty? Duty to whom?"

"Why, my duty to you, Lady Skye." He smiles and closes the door.

To me?

Reaching for the door as quickly as it shuts, I swing it open to see no one. *He's gone.* Sylvester is gone. I take one step onto the wooden porch and look around, but he's nowhere—as if he *vanished.*

My knees buckle before I can take another step. *No.* I grab hold of the knob to support my weight; I can no longer stand on my own. I make it inside, shut the door behind me, lean my back against it, and slide to the floor. *That's it. I'm done for.* Drained past any limit, my legs can no longer carry me. My eyes droop, and my body cries for rest.

I collapse on my side and begin to drift into unconsciousness. But just before the blank, I come to realize that the whispering voice encouraging me to trust Sylvester was none other than *my own.*

CHAPTER 7

Skye

My eyelids lazily part as I gradually withdraw from a state of slumber. My curly hair filters my view, but past the thick strands, sunlight shines through into the room.

Sitting up, I lean on one arm and use the other to rake my hair from my face. Shiny hardwood covers the flooring; to my left sits a round espresso table with three wooden chairs placed against horizontal blinds hanging from a window. To my right, a violet decorative rug lay neatly under a dark wooden coffee table, surrounded by a three-piece gray sofa set. Rays of sun brighten the small living area from a window identical to the one near the dining room. Bolted to the wall is a bookshelf, abandoned by books. Separating the two sites is where I sit, staring down a hallway leading to, presumably, bedrooms, and I can't help but wonder if this is someone's home.

A vintage breakfast bar curves, ending at an opening to enter. Seated on the ground, I have no visual, but it obviously entails a kitchen. Before moving another muscle, I lean back against the door, recalling the events from the blurry night before.

In bed watching One Piece. Wakes up on a boat. There's a man. Yes, that's right, Sylvester. It was dark, nighttime. The voice, "Trust him." My voice. I still don't know how that was possible. He said he was fulfilling his duty to me. What does that even mean? I was exhausted, drained, unlike any level of wear I've ever felt in my entire life. He said to make this my home. What?

The memory of last night returns like a flood, and at the sudden pulse of pain, I rub my throbbing temple with two fingers. Besides the ache in my neck from sleeping on the sturdy surface, I feel recovered—at least as compared to last night's frazzle.

My bladder gives me the nudge I need to ascend from the floor, and I move down the hall to find a bathroom.

It's the first door.

In search of a light switch, my fingers find a button and apply pressure. Warm lighting brightens blue tiles, and the tight space barely holds room for anything more than the three appliances that make up a full bathroom.

I splash my face and rinse my mouth to refresh before glancing at myself in the mirror. I look normal—*I guess. Where is my hair tie?* I feel around my hair until the pad of my finger finds the elastic hanging onto a single strand for dear life. I begin to bring my hip-length curls into a bun but think better of it. There's something akin to security I feel when my hair is down in its natural state—as if my tresses allow me to hide.

I pivot and continue down the hall and see two furnished bedrooms with double windows and burgundy carpeting. They each have but one nightstand to accompany the bed frame. My symmetrical obsession declares these rooms ruined without the complete set. I open both closets to see they're empty. I assume this house is vacant, but if so, why is it furnished?

"Make this home yours." I recall the words of the strange man. *Was this home prepared for my arrival?*

I peek through the blinds of the larger bedroom's window, an expanse of freshly cut lawn extends from the back yard. Further in the distance is a wide range of sea. I don't see much else, so I move toward the front of the house to peep through the blinds over-seeing the curtilage.

People relax in the nearby front yards, and small children are playing. The sight of cheerful youths eases my tension—this place seems to be a neighborhood. *But where?*

Working up the courage to visit outside, I step onto the wooden veranda and then down the three stairs that lead to a walkway extending to a mailbox. I realize the home I'm in is the last one at the end.

A middle-aged woman pulling weeds from a garden in the yard across from mine waves, smiling at me. I return the gesture. It's instinctive, rather than sincere. Atop a ladder of the adjacent house is the back of a blond-haired man, who appears to be fixing a gutter.

I walk closer to the mailbox for a better view and notice no cars, driveways, or garages attached to any of the homes, yet the neighborhood gives off a suburban feel. The road bears no trace of tire tracks, and it's not concrete or asphalt but flattened red dirt, smoothed and neatly condensed—the most leveled dirt road I've ever seen.

A scream in the distance shifts my focus, and I abruptly whip my head only to witness riled-up small children playing. A boy appearing to be no older than six and a small toddler girl run around a water sprinkler while their parents, comfortably settled in lawn chairs, watch them.

Julias. My son. I don't know where I am or why I'm here, but if there's anything I must find out, it's *how to get back.*

"Goods, everyone!" a man calls, and my focus shifts. "Fresh goods from the market!"

Descending the road is an older man pushing a wheelbarrow. As he calls, people leave their homes and scurry through their yards toward him. Taking food items from the wheelbarrow, they thank the man, and he nods in welcome as he continues in my direction. Emerging from the adjacent home is a fair-skinned woman that looks to be somewhere in her midtwenties, lissome, and no taller than my five-foot-three. Coarse red tresses pulled into a loose ponytail fall down her back and sway as she saunters through the lawn.

"Thank you, Mr. Alton." She smiles and grabs a bag of apples.

"You are welcome, dear," he replies.

She turns back toward her home, but at the sight of me, she stops and tilts her head, looking in curiosity—*and I'm just staring. Great. Creep.*

Mr. Alton approaches. "Hello there. Welcome to the Haven Downs neighborhood. My name is Alton Windsor. Might I know yours?"

He's polite. Pausing, I stare before finally responding. "Uh, Skye Cooke?" I'm not sure why it comes out as a question. I'm nervous—I have questions—but for some reason, I'm afraid to ask. The environment is welcoming; instead of feeling like I'm in a strange place, I think the strange one is me.

I take a quick glance toward the red-haired woman. She remains in the same position, *staring* at me. *Okay, now who's the creep?*

"Well, welcome, Ms. Skye. I assure you that you will enjoy this area. Care for any consumables?" he asks. The wheelbarrow holds oranges, apples, raw salmon, onions, peppers, deshelled bags of frozen shrimp, bread, eggs, and butter. *Did he buy all of this? This is a lot of money's worth of stuff.*

"I'm sorry, Mr. Alton, but I don't have any money to give you for any of this," I admit. His broad smile retracts to a slight grin. As he looks down at the things in the wheelbarrow, even that slightest upturn eventually disappears. His lips protrude with the scrunch of his chin, seemingly in thought, but his expression is unreadable.

When he lifts his head back to me, the smile returns—*strange, much?* "I'm sorry, I was trying to recall if I'd ever heard of such an item called *money*. I will have to inquire about it on my next round to the market. However, there is plenty of food, so please help yourself," he offers.

I squint in confusion. *That can't be right.* But, considering the empty fridge, along with my stomach, I grab a few things and then thank him. He slightly bows, but before he walks off, I ask another question. "Sir, what is today?"

"Day 192 of 2023," he responds.

"What?" I regret the bewildered response as it leaves my lips. If I want to find answers, I have an inkling that I need to blend in here—not stand out.

He pushes the wheelbarrow away, toward the home across from mine, where the lady gardens. She stands and gives him a peck on the lips, and he parks the wheelbarrow on their front porch. Before entering the home, he projects his voice just enough for me to hear, "Welcome to Land Sandemia, Ms. Skye Cooke."

CHAPTER 8

Skye

"Hi, I'm Mauria," the red-haired woman introduces herself. "So, you're new here? My husband, Sam, and I are too. We moved here about twenty days ago." She's speaking, but I'm only listening partially, admiring how absolutely stunning she is. "We were voyagers when we married, and about a year ago we discovered Sandemia. When we were ready to settle down, this land seemed like a perfect fit, so we came back to stay. What brought you here?"

I stumble over my words. "Uh, I... I don't remember. And I'm Skye."

"Here, let me help you get those things inside," she offers, after giving me a quizzical look.

"Um. Okay." I accept nervously, looking down at the items hugged to my chest.

We go into the home that is, apparently, mine, and she begins putting things away.

"Did you come here with nothing?" She examines my empty fridge.

"Sort of," I reply. "Well, actually, yes. Nothing but the clothes I'm wearing."

"Well, you came here, right? So where did you come from?" Her questions resume.

Earth. "New York."

She taps her chin. "I've never heard of a Land New York, what waters is that in?"

Waters? What in the name of Mother Mary is she talking about?

Unsure of how to answer, but intent on gaining knowledge without appearing clueless, I conjure a lie that would excuse any reason to question my sanity. "Look, Mauria, right? I don't know how or why I'm here. I was hospitalized after hitting my head pretty badly. It caused amnesia, but I still have some memory issues. I arrived here on a boat. That's all I remember."

Placing a hand to her chest, she gives me a look of sympathy. "I'm so sorry. I'll help you in any way I can." Her eyebrows pull together in a frown. "But, what's hos-pi-ta, whatever that is?"

You have got to be kidding me. "Um, like, where... you go to see a professional for medical attention?" I want to say doctor, but if she asks what a doctor is, I might look like the insane person I'm trying not to be.

She laughs. "Oh, you mean the healers and the healing sanctuaries. Some of them are called care centers. Well, you should probably visit again. They're pretty adamant about full recoveries before release."

Healing what? Wait a minute, did I die? "Um, yeah. That." I nervously agree. Taking an apple from the bag, I rinse it under water before taking a bite. Closing my eyes, I savor the sweet taste, not realizing the extent of my hunger until my taste buds frenzy. "This is delicious."

"So," Mauria begins, "any memory of the boat's description?"

"It had green and blue stripes. The letters engraved spelled *Livity.* And the captain, Sylvester, escorted me here, implying this was my home."

She leans on the counter. "Hmm," she sounds in thought.

"I've never heard of a Livity. Sam and I have traveled to almost every land. I'm not familiar with that line."

Of course, even to a voyager, my situation is strange. Her response stings, and I sigh in defeat. Coming in closer, she rests a palm on my shoulder. "Hey, don't look so down. We'll figure this out."

We?

"You don't have much here. Come on over. Let's eat, and tomorrow we'll pick up some things for your home. We'll even stop at the Media Center and look through some of the books. I'm sure we'll find something."

I don't know why she's willing to help me—I'm a stranger—I could be a nutcase for all she knows. However, there's a sincere benevolence in her aura, as if such thoughts haven't crossed her mind.

A man wheeling around free groceries for the block, and now a supportive Mauria. These people only met me minutes ago. *Is everyone here this nice?*

But, suddenly feeling a bit of hope, I smile. "Thank you, Mauria."

I'm introduced to the tall, blue-eyed blond man I witnessed atop the ladder. He's Mauria's husband, Sam. Mauria explains that she decorated their home herself, and the conspicuous orange of every miscellaneous element hints at her favorite color.

I notice the absence of commonly used electronics. Not a phone, radio, or television in sight, but an outdated CD/cassette player plays music in the living area. To inquire about the lack of electronics, I take an indirect approach. "So, what do you do for entertainment?"

"I read most of the day if I'm not finding ways to redecorate, but I'm currently trying to learn gardening. I browse through the daily Daycomm to see if there are any upcoming events or plays. Those are fun to attend."

"Daycomm?" I ask curiously.

She places a covered baking dish in the oven, sets a timer, opens a drawer, and pulls out what looks similar to a newspaper. "These are the daily communication papers. One is delivered every morning. It holds information regarding shop hours, new openings, news, events, and help wanted. I look out for help wanted, most of the time. If you're up early enough, you'll see someone riding by on a cycle, placing it in your mailbox."

So, it's a newspaper. "Can I see that?"

She hands it to me, and I skim through it. The date at the top reads: DAY 192 OF 2023. *So, their calendar only goes by day and year here? No months or weeks?*

I'm having a hard time wrapping my head around all of this, but the scent of whatever Mauria has cooking in that oven chimes my hunger, and for the first time ever, I actually finished a full plate of food.

Energy regained, I feel back to my normal self again. I don't know how much time has passed, but I've been absorbing all of Mauria's forthcoming information—from details that may hint where on Earth I could be to insignificant things.

Without asking direct questions, I decipher through clues in our conversation that there is no form of trade or currency, and people work based on interest and need. She and Sam are from Land Tikita located in northwestern waters, and they've voyaged together for four years before choosing a land to take up residency. However, now that they've settled, she isn't quite sure what she wants to do, but she'll explore the land more, seeking where she can be of help.

Sam, in contrast, is an active architect, drawing blueprints for new developments in the town and assisting in establishment upgrades. She mentioned that they're residing at one of

Sandemia's prebuilt residencies temporarily until Sam completes the blueprint for the home they'd like to have custom-built.

I find it peculiar that telecommunication ceases to exist on this land, or any other land for that matter, and the primary form of communication is letters by local delivery and *sea mail*. Cars do not exist, however, machinery does. Computers exist, but there is no Internet. Their primary function is to hold information digitally.

Interested in this unusual way of living, I wanted to ask how the land is run, government and all, but there was no question I could present that would allow Mauria to elaborate without suspicion. From the information gathered, I've realized that I am no longer on the same planet anymore—there is no way I can be. This is either *heaven* or another dimension. The only conclusion that makes sense is that I must have passed on, but even then, I'm skeptical, because if this is the afterlife, then why is it that Mauria and Sam were born of this world? This leads me to believe something else is at work here—*but what?*

Mauria pulls me out of my thoughts when she asks, "Are those the only clothes you have?"

"Unfortunately, yes."

"Wait here," she says, then leaves the room.

Reentering the dining area, she hands me a small bag. "There's a pack of toothbrushes, toothpaste, washcloths, a hairbrush, hair and body soap, moisture cream, *anti-sweat*, *skin blades*, toilet paper... oh, and you seem really close, if not the same size clothing as me, so there's a pair of jeans, a shirt, and at the very bottom is a pair of walking shoes with new socks tucked inside."

I walked over with my feet covered in nothing more than my fuzzy pink socks, not that I had any choice, but, *God, how embarrassing.*

"Thank you so much, Mauria. You are my hero right now."

She giggles. "Oh, don't worry about it. We'll get much more stuff tomorrow."

I bid her good night, and she hands me a book on my way out. "Here's so you don't get bored. I noticed your empty bookshelf."

I thank her, then leave, scurrying through the grass toward the property that's apparently mine. I stop at the mailbox before reentering the abode. Inside are Daycomms from the last few days, an envelope, and a key.

Ripping the seal, I pull out the letter:

Land of Sandemia Town Registration
Hello, if you have chosen to take up this residence temporarily or permanently,
please register at the town registration at 15 Norehall Pave.
Temporary: 40 days
Permanent: Indefinite with yearly renewal requirement
Sandemian identification is required for all registrations
Thank you.

Great. Just great.

CHAPTER 9

Skye

"Coffee?" Mauria offers, holding up a thermos.

"Ugh, yes," I grumble, exhausted, needing a cup.

I take a sip of the warm liquid. As it passes through my palate, my taste buds spring to life. I close my eyes, take a deep breath, and feel grateful for the beverage before me. *Coffee is life.* If there's a coffeemaker out there, I want one.

"The clothes fit you well," she mentions.

"Yes, they do. Thank you, again."

We commence our journey at once. When we exit the neighborhood past a sign that reads Haven Downs, I recall the night I arrived. The boat, Livity, docked at the back.

"Hey Mauria," I say. "Do boats usually dock at the back of the neighborhood?"

"Yes," she replies. "There are a few dock points. Haven Docks is located at the very end of Haven Downs. That's where mine and Sam's boats are." She pauses and asks, "Is that where the captain docked the boat, Livity?"

"I believe so," I answer with uncertainty. "We entered the neighborhood from the rear."

She nods. "Yes, that's where you docked then."

We walk for about twenty minutes before we enter a town that resembles something of archaic village life.

Shops and merchant stands are assembled from refined wooden fixtures on either side of the broad strip. Some people walk, others ride bikes, and the guardians of young ones push strollers. It's uncrowded, allowing sufficient room to move, but it's certainly not quiet.

A standing cooler displaying water bottles makes me conscious of the dry taste on my tongue, but as I step toward it, I pause—*can I grab one?*

Mauria, noticing my dither, asks, "Do you want water?"

I nod slowly. As if such actions are prevalent, Mauria opens the cooler door, grabs a bottle of water, and offers it to me. I reluctantly accept it, and her eyebrows knit in confusion. "What? You *are* thirsty, aren't you?"

"Um, yes, I just wasn't sure," I mutter. *Do I look as ridiculous as I feel?* My attempt to blend in is failing miserably.

I quench my thirst, and we continue forward. We walk into a clothing shop, where sale signs and price tags are nonexistent, and, at Mauria's suggestion, I lay pieces that are to my liking over my arm.

"You should pick up more," she encourages. "You have nothing."

Glancing down at my items, I decide—why not? I add more to the pile until the weight of it all strains my forearm, and suddenly worry that I might have overdone it. I'm still skeptical of this "everything is free" notion—there has to be a limit. Someone's labor manufactured these items. How can it possibly be given to consumers without charge?

"Oh dear, you'll need something to help carry that load." A woman approaches from behind.

"Sorry, I'm starting from scratch," I say.

"No need to apologize. A small bag with wheels should help." She disappears around a corner for no longer than a few beats before returning with *a bag with wheels*. But I know it as a suit-case, perfectly sized for a carry-on.

"Um. Is there anything else I need to do?" I ask nervously, still seeking a catch.

"If you have everything you need, then no," she replies. "Please help yourself to anything else. Starting from scratch can be tricky."

What sort of utopian society is this? This is unheard of.

Loading the items in the *bag with wheels*, I thank the woman and search for Mauria.

The cropped lawn of Sheridan Park is filled with colorful shrubs and tall trees, many with benches hanging from their branches. A woman with an infant in her lap gently swings back and forth, while nearby two younger children play a game on a blanket laid on the grass.

Lounging by a small garden are a few middle-aged women laughing; one stands with a watering can, hydrating the plants. The path through the park where Mauria and I stroll loops around a lake where an older man is teaching a young boy how to fish. He smiles as we pass by and gives the boy stern instructions. He's clearly passionate about fishing.

At the exit, we decide to grab a bite to eat before heading to the Media Center. Passing through a children's park filled with inno-cent joy, it appears no different than any I know of in my world—with the exception of the outdated equipment. A few older kids play some sort of kickball sport near an open field. I'd call it soccer, but I'm quite familiar with the sport, and that's not it.

In the distance, a man plays fetch with his golden retriever. The energetic dog jumps for the stick before his owner can toss it, catching him off guard. He stumbles backward, dropping the stick, and his playful pet grabs it and runs in circles, wagging his tail. I giggle at the scene. Smart *pooch.*

I halt when I glimpse an ice cream shop. A craving for the dessert arises as I stare at the people seated around the establishment and enjoying their cold delights.

"Do you want frozen cream?" Mauria asks.

I'm hungry. Ice cream won't do. "No, I prefer food."

"There's a pepax stand by the beach. They have the best shrimp pepaxes," she says.

Pep-what?

As I take in the amiable environment, my mental radar searches for signs of anyone that may stand out. But it hasn't pinged.

The refreshing breeze near the beach is a comfort—my skin misses New York's chill in this sizzling sun. Walking along the boardwalk, more stands offer merchandise and foods, and I fix my gaze on the distant shore that's filled with people.

At this *pepax* stand, the extensive writing over the structure lists the menu items, which notably only consist of various fish choices. Curious about the options, I ask Mauria, "Do all dining places serve the same kinds of foods?" Indirectly, I'm inquiring about other *meat* options, recalling that Mr. Alton's wheelbarrow had excluded poultry options and that fish had been the only source of meat.

"Yes. But this place only serves *pepaxes.* Some restaurants serve dishes like stuffed salmon, fried tilapia, boiled crab, and other entrées. Everywhere specializes in something different. There's one place near Haven Downs where the owner makes the best catfish you'll ever taste," she exclaims as we move through the line.

Okay, so fish only. Got it. Wondering if any of this has to do with Biblical faith, I don't ask. *What if this really is... heaven?*

A man who's been served his food walks by, and I take a peek to see what this "*pepax*" is. Observing the entrée, the thin dough —similar to a tortilla—bi-folds, creating an open pocket that holds the meat, lettuce, tomatoes, sauce, and other ingredients. And I'm immediately dumbfounded.

Pepax? That's a damn taco.

The name given is so far off that I'm having a hard time processing where a name like pepax for a taco could have been derived.

How could it be called a taco? My brain mocks me.

I want to ask Mauria if she's ever heard of a taco, but I refrain. Unnecessary.

"Mauria, I've found nothing," I stress having skimmed through the sixtieth book regarding information about vessel lines.

"Me, neither," she replies.

After spending hours at the library—*Media Center*—I'm not ready to leave, but the sun begins to set, and the pleasant lady announces she's closing soon. We're on foot, so Mauria suggests it's best to head back. We make our way to Haven Downs.

Approaching her home first, I bid her good night. She stretches her arms and brings me in for a hug. "Hey, despite not finding any information, today was fun. Don't look so defeated. We'll find something. Cheer up."

I manage a slight smile. "Thank you, Mauria. I appreciate you."

We release each other, and she slaps the air. "It's nothing. Mysteries and journeys are my thing!"

Optimism finds its way in through doubt at her willfulness to help. I'm aware that everyone is different, but I wonder: Are the ways of most people here similar to Mauria's?

Though I'm eased knowing there's someone in my corner, I fight brewing despondency from taking hold. I could use a shot of something strong tonight.

"Hey, do you have alcohol?" I ask Mauria.

"For cleaning?" *Well, that's innocent.*

"No, like... liquor?" I reluctantly clarify.

"What's liquor?"

"C'mon, even Jesus drank wine," I mutter, voicing my intrusive sarcasm.

"Oh, we have wine!" She puckers up. "But who's *Jesus?*" *If this is heaven, my whole life was a lie.*

"Wine is perfect." I refuse to acknowledge her question.

"Wait here," she directs me before making her way inside.

It isn't in my best interest to be alone with my thoughts, so I'm relieved when it only takes a moment before Mauria is descending her property with a bottle of red wine in hand.

A few glasses to fall into a quick slumber is what I need, or anxiety will keep me up. I will pensively drown myself in thoughts of everything that's happened in the last twenty-four hours and then worry half to death about things I have no control over.

Although this unorthodox environment is welcoming and beautiful, I miss my son. I *need* to return to my life.

I thank Mauria for the wine and walk over to the home where I currently reside. I can't help feeling that while I've worked hard for all that I have in my own world, in this land, I am a squatter.

I push through the door and lock it behind me. I unpack the items I've picked up today. Toiletries, clothing, kitchen items, books, a small bag, a watch, and a calendar. I've paid for none of these items, still somehow, they're mine. I find it challenging to grasp this concept, but hopefully there'll be no need much longer. I head for the bath and wash away the icky feeling from spending the day in a heatwave, then change into soft, pink satin flannel pajamas. Manufactured by a maker, unpurchased by a consumer, yet feels far from cheaply made.

I rest against the headboard of the bed—that is not mine—with a glass of wine in hand. At the first sip, the sweet taste relaxes me.

Exploring Sandemia offered no answers other than the insight that this place is quaint with exuberant people. Yet still, no information surfaced to lead me in *any* direction. Before allowing the uselessness of the day to digest, I reach for my glass and down what's left.

Tomorrow is another day. And with that thought, I slump into dreamland.

CHAPTER 10

Skye

"Tomorrow, Sam and I are sailing to Land Zendovou for a couple's spa," Mauria informs me. "I won't be back until the following day, but I promise to ask around while we're there." She's trying to keep my hopes alive, but despair grows with each passing day.

The sun begins to set in the sky, so we head for Haven Downs after another long day of no answers.

It has been four days, and every day since the first, Mauria and I have set out on the same journey to find information regarding Livity, or the captain, Sylvester. We've asked every neighbor at Haven Downs, except Mr. Alton, because he hasn't been home, and expanded our questioning to owners of different establishments and residents in other neighborhoods. Mauria, sensing my growing gloom, became determined and began asking passersby.

"You know, I'm pretty sure someone knows of this mysterious boat, but sometimes people need to see it with their eyes to actually remember," she suggests. "For instance, sometimes we forget things that we don't consider important enough, but a visual image can jog a memory, you know?"

I process her words and recall having such thoughts recently. Glancing down at the butterfly bracelet I had once forgotten—

locked away in a jewelry box, collecting dust for years—had restored long-gone memories. "Mauria, you are so right." The revelation of what she said hits me. "Maybe I can somehow draw it. I have no idea how to draw, but I can try."

"You may not know how to draw, but Sam does." She grins with a light-bulb expression. "Come in. I'm sure he's home by now."

"Okay, now describe this boat," Sam says, pencil and paper in hand.

Describing the boat as best I can, I watch as Sam's hands glide the pencil over the white sheet. When he's finished, I see his talent for architecture. Despite my terrible description, he made it work.

"I don't know, Skye." He scratches his head pessimistically. "This boat is ordinary and out of date by centuries. There are still plenty that exist for sentimental reasons, but this doesn't strike me as something that would jog a memory. There is nothing unique about it."

Mauria looks down, intertwining her fingers. *She was thinking the same thing.* If I presented this drawing to anyone, they would see it as another boat, nothing memory-jogging, as my bracelet was for me. Nothing *unique*.

Mauria has helped me plenty, and Sam offered a hand and an honest opinion. That is more than I could ever ask from either of them. I won't involve them in the pain that just struck my chest, the anguish that will consume me tonight, or the tears forming in my ducts.

"Thank you, guys. I really appreciate it. Enjoy your day tomorrow." I smile, masking the pain before moving toward the exit.

When I close their door behind me, it swings open again, and

I turn around to see Mauria. She throws her arms around me, her voice quavering. "I saw right through that smile. We'll figure it out, I promise." A tear slides down her face when she releases me. She's showing me her empathy for my situation, and all it does is make me feel like a burden.

I refuse to allow her such sadness on my behalf, so I dissemble. "Hey, maybe I just have to wait for my memory to return. It's just amnesia. There has to be a reason the captain, Sylvester, brought me here specifically."

Her expression lightens, which is what I prefer.

I don't do well with pity parties.

"Right." She puckers up. "We'll start there when I get back!"

Smiling, I bid her good night.

Making my way across the lawn, I notice the dim lights through Mr. Alton's window.

He's returned.

So before calling it a night, I make one more stop.

"Hello, there, new neighbor. Skye Cooke, is it?" Mrs. Windsor answers after the second knock.

"Hi, Mrs. Windsor. Yes, that is correct. I hope I'm not interrupting. I just had a question for maybe you and Mr. Alton?"

"Sure, dear, please come in," she offers. "And you can call me Lorlee."

"No, there's no need. It will only take a second."

She calls for Mr. Alton, and he greets me with a smile.

"Have either of you heard of a boat named Livity? The model of it is centuries old, with green and blue colors on the outside?" I ask.

I don't miss Mr. Alton's nuance. He drops his head as his smile disappears—precisely the same expression from days prior.

"I'm afraid not. I'm sorry." Ms. Lorlee offers. Looking at Mr. Alton, she asks, "Have you, Al?"

Glancing at his wife, then back at me, his smile reappears—*just as before. Why does he do that?* "I'm afraid I don't recall such a vessel. Very sorry we cannot be of much help."

"That's quite alright. Thank you for your time. You all have a good night."

I depart from their property, and they retreat into their home.

Something about Mr. Alton gnaws at me *because* his expression sometimes lacks lucidity.

Or maybe it's just me.

Desperate for a sign, a hint, I could be reading into nonsense, and though Mr. Alton may strike me as strange—*would he lie?*

CHAPTER 11

Skye

Awakening early, I sip coffee on the front porch, reading the Daycomm—*I'm on the front porch, sipping coffee and reading the newspaper. How old am I again?* This is what life is like in a world absent of telecasts, and those of the oldest living generation in my own world are still hard-wired to this once-normalcy.

Refusing to sit around and wait for Mauria's return to attempt finding answers, I down the last drop in my mug, and as my energy spikes, I prepare to go out on my own for the first time.

Watch reading 12:43 p.m., at this hour, the town is filled; I quite hope so. Given the amicable norm, I plan to continue what Mauria and I started—approaching strangers to inquire about Livity.

Dressed in white capri pants and pink sneakers and a pink tank top, my hair is looped in a messy bun at the top of my head. I carry a mini pink crossover purse to hold the keys to the residence and a bottle of water. Exiting through the front door, locking it behind me, I descend the property, and my mission begins.

After three hours of asking around, at the few mentions that Mauria and I had already approached them, I did away with the inquiries. Given the population not being vast, I suppose this was likely to be the case.

However, after another three hours spent at the library, today has already proven to be a bust. Laying the search to rest, I go to the beach, approaching the pepax—*taco*—whatever the hell it is—stand, having not eaten the entire day. But, at my turn to order, dejection replaces hunger, and instead, I request a bottle of water.

Kicking through the sand, I find a quiet area by a small mountain of rocks. Planting there, I take in all the activity in the area, chasing a distraction from the defeat I carry. Sandcastles, volleyball, sunbaths, and swimmers ashore; others sail at high speeds pulling jet skis while surfers ride waves. Laughter and excitement fill the beach, except for one individual—me.

In the presence of sunshine, I sit isolated with a gray cloud of thunder, storming over my head. Thoughts of my family, my son, my life, bring in waves of apprehension as I worry about what could be happening back home.

What do they think might have happened to me? And what does that mean for my son?

My son. I miss him so much. Jason wouldn't dare try to get him, *right?*

No, he wouldn't, and my parents wouldn't allow it without a fight. At the prospect, I grow extremely unsettled. Will I ever see my family again? The people I love? Have I been fated to this life forever?

I came to the beach to distract myself from pondering these very questions, but with every *"no"* and *"I'm sorry,"* every waking day—with not even so much as a clue—the foreboding thoughts become unyielding. Relentless tears spill over like a flood as despair swallows me whole. Pulling my knees to my chest, I bury my face in my arms to muffle the wail that threatens to unfetter. And I sit at the beach, among the surrounding joy, crying my eyes out for my breaking heart.

CHAPTER 12

Skye

Chilling air films my skin as the soft touch of sand cushions beneath. The consoling sound of waves breaking against the shore and the twilight sky of imminent gloom blur in the distance as my droopy lids lazily blink. Slowly rising to an empty beach, I glance at my watch to see 8:29 p.m., realizing my unwitting doze off after a mental breakdown.

Pushing to my feet, brushing off what little sand, I exit the now-empty beach and follow the path to Haven Downs. Having never been out this late, Mauria and I have been wrapping up by six p.m.—and now I see why. Closed shops and covered stands line the strip. The town filled with people during daylight becomes a ghost town by sundown. However, dim lighting behind the glass door of a small diner with a lit sign—*Mrs. Arna's Diner*—remains open, seating customers.

Suddenly remembering I haven't eaten in nearly twenty-four hours, the hunger from earlier, that was veiled by depression, ferociously claws through the mantle. So, I enter the diner in hopes of fulfilling the need, and a bell dings upon my entry.

"Welcome!" the woman behind the counter greets.

"Hi," I reply with a small smile, although it's baffling how I still manage to smile.

A quality of mine for as long as I can remember, I never considered it a valuable trait until employment in customer service, where someone's "I'm having a bad day" is probable cause to be mistreated. I contrast in that manner. Whatever the dismay, my trials are inexcusable to mistreat others.

"May I have a loaded tuna sandwich and a salad? I don't need a drink," I request, placing the card stock menu back on the counter.

"Sure, darling. Have a seat. Will let you know when your order is ready," she assures.

Thanking her, I sit at the square, green-topped table closest to the counter. But at the sound of the entry bell—while a quick glance on impulse is my usual—oddly, I lock on to the man that has just entered the premises.

Sucking the energy out of the room, about an entire foot taller than me, emerald eyes under furrowed brows peer straight ahead, paying not even a glance to anyone seated before him. Frowning, but not hardened in anger—rather a seemingly habitual expression—is *unapproachable and doesn't like to be approached.*

Sharp jawline, sleek shaved; tanned olive skin, his slightly disheveled dark silky hair is pushed back, as if done with the rake of his fingers, but unruly few strands hang down above his eyebrows. The bulge of his muscled biceps causes the sleeves of his ivory shirt to pull tight, and as he passes by, a whiff of mint invades my senses.

Murmuring sounds draw my attention from the intense energy within the vicinity, and I turn to see the women in the diner—their eyes on him—as they whisper among each other. *Seriously? Make it obvious that he's a walking hunk of masculine beauty, why don't you?*

"Mrs. Arna, what'd you got for me today?" he asks the woman at the counter, and his deep baritone passes through my ears, traveling down my center. A subtle difference in his accent— non-distinctive—but familiar, I may be able to pinpoint it, but even then, I wouldn't be sure from where—which begs the question—*who is this guy?*

"Elias, good to see you! How does glazed salmon, asparagus, and a baked potato sound?" Mrs. Arna offers.

Uh, damn good. Where the heck was that on the menu? I ordered a stupid tuna sandwich, and he gets glazed salmon?

"Delicious, I'll take it," he replies, unenthused—not because he's lying, rather apathetic, being his usual.

Elias, huh? So, you get special treatment?

She informs him his order will be ready soon, but he doesn't take a seat, instead turning to the side—*in my direction*—resting his elbow on the counter. Bending one leg over the other, resting it on the tip of his toe, he glances down at his black watch, and his side profile appears as though he's abandoned the frown. However, when he lifts his chin—with a slight turn of his head—his eyes meet mine. *Shit.*

Darting my eyes down, I nervously play with my nails, but the urge for another glance overpowers me, and after a few beats, I slowly lift my gaze only to instantly freeze.

Soul-piercing, emerald eyes under furrowed brows glare at me in disgust. *Holy shit.* His hardened expression—as if I'm a sore to the eyes—unnerves me; a burning gaze sends a chill down my spine, yet somehow, I find it impossible to look away. *Dude, what the hell did I do to you?*

Breaking the stare, he motions to the table adjacent to me, removing a book from his back pocket before taking a seat. *Why didn't I think of that?* My thoughts are envious that, unlike him, I have nothing to distract me. Mrs. Arna brings out orders for the other customers, and when the last one departs, *Elias* and I are the last waiting.

Still focused on the pages of his book, I buy another glance, but when his eyes dart to me, I freeze—again. *Why don't you just stop looking at him?* And as if it were nothing, his gaze drops to his text.

Potent darkness radiates off the handsome man before me; his intimidating, frigid aura differs from the masses, drawing me like a magnet yet shunning me in disdain. And my intuition whispers that his dissimilarity to this world is kindred to mine.

Mrs. Arna lifts two bags in hand, gesturing to us both, and we approach the counter wide enough for two people to stand. Grabbing his food while I stuff napkins in mine, he makes for the door, and I do well fighting the urge to take another peek. But, when Mrs. Arna bids him good night and he offers his thanks with, "*'Preciate you*, Mrs. Arna," I gasp.

Spinning so fast I could have given myself whiplash, my eyes widen, and the dramatics earn me a glance. Not sparing another moment, he exits, and I quickly gather my bag, thanking Mrs. Arna, then rush after him.

The familiar accent. I *know* it. Nonetheless, it's the lingo that confirms. That distinctive, inane lingo reminds me precisely of a place where I used to spend my summers—*Georgia*.

Bursting through the door, jogging toward my left—the direction I saw him go—I scope the surroundings, but he's gone. *Where could he have gone so fast?* My twenty-twenty is no match against the darkness, and the streetlights on either side of the broad path are dimly lit.

"Um, hello?" I call. But silence responds.

Haven Downs is toward the right, and the thought of being out here alone in the dark disquiets my gut. After calling a few more times, I hang my head in defeat once more and make my way back to the neighborhood.

Elias

I *see* her. As I hide in this alley, out of plain sight, I *watch* her.

She's looking for me.

She *noticed* me.

And as her unique aura summoned my attention—I *noticed* her.

Uncertain before, her sudden reaction as I thanked Mrs. Arna confirmed my suspicion. She's from the world that is home to my haunted and dark past. A place I've never been more relieved to never set foot in again, yet a place that still haunts me in the midnight hour.

Why is she here?

She's a reminder of everything I've worked so hard to forget— a life I've left behind. I've been granted a chance, a new beginning, one where I never face a soul of the wretched world I was unfortunately born of.

Now someone from that world has come here, and *she knows my name*. It's time I left.

When she's given up her search, hangs her head, and commences walking away, I move from my hidden spot. Taking a long way home through the valleys and hidden paths, I mentally note things to pack. I've done my fair share of exploring; now it's time to pack up—*again*—and set sail to another land.

A land far, *far* from these waters.

Because now I've *seen* her, *and I never want to see her again.*

CHAPTER 13

Skye

Banging at the front door rudely awakens me. I glance at the clock sitting on the nightstand. 6:52 a.m. *Seriously? Is the sun even awake?*

I crawl out of bed, rub the grogginess from my eyes, and stride to the door. I am met with a very awake, wide-grinned Mauria holding up a Daycomm.

"Good morning," I rasp.

She rushes in, squeezing past me. *Sure, come in, I wasn't sleeping or anything.*

"Skye! You have to see this," she urges.

"What's that?" I ask, still half-dead.

She hands the paper to me. "Read it."

Read? I can barely see right now.

Skimming through, nothing sticks. "Mauria, I don't know what I'm looking for."

"Bottom right."

I squint to focus on the photo at the bottom right corner of the Daycomm. A boat with blue and green stripes sticks out. My grogginess wavers as my interest piques at the sight of Livity. I read the description below the image:

"*A grandfather boat engraved Livity docks at Port Velle on*

Land Sandemia at approximately nine thirty p.m. Disembarking the mysterious vessel is one passenger. A man seeming to be engaged in conversation with himself. At approximately 9:58 p.m., Livity departs. Captain, unidentified."

The date reads, Day 145, *2018.*

"Where did you get this?" I ask.

"Sam and I have collected Daycomms from different lands for years. We have a pile of them," she explains. "I went through them to see if any past Daycomms mentioned such a boat. Sometimes, if a new or unrecognizable boat docks a land, it will make the Daycomm. This one is definitely mysterious; I can see why someone would deem it important enough for an article. I mean, look at it. The vessel is older than time itself."

I stare at the Daycomm in deep thought. *Five years ago?* "Mauria, this is the memory jog people need."

"Yes!" she agrees, enthused. "It's early, we can go now if you'd like."

"Yeah, start a pot of coffee, I'll get ready."

I take the Daycomm with me back to the bedroom and reread the description.

"...Disembarking the mysterious vessel was one passenger..."

"A man..."

"...conversation with himself..."

"...Captain, unidentified."

I encountered this passenger last night. And there's one thing I'm sure of: As he disembarked that vessel, he *wasn't* having a conversation with himself.

Elias

Tossing the last bag of necessities over my shoulder, I make my way down the steps before dropping it near the others to load onto my vessel upon my return. My watch reads six a.m., earlier than my usual, but most shops are just opening, and I prefer to grab necessities before people crowd the town. Chances are, *she'll* be looking for me, so I lock up and head out—the earlier the better.

8:12 a.m. *Not bad.* Sparse with people, the town gradually crowds as the day carries on, but my errands are complete—*time to depart.*

"See you next time, Elias," Mrs. Arna says as I gather my food.

"It may be a while, but I'll see you when I see you."

"Oh? Taking another trip? Will it be three years or longer this time?"

"Maybe, not sure yet."

"Well, darling, may the low tide be with you." She bids me goodbye.

Nodding, I thank her, but before leaving the counter, the question that's been edging the tip of her tongue finally escapes. "The young lady from last night, did she catch up to you? She was in quite the hurry."

Mrs. Arna wouldn't have missed that, but I had hoped she'd keep her curiosity to herself. My terse, *"No,"* doesn't satisfy her, so when she opens her mouth to speak again, before a word leaves, I grimly interrupt, "Have a good day, Mrs. Arna."

I'm not up for any more questions.

I push through the diner's exit, but before hitting a left, I halt in my tracks. Standing at the fruit fixture across from Mrs. Arna's is the reason for my departure, engaged in conversation with a red-haired woman.

My mind suggests that I keep walking, but my legs ask for a moment. I pause and drink her in.

She fans herself with a Daycomm. Her caramel skin glistens in the sun's rays, and jet-black curls hang below her petite waist. My nose recalls lavender near her presence last night, and at the sight of her, it pines for another whiff. Smiling, she thanks the man behind the fixture for the apple he handed her, and the reveal of her perfect pearly whites reflects a smile from the heart, displaying her genuine spirit. Iridescent brown eyes brighten with the upturn of her lips, and their radiance can shine light on even the darkest of souls.

I swear that I'm caught when she lifts her chin, but when she doesn't spot me, I prolong the gaze. *She's beautiful*—magnetic—and like a shot through my senses, I feud with the hankering to approach. Reminding myself she's from *there*, I snap out of whatever the fuck was just happening. I tilt my head down, hoping to go unnoticed, and no longer hesitate to leave the area at once.

I go through the narrow alley between Ms. Arna's and another shop. I hear a shout of "Hey!" and solidify in place.

Shit.

CHAPTER 14

Skye

"I remember that article," the man at the fruit stand recalls. "There has been no mention of it since. It's never returned."

There aren't many people out this early, but the few we've asked recall the article after seeing the picture. Thanking the polite man for an apple, the movement in my peripheral vision captures my attention. One glance in that direction, and there's no question that it's *his* retreating back.

I urgently call to him. "Hey!"

He stiffens but doesn't stop, instead picking up his pace. Powerwalking in his direction, I aim not to lose sight of him. He makes a sharp turn behind one of the shops.

I cut the same corner—he was only a few feet away, but to my astonishment, he's already gone. *What in the Michael Myers? How does he do that?*

Mauria approaches in the distance. "Hey, Skye, where are you going?"

Ignoring her, I follow the sound of ruffling bags a few meters northwest.

"Skye!" Mauria calls again.

I take no notice and dash behind the next shop. Determination consumes me, but at the sharp turn of the next corner, again, there's no one.

A thinning shadow is my cue, and it's become clear that last night, the darkness befriended him, hiding his presence as I searched. However, in broad daylight, the sunlight is the enemy, revealing his outline, guiding my gaze as he so desperately tries to escape.

Another right, straight, left. We've extended the chase to a forest that nearly blocks out the sun—*his perfect playground*—and somehow the connection befits the gloomy man I trail. My pride loathes this lunatic chase after this man, but pride is the least of my concerns. Under normal circumstances, I wouldn't dare approach, let alone chase, but this is far from ordinary. I'm insistent on answers, and my gut assures me he has them.

I lag behind as I dodge lifted roots, twigs, and branches. Intrusive thoughts wonder at what point in life I grew the balls to run through unknown woods.

Open land in the distance drives my legs to push harder. *He can't hide in the open.* And the likelihood of cornering the rat fills me with hope.

Mauria, hot on my heels, continues to shout my name, but never minding her calls, I hasten through these woods. Adrenaline tenaciously ignores every prickling twig. Like a predator for her prey, I'm dedicated to the chase until the first step onto open land, and everything ceases.

Stones line the concrete path leading to the entrance of the two-story brick-front home atop a hill. Colorful shrubs offer life to the cropped yard before the black patio fence lining the edge of the front porch. As if the abode needed it, a second-floor balcony adds luxury to the edifice. Behind the beauty is an endless sea, and docked near the shore are three vessels, and a narrow-cemented path leads to a garage. A movement to my left fails to divert my gaze from the breathtaking home before me.

Mauria, out of breath, finally catches up. "Skye what are you... wow—" She cuts off, distracted by the sight of the elegantly built home. "I've seen many custom builds, but none of this stature. Let's see if anyone is home!" she exclaims and proceeds toward the entrance.

"Mauria, wait," I warn, but she ignores me, and gestures for me to follow.

I remain glued to my position, refusing to move a muscle. She rings the doorbell, then knocks. However, when no one answers, rather than leaving the property, she goes across the patio to the side of the home.

"Mauria!" I whisper-shout.

Inattentive, she attends to her curiosity and disappears into the back yard. Swallowing the apprehension in the pit of my stomach, I creep up the concrete path. Finally, past the patio, I peek around the side of the house and catch a slight view of the back yard.

"Mauria?" I cautiously call. I don't know about this world, but where I'm from, this is trespassing.

"Oh my! Skye, you've gotta see this view!" *Why is she so God-forsaken loud?* However, at the sound of her chipper voice, I exhale in relief.

"Mauria, we can't just intrude on someone's property," I reason, still looking around the corner to see where she's gone.

"I know, but I'll apologize and then tell them how beautiful their home is." *Seriously, that's her plan? Because mine is to take off running.* "Now get over here and come see this!"

I turn on my heels to ensure the coast is clear, and my knees grow weak. A gasp leaves my lips, and I stiffen where I stand as infuriating, soul-piercing emeralds—under furrowed brows— glare at me in utter repulsion.

Elias.

Elias

When the chase neared my residence, I ventured east to lead her away. But, when the footsteps silenced, I doubled back to see that she and her friend had caught sight of my home. She either didn't hear my movement or ignored it.

I'm convinced it was the latter.

Watching from the shadows as she and her redhead friend approached my home, my initial plan was to stay hidden until they realized its vacancy and retreated. But then Redhead motioned to my back yard, and I watched Skye's reluctance.

Skye. I'm presuming that's her name, as her friend yelled it repeatedly during the chase.

As my six-foot-three frame towers over her, the predacious animal who mistook me for one to be hunted gasps in alarm, a hint of *fear* in her irises.

Good.

It's her fear I plan to feed on to get her the fuck away from me.

"Leave," I demand, low and gruff, matching my disdain for this entire morning.

Frozen where she stands, she slightly shakes her head. "No," she voices nearly inaudibly. *She's determined.*

Flames of anger lick me, and I feel the twitch in my jaw as it tenses.

In the same instance, Redhead rounds the corner. "Oh, hi! We're so sorry to be on your property without permission. Your home is extravagant! But again, very sorry."

Her friend babbles about my property, but my eyes remain fixed on *Skye*. She squeezes her eyes shut and blows out a breath. When my gaze falls to her parted lips, I curse my mind for the lustful abomination infringing on my will to despise her.

"Is the interior just as beautiful as the exterior?" Redhead asks, but I'm in no mood for chit-chat.

Without breaking my stare, I address the babbling friend. "Today is not a good day."

"Okay, well, I apologize once again. Have a good day, sir," she replies. "Let's go, Skye."

She's retreating when Skye stops her. "Mauria, the Daycomm."

"Oh right." *Mauria* moves toward me with a Daycomm in hand and asks, "Have you seen this boat?"

I break away to inspect what I'm handed and read the description under the photo:

"*A grandfather boat engraved Livity docks at Port Velle on Land Sandemia at approximately nine thirty p.m. Disembarking the mysterious vessel is one passenger. A man seeming to be engaged in conversation with himself. At approximately 9:58 p.m., Livity departs. Captain, unidentified.*"

Day 145, *2018.* After another look at the boat that I've never seen again, I hand the Daycomm back to her.

Skye, sensing my pending refusal, pleads, "Please, descending this boat is the last thing I remember."

"And apparently the captain's name was Sylvester," Mauria adds.

I tense at the name I haven't heard in years. Mauria doesn't notice, but Skye is keen. Her sorrowful eyes wager her life, and the view sparks something akin to sympathy within me. "Have you received your hourglass?" I ask.

"A what? I-I mean, I'm not sure I understand," she timidly replies.

"*She* shouldn't be here," I suggest, barely above a whisper, and turn my back, retreating to my patio.

I'm referring to Mauria, but I'm unsure if Skye understands that. Whatever answers she seeks, those of this world shouldn't be exposed to our alien existence.

Mauria begins to leave the property, but Skye pauses on the path.

I face my front door with my back to her, blow out a breath, and bite the bullet. "Skye, is it?"

"Yes," she answers.

"Elias," I introduce myself. "Pepax stand. Noon tomorrow."

There's relief in her tone when she responds, "Okay," before she and her friend continue on their way.

Those pleading eyes.

She wishes to return, which I find confounding. I marvel at how she could have ended up here in the first place. Contrary to me, she isn't here in search of anything from this world. She's barely scratched the surface of what's happened. And though I've never laid eyes on that Daycomm, the passenger referred to in the article is, indeed, me.

Skye

"**G**ood morning, Mr. Alton," I call to him as I walk toward the Haven Downs exit.

"Good day, Ms. Skye." He returns the greeting, hands on the bars of his wheelbarrow. "Care for any goods?"

"No money here, huh?" I joke.

He laughs. "I'm afraid not. Is there anything else here that may be of interest to you?"

Examining the wheelbarrow's contents, I pick up a folded piece of ivory paper that grabs my attention. *It's a map.*

Curiously, I ask, "Is this for me?"

"It is for anyone who may find it useful," he replies.

I glance down again, glimpse a compass, and reach for it.

"The two work well when used together," he adds.

I stuff them both in the mini bag crossed over my shoulder, thank him, and after a bow of his head, we go our separate ways. I'm no doorknob, it's clear the contents were specifically for me.

It's 11:42 a.m. When I arrive at the pepax stand, Elias is seated at one of the nearby tables, reading a book. I pause and take him in as I work up the courage to approach.

A crowned lion's head is neatly inked on the curve of his built arm, and his gray tank top does nothing to hide his chiseled body. He wears gray and white plaid shorts and a white bucket hat, and I hate that I have to ask myself, *why is he so hot?* If I came across him in my world, I wouldn't approach him with a ten-foot pole. In my experience, guys that look like him are fire, and when you play with fire, expect to be burned.

Taking a deep breath, I finally get to where he's seated, hoping for answers that make sense of all of this.

"Took you long enough." His eyes never leave the book.

"I'm not late," I reply.

"No. Took you long enough to walk over *here.*"

He knew I was standing there? *Where is the nearest rock I can hide under?* "Yeah, well, I—I was gathering my thoughts." That's the best I can come up with. *Not bad, right? Who am I kidding? That was terrible.*

"Have you had a pepax since your arrival?"

"You mean a tac..." I don't finish my sentence. His eyes quickly dart to me, and his brows pull together. "I had it, it was good," I reply instead.

"Want another?"

I shrug. "Why not?"

"Hold the table," he instructs me, and he rises from his seat to make his way to the pepax stand.

Traces of mint linger in his passing, and I hold my breath so as not to savor it. While he's gone to grab our food, using the time, I immunize my mind to the toxicity threatening to distract my brain. *I need to remain focused.* It's then I recall his frigidity.

He's not obliged to speak to me, but knowing our worlds are alike, his sole reason for meeting me is not courtesy but sheer pity. Suddenly, his handsomeness no longer appeals to me as I question his human decency. The thought of accepting help from anyone offering pity revolts me, but I swallow my pride to obtain the knowledge I need.

He's coming back, holding two pepaxes, and my tense nerves are calm because no longer do I see a beautifully carved man. Instead, I'm sickened by the asshole before me.

"What happened to your face?" he asks impassively, handing me the pepax.

"My face?"

"Whatever you're over here thinking about, changed your face."

Taking a bite, I chew slowly. "Nothing. What kind is this?"

"Octopus," he deadpans.

Instantly, I stop chewing.

"What happened to your face?" he presses.

I swallow what's already chewed to bits and place the pepax on the table and take a gulp of water. "You're here out of pity."

He quirks a brow. "Does it matter?"

Searching his eyes and finding nothing, I lean back in my chair. "No."

Finishing his bite, with a sharp sniff, he says, "And your mistake is assuming that pity holds any influence over my decisions."

Nervously curling my tongue over my bottom lip, I'm stumped. I have no response except for one pending question: "Why did you avoid me?"

"It's pep premium. Think of a gyro but with salmon." He gestures to the entrée.

Sighing in relief, I take another bite, and now that he mentions it, the taste is salmon. His disregard for my question doesn't go unnoticed, but I don't insist. Something tells me I only get one shot with this guy, and unfortunately, he's my only hope for the answers I seek.

"You see that plant next to the pepax stand?" He points. "Look at the leaves."

I scrutinize the plant. "The leaves are shaped like a tac... a pepax."

He nods. "The plant is called the Pepose Auxizima. That's where the name pepax was derived for the dish."

"I've seen that plant before, in my wor..." I begin but pause to correct my statement. "Where I'm from, but I'm sure that's not the name of it."

"Different world, different name, same plant." He takes the last bite of his food. "And Skye?"

I look up.

"Where *we're* from."

CHAPTER 16

Skye

"So, you came here on the mysterious boat Livity as well?" I ask as we walk along the beach. Hardly anyone is here —presumably that's why Elias picked this place for the conversation we're having.

"Yes," he answers.

"That article from five years ago. You were the passenger?"

"Yes."

"You weren't talking to yourself."

"No."

"Was his name Sylvester?"

"Yes."

"Have you seen the boat since?"

"No."

Stopping in my tracks, I assumed the worst. "Wait, you've been stuck here for *five* years? Is there anyone else here like us?"

He stops and faces me. "Like us? Not that I've met. And I'm not *stuck*. I *chose* to stay," he corrects me as if my presumption insulted his presence here.

He proceeds forward, and I power walk to catch up. "Well, how do I choose not to stay? I can't stay here."

"Can't or won't?"

"Both."

"The time will come when you will need to choose."

I halt again, frustrated with his curt responses. "Well, when is that? Because I was supposed to pick up my son from his grandmother's six days ago."

He gazes at me with a softened expression, as if he's just come to cognizance. "From the moment you arrive, until it is time for you to choose, time as you know it—in the world you are from—will remain frozen," he states as if repeating the words of someone else.

"How do you know?"

"Because those were Sylvester's exact words to me the night I arrived."

"He didn't tell me any of this," I mutter.

"You didn't ask."

"Uh, yes, I did," I say defensively.

"Okay, what did you ask?"

I'd like to stick my foot up his imperious ass right now. "I *asked* him where I was."

Crossing his arms, he faces me. "And what did he say?"

Recalling the night and the dialogue between Sylvester and me, "... *Aboard my transport*" ... "... *Call this Land Sandemia*." Okay, so he *did* answer my question—directly—but I'm not admitting it to smartass over here. I roll my eyes and continue walking. "Whatever," I murmur.

"Well, when will I know..." I begin but pause when the question he asked me yesterday comes to the forefront of my memory. "The hourglass."

He nods.

Knowing that time is frozen in my world until my return brings me relief, but how I ended up here, and most importantly, *why,* bewilders me. I'm no conspiracy theorist. I have faith in a higher power. But this is beyond my comprehension. Being freaked out won't solve anything.

It exists, and that's it, but the fact remains astonishing. No one would ever believe this back home. I'd get thrown in the looney bin, for sure.

The people here are born of this place, but Elias, who has resided here for five years, is quite intuitive—he perceived my dissimilarity immediately. So, if he hasn't encountered anyone else from our world, then why are *we* here? And why did he choose to stay? My assumption is he's a rare case, having no one of sentimental importance for him to return to. However, even if I didn't have a child, my family, relatives, friends, people I love—I couldn't fathom living my entire life and never seeing them again. If Elias honestly had no one, I understand his decision to stay. This place gives elation and comfort. But, of all the words in the dictionary, blissful is the last term I'd use to describe him.

"Why did you avoid me?" I ask again.

"In your position, I would have chased any clue regarding my being here. But, until now, I've yet to meet anyone from *there.* You are a reminder of a world I loathe with every fiber of my being." His words are disconcerting, but he speaks them with conviction.

"It's not so bad, you know. It may not be like this one, but there's beauty in our society as well. Life is what you make it."

"Oh yeah? Then why are *you* here?" Sarcasm laces his mocking tone.

I ignore it. "And that's just it. I don't know why. I have a good life, a supportive family, and a solid career. I'm stable and fulfilled."

"Who are you trying to convince? Me or yourself?" He scoffs.

What the hell is that supposed to mean?

I halt, needing a moment to process his offensive remark. He continues moving forward, unbothered. My gaze burns holes into his back, and my hands ball to fists at my sides. He's exasperating, and his supercilious disposition is sure to make me blow my top soon.

He knows nothing about you, Skye. Just calm down.

Nope, go off.

I march toward him, cut him off in his tracks, and face him. I jab my finger in his chest, and I snap. "I don't know who you think you..." But my words are cut short and replaced by a gasp when he quickly grabs my wrist and, with a firm grip, jolts me forward.

His emeralds grow dark. "If you like this finger, I suggest you keep it to yourself," he grits.

My heart pounds in my chest as the sound of his ferocity reverberates through me. I search his eyes. I've never seen someone so full of rage. The darkness that oozes from this man is buried in his roots and sprouts through his veins. It's then I realize that he isn't intentionally trying to keep others away; that's just a side effect of the murk surrounding him.

I may have poked the bear, but this is a distinctive reaction to *something else.*

He releases my wrist and walks past me, but I remain stunned, holding my hand against my chest and rubbing the wrist that was tethered in his grip.

He stops and takes a deep breath. I turn around and face his halted back. He jerks his chin up and says, "I'm sorry."

"No, I'm sorry," I begin. "Offended or not, I had no right to lay a finger on you. It was out of line."

He turns around, and his eyes drop to my chest, where I hold my wrist. "Let me see that." He gestures to my arm.

"No, it's fine. I'm okay, really. I..."

"Let. Me. See." He interrupts my road to a ramble.

I hold out my arm, and he takes my wrist and rubs a thumb over the slightly reddish area as he examines it. "Put ice on it tonight," he instructs me and then releases my arm. We continue walking along the shore.

"You've got a strong grip," I joke.

"You've got tiny wrists."

Rolling my eyes, I smirk. "Oh, so now it's my wrist's fault? Maybe I'll get fat so they won't be so tiny."

"Who said you weren't already fat?" he deadpans and glances in my direction.

The daggers I stare at him could pierce through his being, yet he finds the sight amusing and bursts into laughter.

His laugh. A cool breeze on a blistering day, a smile illuminating his features, betraying the darkness that clouds them. It's only there for a moment before it dissipates, but it's then I catch a glimpse of the shrouded light that begs to shine. And revealed before my eyes is the perfectly carved man.

Sincerely, I begin to wonder: *What happened to you, Elias?*

CHAPTER 17
Skye

"Is this a pescatarian world?"

"Pretty much. I've traveled to many different lands; the only source of meat is seafood. However, they eat hen eggs but not chicken. Never understood that, but I don't question it," Elias replies.

We walked through the beach for a few hours as Elias explained the lay of the land. Although there are no personal or public motor vehicles, leaders of *most* lands have discovered decades ago ways to make construction easier, and so construction vehicles were introduced. People get around by foot or can ask for assistance for long distances by horse and carriage, depending on time and availability. Some have their own stables, but most lands have a large public stable where horses are raised.

Suddenly at ease that I *will* return home, I'd like to journal my experience in this dimension. Elias and I stopped at a shop, and now in my possession is a pink butterfly journal that I couldn't resist.

"I don't understand the absence of currency, trading, or bartering. There is no form of payment for goods and services. Do people just work for free? Live for free?" I begin questioning this world's concept. "I mean, the homes, someone's labor hours built them, yet there is no rent or mortgage? No tax on the land? Someone has to own it somehow. The people who pick the fruits and vegetables, catch the fish, maintain the land, they have to be paid somehow. Is there education? If so, who pays the educators?"

He sighs. "Unfortunately, that's all you know because that is the society of our upbringing."

"Yes, but things have to be that way, or people will take advantage. People will take and take until there is nothing left," I assert.

"I had these very questions when I arrived, but to understand it, you have to open your mind to a new way of thinking, a different perception of people." He pauses for a beat, then asks, "What do you do for a living now?"

"Finance manager," I reply.

"Pays you well?"

"Well, yes. I live quite comfortably, but I had to work my way to that position to earn such salaries. Nothing was simply *handed* to me. How can you value something that you didn't work for?"

He glances down at my wrist. "That bracelet on your wrist, do you value it?"

Lifting my arm, I look at my pink butterfly bracelet. "Yes, of course."

"Why?"

"Because my grandmother made it for me."

"So, you didn't work for it, but for the sentiment of gratitude, you value it. Your grandmother, aware that you value it, feels the same gratuity, but it is within a sense of purpose," he explains. "Now think of this on a wider scale among the masses in general."

Considering his elucidation, I ponder the idea that a stable civilization could operate this way. "So, people provide goods and services for the gratification of pleasing others?"

He doesn't answer immediately. Instead, he seems to be thinking about how to answer me appropriately. "Would you work, doing what you're doing now, if you didn't have to?"

I shrug. "No, who would?"

"Why not?"

And that's when it makes sense. He must have noticed the enlightenment in my expression, because he slightly grins.

"Cultivating gratitude and altruism gives us a sense of purpose. Even in the society we're from, helping someone still fulfills some sense of purpose within us. However, it's heightened *here* because there is no concept of money." He pauses. "The concept of money places *tangible* value on goods and services. While that may not seem inimical, over the years, it has chipped away at our humanity piece by piece. Simple gratitude no longer holds value because it is *intangible*. However, it's that intangible asset that is valuable to our humanity."

I never imagined a society where this could exist. I begin to grasp the concept and input my understanding. "So, people don't take advantage because helping each other like this has been their way of life for centuries."

He nods. "Through their passion, everyone caters to their own purpose, and in doing so, the needs of the community are fulfilled. The *value is to the soul*."

I recall what Mauria expressed the day I met her about helping where she could. "And those who do not quite know what it is they want to do, they offer help where needed, fulfilling their own sense of purpose to the community."

"Now you understand," he says, and it almost feels like praise. "If you love what you do for a living—if it was your passion— you'd never work another day. Similar to the people here."

"What about the land?" I ask.

"Let's go to the library," he suggests. "The founder's book of Sandemian history may answer plenty of your questions."

"What part of town are you residing in?" Elias asks.

"Haven Downs," I reply. "Is that where you arrived as well?"

He hands me the history book of Sandemia. "No. When I arrived, there were no residences available. We docked at Port Velle, near the visitor's lodge, and Sylvester instructed me to ask the woman for a room."

I browse through the fantasy romance and suspense novels and stack a few on my arm to check out. "She couldn't see him?"

"No one could. Hence the article's assumption I was talking to myself," he validates.

I recall a few of Sylvester's words for a moment. "He said he was doing his duty to me, to serve me. I still don't understand that."

"Again, you didn't ask."

"He witnessed my state of panic. He could have been forthcoming."

We head to the front counter and check out the books. Elias continues, "I concluded quickly that Sylvester only directly answers what you ask. In a state of panic, logical thinking defers."

"Who wouldn't panic waking up on a strange boat at sea? Especially at night," I say in my defense as we exit the library.

He gazes at me with dark eyes. "Panicking gets you *killed*."

We approach where I reside as the sun begins to set. "I'll come back in two days. I'm spending the day at the shipyard tomorrow; help those guys with maintenance."

"Was that your passion in our world, too?" I ask.

"It was cars."

"No cars here, so you work on the sea vessels?"

He nods.

We stop at my mailbox. Before bidding him good night, I entertain my curiosity. "Why did you stay?"

His eyebrows raise. "After all I've told you about this world, you have to ask that?"

"Yeah, but what about people? Loved ones? Don't you miss them?"

His lips form a straight line. "No."

"Come on, everyone has someone," I engage him.

"I'm quite content alone." His response is absolute, but I can sense the dark energy behind it.

"Who are you trying to convince? Me or yourself?"

"Good one." He smirks. "Read that book."

I hold up the Sandemian history book with a plastic smile. "Got it, history lesson homework."

Half smiling, he bids me a good night.

"Thank you for today, for enlightening me. You didn't have to do that, but you did."

With a curt nod, he continues on his way, but I remain where I stand and stare at his retreating back, admiring his broad shoulders and slightly hunched posture. He lifts a hand to push his hair back from his face; even from behind, the motion is appealing. I walk away the moment I realize my teeth are biting down on my bottom lip.

There's a small package outside my door. I carry it inside and use my key to cut through the brown tape. I unravel the paper wrapped around the moderately weighted item, and there it is—officially delivered—a glass curved in the center, lined with wood, indicating the countdown has begun.

The hourglass.

CHAPTER 18

Skye

I spent the majority of the night reading the history of Land Sandemia. An interesting read, illustrating the idiosyncratic customs of this world as related by Elias yesterday.

Two centuries ago, a syndicate was founded by voyagers, including an architect, a farmer, a fisherman, an electrician, and a carpenter, on a discovery mission. They discovered an uninhabited island, and through their shared passion, they began construction on this island to create a new civilization. They sent word of their endeavors to neighboring lands, and in due course, others sailed in and joined in the labor, bringing with them materials and skills. After innumerable days, they were content to witness their plan come to fruition. They paved paths, built homes, shops, visiting lodges, and a park, and they began growing crops. The once-wild forest became an established development and was added to the map as Land Sandemia.

Soon, more people moved to Sandemia, and the once uninhabited land became a small village. With enhancement, a rise in industry, and a growing population, a civilization was born.

I suppose this is the way the lands of every world were built. I question how such a toil can go without reward, and I recall Elias's words: *"Through their passion, the needs of the community are fulfilled."* Ambition and pursuing passion know no dollar amount; it's the internal soul's desire. Watching Sandemia come to life was the reward for the founders' efforts in building the nation.

In the society Elias and I were born into, we measure such successes in dollars. Supposing that the timeline of both universes is parallel, the absence of currency and trade is why this world lacks some technological advancements relative to ours. But how important is such amelioration if the citizens are jovial?

A knock at my door pulls me out of my thoughts. I close my journal and place it on the coffee table. I lift myself from the sofa and move to the door. On the other side of the peephole is Mauria.

"So, how'd it go? Do you remember anything?" she asks when I open the door.

I step to the side and let her in before answering. "It went well. I remember quite a bit, but not everything."

She heads toward the kitchen and pours herself a cup of coffee. "That's great! Something is better than nothing. So, this Land New York, are you going back? What about the captain and Livity?"

Damn it. How am I going to flip this? "Well, uh... so, Land New York is not the place I'm from. I used to write. My memory was jumbled in the book I was working on. Land New York was what I named the place." *Believable, right?*

Her eyebrows shoot up. "Oh, so you're a writer? What about the boat?"

"Elias said it's for patient transport. I must have told them I was from here."

"Oh, why didn't I think of that? You have a head injury, it would only make sense," she says. *I'm not even sure how I thought of that, but now I have to tell Elias that I lied on him.* She takes a sip of coffee. "So, what land are you from?"

Damn. More questions. "Uh. That I don't remember... yet.

"Oh well, it'll come back. Soooo." She shrugs, then smacks her tongue. "This Elias guy, what's his deal?"

"Um, he's a shipwright?" I reply, but it comes out as a question. I don't know what she's asking exactly, but that answer seemed safe.

"A shipwright?" she says, seemingly impressed. "Well, that's cool. Wanna know what else I think is cool?" She has an impish look on her face, which makes me curious.

"What?" I tilt my head.

"Mmm. The way he looks at you." She smirks.

I gape, raise an index finger, and move it back and forth, gesturing that we stop right there. "Oh, no. Nope. Not at all."

"Listen. I was speaking to him, and the man barely glanced at me. All eyes were on you. It's like I wasn't even there!" She opens the fridge and grabs a bottle of water. "Like, come on. Have you seen me? My usual is holding up my hand to show my marriage ring, and this one acts like I'm not even worth a glance," she sasses dramatically, then moves from behind the counter with a hand on her hip and slaps her chest. "I'm actually a little hurt right now."

I lean on the couch, my jaw slacking as I stare in stunned disbelief at her total change in demeanor. *She is a totally different person.* Here, I thought she was oblivious and innocent. This girl is a firecracker, and... *I freaking love it.*

Her eyebrows draw together as her sass continues, "Why are you looking at me like that?"

Immediately, I burst into laughter. "Mauria, you are so funny."

"Oh, sure. Laugh at my pain," she says sarcastically.

So *petty* exists here too? Awesome. I'm enjoying this stark difference from her usual amicability. "Sorry for laughing at your bruised ego," I joke.

At the narrowing of her eyes, I laugh again. Mauria gives me a feeling akin to home.

Yeah, this vacation will be fun.

CHAPTER 19

Skye

"She's from Land Kairos as well. I didn't recognize her the other night—it had been years," Elias explains to Mrs. Arna after she welcomes me to Sandemia. His response gives me the impression she previously inquired about my hasty exit the other night.

"Enjoy," Ms. Arna offers, serving our food.

Sitting at a table near a window, I cut into my glazed salmon, then take a bite. "Oh my god, this is delicious," I express.

"The best in town," Elias says before bringing his fork to his lips. "So, what did you think of the book?"

I take a sip of water. "Interesting, really. The history specific to this land reflects the attributes of this world's society as a whole."

He swallows his food and nods. "Manifested the reality of what I was conveying to you the other night."

Scrunching in thought, I ask, "What about bad people?"

He clears his throat and then gazes out the window. "There's good and bad in everyone. No one is perfect, even here." Turning his head back to me, his eyebrows knit. "But that's not what you're *really* asking. There was a situation on another land, affairs of the heart. A man set fire to another man's boat. Would you color him a bad man or a man who made a bad decision?"

I shrug. "Affairs of the heart can be tricky, but I wouldn't consider him a bad man. But what were the consequences for that?"

"It's society's responsibility to understand its people and mold good citizens. I suppose he received the support needed after such actions. Crime may not exist to the brutal extent we've been exposed to, but conflict does. We still battle the internal pull of good and bad within ourselves as humans."

I chew another bite of my salmon slowly, cogitating the absence of heinous crimes. I begin to consider the exclusion of currency. "Is brutality nonexistent because this world exercises humanity?"

He swallows a sip of water and dips his chin. "That's actually an upstanding theory. In addition, it could also be a ripple effect."

"What do you mean?"

"The makings of this society didn't begin with subjugation or eradication. As a result, such actions don't affect future generations."

I consider his theory. "Killing has been the way of our world for centuries. It's how the leaders before us conquered. Even to this day, as unlawful as it is, it's still practiced. We've been exposed to it time and time again, so it's no longer 'the unthinkable.'"

He nods. "In contrast, civilization here began with people working together as one, so it has had a ripple effect for centuries to come."

I raise my chin and contemplate his theory in addition to mine. "This place is a paradise."

He uses a napkin to wipe his mouth, balls it up, and throws it on his plate, then settles back in his chair. "Only to us. But to the people here, it's simply a way of life. How would you know paradise if you don't know hell?"

I take one last bite before pushing away the remainder of the salmon. As delicious as it is, my stomach can't take another bite. "Do you think our world could ever be this way?"

He shakes his head. "If they tried to change where we're from to a place like this, I wouldn't want to be around when the ripple starts."

The ripple effect. "We're too far gone."

He nods. "We would have to go back to the beginning, where it all started."

"So, have you traveled to this 'Land Kairos,' where you've claimed *we're* from?" I ask as we walk past the entrance of Haven Downs.

"I've traveled to many of the islands here. They're all unique in their own way, but Kairos deviates significantly."

"How so?"

He tilts his head down, and his dark hair sways forward, obstructing the view of his upper side profile. The sight is striking. I honestly wish he wasn't so damn fine. "They're different. Many consider their livelihood unnecessary, but it's because most don't understand their culture."

We arrive at my residence and pause at the mailbox. Mauria is in her yard and waves in our direction. "Let's have brunch tomorrow before Sam and I take off to Land Yemen!"

I wave and shout back, "Sure!" She retreats to her home.

"You've made a friend," Elias observes.

"Yeah, I like her." I smile. "She's definitely a character. What about you? Do you have any friends here?"

"Not my thing," he deadpans before bidding me good night and walks away.

"Elias?" I call his name, but it's in the form of a question. He pauses and turns back around. I grow nervous about my next words. He's someone who appreciates his own space, prefers to be unbothered. In my desperation, I barged in on his contentment. However, in a break from his norm, he's helped me understand the situation, even if I'm still perplexed as to *why* I'm here. He's taken the step to further educate me on this society's norms and inspire me with a new perception. There's nothing more he needs to do, and technically, I can take it from here.

I *should* take it from here.

But I want more.

So, without expectation, I express an aspiration. "Um. I'd like to do what you did. Travel to different lands here." I pause for a moment to study any change in him, but he remains stoic, so I continue. "Can I do that?"

He raises his chin, but his expression remains blank. Glancing down for a moment, after a sharp inhale, he gazes at me with softened features. "An adventure, huh? Alright, give me a few days."

I smile so wide I can feel it in my ears. Excitement sets in, and the giddy girl beneath my layers of maturity skips up and down. He notices my reaction, and a slight grin forms on his lips.

"You're awesome sauce!" I exclaim excitedly.

Chuckling, he shakes his head at my overbearance.

"Well, Mister Lonely. Now you'll have me!"

I watch his lips turn down from a half-smile to a straight line, and his habitual frown returns. "Have a good night, Skye." He stuffs his hands in his pockets and walks away. "A few days, eight at most."

"Got it," I reply to his retreating back before proceeding toward my front door.

His sudden change in demeanor remains at the forefront of my mind. It was a mindless declaration of a beginning friendship between us. He had to know I meant no harm; it was sincere. Pondering his reaction further, I get the feeling that Elias opposes companionship.

But why?

I want to know more, but I won't push—*at least, not too hard.*

Elias

Mister Lonely, huh? Lonely people are miserable with disassociation. They crave confidants. Contrasting by a landslide, such relationships are not unprecedented to me. I've known companionship, friendship, love, all of the above.

I've experienced enough to know I prefer to be without it.

She misunderstands me.

I'm isolated, *not* forsaken. To be alone is a choice.

People never truly care for you, only for what you can do for them. Even love is a contract with terms and conditions, and all contracts have loopholes.

They can be bought out.

So grace no one with endearment, and you won't fall victim to the escape clause.

I pivot toward the exit of Haven Downs, and an older gentleman greets me. "Good evening, young man."

Pausing, I acknowledge him. "Evening, sir."

"Name's Alton Windsor. Might you be new here too?"

"Elias Crawford," I introduce. "No, just accompanying someone new home."

He raises his chin. "Ah, Ms. Skye." He clearly recalls the only newcomer to Haven Downs. "You know, I am in search of this 'money' she speaks of, but to no avail." He curls his fingers under his chin, perplexed.

Rubbing an eyebrow with a thumb, I clear my throat—a delay while I devise a fabrication. "She's, uh, having some memory issues and mixes words. She had a mongrel dog some years ago and likes honey in her tea. Believe she may have confused the two, regaining her memory."

He nods. "I had no idea. Well, good to know. I hope her memory recovers soon."

He gestures with his hand for a shake. I extend mine and accept. "Good to meet you, Mr. Alton. Have a good night."

His lips curve into a smile, and he bids me good night. I proceed to exit Haven Downs.

Mongrel and honey? Stupidest fucking lie on the planet.

CHAPTER 20

Skye

"Shouldn't that kid be in school?" I ask Mauria after we're greeted by a minor at the restaurant entrance. The afternoon skies are clear and the weather is pleasant, so we sit outside.

Mauria lifts the menu. "It's a fifth, so the kids are out of school today. His parents own this place, he's helping out."

I have no idea what that means, but I don't ask. "Oh, well, I didn't read the Daycomm this morning, so I lost track."

Her eyes dart to my watch and then back at me. "You need an upgraded watch. One that actually shows the day *and* time. Yours is totally outdated."

Digital watches exist here? I glance down at the watch I picked up the first day we ventured out on the town. "Yeah, I guess I do."

"Memory loss or not, sometimes I'm convinced you live under a rock."

They still communicate by letters, and I'm living under a rock? How ironic. "So, I'm from Land Kairos, by the way."

"Oh, so you do live under a rock," she mutters.

I give her a quizzical look. "What do you mean?"

Closing the menu, she gazes at me as if she's about to teach me a lesson. "Look, I don't want to speak ill of your land, but they are so detached from society. Come on, you know, that's probably why you're here. Their way of living is entirely unorthodox. Kairos is the largest of all the first founding lands, yet they refuse to utilize its full potential. The population continues to decrease because its citizens are realizing that they could live better lives, especially after the fire twenty-five years ago. People evolve, but the leaders and people of Kairos choose to stagnate. It's pretty sad."

I consider her words but refrain from asking any questions—because I'm *supposed* to be from there. I recall Elias mentioning, "*Most don't understand their culture.*" Seemingly, Mauria is one of those people.

"Seriously, it's 2023, and they're still living extremely primitively. Land Tikita, where I'm from, isn't as developed as Sandemia, but they're upgrading and continuing to develop. The people of Kairos have chosen to keep things exactly how they are since the beginning of time. So weird." She quirks her eyebrows and twists her lips. "It's a good thing you're not there anymore. You are way too young to be living in a tenth-century land. Stick with me, I'll show you all there is to the *real world.*"

If only she knew how much I wish this was *my* real world.

After brunch, we stop at an accessory shop, and I pick up a bag, a silver *digital* watch, jewelry, sunglasses, and other neat things. I show the owner the items I'm taking, and I thank him sincerely. These products look like they would be quite expensive in my world; not paying for them feels like theft.

"We have to head back by two p.m.," Mauria mentions as we leave the shop. "Sam and I are sailing over to Land Yemen for some furniture. We'll be back in the morning."

We're passing by the Town Register when she asks, "Hey, have you registered your home?"

Damn, it totally slipped my mind to ask Elias about that. "Um, no. I mean, I don't remember. I'm supposed to, right?" I didn't think my response through before speaking, so total rubbish just left my lips.

"Have you never lived on your own before?"

"Uh…"

"Oh dear, you poor thing. You've lived a sheltered life."

She's sincere, but I'm fighting back a laugh. *She doesn't know what a phone is, and I'm sheltered?*

We walk toward the Town Register and enter the small establishment. It consists of a counter, a very old-looking computer, and a door leading to an office.

"Hi, Mrs. Donnell," Mauria greets the middle-aged woman. "Is 12 Haven Downs registered for occupancy?"

Mrs. Donnell's eyebrows knit together in thought. "I don't believe so. I've sent letters there requiring an occupant to register since I've noticed current water usage. Give me a second. Let me double-check."

She moves toward the back while we wait by the entrance. Mauria shakes her head. "You're a squatter. Terrible." I narrow my eyes at her and that unfiltered mouth.

"Ah yes." Mrs. Donnell returns to the counter. "This morning, this home was temporarily registered to Skye Cooke."

Wait, seriously? "Hi, I'm Skye Cooke. Are you able to tell me who registered me?"

"Mr. Windsor did. Would you like to register for this residence permanently? I am only able to hold temporary residence for forty days."

Alton Windsor? Why would he do that? "I don't have identification at the moment. I'm from Land Kairos. I believe I may have forgotten it there." I recall the letter I found in the mailbox days ago.

"Tell you what," she begins. "I'll hold the registration for twenty extra days. Kairos is a twelve-day sail. If you can have a family or friend mail you your Kairos birth identification, it will take around twenty or so days to arrive."

Just like that? She doesn't know me. I still have no idea how I'll get any birth papers from Kairos, but I'll figure something out. "I appreciate that so much, Mrs. Donnell."

She smiles. "You ladies have a good day now."

"Well, that was nice of Mr. Alton, but seriously, you don't have identification?" Mauria questions as we exit the facility.

Unsure how to respond, I shrug. "Maybe I do. I just don't remember." I use my excuse for everything I don't have an answer for. We're just about to walk toward the main road when I look up and spot Elias in the window of a shop across the street.

Pausing, I study him for a moment. He's casually dressed in a white cap, an aqua blue t-shirt, white jeans shorts, and white sneakers with the *Sandemia* logo at the side.

"What are you looking at?" Mauria asks, but my eyes are glued to Elias's side profile.

Following my line of sight, she also spots him. "Oh, so you like him too?"

Her question snaps me out of my daze. "What? No. And he doesn't like me either."

Crossing her arms, she rolls her eyes. "Well, I wouldn't blame you, the man is total eye candy. I mean, just look at those arms. Those are 'pin you to the wall' arms."

My eyes widen at her blunt remark. "Mauria!"

"Oh please." She shuts me down. "You were thinking it."

"No, I was not."

Her hands drop to her hips. "Well you were totally eye fu..."

"Mauria!"

"Fine. But you were."

How in the world is she like this? I would not expect those terms to be used here, but apparently they are, and Mauria does not hold back.

Elias places the items in bags, nods to the person at the

counter, and moves to the entrance. He spots us as he presses through the door.

"Well, hello there, big guy with the big house." *And here comes the girl with the big mouth.* "I didn't get a chance to formally introduce myself. My name is Mauria Huxley."

"Elias Crawford," Elias replies.

"Look, I know we met on awk..."

"All is forgiven," he interrupts and then gestures to me. "What brings you over this way?"

Remembering that I'm in a pinch, I reply, "Well apparently I didn't register my..." I begin but remember it's "*my*" nothing. "The house I'm in."

He protrudes his lips and lifts his chin slowly, as if recalling something he missed mentioning. "How'd that go?"

"Temporary for sixty days."

He nods. "Okay. Should give you enough time."

Nodding slowly, I squint. "Rigggght." I draw out the word, curious to know if he will clue me in on the plan.

"So, your home is a custom build?" Mauria cuts in.

He nods.

"Would you allow me to tour? My husband, Sam, is an architect, and we're currently working on the blueprint for a custom build. Your home could inspire some ideas."

"I've got time today," Elias says.

"Damn it." She huffs in disappointment. "I can't. Sam and I are leaving for Yemen soon. Maybe when I get back?"

"Just let me know." He looks in my direction. "Want to tour?"

"You can come with us if you'd like, Skye. Have you ever been to Land Yemen?" Mauria asks.

I hear Mauria, but my eyes are fixed on Elias. I get the impression he's exhorting me to come with him. Breaking from his gaze, I turn to Mauria. "Maybe some other time."

"You are so lucky," she says, then addresses Elias. "Hey, this doesn't mean I don't get my tour."

He smirks and peers at her from the corner of his eye. "Yes, ma'am."

"Wait, I have to walk back with you," I tell Mauria.

She gives me a puzzled expression. "Why? I walk by myself all the time. It's not as boring as you think. Elias lives far away. That'll be pointless."

"I'm not going to let you walk alone, Mauria."

"What?" She cringes. "You're acting like something's going to happen to me."

Elias crosses one arm and brings his fingers to his mouth, curling them under his nose to cover his smirk.

"Well, you could like... I don't know... hit your toe." *That was so stupid. I'm an idiot.* I suck at making sudden excuses.

Mauria stares at me dumbfounded, and I hear Elias snicker.

"Skye, I'm wearing sneakers."

Elias struggles to suppress a laugh, and his snickering becomes audible. I stare daggers at him. I want to smack that smirk off his face.

I shift my focus back to Mauria. "Well, I mean, you could fall and hit your head and end up at the healers."

Her expression becomes concerned. "Oh no, is that what happened to you? Memory loss from simply walking and falling? That's terrible! I certainly don't think you should be walking alone." She shifts her attention to Elias. "Hey, make sure she's okay."

Well, that escalated quickly.

Elias can't hold back anymore. He covers his face, hangs his head, and suppresses his laughter in his palm.

"Hey, I'm serious," Mauria says.

Lifting his head, he exhales as his amusement subsides. "I know. She's safe with me, Miss Mauria."

Mauria places a hand on my shoulder and brings me in for a hug. "I'll be fine, girl, don't you worry. Have fun." She releases me. "See ya, Elias," she says and proceeds toward Haven Downs.

I stand stupefied. "What... just happened?"

Elias grins slightly. "You have a lot to learn, sunshine."

"Like what?" I ask, still in utter confusion.

"Like new norms."

Stopping, I turn to look at him. "No, I mean, I didn't think—"

"Then what is it?" he cuts in.

"Well, she's…" I stop speaking because I'm not even sure.

"Too trusting? Naive?" He quirks his eyebrows and dips his chin. "A woman."

I press my lips together, speechless.

"You know what else is not normal?"

I tilt my head, awaiting his response.

"People fearing *other* people."

CHAPTER 21

Skye

"How long did it take to have your house built?" I ask when we arrive at Elias's home.

"Equivalent to six months."

"There's no way you did it alone."

"I fix ships. Not build homes." He searches his pockets for his keys.

"How did you possibly get people to…"

"I didn't *get* anyone to do anything," he emphasizes as if my question assumes he somehow deceived others.

I wasn't implying that he did, but I presume it may have sounded that way. But there is no form of monetary payment for such builds, so I'm curious how a man who keeps to himself could have asked people to build him a home of this stature. That was most definitely a time-consuming, laborious task. "You had to be convincing somehow." He may not appreciate it, but I push for a response that will satisfy my curiosity.

He removes the keys from his pockets, but before inserting them into the lock, he huffs. "I formerly worked on large ships on Land Samoa. At the time, there were no residencies available there; I lived at a visitor's lodge. There's a group of guys whose vessels I maintained. For two of them, I built their boats. I did this on Land Samoa for about a year. They had discovered I was staying in a visitor's lodge for as long as I had been there. Together, they offered to build a home for me. I told them I planned to voyage before settling, so raincheck. When the time came, I informed them that if the offer still stood, I would like to reside on Land Sandemia."

They sound like they're kind-hearted people. "You mention them as if it were of no significance, but it sounds to me that they were really good *friends*."

I wait for a response, but he gives none, instead inserting the key into the lock and turns it. "Officially, welcome to my home," he offers, and opens the door.

Stepping inside, the first view is of a spacious living room with a black faux leather sectional and an ottoman surrounding a gray stone fireplace; a canvas matte portrait of a woman is over it, and a large bookcase accommodating hundreds of books sits against another wall.

I follow him to the kitchen. Black granite counters sit atop the cabinets, and a large island stands in the center with four barstool-height chairs. To the right, a rectangular glass-topped table sits in the middle, with four dining chairs on either side. "Your home is immaculate, but may I ask why you chose to have such a large one?"

"I wanted my own home, not a prebuilt one. Even in our world, I knew that whenever I was ready to become a homeowner, I would buy the land and have one built."

He leads me upstairs. Three of the four-bedroom doors are open, and I assume behind the closed door is his bedroom. He doesn't show me that one. Two other rooms are empty, but one is fully furnished. "Do you ever have visitors?"

"No."

"Would you allow visitors?"

"You're here, aren't you?" Not the answer I was expecting, but I'll take it—he's actually serious.

We exit through the backdoor. The view from his back yard is paradisiacal due to the home sitting on a hill, allowing for a clear, elevated view of the sea. Following a narrow path leading to a small garage, I ask, "What's that for?"

"Where I pull my boats in and work on them."

The garage is at the end of the path, near the shore. Inside, hoisted on a stand, is a midsize yacht. "This is luxurious. Did you build this?"

He smiles. "A beauty, isn't she?"

With raised eyebrows, I agree. "Yes, indeed."

"It's my offshore cruiser. She can sail for up to ninety days nonstop. We're taking this baby to sea. Want to look inside?" His eyes sparkle as his attention shifts to his vessel. He's proud, and it's clear this is his passion.

We climb aboard. I walk through the sizable cockpit lined with cushioned seating. Three steps lead down to a small cabin with a bedroom, a small kitchen, and a bathroom. The bedroom is cozy, with a window to the outside. "This is incredible, Elias," I say and leave the cabin, walking toward the top deck.

He half smiles, pleased with my admiration of his work. "You'll be quite comfortable while we're out at sea."

"I see! I'm super excited." I grin with enthusiasm. I've never been on a cruise.

He chuckles, and I don't miss it when his smile grows wide before he focuses his attention elsewhere. Once again—just for a moment—I caught another glimpse of the light caged in his depths.

Sitting in the garage, I watch as Elias diligently works on his pride and joy. "So, Mr. Windsor registered me for temporary residence this morning at the Town Register. I plan to ask him about it. He also gave me a map and a compass, claiming it was for anyone it could be of use to, but I know it was actually meant for me. I mean, it's all nice of him, but why not just be upfront and say it?"

He pauses his toolwork and looks in my direction. "Speaking of Mr. Alton, I met him. If he asks, you once had a mongrel puppy and like honey in your tea."

I'm so confused. "What?"

"He keeps looking for money. Told him your memory loss has you jumbling mongrel and honey, and you call it money."

"That's the stupidest..." I shut my mouth when the abrupt turn of his head is accompanied by a furrowed glare. He must have known it was stupid when he said it. "I don't even like tea."

He shifts his attention back to his boat. "Yeah, well, you do now."

"He's strange to me. Not in a creepy way. Just... strange."

"Nah, he's not. He's like any other citizen. Skye, you try to blend in, but it's obvious you're different and unfamiliar. I'm sure he's picked up on that, but he probably notices you try to hide it, so he doesn't confront you. He just attempts to help in whatever little way he can without offending you."

I shrug. *Well, that solves that.* I trust Elias. I'm not sure why, but I do. The darkness he carries within stems from whatever he may have experienced in our world, but I feel that, overall, he's a decent human being.

A decent human being, hard-shelled, with an uncharitable demeanor that rejects companionship and is sporadically brooding, morose, curt, and impertinent. *Okay, so maybe his entire personality screams "run,"* but my gut tells me that, beneath all of that, he's genuine. "Okay. I trust you, but I'd still like to ask him about it, even thank him."

Pausing for a beat, his jaw tenses after my response. *Was it something I said?*

"I'll get a birth record with a Land Kairos seal. You'll be able to get a Sandemian ID and register your address for permanent residence until your time is up and you return."

His manner switched. It's hardened, and although his plan is benevolent, his tone is discourteous. I know I'm going back—I have to—but there's something about the way he said it that slightly pinches as if he'd be happier if I left tomorrow. I'm not sure why the sudden shift, but his dark energy stifles a room in an instant.

Pushing down the unsettling reception, I focus on my curiosity. "So, why Land Kairos?"

"They're behind the times there. It'll be easier to get into the records office, make a birth record, and sneak out."

"Is that how you made yours?"

"No."

That's it. No explanation, nothing. *Here we go again.*

"Well, how are you so sure you'll be able to do that?"

He glances at me with a frowned expression—*his usual.*

"Look, I just don't want you getting into any kind of trouble over this—over me. I'm not here permanently—you are. So, if it means you're risking any sort of repercussions that could affect your future here, don't bother," I quickly explain.

This is what perplexes me about him. So cold, yet so humane. If his gruff exterior could be penetrated, I might find an affable Elias.

His expression softens slightly, and he turns back to his work. "A forest fire broke out at Land Kairos twenty-five years ago. Many of the birth records were disintegrated. Most citizens have copies of theirs. I claimed to have lost mine, and one was created for me."

"Well, can't we say the same happened to me instead of you sneaking in there?" I suggest.

Sighing, he says, "You're not staying. Not only will they make a copy for you, they'll create one to retain in their records."

He has a point.

"So how long do I have in the hourglass? It moves incredibly slow."

"One hundred twenty days."

"So, is your age current in this world as well?" I ask. "The fire at Kairos happened twenty-five years ago, so you had to be older than that for them to believe you."

"I would have lied if necessary, but I didn't. I was twenty-seven when I arrived here."

"So, you're thirty-two now? You're old."

"Old? What are you, twelve, to be calling me old?" He scoffs.

"I'm thirty-nine," I deadpan. The swift turn of his head toward me warrants my expulsive laughter. *He was totally not expecting that.* "I'm twenty-eight, but your reaction was priceless! That was awesome."

With a short laugh, he shakes his head at my silliness. There goes that cool breeze on a blistering day—again, only there for a moment. But I wish he'd find more reasons to laugh. It suits him.

Elias

"You know, you could've made a solid career out of this in our world. As long as there are cars, mechanics will be in demand." Skye walks around the garage, inspecting the equipment.

"You don't think it makes me a grease monkey?" I smirk.

She chuckles. "That's actually funny, but you'll be a successful grease monkey." She turns on her heels. "That would actually be a pretty cool business name." She extends her arms and flexes her fingers, holding an invisible sign. "Grease Monkey Auto. Pretty cool, huh?"

I chuckle inwardly. "Yeah. Would've been."

Sitting back down, she places her elbows on her knees. "Most people don't know what their passion is. You have clearly known yours for a while. Did you never try investing in opening a shop?"

I don't want to get into this conversation, but I'll answer. "I *did* have a shop."

"What happened?"

"Just didn't work out."

"Well, why not?"

She's prying; I shut it down. "Skye." One hardened glance and a steel tone, grim and absolute. I don't know why she trusts me as she does. I may have helped her, but I haven't been pleasant. I trust no one, not even the woman with pure ambiance sitting before me, evidently fascinated as I work. She can kill her interest in obtaining knowledge about me prior to my arrival here. The only thing she's getting is whatever she witnesses. She can Internet search me or some shit when she gets back. I won't care because I'll never see her again.

She tucks in her bottom lip, darts out the tip of her tongue, and tilts her head down. It's clear she's become unsettled. While I revisit my work, in my peripheral, I see her stand and inspect the equipment again. After a few minutes, she leaves the garage. I watch her retreating back as she makes her way to the shore.

After a few hours of maintenance work, it's finally complete;

my vessel is ready to take sail. I'm setting tools away, but I pause when I glance over to the shore, and my eyes land on Skye.

Leaning on the garage opening, I watch her for a moment. She's strolling around one of my other docked boats, examining every area, opening compartments, searching. She finds my spyglass and proceeds to climb to the highest point of the boat. Bringing the spyglass to her eye, she focuses far out over the sea. I am struck by the sight of the wind blowing her lengthy spiraled tresses. The lift of her arms causes her white shirt to pull tight at her back, revealing her well-proportioned figure.

She'd fit like a glove in my arms.

She begins to circle, taking in her surroundings with magnification. Facing my direction, she points the glass down and slightly jerks, removes it from her eye, climbs down, and jogs toward me with a wide smile.

That smile again. It's unique to her. One can't remain in a state of gloom if she beams at you. It's irresistible and makes her one with the sunshine, enhancing her beauty, exposing her pure soul. It remains a mystery why she's here. Her aura is the reflection of someone who is cherished and cherishes others. *So what happened?*

"Your head was like super big in the scope. So unexpected." She laughs.

"You have to adjust it with your movement, or you'll see a bee the size of a gorilla and piss yourself."

"Yikes."

I turn to close up the garage. "Hungry yet?"

"Starving!" She grimaces.

"Pepax?"

"Pepax, taco, whatever. It sounds delicious right now."

We eat our pepaxes as we walk in the direction of her neighborhood. As we enter, I notice how active it is. The majority of her neighbors are outside and socializing with one another. Mr. Alton's home is across from Skye's, he and, I presume, his wife are gardening in a small section near their patio.

"That's Mr. Alton's wife, Ms. Lorlee. Really nice lady," Skye confirms my thoughts.

We arrive at Skye's home and linger on her patio for a moment. "So have you thought about why you're here?"

She shrugs. "Not really. I told you my life was fine. Last I remember, I fell asleep watching *One Piece*."

"*One Piece*? The anime?" I quirk an eyebrow, recalling the show I hadn't watched since my younger days. But, back then, I'd made it a priority to catch the weekly release episodes of Naruto.

"Yep! Sort of ironic, don't you think? Fall asleep watching a show about adventure by way of sea transport, then wake up to vacation in a similar world?" she says excitedly.

I stuff my hands in my pockets and shake my head. "You didn't end up here from watching an anime, Skye."

"What about you?" she diverts.

Not happening. "We're not talking about me."

She crosses her arms and sasses, "Yeah, well, how about we talk about you? What brought you here? And why'd you stay?"

Damn, she's persistent. But I made my decision to stay, so the *why* is no longer important. I can't return, and I have no interest in returning. "I've made my decision."

"So did I."

She's stubborn as shit. "You have those you love and cherish back home, am I right?"

"Yes."

"Okay, so no issue there." I gaze directly into her brown eyes. I am unsure why, but there's a pull within me that wants to help her. "There's another reason, something deep down. You're either unaware of it, or you are but refuse to accept it. But if you don't face it while you're here, you'll return more miserable than when you arrived."

Her features contort into a deep frown. "I'm not miserable!"

Now we're getting somewhere. I've struck a nerve again. I search her eyes—she's brewing with anger. *She's got walls up,* convincing herself she's happy. "So, *One Piece* brought you here? Okay Skye." Mocking sarcasm laces my tone, and she reddens with anger.

She takes a breath to calm down, but it helps only a minuscule amount. "No, I was watching *One Piece,* and for a moment, I thought of myself in Luffy's shoes. Exploring the world. Sure, I would like that, but it doesn't make me miserable in any way. It just *felt* good."

"It's more than that. You're in denial," are my last words before I turn to leave.

"Excuse me?" she says, clearly offended by my words. I face her again.

She's utterly still, fumes blowing from her ears, fists balled at her sides. *Someone's enraged.* She steps into my bubble. At the first glimpse of her rising arm, anger shoots through me. "I swear to God, if you jab that finger at me again, you're going to regret it."

"I wasn't going to!" she snaps.

"Then back up," I demand. And she does.

I won't push any further, *for now*; it may cause more harm than good. She doesn't want anyone to see beyond her superficiality, but I see it in her volatile reaction to any attempt to peek through her barriers. All that "*my life is perfect*" bullshit she claims is transparent. However, for right now, I'll let it go. "I'm sorry. I didn't mean to upset you. Have a good night."

Not responding, she pushes through her door and slams it shut. I leave her patio, making my way to the Haven Downs exit.

Thrill creeps in as a new challenge arises.

I'll shatter those defenses, Skye Cooke, if it's the last thing I do.

CHAPTER 22

Skye

I've spent the next three days with Mauria, and she has inquired about Elias's home at least once each day. She keeps insisting that I describe his home to her, but I refuse. If I tell her, she'll be incredibly eager to—and chances are, she will—show up unannounced. The woman can be quite audacious, but Elias doesn't strike me as someone lenient about being imposed on. I'd have a guilty conscience if she shows up and he's rude to her because I didn't follow my gut.

"Maybe we'll run into him again at some point, and you can ask." Heavy on the *you ask* because I'm certainly not doing it.

"But what if we don't run into him?" She pauses for a beat, then puckers up. "Oh, I have an idea! Maybe he's not busy right now. Let's go visit."

And my gut wins. "Mauria, that is *absolutely* not a good idea. Elias lives quite the distance from everyone else for a reason. He won't appreciate us popping up and requesting to tour his home. Why don't you write him a letter? This way, he can plan a day and prepare for a tour of his home."

She nods. "That's actually a better idea. Now that you mention it, I'll write and ask him if Sam and I can both have a look. Sam is the architectural genius, not me. He'll know how to adjust the plans if anything in particular inspires him. I'll speak with Sam tonight and send off a letter."

Relieved, I pause during our stroll through Sheridan Park when the stables come into my field of vision. There are children with their guardians for leisurely purposes. A young boy, who looks to be no older than six years old, is currently riding one of the horses while being chaperoned by an adult. "Mommy, I want to ride next!" a little girl yells while pointing at the boy.

My son comes to mind. He'd enjoy horseback riding. *I'd enjoy it.* The closest thing to a horse I've ever ridden was on a merry-go-round. *"I'm going to take Julias horseback riding when I get back,"* I declare to myself.

"Do you like horses?" Mauria asks, pulling me out of my thoughts.

"Uh, yeah. Well, I don't know, but I'd like to go horseback riding."

Her lips stretch to a wide grin. "We'll put it on our list of things to do tomorrow."

"There's a list?"

"Yup! So, we'll go to the stables tomorrow morning, then we're going to sail to Zendovou. There's an amazing spa there. It's where Sam and I went recently for our couple's massage. You'll love it."

Now *that* I'm totally looking forward to. However, I know *diddly squat* about sailing, rowing, boats, yachts, ships, any of it, so I certainly hope she does. "I love that plan," I say.

"Great. You'll meet my friend, Belva, and my sister-in-law, Shimi. You'll like them."

What? More people? Suddenly, the idea doesn't sound as gleeful. An unwelcome feeling sets in as my mind spins. *What if they ask questions about things that are common knowledge in this world, and I'm clueless?*

I push down the spewing doubt. *It's a spa day, not an interrogation. Relax.*

"Hey, are you okay? You look flustered." Mauria's concern grabs my attention.

"Yeah, no, I'm fine. Just a little exhausted. We've been on the move all day." I'm not so handy with instant fibbing, but that was a good one.

"You're right, let's head back," she suggests, and we round the curve leading to the park exit.

"Alright, we're up early tomorrow. Eight a.m. sharp. We'll grab a morning meal, head for the stables, then Shimi and Belva are going to meet us at Haven Docks by twelve," Mauria informs me before we part ways.

"Got it," I acknowledge.

On my way home, I glance across the road to see Mr. Alton and wave. When he returns the gesture, I proceed toward his yard. "Good day, Mr. Alton."

"Ms. Skye, how are you on this fine day?"

"I'm well. Hey, question for you." I get straight to the point.

He nods. "Sure."

"Did you register my name for temporary residence?"

He answers without hesitation. "Ah. Yes, I did."

"Oh. Well, thank you." I'm not sure what to make of any of it, so I simply offer my gratitude.

"I am terribly sorry if my doing so was out of place. Please forgive me, but you appeared to be a bit out of sorts when you arrived. I thought it might have helped as you become acclimated," he explains.

It's just as Elias said. It's obvious I'm unfamiliar, although I attempt to keep it hidden. "Please don't apologize. I appreciate it. Is that what the map and compass were for?"

He nods.

"My sincere apologies if I came across interrogating. My memory is still quite foggy. I'm from Land Kairos, the developments here are new to me."

He smiles. "Ah, Land Kairos. One of the homelands." He says it as if being from Kairos is a valid excuse for my discernible differences. "I trust you'll like Sandemia as you frequent the town."

"I trust I will. Thank you again, Mr. Alton."

"No worries, dear. Have a good evening."

I'm a fraud. I need to visit this Land Kairos I keep claiming to have come from. I also feel terrible for calling Mr. Alton strange, for approaching and questioning him with suspicion. I should have simply led the conversation by offering gratitude. He was being considerate, a normalcy in this society. He didn't announce what he'd done, expecting nothing in return. Elias explained that I needed to have a new perception of people, and I understood it, yet I still make assumptions based on the biases of the society I was born into. I must disregard that worry and simply enjoy my time here.

I try to reframe my mindset and remember that I'll be meeting new people tomorrow, and excitement replaces the apprehension I felt earlier. After preparing for sleep, I sit up in the bed, lean back against the headboard, pick up the journal that sits on my nightstand, and turn to a blank page. Every night before sleep, I write about a new experience. Tomorrow, I'm meeting new people, and *I'm looking forward to it*, so I write.

CHAPTER 23

Skye

The constant ringing of my doorbell draws me out of sleep. My droopy eyelids part, I turn over on my back, rub my eyes, and still in a sleepy state, I glance over at the alarm clock. It blinks 8:02 a.m. I shoot up.

Shit, Mauria. Damn, she's punctual. I definitely set the alarm for seven, but I must have hit it when it dinged and drifted back to sleep.

I drag myself through the hall and open the front door to a wide-awake Mauria while I stand barely alive. As the sun beams, I scrunch my face and avert my eyes from the stinging rays.

Mauria's wide grin turns down. "I said be ready by eight, not get up at eight!"

I leave the door open for her, drag myself to the couch, and then plant myself face down, placing a pillow over my head. "Stop yelling at me!" I childishly babble, my voice muffled into the sofa.

"No! Get up, Skye!" Mauria grabs the pillow and hits me with it.

"Oweee!" I let out, pretending it actually hurt.

"Now we don't have time to have a morning meal at Buck-wheat's!"

I don't know where she went, but her voice is echoing further away. When I feel her hands grab hold of my ankles, I tense. She drags me by my legs until I'm off the couch and hit the ground. Turning on my back, I look up and see her frowning face hovering over me, her hands on her hips.

I begin to stand, using the sofa as leverage. "I'm sowwy," I say innocuously. Her frown doesn't budge, so I pucker my bottom lip and attempt puppy eyes. She holds the frown, but I see the struggle.

Finally, she giggles. "Get ready." She grabs my hand and pulls me toward the bathroom, pushes me inside, and shuts the door behind me. "I'm making coffee, so hurry it up!"

I go through my morning routine until, at the very end, after the last drop of coffee, my energy springs to life. We head out, stop at a few shops, and I decide to pick up a camera to capture every moment spent in this world.

Mauria and I finally arrive at a fence surrounding a large field with carriages lining one area. We enter the stables, where a mocha-toned, slender man brushes one of the horses.

"Hi, sir," Mauria greets.

Pausing his work, he turns to us. "Hello, ladies."

"I'm Mauria. My friend Skye here has never ridden a horse."

"Destry," he introduces himself. "Really, never?"

I shake my head.

"Alright. Well, let me saddle two of them up, and I'll meet you by the carriages."

We thank him and wait outside.

Destry motions toward us with two brown horses, and Mauria immediately climbs onto hers. She's preparing to signal the horse to take off, but I stop her. I remove the camera from my bag and ask Destry if he would be so kind as to snap two pictures after helping me climb my horse. Mauria tilts her head and smiles. I return her grin before we begin riding.

"Come on, faster!" Mauria calls, urging me to pick up the pace. Destry walked alongside me for a bit until I felt comfortable enough to ride alone. Mauria has her horse galloping like a beast, and I'm envious, but I don't have the guts. I lightly bring my legs inward, and my horse trots. I smile, delighted that I'm getting the hang of this, and continue at a steady pace. Mauria laps me, mouthing, "Boo you chicken!"

Chicken? So, she thinks I'm scared? Here I am, enjoying the idea that I'm actually on a real horse for the first time in my life, and Mauria is poking at my internal competitiveness. I keep that reserved for those who challenge me. *Well, whatever, it worked.* Slightly leaning my torso forward and loosening the bridle, I signal my horse to pick up the pace. He does. I grow a bit nervous, but I keep my body centered while he canters.

"That's the spirit!" Mauria shouts.

As I pick up speed, the unease subsides.

My first time on a horse and it's in another world. Why have I never made time for this back home? The thought of going horseback riding had never crossed my mind, but as I ride the intelligent and agile creature, I'm flying, though I have no wings. All worries dissipate, replaced with invigoration. When I go back home—to my world—I must indulge in such liberation once again, even if it's for a simple reminder of this beautiful place.

At Haven Docks, I'm introduced to a blue-eyed fair blonde, Shimi, just as her brother, Sam, and Mauria's friend, a curvaceous mocha, Belva.

"So, you're new to Sandemia?" Belva asks.

"Yes," I reply.

"Welcome, it's definitely a great place to live."

Thanking her, we proceed to climb aboard Mauria's boat. "Let's wait a moment, I invited Al," Shimi mentions.

Mauria narrows her eyes and asks, "Why?" She seems averse to an invitation being extended to this 'Al' character.

Shimi, exasperated by Mauria's reaction, replies, "Oh, c'mon, he doesn't mind. It's so that he can sail, and we can enjoy ourselves. He'll tour until we're done."

"I suppose." Mauria rolls her eyes.

We're setting our things down near the cockpit when we hear a baritone voice. "Ladies?"

"Al! You made it! Thanks for coming," Shimi greets.

"Ey, it's nothing, I could use a quick trip." He greets Mauria and Belva as he approaches and turns to me. "Who might this be?" he asks flirtatiously.

Well, he's definitely visually appealing. Muscular and beefy, with bronze skin and hazel eyes. He wears a hat, but I'm almost positive that's a temple fade beneath. "I'm Skye," I introduce.

He gestures with a handshake. I extend my arm, and my eyebrows shoot up when he bends and kisses the back of my hand. "Pleased to meet you. I'm Aldrin, but you can call me Al. You're a sight for sore eyes, Ms. Skye."

His lips contort into a charming smile, but I feel awkward rather than charmed. "Uh, thanks. Nice to meet you," I say, and he releases my hand.

"Okay, introductions complete. Let's set off," Mauria announces, still appearing disapproving of his presence. I'm quite certain Mauria knows Al is a charmer, and she may be under the impression it would annoy a girls' trip.

Cushioned seating lines the small area of the front pit where the women and I lounge, and Al sits in the main cockpit, steering. About a half hour has passed, and while they engage in conversation, I'm zoned out and admiring the open ocean view.

"Hey, Skye. Are you alright?" Shimi calls.

The sound of my name pulls me out of my daze. "Huh? Yes, I'm just taking in the scene."

"Have you never been on a boat?" Belva inquires.

Why am I so awkward? You couldn't just wait until your travels with Elias to daze out in admiration? "It's just been a while, is all."

"She's from Kairos," Mauria adds as if that makes me some exception to a rule.

"Oh," Shimi and Belva voice in unison.

Okay, now I must visit this Land Kairos. Seriously, why does my being from this land absolve me of all social sins?

After about an hour, we dock near a wooden bridge, and all, except Al, exit. "Meet us back here by four, Al," Mauria instructs.

"Sure thing. You ladies enjoy," he offers.

"Where's he going with the boat?" I whisper to Mauria.

She chuckles. "You're so cute. He's going to the main dock where the other vessels are."

"Oh." *Why the hell did I even ask?*

Ahead of the bridge are trees and a deserted beach. A barely visible path leads through the woods in the direction we're heading. I'm questioning where this *"amazing spa"* Mauria claims is here. However, it's not until we've completed the journey through the trees that my eyes damn near pop out of my head.

A statue of a man on a horse stands tall between two waterfall fountains. Large flowerpots line the edges, separating the beginning of the pavement from the natural grounds where we stand. Beyond the statue are large gray pillars lined about twelve feet apart. Near each pillar is a different stand, displaying various items, and beyond those are shops and establishments. They're modern in comparison to the shops in Sandemia. There are sturdy chairs, benches, and tables spread throughout, and people are seated in most of them, lounging and socializing.

"Zendovou. The Sinking Land," Mauria comments.

"Sinking?" I ask.

"Come on," she instructs me. We proceed past the pillars and stop at a gate. Below, people in canoes row to and around tall brick buildings with foundations submerged beneath the sea.

"Those structures are homes. That's how they house people here. People live above, below, and side by side, from the entrance of the building to the very top," Mauria explains.

They're called apartments, and I used to live in one, but okay. By the sound of it, this isn't a norm for most lands.

"Rumor has it that due to overuse of heavy material like brick, metal, and concrete, the land can no longer support such weight. So it's sinking. How true is that? Not sure, but they will be totally submerged in another century or so," Shimi states.

Such a beautiful place. It's disheartening to think that's what may become of it.

We walk for a few more minutes to the glass doors of a three-story parlor with the name "JuliSpa" plastered at the entrance. A notice at the front counter reads, Appointment Only, which would explain why the establishment isn't crowded. I mean, seriously, free spa? I'd be here every day.

"Welcome, Mauria and friends. Right this way," an older woman greets us.

"I asked for a four-hour day consisting of nails, toes, full body massage, and hot tub time. You've got your swimsuit?" Mauria whispers to me.

I nod. This sounds incredible. They really enjoy offering these services free of charge? I'm uncertain as to why, but I find great pleasure knowing that this is a passion for them, not just a means to live.

In my world, I've seen people walk into a place of business with a sense of entitlement because of the money in their pocket, as if the tangible green material wields power. However, when one provides a service simply to fulfill their sense of purpose, currency is no factor; there is no loss when one refuses to deliver for someone who is ungracious. Frankly, one will even provide the service to the best of their ability. Not because they're required to, but to serve their passion by doing so.

After hours of pampering, our last hour is spent soaking in the hot tub, sipping wine, snacking on cheese and crackers, and chatting about everything and nothing. Appreciating Mauria for inviting me to this outing, I'm sure I'll miss her when I return home.

"So, looks like Al has a thing for you, Ms. Skye," Belva teases. I'd like to avoid this topic as much as possible, so to delay my response, I bring my glass to my lips.

"Oh, totally," Shimi adds as she grabs a piece of cheese. "He was more focused on her than he was steering the boat."

Mauria rolls her eyes. "Oh, he's a charmer, alright. Don't fall for it."

"Oh, come on, he's a charmer, but he's no heartbreaker." Belva rebuts Mauria's implication. "Al is hot stuff, and he's single. Are you dating someone, Skye?"

I don't want to answer. *Can someone add something else now? No? Fine.* "Uh, no, but..."

"Not yet," Mauria corrects, emphasizing the "yet." "There's Elias."

Nearly choking on my wine, I shake my head. "Mm-mm," I sound as I focus on catching my breath to refute such claims.

"Oh," Shimi begins. "Who's Elias?"

"No one," I force out. Talking about Al doesn't seem like such a bad idea anymore. I absolutely do not want to talk about Elias.

"The man's house is the best custom build I've ever seen. I just know he did the mock-up himself." Mauria pauses to take a sip of wine. "Oh, and you think Al's hot? Elias is on fire." *Damn it, Mauria.* She had to add that in there.

"Oh," Belva says, intrigued. "And this is who you're dating, Skye?"

"No, we're just frie... acquainted." I make sure to correct myself. Elias is opposed to companionship in any form. He calls no one a friend. If the tables were turned and someone asked him about me, he wouldn't call me a friend. The realization sets in that I should probably tread carefully with how close I let myself get to him. We'll never be romantically involved, but it would affect me a great deal to know that I would leave here missing a friend, even if he wouldn't regard me in the same light.

"Well, hello, I'm single. I'd love to meet this fire of a man," Belva says boisterously.

While they laugh, I put on a fake smile. For some reason, her admission leaves a hollow feeling in the pit of my stomach.

CHAPTER 24
Elias

I've gathered supplies out on the town to prepare for my upcoming trip with Skye. I haven't seen her since our quarrel. She's had a few days to cool off, and I wonder if she's still up for the adventure. But I don't doubt it. Her fury only lasts a moment, and only when her barriers are threatened. Everything else, she brushes off—or appears to—and that may be another issue, but not one I care to investigate.

After receiving a letter from Mauria asking if she and her husband Sam could tour my home for inspiration for their own custom-build endeavors, I think better of writing back. It's time I pay Skye a visit. Mauria and Sam are her neighbors.

Two birds, one stone.

It's five thirty p.m., and she's not here. Sunset's in about two hours. She'll be back soon. The door opens at Mauria's home, and a man with blond hair steps out, beer in hand. Presumably Sam, he glances over and raises the drink, hailing me.

"They should be returning shortly from Zendovou," he says.

Zendovou? That's an hour's sail. I hope they've left already.

I go toward Sam, cutting through the grass that separates the two properties. "Sam, is it?"

He nods. "Yes, sir."

"Elias."

"Oh!" he gushes. "Good to meet you, man."

"Likewise." We shake hands.

He gestures for me to join him on his patio. I walk over and take a seat. "Yeah, they went to Mauria's favorite spa with my sister Shimi and their friend, Belva," he informs. "Hey, want a brew? It's cold."

"Yeah, why not?" I accept, and he retreats inside.

Sounds like some girls' day. Good to know she's becoming comfortable enough to associate with others, but she should be wary of building close relationships. She'll be departing to never return, causing grief for herself and the parties involved.

Returning, Sam hands me a beer. I pop the cap, chug for a moment, and after I remove it from my lips, a belch releases. "Good stuff, 'preciate you."

"Yeah, M-Tallen's the best." He takes a seat in the adjacent chair. "Since Skye moved in next door, Mauria drags the poor woman everywhere. The girl can't catch a breather."

"Yeah, well, Skye doesn't get out much, so I'm sure she appreciates it. By the way, I received Mauria's letter. You two free tomorrow?"

"For sure. Does ten a.m. work?"

"Fine with me."

"She told me about her intrusion. My wife can get ahead of herself sometimes, I apologize for that."

I brush it off. "All good."

Laughter echoes in the distance in the direction of Skye's home. They must have docked at Haven Downs.

"Sounds like them." Sam rises to his feet.

"They docked at Havens."

"That's where my boat is. That particular vessel is a shoreline and needs some work. It's not meant for the open ocean, but Mauria runs it every time." He shakes his head. "Trust my wife won't listen, but on a day where the sea is calm, and only traveling to Zendovou, it's not too bad."

We step down from the patio and make our way to the edge of the yard. "Bring it over one day, I'll take a look at it."

"You're a shipwright?"

I nod. "I am."

"No kidding. Yeah, I'll do that."

I gaze in the direction of the voices. Four women and a guy walk toward us. I'm introduced to Shimi, Belva, and Al, and Sam informs Mauria they're visiting my home for a tour tomorrow. Mauria thanks me with a huge grin, then chiming in is an enticed Belva. "So you'reeee Elias."

Quirking a brow, I glance at Skye, who crosses her arms. "Don't look at me. Look at Mauria." It's clear she prefers no involvement.

Belva draws near to me and extends her arm, gesturing for a handshake. "I'm Belva."

My eyes dart to her hand and back up to her eyes. She's flirting. I shut it down. "Yeah, you told me."

"Oh... uh..." She retracts her arm and steps back. I look over to see Mauria fighting back a hysterical laugh and Skye covering her face, embarrassed for Belva.

I personally don't give a shit.

Sam breaks the silence. "Dark is approaching soon."

"Ugh, we should've scheduled a carriage ride," Shimi grumbles.

"Or we could extend this girl's day to a girl's night," Mauria poses, and looks intently at Skye.

Skye's eyebrows raise, nervous as their eyes rivet her, awaiting her response. "Uh, yeah, sure. But like, I don't have much."

Mauria palms the air. "Don't worry about that. I've got snacks and games. We'll bring them over."

"Okay." She smiles, her apprehension subsiding.

"Well, alright ladies, I'm off." Al bids his farewell. "Later, Sam. Good to meet you, Elias."

I curtly nod, but before making his exit, he gives Skye a lingering glance with a look of intent. This pokes a nerve.

"And Skye." He charismatically gestures for a handshake—fully displaying interest in her. She lifts her arm and accepts the shake. But just as I thought it would end there, he bends and presses his lips to the back of her hand. Skye is not in the least bit surprised and not rapt. *He's done this before.* He rises only slightly so that he's at eye level with her. "It was a pleasure to meet such beauty today. I hope to see you again."

Heat rises in my chest, and hostility brims toward the disproportionate bulky fuck that's overdone the lift, he can barely reach his sack. Irritation pricks and a woken bitterness festers, and I'm uncertain as to why, but Brick Face can go now.

Skye offers a subtle smile, and Brick Face releases her hand, finally taking off.

"Alright, you two, help me grab the stuff," Mauria instructs Belva and Shimi. "Skye, we'll meet you at your place soon."

She nods, and I bid the women and Sam good night before walking with Skye toward her home.

"You have an admirer." I smirk.

"Yeah, seems like you do too," she says.

"Speaking of, you're making friends, but be careful getting—"

"Yeah, I know. I've already thought about that," she cuts in. "Hey, about the other day. I'm sorry. You apologized, and I still slammed the door on you. That was rude of me."

"All good. Are you ready for the trip?"

Her features brighten at the mention of our travels. "I am."

She unlocks her door, and we step inside. "Come by with Sam and Mauria tomorrow."

"Wait, we're leaving tomorrow? I should probably pick up some things first, don't you think?"

"We're not leaving tomorrow, but yes, you should pick up some things to prepare."

Her eyebrows pull together as an expression of perplexity contours her features. "Sooo, why am I coming over with Sam and Mauria tomorrow?"

Her question stumps me. *Wasn't expecting that.* Refusing to ponder her question, I don't respond. Instead, I just... look at her. She's anticipating a response—one I'm not offering. My lips remain sealed as I gaze into her brown eyes. I'm not one to stumble over answers or overthink until I find excuses. She's either coming or not, but I'd prefer it if she does. "Are you coming, or not?"

"Sure, as long as you tell me why." She's amused that she thinks she's onto something.

"There is no 'why,'" I deadpan.

She draws near, and I catch a whiff of lavender scent. "Just admit it, you enjoy my company, Mr. Lonely," she teases. "Are we becoming *friends,* Elias?" A grin forms on her lips as she emphasizes "*friends.*"

"Don't get ahead of yourself. I'm only helping until you return. If I'm to spend more than thirty days out at sea with you, I need to be able to tolerate your company," I impart, padlocking her assumption.

Her grin turns down, and an expression akin to dispirited forms in its place. The sudden sting at the sight is unwelcome.

"Fair enough," she says.

She smiles again, but it's synthetic, lacking her usual glow, and doesn't reach her eyes. She's hiding the blow, but it's noticeable because I've seen her true smile. I've been on the receiving end of its authenticity.

She breaks eye contact and heads for the kitchen. "Yeah. I'll be there. Hopefully the girls won't keep me up too late."

I make for the door. "Alright. Have fun." I place my hand on the knob but don't turn it. That sting in my chest is unabating. I can't put my finger on why the fuck I care, but I turn on my heels and stalk toward her. "If I consider you a friend, will you stop doing that?"

She appears confused. "Stop doing what?"

"Stop—stop being butterflies and sunshine and shit that you do." I don't even know what the fuck I just said, but she gets it because she laughs. That laugh is music to my ears, and with that smile, the glow returns—*that's hers.* The sting dissipates, and I welcome relief.

"You think I'm butterflies and sunshine?" she says with a wide grin. *Oh, but you are, and you don't even realize it.* "It's okay, Elias. I'm not begging you to be my friend. I just really appreciate all that you're doing to help me enjoy my time here. I do like the idea of you finding a friend in me, but I also know that I'm leaving, and you're opposed to such associations." She pauses for a beat. "I'm a tough cookie. You don't have to worry about hurting my feelings over something so trivial. I've been through worse."

Her admission brings me no comfort, but I know it's her intent. As I quirk my lips to respond, a knock at her door stops me. I open it, and let the women in.

"Oh, hey, Elias," Mauria greets. "Didn't realize you were here. We can come back."

"No, I was just leaving." I turn my head to Skye. "See you tomorrow?"

She nods.

Shimi motions her fingers between Skye and me. "Acquaintances, right?"

Glancing to Skye, she rolls her eyes. That must be what she told them.

"She's my friend."

Her features soften at my disclosure. I bid them good night and proceed through the door, closing it behind me.

CHAPTER 25

Elias

SIX YEARS AGO

"Yo, El!" my best friend Travis calls from outside.

It's a Friday evening, and I'm still at my shop two hours past closing. For Travis to travel all the way to Lithonia to seek me out, the guys must be searching for me.

"Yo," I curtly reply, projecting my voice for him to pinpoint my whereabouts as I continue my work under the hood of a client's vehicle.

He enters the garage. His gold and silver Rolex comes into view first at the corner of the hood. He's still dressed in a finely tailored gray suit and black polished leather shoes; it's clear he traveled here right after leaving his office—which is the size of my apartment. "Dude, what are you doing?"

Gaze never faltering from my work, I reply, "Finishing a spark change. What's up?"

"What's up? Bro, you've been MIA for weeks."

I tighten the cap over the coolant tank and finalize checking all the fluid levels. "Business picked up quickly. I've been busy."

He walks around the shop, inspecting the devices. "Well, I'm glad to hear business is booming, but you're missing out."

I shut the hood of the '98 Civic. "On what? Strip clubs and getting piss-drunk?"

He turns on his heels. "Ah, don't be a party pooper. You missed Mrs. Tori's potluck last weekend."

"Shit, that was last weekend?"

He stuffs his hands in his pockets. "See what I mean? You're out of touch, El. I bet you don't even check the group chat anymore."

I set my tools away and grab my bag. "I silenced it. Y'all talk too damn much." We exit the garage, and I lock it up.

"Come to the lake tonight. You ain't been there either," he says.

"Alright, I'll be there."

He looks around the lot and asks, "El, where's your car?"

I press the unlock button on my key. The lights of my '07 Mitsubishi Lancer light up.

Travis cringes. "Tell me that's just your work vehicle."

"Nope. I only have one vehicle. That's it."

"What the hell happened to your Camaro?" he asks. My current ride confounds him.

I walk over to my vehicle. "I sold it."

"You what! For this?" His outburst is ticking me off. "Is this some rebellious act to get back at your pops about your trust fund?"

His assumption is offensive to my efforts, but I don't address it. "Hell no. Screw him and his money. I don't want it."

"Does he know you opened your own shop?"

I open the door and throw my bag inside my car. "Don't know. Don't give a fuck." Sighing, I turn to him and decide to give him the reality. After all, he is my best friend. "Look, I sold the Camaro for the cash. It took sacrifices to get the business running. Cutting back on unnecessary expenses is vital right now."

Nodding, he considers my stance. "Alright, understandable. But how does Jessica feel about all this?"

"I mean, I don't expect her to move out here. But—"

"Wait," he interjects, holding out a palm. "Dude, you moved out here? What happened to the condo?"

I take a deep breath. "I sold it, Trav."

"Ah, get the fuck outta here, El." He throws up his hands and lets them fall to his sides. "What? You're gonna tell me you live in a studio apartment next?"

My silence gives him his answer.

"Alright." He finally simmers the dramatics. "Jessica?"

"Bit of a pushback, but she'll get the big picture soon. She's busy pursuing her acting career. Her schedule is as tied up as mine."

"You sure about that, man?"

I frown at his ambiguous response. "The hell is that supposed to mean?"

Slapping the air, he gestures that I let it go. "Nothing man, just... you should make more time for her."

Narrowing my eyes. "Travis, what is it?" I press.

He shrugs. "Nothing. Just looking out."

"I know when you're lying, dipshit, now spit it out," I demand.

He turns his head away for a moment, as if contemplating divulging whatever it is, then faces me. "I shouldn't have been eavesdropping, but she mentioned something to Miranda about not knowing how to support you."

That's only part of whatever is on his mind. "What else?"

He clears his throat. "Look, why don't you reconcile with your dad? Learn the ropes of the company, gain his trust. Once he gives you your money, he can't take the shit back. Then do your own thing. It doesn't have to be this way."

Shaking my head, I enter my vehicle. "That's deceit, Trav. I ain't made that way."

"Alright, whatever. Meet us at the lake by nine," he says, walking backward in the direction of his Porsche Panamera. "And bring booze!"

I buy two twelve-packs of beer and flowers before heading home to freshen up. Travis's words about Jessica's conversation with Miranda replays in my mind as I drive down I-85 to her condo.

If she feels insecure about us, that's my doing. As of recently, my life has pivoted around my shop, but if she expects I need anything more than her moral support, she couldn't be more wrong. Our exacting schedules limit the amount of time we've grown accustomed to spending together, however, only in that aspect will I heed Travis's advice. I'll set aside more time for my woman outside of the grind.

Ringing Jessica's doorbell, I wait with the flowers in hand. When she answers, a wide grin forms on the lips of my five-foot-seven, brunette, supermodel-figured girlfriend. She throws her arms around my neck, and I pull her flush against me, squeezing her tight. "Hey, beautiful," I voice in her ear.

"I've missed you, Ellie!" she exclaims, using her nickname for me.

"I miss you too," I tell her, pressing a kiss to her lips.

I follow her through her expansive, elegantly decorated condominium, and a savory scent lingers. "What are you making?" I ask, leaning over the island counter.

"Soft tacos for the lake tonight." She unravels aluminum foil. "You know the guys, always remembering the booze but never the food." They'll order pizza, but Jessica finds any reason to cook. Aside from being the focus of the lights and cameras, she favors experimenting in the kitchen. "Are you going?"

"Yeah, Travis summoned me. Much to my surprise, he came to the shop."

She cuts the stems of the flowers to fit them into the empty glass vase resting on the counter. "You've gotta make time for your friends, babe."

"Yeah, well, I don't have the kind of time they do, and their favorite hobby is futile splurging," I say pointedly.

She places the flowers in the vase. Examining them, she smiles. "They bring my kitchen to life. Thank you."

I slightly grin. "Anytime."

"Anyway, you know you're choosing not to have it like the rest of them," she carries on.

I inhale deeply and blow out a breath. "I don't wanna talk about this. I need to grind right now and save as much as possible. They need to understand that."

She's wrapping individual tacos in foil and placing them in a large glass container. "You know they'd be willing to cover your part. You just need to show up."

The fuck? "You think I'd be okay with that shit?"

"You should at least try to mend things with your father. Mr. Crawford only means well."

I'm in no mood to talk about *him*. I'm done with this useless topic. I'd rather enjoy my time with her. Rounding the island, I walk behind her, place my hands on her hips, and press a kiss to her shoulder. "How is the new role coming along?"

"It's okay so far. Fairly easy. My agent says the more roles, the better, whether big or small, to gain experience."

My kisses trail up her neck. "Better not try and slip away when you go all Hollywood." I feel it when she stiffens. Her movements slow as she wraps the tacos. "Hey, look at me." She turns around and tilts her head back to look at me. "I was joking. Is everything okay?" I search her eyes; something is bothering her.

"Ellie," she says despondently. "It's just—I don't know how Hollywood would fit into *your* world."

I retract my head and frown in confusion. "What do you mean?"

"I mean, you want to be a mechanic. How does it look if I'm Hollywood and my boyfriend is..."

I step back from her, in disbelief at what I'm hearing. *What the fuck?* "Seriously, Jess? Is that your concern?"

She gazes at me with pleading eyes in the hopes I'd understand this utter bullshit. "It just doesn't..."

"Doesn't what?" I interject. "It doesn't fit into the superficial shit you see plastered on social media?" I grip the counter opposite of her, sending my frustration to my fingers.

"Ellie, I just don't want you to get hurt if this whole thing crashes and burns. I mean, you gave up your condo for an apartment. You sold your Camaro, your most prized possession. When was the last time you traveled, did something nice for yourself? Spent without calculating? It wouldn't be so bad if your budget wasn't so steep. Ellie, that's no way to live! You're giving up valuable things for this... this obsession!"

"Obsession?" Anger swirls, but I tank it. Instead, I choose to help her understand. "This is my passion, Jess. This is only because I'm doing it alone. Your concerns are regarding things that are of little significance. I know since opening the shop, things have changed. I've become strict in certain areas of my life. Those are simple desires that can be obtained later. Currently, I'm investing in my future."

She won't directly say it, but I know this isn't just about my prior costly possessions. She misses the life I had before opening the shop. The life *we* had. Commonly, I've spent a hefty penny treating her, but I've recently abandoned such spending habits. "I'm sorry that I can't take you on those extravagant trips anymore or treat you to the finest, but it's temporary."

Tears shimmer in her eyes.

Drawing near, I hold her. "Just give me more time, Jess. It won't be like this forever, I promise." I hold her as she buries her face in the crook of my neck. "Look at me," I whisper. When she looks up, I gaze into her blue eyes. "I love you."

"Okay," she squeaks. "I love you too."

I kiss her tenderly. She pushes up on her toes, wanting more, and I intrude with my tongue. I grab her by the hips, hoist her up against me, and she wraps her legs around my torso. My lips move to her neck while I carry her to a clear counter, pull a condom from my pocket, and take her right here in her kitchen.

CHAPTER 26
Elias
SIX YEARS AGO

We drove Jessica's BMW X7 to the lake because she was determined that we do not drive my *"that,"* which is what she called my car. It didn't matter to me.

"You came out! Looks like traveling across town was worth something," Travis greets me. He gives Jessica a hug, and we descend the path leading toward the lake house.

"Eyyy! What's up, grease monkey! Where you been?" My buddy Tyler boisterously greets me when I enter the house.

"Busy being a grease monkey. What's up?" I smirk as we pound our fists together and then hug.

"Finally got the approval for the hotel down Main. How's the shop coming along?"

"Sweet. Business picking up. Might need to hire help soon."

"Elias! How are you?" I hear a woman's voice behind me. I turn around, and it's Miranda, Jessica's best friend.

I extend my arms and give her a hug. "Good. Yourself?"

"I'm well. Where's that girlfriend of yours?"

I inform her that Jessica is outside, then grab a beer, pop the cap, and chat with Travis and Tyler for some time.

While it was owned by Travis's parents, over the last few years, the lake house has become our Friday night carouse spot. Located in a secluded area near campgrounds, through the back door is a path leading to a large gazebo standing by the lake. There, we spend most of our time drinking, talking shit, and playing music.

Before throwing myself into my career goals, every Friday night, after a long week, I'd join my crew at this spot. Here we've shared goals, pains, happiness, and sadness. Whatever bullshit is going on in our lives, this is where we release our tension. This lake house is home to formed friendships and forged bonds. It has witnessed us through many stages, gracing us with peace during conflict and wisdom when we were foolish. This home holds a special place for all of us.

Travis, Tyler, and I step outside and greet Mike, Bart, and Neil —the remainder of the crew. A woman I'm not familiar with accompanies Mike, but it isn't uncommon for him to show up with a different woman every now and again. While the rest of us stand six-foot or taller, Mike stands at five foot six, and his vertically-challenged insecurity compels him to prove that despite his height, he could still attract pretty women.

"Yo, Barf! Wifey let you out tonight?" Tyler shouts, mockingly greeting Bart.

"Dude, do you hate me? When are you gonna stop calling me that?" Bart gripes, obviously displeased.

Tyler takes a sip of his beer and places a hand on Bart's shoulder. "Bro, I'm not the one who hates you. Your parents did when they named you Bart."

Bart shrugs Tyler's hand off. "Where's the beer, dickhead?" We all snicker.

We're in the gazebo when Jessica descends from the house with the glass container. "Tacos, anyone?" she offers.

"Oh, hell yeah." Travis reaches in first.

She hands him the bowl, and they pass it around, each grabbing one before she takes a seat beside me. I wrap one arm around her shoulder. She leans into me, and I press a kiss in her hair.

"So, El, when are you gonna let me floor the 'Maro?" Mike asks.

"When you hit puberty," I deadpan, and everyone snickers again.

"Yeah, whatever, ugly fuck," he bites back.

"Not according to your mom."

My comment stirs an outburst of laughter, primarily because it's true. Mike's mother, Mrs. Jenkins's, nickname for me is "Handsome El." However, the adjective isn't the problem. It's the conspicuous flirtatious manner in her greetings. I don't suppose she'd ever take it a step further, nonetheless, she gives *"if given the opportunity"* vibes, and the thought is repulsive.

"Dude, Mrs. Jenkins be lookin' at El like, *'if only I was thirty years younger,'*" Travis mimics Mike's mother.

"Mrs. Jenkins be like *'Hi, Handsome El.'*" Bart mimics Mrs. Jenkins's flirtatiousness, then deadpans when he turns to Jessica. "Then, *'Hi, Jessica.'*"

Guffawing after a few drinks is the usual. Let the incessant shit-talking and hysterics begin. "Shut the fuck up, Fart!" Mike barks at Bart, and the contagious laughter reaches me.

Neil breaks the laughter when he says, "When I didn't see the Camaro, I thought you skipped out another Friday."

"Nah." I clear my throat. "I sold it."

"You what?" Tyler sits up, baffled. "After all the work you put into it?"

Except Jessica and Travis, everyone's eyes are on me. I feel it when Jessica grows uncomfortable against me. "I had to..." I begin, but Jessica abruptly shoots to her feet, so I pause.

"Anyone want some water?" she asks, but we just stare at her in silence. "Well, I'd like some water." She scurries away. Her friends, Miranda and Rachel, sense her discontent and leave the gazebo as well.

"Um. Bathroom break," the woman Mike brought along says, and then proceeds in the direction of the house.

"How do women do that?" Neil questions, perplexed. "It's like they just read each other's minds."

"Now give me one good reason why I shouldn't kick your ass for selling our baby?" Tyler scolds.

I lift a brow. "Our?"

"Hey, I helped install most of those upgrades. I should have been notified and in full agreement before such actions had been taken."

I chuckle. Tyler takes nothing seriously.

Bart shakes his head. "Damn. We've had some good times in Dyno. Drop-top cruising, being fucking stupid. Remember the Miami trip?"

"When you heard the rev down the block, you just knew it was El pulling up," Mike recalls.

A comforting nostalgia washes over me, but I push it down. I did what was necessary.

"Why'd you sell it?" Neil asks.

I lean forward, resting my elbows on my knees. "To cut back on expenses. After opening the shop, I exhausted my resources, so I sold the car."

Tyler frowns. "Um. *That car* had a name."

I chuckle inwardly. "Dynamite," I utter the name I gave to my red and black, once-prized possession. "I live near the shop now, so unless I rent a garage to park it, keeping it in a parking lot would just mean dealing with vandalism and theft."

"What do you mean, you live near the shop now? What happened to the condo?" Tyler asks.

"Sold it."

They all stare at me with wide eyes. "Yo El, what the fuck?" Bart expresses his disdain.

"Dude, why didn't you say anything? We could've helped," Neil offers.

I remain composed as they discount my life. "Bro, I'm not homeless. I'm living within my means. It may not be our customary opulence, but for what I've gained, it's enough."

"And what? You take the bus now?" Neil quips.

"No, jackass, I have a vehicle," I snap.

"Barely," Travis mutters.

They want me to elaborate, so I do. I really don't give a shit. They're hard-pressed, but I'm not, and it's my damn life. "'07 Lancer and it runs like new."

Tyler dramatically throws himself back in his seat, faking a distressed cry. "Oh, no, no, no, no, how could you? Dynamite, he gave you up for a hoopty." *It's not a damn hoopty.*

"Damn, bro," Bart begins. "I knew you were cutting back to start the business, but I didn't realize you were down this bad."

Growing defensive, my jaw tightens as frustration sets in. "I'm not down bad. I just have my priorities set elsewhere."

Neil takes a sip of his beer and swallows, then smacks his mouth and says, "El, you're in denial."

I firm my posture and prepare to face off with them because, what the fuck? They're pitying me, and pity is the last thing I feel for myself.

"You're broke, Elias. Just admit it. This dream of yours is draining you." Travis objects.

My blood boils, and I snap. "Don't fucking pity me! I'm not broke. I worked my ass off to pursue my own goals, not become my father's bitch for his coins. I started working for an auto shop, and now I own mine. You see failing, I see progress. Don't discredit me. I didn't get access to a trust fund or hefty allowances after college like you fucks did, all because the piece of shit disagreed with my major. So, I'm doing it my way, independently, and I have no goddamn regrets!"

I charge off. I'm flaming inside. "How would your mom feel about this?" Travis shouts at my retreating back.

Halting, I ball my fists and fight the urge not to go over there and knock his jaw loose at the mention of my mother. Instead, I say, "She'd be damn proud that I chose my own path." And with that, I pivot toward the house. It's the truth. All my mother had ever wanted was for my brother and me was to pursue our passions.

"We're leaving." I burst through the door of the lake house. Jessica senses the oozing tension and doesn't ask questions. She grabs her things, bids her friends good night, and follows me to the driveway.

"Yo, El!" I hear Tyler calling from behind, but I continue walking. "Elias, wait up." I turn around. Tyler continues. "Look bro, I know you know what you're doing. I just hope *you* know what *you're* doing. Regardless, I trust you." He gives me a look of deep concern. His words seem equivocal, but I'm too fired up to give it much thought. He glances at Jessica, but I presume he's speaking to me. "And I hope you do the right thing." Darting back to me, he continues. "Just don't want to see you get hurt, bro."

"Alright, I hear you," I acknowledge. We shake and hug before Jessica and I get into her vehicle and take off.

Though Travis holds the title by default because we've known one another longer, oftentimes I feel as though Tyler has become more of a best friend than him. We share similar interests, and our bond has strengthened throughout the years. We've fixed many cars side by side, but what is a simple hobby for him is a passion for me. Regardless, I've had his support, despite what my pursuit would entail. He may be disappointed in the loss of Dynamite, but I didn't miss his reaction to my stance differing from the rest. My choice to abandon superfluous statuses and luxuries is an unreasonable reason to criticize my decision to continue forward, understanding that the larger picture matters.

"What's up with you and Tyler?" I ask Jessica, recalling the sharp glance of contempt he offered her. I recall the night in its entirety. Everyone interacted at some point, but the otherwise outgoing Tyler avoided Jessica like the plague.

"Nothing, why?" she replies nonchalantly.

"You two didn't exchange words all night."

She insouciantly shrugs. "Oh, I don't know. I guess I was just busy with the girls. Didn't notice I hadn't spoken to him."

She pulls out her phone and mindlessly scrolls. It's a compulsive effort to distract herself, to appear preoccupied when she's dodging a conversation. That impulse alone tells me one thing: *She's lying.*

CHAPTER 27

Skye

"Yeah, I have no chance with Elias." Belva pops a grape in her mouth.

Mauria smirks. "Told you."

"Well, you weren't lying. He's hot stuff for sure," Shimi adds.

Belva covers her face with her hands and shakes her head. "I embarrassed myself."

I reach for the bottle of wine and refill my glass. "I did not expect him to be so blatantly uninterested."

Belva drops her hand to her thighs, makes a loud clap, and gives me a dumbfounded look. "Girl, did you even see the glare he gave Al when he kissed your hand?"

Mauria laughs. "I saw that."

"He wasn't even discreet about it. Blades for sure," Shimi adds.

When was this? "I did not see that."

Belva reaches for the bottle next. "Yeah, well, the friendship role is totally a front. He's got eyes on you."

Whether that's true or not, Elias and I could never be anything. Not just because it would be a disaster at my departure. They aren't aware that Elias is cold, and though I know there's warmth at his core, I'd need more than the days I have left to crack that iceberg.

Last night was a pleasure. We played games, talked, laughed, and sipped wine until we grew too exhausted to stay awake. A girls' sleepover.

I hadn't had one of those in years. I'm too close to thirty to revel in youthful activities like sleepovers, *right?* Or so I thought. Perhaps youthfulness isn't what ends enjoyment like sleepovers in my world, but adulting. *Yeah, adulting in my world sucks.*

I recall the endless times my friends back home have reached out, and I've either ignored them or declined invitations. I've wrapped myself in work for the sake of financial stability for myself and a prosperous future for my son.

But that isn't the issue. I've never created a timeline as to when I'd be able to start seeing them again. Did I plan to live that way forever? Slaving away to the dollar in hopes of a free future? How can one ever truly be free if precious time is traded for money? I ponder how I've been living, how exhausted I've become, the relationships I've abandoned, the amount of energy I've spent on work, and how, when a free day comes around, I prefer to be alone.

My life has lacked balance. *But why?* The people here may work for pleasure, nevertheless, it's still work. No different than what I do every day.

Elias's words echo in my brain. *"... if it were your passion, you'd never work another day. Similar to the people here."*

I pick up my journal and write about yesterday. My first time horseback riding, *my very first time on a yacht,* my thoughts of Land Zendovou, and the sleepover. I write about how it all felt, how I've been feeling since arriving. As I adapt to the characteristics of this society, I almost wish I could bring my loved ones here and stay forever.

Curtaining the thought before savoring it, I remind myself that my goal is to enjoy my time here while it lasts; allow myself to relish in the adventures and capture every moment, but to stay grounded, remember where I'm from, where I will return, and all I have to appreciate. I close my journal, place it back on the nightstand, and get ready to head over to Elias's with Mauria and Sam.

CHAPTER 28

Skye

While Elias takes Mauria and Sam around his home for a tour, I stroll around his back yard. I had never recognized the excessive lilacs planted around his yard.

I'm plucking from the shrubs when Mauria enters the yard to inform me she loves the place and that she and Sam are leaving.

Soon after, Elias comes out. "I hope you don't mind." I raise a handful of colorful blossoms.

"You like lilacs?" he asks.

"They're my favorite. Your yard is filled with them. You like them too?"

He stuffs his hands in his pockets. "Yeah."

"Are they called lilacs here?"

He steps down to meet me halfway in the garden. "No. Animas."

I tilt my head. "Interesting name. You know, it's been said, the color of a lilac bloom has a distinct meaning."

He dips his chin. "I did not know that."

I stride around the garden, explaining, "White lilacs represent purity, purple symbolizes spirituality, blue, happiness, and magenta, love. The primrose, or yellow, lilacs are the rarest of them all. They hold no definite meaning; however, some may say they represent nostalgia." Walking over to where he's standing, he appears to be attentive to my words. I hand him the yellow flower. He takes it. "Some of your lilacs are purple, but most of them are yellow."

He twirls the flower between his thumb and index finger. "You know a lot about lilacs."

I take a prideful breath. "Yeah, well, I'm from Rochester, New York, the lilac capital of the world. I live in Webster now—just outside of Rochester—but my mom and I religiously attend the Lilac Festival hosted in Rochester every year."

The twirling of the flower comes to a halt. My eyes drift from his fingers to his face—and my heart drops. I'm met with a hardened expression and furrowed brows over darkened emeralds. The ultimate intimidating, soul-piercing gaze.

"What's wrong?" I ask reluctantly, feeling with every bone in my body that he won't divulge whatever it is.

"Let's go," he demands sullenly and turns and stalks inside through the door.

I stand in place, stunned. *What the hell just happened? I* swing open the back door to see him walking back outside through the front. "Elias," I call, but he continues forward.

Halfway through the front yard, I jog to catch up. *How does he walk so fast?* "Elias!" I call again, louder this time, but he's ignoring me.

I finally catch up, but one of his strides is three of mine. I grab his arm, and he turns around in a huff. I instantly regret it when I catch sight of abhorrence beneath acute darkness. "Elias, what the hell?" I ask, my chest heaving. He's blocking me out with a dense shield of ice, but I don't care. I'm determined to know where the hell we're going and why.

"Let's go," he demands, motioning forward again.

"Not until you tell me where we're going!" I snap.

He halts and faces me again, his jaw tense. "The stables. You're going home."

"Okay, why?" I cross my arms. No response. He turns and continues, so I follow. *God, he's insufferable.*

We arrive at the stables, and Elias asks if there are any carriages available. I recognize Destry, and we greet each other.

"Will you be back to ride again soon?" Destry asks.

"Hopefully, I really enjoyed it. Thanks again for your help with that."

"Anytime," he says. He turns to Elias. "Just give me a moment, I'll prepare the horse and carriage."

Elias nods, but as Destry walks away, I stop him. "As a matter of fact, Destry, I think I'd like to take that ride again today... if that's okay."

He nods. "Sure, I'll saddle one up." He turns to Elias again. "Would you still like me to prepare a carriage?"

"The carriage is for me to head to Haven Downs. It's where I live, but I'm not quite ready to go home." I answer the question directed to Elias.

Destry smiles. "Okay, Miss Skye."

I thank him, and he heads to the stables.

"What are you doing?" Elias asks, annoyed.

I cross my arms. "Going horseback riding."

"I'm not staying here."

"Then don't. I'll ask Destry to take me home after."

His jaw tenses. He walks off and leans on the fence.

Destry comes out with a saddled horse, and more like a pro than a beginner, I climb the creature and take off. Elias gets under my skin, and if I didn't care, it wouldn't bother me, so I won't deny that I do care. However, my time here is limited; I refuse to allow his energy to consume me.

If I return to my home at Haven Downs under this tension, it'll eat at me the entire day. So, becoming one with the beautiful, strong steed, I ride. As the air hits my face, my mind clears, and with every gallop, the tension melts away, *and I'm free.*

After I've had my fill, I climb down off the horse and pet the beautiful brute. "Thanks, big guy. I needed that."

Turning to Destry, I hand him the bridle and thank him. Nodding, he informs me that he'll prepare the carriage. I look over to see Elias still leaning on the fence. *He stayed.* Hoping his tension has subsided, I make my way over to him.

"You didn't have to stay," I say.

He gazes out at the field. "Riding the horse, it made you happy." It doesn't come out as a question, but he is asking.

"It did."

He nods.

"Can you tell me what happened?"

He peers down at me, but I can't read his features. He inhales sharply. "Look, Skye, we're not going on any adventure. It's not a good idea. It's good I figured it out now and not while we were on route."

Heart dropping to my stomach, his admission hits me like a ton of bricks. "Elias, I only have so long. If I can't get to enjoy it to the fullest, at least tell me why."

He looks toward the sound of the approaching carriage before looking back to me, and his features soften. "Listen, people from our world don't just end up here. They must have an undoubted belief that it exists. They *need* it to exist. That feeling to be somewhere else, *to live a different life*, has lingered deep within you, and you've ignored it. At some point, even just for a moment, that feeling you've kept caged at your depths breached the surface; that's why you were sent here."

I narrow my eyes. He's insinuating I'm miserable again. "It was a simple fantasy about exploring."

He shakes his head. "It was deeper than that, and you refuse to admit it. You didn't fantasize or just *imagine* yourself exploring. For a moment, you unwittingly acknowledged your *soul*. The universe somehow responds to this intense energy and offers you a choice."

I push down the brimming irritation that he assumes I'm in denial. "I don't have a choice."

The carriage comes into sight, and he lowers his voice. "You do. You know you can't stay, but my advice is that you allow this world to inspire you to make a change in your own life when you return."

"I didn't ask for your advice."

He sighs heavily. "Take it or leave it. Goodbye, Skye."

I climb onto the carriage. As I'm seated, Destry signals the horses to trot away. I look back at Elias; he stands in place. We gaze at each other as the distance between us grows. Breaking eye contact first, he stuffs his hands in his pockets, hangs his head, and walks off in the direction of his home.

Facing forward, I bring my knees to my chest and bury my face.

What happened?

Elias

I hope she heeds my advice because I can no longer take the time to peel back her layers. A path of destruction for us both, I can't risk us growing any closer.

A primrose lilac lay on the path leading to my patio—Skye must have dropped it. Before today, I had no knowledge this was a rare lilac, nor of its name. I pick it up, look to the skies, and whisper. "I miss you, Mom. You'd have really loved it here."

I reminisce about what it felt like to hear my mother's voice, to feel her kiss on my cheek. I remember her last words: "*I'll always be with you, my sweet boy,*" and her last words of encouragement: the lyrics to her favorite song, "I Hope You Dance," by Lee Ann Womack, which inspired me to follow my dreams, my soul's desires, no matter what.

I take a deep breath and glance down at the yellow flower resting in my palm. A sudden epiphany hits me as I recall Skye's words regarding the primrose lilac—*nostalgia.*

CHAPTER 29

Elias

SEVEN YEARS AGO

Today is my younger brother Elijah's birthday.

He's twenty-one, so it's a big deal. Jessica began planning a surprise party for him, but my brother had other plans—*specific plans.* He rented a cruise ship, and he invited damn near Atlanta's population, all on my father's dime. However, I haven't received so much as a "happy birthday" greeting from my father since I was sixteen.

Unlike me, my brother's college tuition was paid for by our old man. Majoring in business law, he plays college football and expressed to our father that if he doesn't get drafted, he'd like a career at his investment firm.

Imagine my father's excitement at that.

If he gets drafted to the big leagues, our father would be equally proud, because that's an accomplishment *worthy* of honor.

As for me? David Crawford would disown me if he could. He can't brag about the son who owns a mechanic shop. *Oh no, that's disgraceful.* Nonetheless, there's one person, if no one else, that remains proud of my pursuit of passions.

I haven't had the time to visit Mom lately, but today I made time. My mother, Elizabeth Crawford—my biggest supporter—

refused to let me give in to my father's ridicule of my career choice. She preached to my brother and me to follow our dreams, whatever they may be.

I was fascinated with cars for as long as I could remember. By the time I was nine, I had begun exploring their mechanics. My uncle Eric—my mother's brother—used to dismantle and reassemble vehicles, and when I had gotten a little older, I'd ask my parents to spend weekends at his place to watch him diligently work under the hood of multiple makes and models—educating me during his processes.

My father had utter disdain for my uncle Eric. One might consider his reasoning justifiable, as my uncle was reckless. Countless speeding tickets from racing eventually prompted the revocation of his license, yet it never stopped him from getting behind the wheel. His improvidence landed him in the county jail many times, but my mother was a lawyer—and a good one.

Regardless of my uncle's imprudent behavior, he was good to me. He owned a '69 Camaro, and his favorite words were, "*Every lane is the fast lane.*"

At the age of sixteen, I expressed to my parents my plans to attend a technical college and major as an automotive technician. This was no surprise to my mother, but my father raged at my declaration.

I park my vehicle, take my mother's most favored flowers in hand, and recall the life-changing events that shaped the last ten years of my life.

"This is your delinquent brother's fault!" my father yells at my mother, hours after I've announced the news of my chosen major.

He charged into my room that night and made it clear that I'd better choose a different major, or he wouldn't be paying my tuition. That was the night our relationship took a turn for the worse. He began deliberately displaying more affection toward my younger brother, ensuring that I'd notice. My new nickname became "disgrace."

"Come get your shoes out of the hallway, you disgrace."

"Shut the hell up, I'm talking! You disgrace."

"You better make it to your brother's game, you disgrace."

As graduation drew near, the letter that I had been accepted into the Automotive Technician program at Georgia Tech came in the mail, and he *flipped*. While he exhibited imperturbable composure publicly, within the walls of our home, my father could be an ill-tempered brute.

He stampedes to my room.

"No, David! Leave him alone," my mother cries, following closely behind my father.

"You fucking disgrace! Are you trying to embarrass me?!" he snarls, bursting into my room, grabbing my shirt in his fist.

"Stop, Dave! You'll hurt him!" My mother pulls his arm, attempting to placate him. My mother is four foot ten to my father's five foot eleven, and he shrugs her off effortlessly.

He releases my shirt and begins jabbing his big-ass sausage finger into my chest, yelling about how much of a disgrace I am to his lineage. I'm uncertain about the pain in my chest. Is it from the continuous jabs of his finger or the incessant insults? Regardless, resentment grows within me like a tumor. My hands become fists at my sides. Fury vibrates through my being. He's yelling, but his words fall on deaf ears. The only thought thrumming through my head is that if he jabs that oversized Vienna sausage at my chest one more time, I'm going to gut him like a fucking fish.

As if my mother could sense the shift in the air, her pleas to my father ceased, and she focused on me. She grabs my arm, pulling as hard as she can. I stumble where I stand. I'm seventeen, having reached my full height and being fit, and somehow my mother found enough strength in her small frame to nudge me hard enough to derail my attention.

My father, having finally released all his anger, turns and stalks away from my room while my mother holds my clenched fists in her small hands, softly sobbing. "That would have turned out so badly. Baby, I couldn't let that happen."

In retrospect, I believed it was the words and actions of my father that anguished me. However, there were knives to my chest when my brother entered my room that night, his face twisted in contempt as he uttered, *"This is all your fault."*

The following day, I attended school with a burdening weight on my chest. The contention with my dad, the distressed state of my mom, and the comment from my brother. I was beginning to question if my pursuit was worth this, but then I thought of my mother. She wouldn't be pleased if I chose to switch paths. She'd know it wouldn't be for the right reasons, and she'd rather argue with my father over my following my dreams than argue with him because his outrage took hold of me. Adhering to my father wouldn't ease the ferment, it would contrive another.

I wonder if my father thought my actions would become similar to Uncle Eric's. If so, then he simply doesn't understand me. That evening, I waited in the kitchen for him to return home from the office.

"Dad, may I speak with you?" I ask as he enters the kitchen.

Giving me a look of disgust, he reaches into the cupboard and removes a bottle of whiskey. "What is it?"

"My major..." I begin but pause when he gazes at me attentively, anticipating my next words. Inhaling, I continue. "Look, my major in automotive technician, my aspiration to maintain cars... I won't become like Uncle Eric." A thorn of guilt prods me to speak of my uncle in a negative light, but it's my best attempt to communicate with my father. He takes a gulp from his glass and slams it to the counter. To my surprise, it didn't shatter.

Shortening the gap between us, I want him to see me—really see me. "I promise, Dad. I want to work on cars, fix them, and open my own shop."

When he doesn't respond, I continue pleading. "When business flourishes, I'll have a team, employees. I... I'll open more shops. Expand. Become a brand."

He remains impassive, but I take the slightest pleasure in his still being here, looking at me, listening. I suck in my pride and tears well in my eyes as I grow determined to reach the part of this man who once considered me his son, not his disgrace. "Dad, I can do this, please. But the road will be harder without your support."

Taking another gulp of his whiskey, he laughs; the reaction confuses me. "Elias, I've never doubted your ability to achieve and accomplish." His eyes dart down to his glass before they raise back to me. "As a matter of fact, my biggest fear is that it is within your capability that you'll actually succeed in this pursuit." His admission dissipates my despondency, replacing it with bewilderment.

However, it was my father's next words that paralyzed me.

"But what kind of man am I, in the face of my peers and subordinates, if the son I so highly endorsed to take my place instead wasted his potential to become some blue-collared grease monkey?"

It was then I realized it was never about me.

I started college in the fall and moved into a campus residence. My father kept to his promise that he wouldn't fund my college expenses, but my mother did.

I began employment at Kauffman Tires so that it would appear that I was working to pay for my own education. My mother insisted there was no need. However, I wouldn't stand by and pretend as if a wedge wouldn't form between my parents if my father knew that she'd acted against his will. Nevertheless, working for Kauffman's became a good experience for my resume, and since my mother saw to all my expenses—including her weekly discretion deposits—I saved every penny earned from my day job.

For my twenty-first birthday, she gifted me a red and black, brand-new Chevy Camaro ZL1. She, my brother Elijah, and my uncle Eric drove it to my residence the morning of my birthday. Enraptured by the beauty that stood before me, I called her Dynamite.

"Lucky bastard," my brother joked as he wished me a happy birthday. Although we reconciled our differences, my father had him wrapped around his finger, so I treaded carefully with information around him.

A week later, my mother purchased a condo, another gift—my own residence.

"Do you like it, honey?" my mother asks, more excited about this immeasurable gift than I am. Granted, it's stunning but unnecessary. Still, I appreciate it.

"Yes, Mom, but why?" Hesitant in her response, I begin to assume she's doing this because graduating college was the stipulation for receiving my trust fund. But we both know my father won't be giving me access to mine. "Are you doing this because—"

"Because I want to," she interrupts. "So, tell me, how's college life treating you? Are you ready to graduate? I feel like we don't talk as much anymore."

I chuckle. "Mom, we talk every day."

"Yes, but the conversations are shorter. So, tell me, any girls?"

I raise my eyebrows at my mother's sudden forwardness. "Okay... no... well, no, we're not talking about this." I trip over my words to refrain from lying. I'm uncomfortable with the topic, but my grin reveals all she needs to know.

Her hands fly to her mouth, and she gapes. "Oh my god! There is! Tell me all about her."

I chuckle at her excitement. "Her name is Jessica. She goes to Georgia State."

She grins. "Oh, so where'd you meet her?"

"One of Travis's functions."

"Okay, so are you guys official? Dating? Are you being safe? Condoms? You know when me and your father—"

"Okay. Mom." I stop her before she goes off the rails. "We're not official yet, and it hasn't gotten 'there' either."

Her expression turns serious as if she's about to offer must-heeded advice. "Okay, well, make sure the size you get—"

"Mom!" I cut her off again. "I know, I understand. New subject, please."

If she thinks I'm a virgin, I'm okay with that, but we're not having this conversation.

"Okay, honey, I know you don't want your mom all in your beeswax, but I just want to make sure my baby is safe."

I chuckle, my mother is adorable.

I spent that entire day with my mother. We shopped for furniture, ate lunch, and had ice cream before calling it an evening.

Two weeks later, while leaving work, my phone vibrated in my pocket. I pulled it out to see my father's name lit on my screen. He never called. I was reluctant to answer, but I did.

"Hello."

"Elias, you need to come home now," my father demands.

"Why?" Who the fuck does he think he's talking to, demanding me?

His tone changes from demanding to concerned. "It's your mother."

My movements to my car halt at the mention of Mom. "What's wrong with Mom?"

"She's not well. She's asking for you. Come home."

Exchanging no further words, I end the call, jump in my Camaro, and floor it to Milton.

What the hell does he mean, she's not well? I swear for the life of me, if he's done something to her, I'll kill that motherfucker.

Whatever it is, Mom, just hold on. I'm coming. I'll fix it.

The sight of my mother that night would be etched in my brain forever.

I arrive at the place I once called home and burst through the front door. I see my best friend, Travis, our friend Tyler, my brother, and Uncle Eric.

"Where's Mom?" I ask.

"Come." My uncle gestures, and he leads me to the first-floor guest room and pushes through the door. My mother lies on the bed with an IV bag over her. A nurse stands in one corner, and the waste of space that is my father stands in another.

I slowly approach the thin woman lying on the bed. She only barely resembles the healthy, lively woman I spent the day with two weeks ago. I take her hand in mine and blink away tears.

"Elias," she whispers.

My voice begins to quaver. "Tell me what to do, Mom."

Tears spill from her eyes when she says, "My sweet boy."

I abruptly cut my head to my father, ready to rip him a new one. "What did you do?"

"Elias." I shift back to my mother as my name leaves her lips. "I've been sick for some time now, honey."

"What? No, I just saw you two weeks ago, you were fine. Mom, don't cover for him."

"No, honey, your dad has been taking care of me. The best treatments, the utmost care, but..." Pausing to catch her breath, she coughs strenuously. I can tell it pains her. "The cancer. It spread faster than anticipated."

Cancer? What? When? "How long? Why did no one tell me?"

"That was my doing. I didn't want you to know. Not yet," she barely voices.

Unrelenting tears flood my eyelids until they pour. Sorrow encapsulates me as I gaze into the eyes of my feeble mother.

She places a palm on the side of my face, and I place a hand over hers. "Follow your dreams, honey. No matter what, you don't give up—you dance. Your passion, your purpose, are yours alone. Even if no one understands it, follow the light within you and dance. Live, love, and fulfill your heart's desires." Pausing to cough the dreadful cough of approaching demise, she continues. "I hope you dance, Elias. I love you, and I'll always be with you, my sweet, sweet boy."

"Mom..." I croak, but the words are stuck in my throat as I drown in despair. I push to my feet and approach my father. "Save her," I rasp.

"Elias..."

"I know you can! I'll do whatever you want. I give you my word. Just save her."

He's silent, looking at me with eyes full of remorse and something else—empathy, an emotion I didn't think the bastard was capable of feeling—but he remains silent. I storm out of the guest room—where my mother lay dying—and charge upstairs to my room. Unbearably glaring pain takes hold of me, and I'm losing my ability to contain it. Anger rises in me like a tide, and I start kicking shit.

When nothing eases the pain, I plummet to the floor, dropping my head in my hands, grabbing fistfuls of my hair until I feel the pull at my roots.

My room door opens, and it's my uncle. He sits next to me, pulls me in, and places a hand on my head. "Let it out, El," he says. With that, I release all my emotions in a painstaking bawl from deep within my chest.

She passed away three days later. With every lowering of the casket, the ache in my chest grew. *What a cruel universe*, I thought. If there's some God or higher power he hates me. The sweetest soul of them all, the one person that loved me unconditionally, was ripped from me. A large part of me harbored anger. I never imagined losing my mother so soon.

I suppose it's different when you're given the opportunity to prepare for the loss of someone you love. I'll never know, because it wasn't the case for me. She was here today and gone the next. Had I known, I would have come home, withdrawn from classes, and cared for her. Understanding that's why she kept it from me didn't make the loss any easier.

It wasn't until much later that the realization set in that the sudden purchase of the car and the condo were because I confided in her that when my business took off, I would treat myself to such lavishes. Knowing she wouldn't be around to witness that, Christmas came early.

After the funeral, Travis and Tyler approached me. "It hurts now, El, but you're gonna be okay."

I face the ground and stuff my hands in my pocket. Travis touches my shoulder and says, "El, you will be okay."

Looking up, I nod. "Yeah, um." I take a sharp inhale. "I'm gonna take a semester off."

"Nah, can't let you do that." Tyler shakes his head.

I narrow my eyes. "What?"

"That's not what she wanted. That's why she reached out to us. You'll get through this, bro." Travis tries to console me.

Tyler grips my hand in a solid clasp, reeling me in for a hug. "We're here for you. You're not alone." Emotion is raw in his voice.

Tears form, but I tighten my jaw and bite them back. Travis places his hands on both of us, and when the hug breaks, he nudges our heads together. "It's not your burden to bear alone. We're in this together."

He pats me on the back, and as my tears dry, we begin to exit the gravesite. As we're walking away, I spot my father in the distance.

He stands rigid, watching our interaction. I almost feel as if he wants to say something. I hold his gaze. Breaking eye contact first, he makes for his vehicle. He can't bring himself to say a damn thing to me. What unshaken pride he must have.

I lay fresh lilac flowers beside my mother's headstone. Every year, until she passed, we visited her hometown, Rochester, New York, during the week of their annual Lilac Festival. We would enjoy the festivities and take an abundance of photos near her favorite flowery shrubs. After she passed, my brother Elijah and I made it our priority to visit each year in her honor. Over the last three years, life changes have made that difficult, but I'm sure to visit again soon.

I press my lips to my index and middle fingers and transfer the kiss from my fingers to the top of her headstone.

"For you, Mom, I'll dance."

CHAPTER 30

Skye

Elias's words replay in my head.

"My advice is that you allow this world to inspire you to make a change in your own life when you return."

I make my way to the kitchen, pop a bottle of red wine, pour a glass, and take a long sip. The fine red liquid passes through my lips, and my frustrations ease. The heavy disappointment of no longer exploring slowly lifts.

I sip more, pour more, sip again, and the bottle is half empty.

All this talk of passion, purpose, *my soul*. He wants no conversation about either of our lives from our world, yet he chooses to sum me up with no intent of actually knowing me. I'll take his perspective on this land into consideration, as he's lived in this society for five years. Notwithstanding, he doesn't know a damn thing about my life to advise me of anything.

"You unwittingly acknowledged your soul." No matter how many sips I take, his words aren't diluting, only replaying at the forefront of my brain. In my tipsy state, I begin to ponder them.

"That feeling you've kept caged at your depths breached the surface; that's why you were sent here."

I pick up my journal, open to a new page, and, taking a dive into my depths, *I begin to write.*

The next morning, I reread what I had written before ripping those very pages from my journal, balling them up in my fists, and tossing them in a corner.

I had become subdued and allowed Elias's words to induce skepticism of myself, to bring me to a dark place, and I'm utterly disgusted in myself for allowing his gloom to envelop me. *No more wine for me.*

The next two days, I stayed home—I should really stop referring to it as "home"—but I stay in, reading. Elias hasn't shown up, so I suppose he's serious regarding parting ways for good. I just wish I knew what triggered such a rash decision.

The truth is, I've glued myself to books so as not to contemplate his actions, because what would that change? Another part of me feels resentment toward him for his repeated assumption that my being transported here is by reason of internal desolation.

That may be his narrative, but it isn't mine.

I will enjoy my time here while it lasts. I consider this place a paradise, despite the fact that it could never mean forever for me. Without my son and my loving family, I'd brim with grief and suffer from loss. The thought alone disheartens me.

He tethered himself to this utopian society, asserting his unwavering content, yet still darkness lingers. He has to become aware that fleeing did not end his internal war. He may have anticipated that remaining here was the best decision, and it may well be—for someone else—but for Elias Crawford, it is as plain as day that it was not.

I further mull on his actions from the other day.

The primrose lilac.

The meaning of the yellow flower. *Nostalgia.* Observing the abundance of yellow lilacs in his yard, at the mention of their meaning, his demeanor flipped like a switch. What if his truth is that he *does* regret his decision to stay?

The ring of the doorbell pulls me out of my thoughts. I go down the hall and see Mauria in the peephole.

"I think Sam and I are ready to show the blueprints to some builders!" she says exuberantly when I open the door.

"That's awesome," I respond with as much enthusiasm as I can work up before stepping back to let her in.

"Okay, what's wrong?" she asks, placing her hands on her hips.

"Huh? Nothing. Why would you think something is wrong?" I attempt to appear normal.

"Don't wanna hear it, liar. What happened?" She's not falling for it. I totally stink at fake impressions.

I take a reproachful breath. "Elias and I were supposed to take a long trip, exploring some of the lands."

"Okay, and? Why are you still here?" she asks with her usual sass.

"He changed his mind," I admit, shrugging it off as I head to the kitchen.

"He did what?" she snaps and marches toward the front door. "Oh, no, I've got a thing and two for him."

I run to her and grab her arm. "No, Mauria. He's got some other... stuff."

She crosses her arms and frowns. "What other *stuff*?" Her current stance insists that if I don't give her a good explanation, she's charging over there.

"It's really hard to explain, it's even confusing to me. Don't approach him, please?" I plead.

"Fine." She shoots up her index finger. "But only because you said please."

I chuckle. She walks into the kitchen and opens the fridge. "And did you plan on leaving without telling me?"

"No. I planned on telling you the day you guys toured his home, but that's the same day he canceled." I pause to take a sip of water. "There was nothing to tell when I returned, unfortunately."

She gives me a look of pity. "You poor thing." She stretches her arms to give me a hug, and I accept and hug her back.

My mind revisits what she mentioned about leaving and not notifying her. Sooner or later, I will be leaving—forever, and suddenly the weight of that knowledge burdens me.

I really am going to miss her.

CHAPTER 31

Skye

It has been twenty-three days since Elias and I parted at the stables.

After eight days without seeing him, before agreeing to the five-day trip to Land Tikita with Mauria and Sam, I visited his home to see if he'd be there, but to no avail. One of his boats was gone, and not a hint of light shone through the windows. I wonder if he's decided not to return until my departure.

I can't help but think that this is my fault—not for his reaction, but for having thought he'd ever regard me as anything more than the distressed woman that needed his help, much less a friend. While I only spent a short period with him, the longing exists. Unfortunately, it's one-sided.

He truly does have a brutal and hardened heart. Coming to terms with the fact that I wouldn't be seeing him again, I hung my head when I left his property. *So long, Elias.*

"So, Land Tikita is not like Land Sandemia, but it isn't like Land Kairos either." Mauria pulls me from my thoughts. Still, this Land Kairos, I've yet to visit. *Oh, but I was born there.*

"How so?" I ask.

She takes a bite of her plum, and her chewing sends a signal straight to my empty stomach. "Well, Tikita is more populated than Sandemia, but it isn't as modern. They're making small upgrades here and there, though." I want to ask how it differs from Land Kairos but think better of it.

We are riding aboard a larger vessel instead of the boat Mauria used for our spa day trip to Zendovou. Sam informs me this one is meant for long distances at open sea. I wouldn't know the difference, but the height gives a prominent view of the distance—and it's incredible.

The grassy earth of Mauria and Sam's homeland, Tikita, is lined with small log cabin homes that aren't in terrible condition. But still, I'm in agreement with Mauria—an upgrade could be useful. Unlike Sandemia, where the trees are tall and well-kept, the grass is shaved, and the shrubs are groomed, here there are no distinct paths, grass covers the land—it resembles a large back yard.

We stroll through the town. The shops are exterior stands, and the outdoor lighting comes from wooden torches instead of the tall metal poles on Sandemia. Nonetheless, the people are amicable, but I gather that is common among all the lands.

Mauria introduces me to a few of her relatives and old friends before we make our way to her old residence to greet her parents. Their home was upgraded, in contrast to the others in town, with the exception of a few. Mauria elucidates that she and Sam began dating while he was completing his architectural education, and her family home was his first project. Having no qualms about his inexperience and trusting he'd do his best, it proved to be enough. They loved the upgrade, which included an extra bedroom, an extended kitchen, a separate dining area, and a back patio.

"They're upgrading the schools, building outdoor activity areas, and creating pathways," she informs me as we tour construction areas.

"Are the people in agreement with these new advancements?" My question may seem outlandish, but with no knowledge of government proceedings, I'm curious.

"Of course," she says. "When an idea is proposed, usually

through one of the leaders, the community chips in. If they were against it, the work couldn't begin."

"Hm. Interesting."

"It's usually travelers native to the land that return with inspiration and bring it to the leader's attention. The leader decides if the change, or addition, would be of benefit, then communicates it to the people."

"Oh, so that's how that works." I regret the words as they leave my lips. It was a thought, meant to remain a thought. *Why do you talk to yourself so much, idiot?*

Mauria gives me a quizzical look. "You didn't know that?"

Get yourself out of this one, you suck at sudden excuses. "Well… I mean, it's just all I know is Kairos." The amnesia excuse isn't at my disposal any longer, so I make use of the lie that excuses my ignorance.

Mauria nods. "Understandable. Maybe, being that's your homeland, you could convince them that change isn't so scary."

Okay, so that worked. Thank you, Land-I-know-nothing-of.

After three days of touring Land Tikita and another five at sea, we've finally arrived back at Sandemia, and as I've taken a great deal of photos, I wonder how much space is left on the small chip in the camera.

I check the mailbox before entering the home. There's nothing more than Daycomms and a reminder that my temporary registration will expire in twenty days. *Great, now what?* Bending to see if there's anything else, I realize there's another envelope addressed to me without a sender. I open the seal and remove a thick white folded paper. Upon unfolding it, my eyes widen.

Skye Cooke

Birth 101 Day of 1995
Land of Kairos
Mother: Rain Cooke
Father: Lester Cooke

At the bottom right corner is a Land of Kairos seal.

Elias.

He's back. He traveled all the way to Kairos to obtain this for me? That's a twenty-four-day round trip. *That's why he wasn't home.* I run inside and grab the bag I had originally packed in preparation for our original travel plans.

It isn't much, but it's enough.

I write a note to leave in Mauria's mailbox and grab my fake birth paper.

It's three p.m. I have time.

On my way out of the bedroom, I halt, catching sight of the balled-up journal entry from the night I allowed Elias's darkness into my depths. It still sits on the floor in the corner of my room, and I question why I haven't bothered throwing it out. I pick it up, smooth the sheet to the best of my ability, and read over it again.

These words are not my own. Empathy for Elias festered that night, and during a frivolous state, I wove the threads of his murk into my own life. Putting the pen to paper, I mindlessly journaled it as if the experience were my own. Under this notion, the pages no longer spark anger but rather insight. I further straighten the page before folding it neatly and place it inside my bag before heading through the door.

I arrive at the town registration and get a picture ID, then register 12 Haven Downs as my home indefinitely. I stop at a nearby accessory shop to pick up another chip for my camera, then grab a fish sandwich from a place nearby—I'm starving. I walk as I eat, then dump the foil in a nearby trash, guzzle a bottle of water, and then pop a mint.

I've got a thing or *ten* to get off my chest; I'd hate for it to be with fish breath.

My watch reads 5:17 p.m. Still enough time to get there and head back if this goes south. I walk through the tree-filled path until it ends at a grassy field and gaze upon the large brick-front home with the stone path leading to the front patio. I walk through the lawn until I am a step from ascending his property and glance over to the shore. The missing boat has returned. Closing my eyes, I take a deep breath, and upon opening them, I continue, preparing for the worst.

I want answers, Elias Crawford, and you're going to give them to me.

Elias

She shouldn't have come here.

CHAPTER 32

Skye

Before I can ring the bell, Elias swings open the door. He gives me a brooding glare. "Leave," he demands, austere and intimidating, but I'm not intimidated. Not this time.

I came ready for war.

I reciprocate his energy. "No."

"I wasn't asking." He starts to close the door, but I stop it with my foot. This earns me a deepened frown.

"I'm not done," I retort.

"What do you want, Skye?" he asks discourteously.

I push the door open and toss my bag at his foot. "I *want* to go on the adventure you promised."

His eyes dart to my bag, then back to me. "I didn't promise. Things change."

"Yeah? Well, *what* changed?"

"Not up for discussion."

My patience is growing thin. His haughty tone is pissing me off.

Stay calm, Skye. Remember, you showed up at his door.

No, go off. "What the hell is your problem?!" I snap.

He begins to respond, "I'm not the—"

"Shut up!" I cut him off.

Raising his eyebrows, astonished at my outburst, he silences. *Good, I've gained control.*

"You know, you tell me to find inspiration here and make a change. You're convinced I'm the miserable one, but it's not me, it's you." I take a breath. "You don't think I notice your change in temperament at the least mention of any form of friendship? Your choice to be isolated, to reject anything or anyone that could mean something to you. You act like I have a problem, but no, you have a damn problem!"

His front door is now wide open, but his frown doesn't waver. Arms crossed, he stands rigid, but his silence continues— and *I'm not done.*

"You claim you chose to stay, how much this place is a better life, but I call bullshit! I don't know what the hell happened to you in our world, but changing worlds didn't help you. You carried that hurt with you here. The place changed, but the man didn't!" My chest heaves as adrenaline pumps through me. I'm uncertain if it affected him in the slightest, but he hasn't moved a muscle.

He unfolds his arms. "Are you done?"

My erratic breathing slows, and I nod in defeat. I've made a fool of myself. *How is he this impenetrable?*

I reach down for my bag, but he puts one foot in front of it and kicks it behind him. Before I can look up, Elias has a hold of my wrist. In one swift movement, I'm being pulled inside. The door shuts behind me, and now my back is against it. *How the hell did he do that so fast?*

My heart hammers in my chest. I tilt back my head to see dark emerald, soul-piercing eyes staring back at me. He's so close. His masculine energy engulfs me. Mint invades my nostrils, and palpable darkness permeates the air around him. Everything about his intense aura screams danger, yet I am all but afraid. His hold on my wrist stays, and in a low and deep baritone, he utters, "Good, because now it's my turn."

Elias

She's so close. Her lavender scent nearly sways my stance. Her palpitating heart thrums through me, but she's not afraid. Her feminine nature of nurture is inviting, beckoning me to take shelter beneath her. Her sparkling essence threatens the void I take comfort in.

She set out to level the ground between us, substantiating her moral fiber as she's grown impatient with being the patronized novice. My sudden disaffection brought about a will to turn the tables, *to become the patronizer,* and she's been patient, hoping I would divulge something. But I won't budge. So, she chided me from her own presumptions. And I watched as her sunshine blazed into a fire with her determination to get even.

And it *electrified* me.

I loathe how much I enjoyed it.

Her accurate discernment is commendable. She has inadvertently proven, time and time again, that she is indeed sunlight to my darkened core. I can't allow her to be that.

I fear it.

So preemptively, I insisted we part.

My conjecture is that she's *here* because she's confined herself to a lackluster life for undisclosed reasons, oblivious to the authenticity that she's kept under lock and key. Well, now the beast is primed to be free; the cage has rattled for far too long.

Incarcerating her originality is becoming her undoing. *That's why she's here.* While I may be aware of this, until she concedes this, she'll return to our world, craving this place above the love she feels for anyone. In her time here, she slowly opens the cage, providing deliverance for her individuality as she learns a true sense of freedom, the way it's manifested in this world.

To then impede the tortured embodiment of her soul after it has tasted liberation will cause an endless war to rage within her.

She may think we're going to talk about me, but the moment

she stepped foot in my yard, I already had quite the opposite in mind. In about a minute, she'll regret coming here. I'll live with being the bad guy. It's for her own damn stubborn good. She won't betray her defenses indisputably, not even for her tormented soul, because she's grounded within her obstinateness.

It's unfortunate that I find this very aspect of hers comparatively attractive since I'm preparing to shatter this defense mechanism of hers into pieces.

"Why are you here?" I demand her truth.

"I already told—"

"I said... why are you *here*?" I interrupt.

Pausing, she narrows her eyes, searching mine. Comprehending what I'm *really* asking, her defenses slowly rise.

Well, I don't give a shit. Let them.

"I. Don't. Know."

"Yeah?" I ask daringly, then bend to her ear and whisper, "Well, you're lying."

She begins to twist the wrist imprisoned beneath my palm. When I move from her ear to her face again, she's fuming.

"What's wrong?" I bait her fury. "Couldn't handle your miserable little life?"

She's simmering with anger, and the sight entices me. "You're the one miserable. Don't project your misery onto me."

She's deflecting, so I go below the belt. "At least I'm not some mockery of happiness."

Her breathing halts, she stills, and I know what's to come. Grabbing her other hand before it connects to my face, I pull her from the door to the sectional couch in my living room.

Her and those fucking hands.

Barely balanced, she plops onto the couch. I crate her in with one arm by her head and the other on the armrest. She slightly raises in a small attempt to get up, but I'm hovering over her. I lean in, and she instead sinks back into the cushion.

"You wanted contention when you showed up at my door. Well, now you've got it," I say through clenched teeth.

"Who are you?" she asks in a shaky voice.

"Your worst goddamn nightmare," I hiss.

"I... I won't come back. I promise. Thank you for the birth paper from Land Kairos."

No.

I've been looking at her—glaring—but not *paying attention.* A burning sensation forms in my core. My entire self screams to abort the defense-shattering mission. I witness *fear* flash in her eyes, and my chest tightens. I step back from her.

Why the fuck did I do that? I didn't account for what would happen if I went as far as striking fear in her. I expected pique, outrage, anger, all of the above, as I forced through her barriers of denial. I could deal with them all as akin to mine.

But fear?

No, she can't fear me. How could I expect such tenderness to contest the callousness I unveiled?

Gingerly, she rises from the sofa and moves toward her bag.

"Skye," I call to her retreating back, low and full of contrition.

Suspending her movement, she answers. "Hm." It's nearly inaudible, trepidation in the mere sound of her voice. I slowly approach her, and she turns, facing me. I still see the lingering fear. *Damn, El, what did you do?*

"Skye, I'm sorry."

"No, I... I shouldn't have... I'm sor..." I stop her from finishing by curling my fingers under her chin and placing my thumb over her lips. She's being careful with her words, apprehensive of an unexpected me.

"Skye, don't be afraid of me, please. I went about this all wrong. I pushed you away, opposing how good you are for me. I despise it." I admit my truth. "Using aggression to get you to lower your defenses, I went too far."

A tear falls from her eye. My gut twists.

"Please, don't fear me." I whisper my plea. "I can't take it."

Another silent tear falls, and I bring her into my arms. She buries her face into my chest and softly sobs.

For as long as she's here, I'll never resort to that again. There are many who deserve the worst from me. She's not one of them.

CHAPTER 33

Skye

I'm uncertain as to why I ever thought I could rival Elias's energy.

This level of darkness is unknown to me. As it bared its fangs, I witnessed a hostile beast with which I could not conflict.

But that's not him.

That's the surface he hides behind.

When it roared at me, had I thought of this sooner, I wouldn't have been afraid. The beast is a veil that protects him—*the real him.*

I suddenly get the feeling that his resentment stems from those he once held close. He has to free his heart, or those who begin to cherish him will in turn be on the receiving end of his harbored hate.

He refuses to let anyone in. However, that's no way to live and expect to truly be at peace.

A life without love is not living, it's *surviving*.

To protect your heart is to fill it with joy, allowing it to love. To refuse to love is to stifle it.

I wish he'd let the iron chains wrapped around his core crumble, because beneath Elias Crawford's steel barriers is a *heart of gold*.

Elias

When her sobbing subsides, she lifts her chin and meets my gaze. I don't expect forgiveness, but at the sight of her glassy eyes, I'm comforted by the absence of fear.

"You can slap me now, I deserve it."

She slightly giggles, and relief surges through me. A hint of a smile from her is oxygen to my lungs.

"Would you like a glass of water?" I ask.

She nods, so I make for the kitchen.

When I reenter the living room, Skye studies the large portrait over the fireplace. I walk over and hand her the glass of water. She thanks me before taking a sip.

"This woman looks oddly familiar. Who is she?"

"She's from Rochester as well. She's my mother."

Her head abruptly turns in my direction with an expression that suggests she's put the pieces of a puzzle together. "Is that why you...? The lilacs."

"Yes. Every year during Rochester's spring season, we'd visit for the Lilac Festival," I reveal before stepping back toward the couch.

"Well, is she back in our world?"

"Yeah," I say. "Her headstone is."

"Elias, I'm sorry." Sympathy covers her features.

"Don't be. She's no longer suffering," I stoically mention.

"What was..."

"Cancer. Eleven years ago." I know what her question will be. Recalling her words from moments prior, I ask, "Skye, did you say my mother looked familiar?"

Facing the portrait again, she sighs. "I can't quite remember where, but I've seen her before. I may have even interacted with her." She glances back in my direction. "What's her name? And are you from Rochester too?"

"Elizabeth. And no, I was born in Sandy Springs, Georgia. We moved to Milton when I was ten. You may not have been born when she left Rochester."

She rolls her eyes. "I totally forgot, it was that irking Southern, *'preciate you*, lingo' that confirmed my suspicion of you."

I chuckle. "So you're familiar with the South?"

"My grandparents moved to Griffin when I was twelve. I spent every summer there until I graduated high school."

When I internally question how this information hadn't been introduced prior to now, I recall that I chose to shut down any conversation regarding my history from that world. In doing so, she didn't impart hers, either.

She raises her glass to take a sip of her water and pauses in motion. Instead, she lowers her arm, scrutinizing the glass of water.

"Something wrong with the water?" I ask, concerned.

She places the glass on the fireplace surface and gazes down at her wrist, or rather, she inspects her butterfly bracelet. Her brows furrow in concentration. Unsure what to make of this nuance, I say her name. "Skye?"

She remains silent and glances toward my mother's portrait, then again at her bracelet, then back to the portrait, squinting, seemingly in deep thought.

I rise from my seat but don't approach. "Skye, is everything okay?"

"Do you have a brother?" She's asking *me*, but her mind is elsewhere.

"I do?" I answer, but it comes out as a question.

"Growing up, who was taller?"

"I've always been taller than him," I answer, growing impatient. "Skye, what are you doing?"

"He called me stupid," she says, still gazing at the portrait.

"What?"

"Your brother. The lilacs were blue. Her husband... he yelled at me, and I cried." Though she speaks, she's not here—it's as if she's revisiting a memory in real time.

"Whose husband? My mom's?" Wherever she is right now, I need to be there, but she's in some sort of trance.

"Dave. That's what she called him."

My father's name leaving her lips sparks my temper. *What the fuck does she mean he yelled at her?* I step in front of her, blocking her view of the portrait, and place my hands on her shoulders. "Skye?"

Blinking rapidly, she focuses on me as she leaves her daze. "Sorry, sometimes to remember something I've forgotten completely, I have to revisit the exact moment."

"You have to relive it." I voice my comprehension.

She nods. "It's funny how that works. You completely forget something, but then a sudden scent or sight triggers a memory in the brain, and it all comes back. A lost memory you never knew existed."

"Do you know what you were saying? My father yelled at you? My brother called you stupid? Can you tell me what you were remembering?"

She chuckles. "I know what I was saying, I wasn't in a trance." *Could've fooled me.*

"I was just really focused on remembering, and you kept interrupting, so I mentioned small things as I remembered them." She gives her bracelet another glance and then raises her chin to look at me. "I met your mother, Miss Elizabeth." She smiles. "Looks like you and I have crossed paths before, Elias."

She moves back to the couch and takes a seat.

"When?" I itch to know.

"It was only for a moment, but at the Lilac Festival twenty years ago."

CHAPTER 34

Skye

TWENTY YEARS AGO

"Mommy, look! The lilacs are blue!"

Mom says the blue lilacs mean happiness, but I'm not happy right now. I lost my pink butterfly bracelet Grandma handmade for me, and I can't find it anywhere. There are so many people walking around, and I know someone kicked it.

"Mommy, we have to find it. I dropped it over here somewhere."

"It's okay, Skye. Grandma will make another one for you."

"But I don't want another one, I want that one," I pout.

"Okay, but we won't spend all day looking for it," Mom agrees.

We walk through the area where I dropped it, searching the path and the grass, but I don't see it and neither does Mom. There are so many people, and I wish they'd all just go away so I can find my bracelet, but when Mom says it's gone, I begin to cry.

"It's okay, sweetie," she says, hugging me.

Mom and I continue through the park. She's no longer looking for my bracelet, but I still keep an eye out. We stop for a frozen custard, and while she orders, I look around, and there it is.

My bracelet.

I take off from Mom's side, running full speed toward my bracelet, but someone kicks it.

Inches away, I slam into someone—a man—and he spills his drink on himself.

"Shit!" he curses, looking down at his shirt. "Watch where you're going!" he yells at me.

"I... I'm sorry, Mister. It's just my brace—"

"I don't give a damn!" he yells again. He's looking at me so angrily. I begin to cry. Why is he being so mean? I didn't mean to run into him.

"Oh, stop it, Dave. She's just a kid," a lady, *a really short lady,* with two boys next to her says to the mean man.

"Yeah, a stupid kid." The shorter boy smirks at me.

"I'm not stupid! I just wanted my bracelet," I snap at him while I try to stop crying. I hate boys. They're all mean and stupid.

"Elijah, stop it. Say you're sorry," the short lady commands him.

He tries to say something back to her, but she gives him a mean face. He looks back at me. "Sorry," he says, holding his head down.

The woman puts a hand on his shoulder. "Sorry for what?"

"Mom!" he whines like the baby that he is. She gives him another mean look, and he turns to me again. "Sorry for calling you stupid."

He's walking away, and the taller boy teases the short, mean one. "Now look who's stupid?"

"Elias." The woman eyes him sternly. The tall one stiffens and quickly says, "Sorry, Mom."

"Now was it this you were after, honey?" The woman looks at me with a smile. My bracelet rests in her hand, and excitement fills me.

"Yes, miss, thank you so much!"

"It's no problem, dear. I saw you running straight for it. It's a pretty bracelet."

"Thank you. My grandma made it for me."

She places it on my wrist. "Be careful not to lose it next time. You might not find it."

"I won't, thank you again, miss."

"Elizabeth." She tells me her name. "What's your name, hun?"

"Skye."

"Okay, Skye. Where are your parents?"

"Oh, my mom is—" I look over to the area where we were getting custards, but my mom is no longer there, and the happy feeling isn't there anymore. I'm getting scared. Where is my mom? I turn back to Miss Elizabeth. "We were just getting custards. I don't see her."

"Don't be scared, she's more than likely looking for you. Let's go wait for her where you were last with her," Miss Elizabeth instructs.

Taking my hand, she tells the mean man and the stupid boys that she will meet them at the car, then walks with me near the custard stand.

"If you ever get lost, wait by the last place you were with your parents," she tells me. "And you shouldn't run off from your mom, okay? I can only imagine her worry. It's dangerous to do that."

I nod and begin to cry, and she hugs me. "Don't cry, honey, everything will be alright."

"Okay," I say through my cries, hugging her back.

I really like Miss Elizabeth. She's really nice.

"Skye! Oh my god!" my mom cries, hugging me so tight I can barely breathe. "Don't ever do that again! Where did you go?" Mom looks so scared, her face is wet with tears.

I'm about to answer, but Miss Elizabeth speaks first. "Hi, I'm Elizabeth. Your daughter, I presume?"

Mom holds me close. "Yes," she answers.

Miss Elizabeth smiles. "She bumped into my husband, running after her bracelet."

I hold up my wrist. "Look, Mom, I found it!"

"Okay, Skye, but running off is never okay. Do you understand?" Mom scolds me.

I nod. "I'm sorry."

"Thank you so much, I was worried sick," Mom says to Miss Elizabeth. "I'm Sylvia."

"Nice to meet you, Sylvia. Don't thank me, please. I'm a mother of two very energetic boys."

"Well, can I get you anything? Perhaps a frozen custard?"

"Oh no, I've had enough delights for one day." She laughs. "It's my pleasure to see mom and daughter reunited. My husband and boys are waiting for me at the exit."

Mom thanks Miss Elizabeth again.

"Stay near your mom, Skye," she says before walking away.

I wave goodbye, and Mom and I finally get custards. We enjoy the festival, and I have my bracelet.

The blue lilacs are perfect. Even though I was sad, they told me not to worry because the day would end in happiness.

CHAPTER 35

Elias

kye's recollection festers a mix of emotions.

I never thought I'd ever meet anyone from Earth ever again, let alone someone who would share a memory of my mother.

"She's an angel, for sure," Skye mentions with a soft smile.

I gaze at the beautiful soul before me taking a sip of water, and a throbbing begins in my chest. My mother was good to her in the moments they'd met, yet the three Crawford men have been jerks. My brother was just a dumb kid, but for my father to snap at an eight-year-old? *Pathetic bastard.* Twenty years later, we meet again in an entirely different universe, and I scare her to tears while she trusts me.

She trusts me.

The very thought brings forth an idea. A different approach to take with her denial.

"Skye, why do *you think* you're here?"

She looks down at her glass but doesn't jump to the defense immediately—a good sign. There's something on the surface she's not saying as she lightly taps her cup in thought.

"Look at me," I softly voice.

She raises her eyes to mine. I search them with my own. "If I offend you, you can slap me, but can I tell you what I think?"

"I'm not miserable," she says defensively.

I shake my head. "No, you're not. You're content. However, *content* isn't *your* form of happiness. 'Just enough' isn't *good* enough for your soul."

"I don't know what you mean." She abandons the defensive tone, looking to understand.

The entire time Skye has been here, she has taken an interest in learning, understanding, then putting things into perspective based on such knowledge. I've done this with her since we've met, yet when the topic of her own situation arises, I switch gears. Instead of knowing her and feeding her what she needs so she can decipher it for herself, I've chosen to scold her. She's intellectual. Such an approach is an insult to her intelligence.

Taking a breath, I proceed with caution. "Can I ask about your happiness? Why do you think you're happy?"

She downs the rest of her water and places the glass on the ottoman. Inhaling deeply, she relaxes her shoulders and lifts her chin. There's a change in her posture, an air of self-assurance suddenly surrounding her. "Look, in our world, landing a job is important. We all need money. However, obtaining a career is respected. It takes substantial effort to attain. Fortuitously, I landed a job in my field soon after I graduated college. I've climbed the ladder in a short time, unremitting in my pursuit. I'm not rich, but I'm paid well, I save well, and I can provide for my son. I've become established and will be set for retirement. Continuing my steady path, I'll be able to put my son through college, and my efforts to achieve such stability have and are coming to fruition."

"Sounds like the American dream. What's Skye's dream?" I regret the words the instant they leave my mouth.

She narrows her eyes and pushes to her feet.

Shit, wrong move. I responded truthfully, yet mindlessly.

"I'm leaving," she says, expressionless.

I stand too and approach her. "You didn't answer my question, Skye. I asked about your happiness, not your complacency."

This earns me a halt. She turns, facing me. "Complacency?"

"There are those who do just as you do and are content. Such complacency is parallel to happiness for them. But then there are those whose souls require more; those people are us." She's attentive, taking in every word. "If you had no one to return to, no pull of the heart, would you go back?"

"I could never truly be happy here without the people I love," she says, but it's another deflection.

I motion toward her. "But if they weren't there, would you return?"

When she doesn't respond, I have my answer.

"I'm not saying you don't have a good life. But is it everything you've ever wanted out of life? You're progressing at a rate at which society says you *should* be happy; in turn, your soul suffers. You're ambitious in your endeavors, but you lack passion, Skye. You may believe you're able to live this way forever, but you can't. Your soul has already begun to fight back."

Stuck in place, her eyes grow glassy. I get the feeling her being in this world has already caused such introspection. Even so, she knows she must return, so she pushes it down. *Ignores it.* But there's something else there. Something she holds in her very core. Proceeding with caution, I ask, "What's stopping you?"

She doesn't respond. Defeat prickles when she turns around and moves to her bag. She bends. But doesn't grab it. Instead, she unzips it and removes something. Turning toward me, she approaches with a wrinkled, folded paper in her hand. She glances down at the folded sheet, then lifts her chin and swallows, fighting back tears. Her shimmering eyes concern me.

"I trust you," she says in a voice barely above a whisper.

I know you do. And damn, am I sorry I almost broke that today.

"The day we parted at stables, I had a little too much to drink that night. Your words from earlier wouldn't leave my head, so I began to write." She stretches her arm to hand me the folded sheet. "I balled it up the next morning, revolted at the idea that I could ever feel this way. Then I convinced myself that these words are not my own, that I had allowed your darkness to protrude and mistook it for my own deep feelings."

"But now you're not so sure," I add.

She nods, and a tear falls.

I gesture for her to sit. She does, and I seat myself beside her. She hugs herself and hangs her head, letting her hair fall to purposely cover her face—to create a barrier. *She's hiding.* Whatever is written in these pages, she's ashamed of it. She's revealing it to me because she feels only I would understand it without judgment. *It's her trust in me.*

Wordlessly, I unfold the crinkled page and begin to read.

I've never thought about what would truly make me happy. Perhaps I don't know. According to the ways of society, I'm supposed to be happy. I'm walking in my purpose, right? Or is "purpose" even a real thing?

I make my living managing the accounts of those whose net income quadruples my own. If "purpose" is real, what a sick joke for that to be mine. Those with millions of dollars, whose accounts I manage, they've taken risks. Risks I can't afford to take. For others, such wealth has been passed down through generations.

Well, my family are immigrants.

They escaped a life of poverty and passed down an opportunity unknown to them for a better life, for which I am grateful. I've taken a risk before, and all that risk did was lead me to depend on the people who love me to bail me out. There are many who do not have that level of support, so now I tread carefully in the risk department, taking the path of least resistance.

I do as I am expected. Society teaches that this is the path to stability and financial security. The "safest" path, that is.

I have a son that depends on me and a family I refuse to allow to bear the burden of my consequences ever again.

I'm stable.

Continuing this journey will result in a future of absolute security. In a society such as ours, unless you're born with the financial freedom to take risks in hopes of finding your passion, you must be diligent. Those without? Our world says it's their own fault, that they make their own struggles. I just happened to be lucky I didn't fall on my face when I made mine, and it is with great appreciation for the love of my family that surrounds me.

Oh, right, love.

I may be a restless soul, but my heart is why I am able to endure. My love is powerful, and the love that exists around me is unwavering. It is why I am able to continue, content with my internal weariness.

For as long as I live, I'll smile because I'll be okay. Right? Because of my establishment, I am happy. Or I should be, right?

I'm a prodigy of my family's hopes and dreams that couldn't be achieved. Their investment in me did not go to waste, and superficially, I am elated and thriving. However, never can I be prodigal.

When my eyes are closed, my world is perfect. I escape to another land, another society, one less demanding. One where I have the freedom to explore the desires of my soul, whatever that may be. I fantasize about that sort of liberation. What would I do with such freedom? I'm not sure because I have no sense of passion.

I do not know my purpose, and I don't have the means to find out. I will never breathe a word of the havoc that reeks within me because, for me, to be unhappy is to be ungrateful. However, to soothe my aching soul, I look forward to the faraway place I visit when my eyes are closed. For it is only then, and only for a few hours, that the caged bird that is my soul is set free.

Until the night my dream became a reality, but I can't stay.

The words on this paper are none other than her agonized soul; I'm honored that she shared it with me. Refolding the sheet, I place it on her lap. "Skye," I say calmly.

"Hm." She doesn't move a muscle.

"Look at me."

She slowly lifts her head, and I gaze into her glassy brown eyes.

"These are the words of your tethered soul, ready to be set free. This isn't darkness, this is truth."

"I've always drowned out reality in books or anime. I'd fantasize about a different world, but I've never correlated those reveries with unhappiness. Not until the night I wrote that journal entry," she reveals.

I put my arm around her and bring her close.

Mission complete.

She's accepted that she's caged her soul. Yet there's still a pull. This was hard for her, but there's something else I want to know. I should stop here, but I don't. Suddenly, I have a duty to see this through—to help her.

Resting her head into the crook of my neck, I lean back, sinking us into the cushion. "Skye, can you tell me why you think acknowledging your soul implies that you are ungrateful?"

She tilts her head back to look up at me. I don't move. Our heads are close enough. Dare I look down and refuse the lips that compel me? She leans upright, and I silently ache for her to be against me again, but the distance is needed.

"You won't get it," she says drearily.

I gaze into her dispirited eyes. "Try me."

She shuts her eyes and takes a deep breath. "You'd have to know love and compassion as I know it—as I feel it—to understand my *why.*"

I lean upright with her and hold her gaze. "Try me."

Observing her nuance, before her lips quirk, I see the part of her that trusts me.

CHAPTER 36

Skye

FIVE YEARS AGO

My heart drops to my stomach when I see the second line appear on the stick.

Pregnant?

Damn it. This is so bad. I guess we didn't wait long enough for the birth control to actually work. *No, we were definitely careless.*

Jason and I had always used protection, but then one night—and one too many drinks—happened, and we didn't. We continued when nothing came of it that month, nor the month after, nor the month after that. Then the months turned into an entire year of no protection other than the pull-out method, *most times.*

After giving our reckless sex life deeper thought, I brought it to his attention one night.

I live with my parents, work part time at a diner, and attend college. A child is the last thing I need. I expressed to him that, at some point, our luck will run out and that I'd better get started on some sort of birth control. He said I could if I wanted to, but he wouldn't care if I got pregnant because he loves me. As much as that swelled my heart, right now was not the time.

I had just begun taking birth control this very month. *Damn it, Lady Luck, couldn't you have given me a sprinkle one last time?* My parents are not going to be happy about this. It's bad enough they don't like Jason, especially my father.

I had delayed college immediately after high school. I wasn't sure what I wanted to do yet. However, after working at the bank for two years, I grew to like my job, and the idea of becoming an accountant didn't seem awful.

I expressed this to my parents, and they were overjoyed. My father offered to pay my tuition fees. I didn't hate the idea, but my parents are average middle-class working people, and college isn't exactly affordable. I told my father I would take out a student loan if aid doesn't cover everything, but my mother insisted that I don't, warning that I'd be repaying those loans for the rest of my life.

My parents emigrated here as adults. My mother, Sylvia, is from Guyana, and my father, Delroy, is from Trinidad. Neither of them has *official* education past grade school. Nevertheless, they are far from uneducated people.

They came here and took advantage of the opportunities, gaining employment to build a stable life for a promising future. My mother has been a flight attendant for as long as I can remember, and my father is an armed security officer.

The road has never been easy, but they've strived to ensure that my brother and I grow up in a far different environment from theirs, which was poverty. They've had high hopes for us and preached the importance of education and obtaining a career.

"We want you to be better than us." I've heard that more times than I can count, but they've never once attempted to choose the path for us. Still, I feel an obligation to make them proud, and in doing so, I am proud.

But now, here I am, unmarried, pregnant, and unable to live on my own. My parents are spending from their savings to put me through college, and all I did was be reckless. *Idiot.* I quit my job at the bank because, as a full-time student, the inflexible hours didn't work for me; now, working part time at Hoyt's

Diner as a waitress, I make pennies—certainly not enough to care for a baby.

I decided to stop beating myself up about it. It's not solely my burden to bear, Jason will be picking me up tonight. I'll break the news to him, and maybe we can come up with a plan.

We're in Jason's room in the two-bedroom apartment he shares with a roommate, sitting up against the headboard with takeout in our lap while he looks for a movie for us to watch.

I open the container of sesame chicken and cringe at the awful smell. Closing the lid, I place the food on the nightstand beside me and take sips of the lemonade instead. *So, we don't like takeout anymore, got it.*

"What's wrong?" Jason asks.

"Not really hungry."

He places his food on the nightstand beside him and takes one of my hands in his. "Skye, you've been distant all night, what's the matter?"

I gaze into the dark-brown eyes of my handsome, high-yellow *Rican* boyfriend of two years, and all I see is genuine concern. I have been distant the entire night. He doesn't deserve that, but this is a big change, and I'm not sure I've accepted it. Telling someone—*telling him*—just makes it so much more real. *That and the fact that my love for sesame chicken is gone.*

"I need to tell you something," I utter, low and disinclined.

A frown forms as if apprehension is rising in him. "What's up?"

"I'm pregnant."

He dips his chin. "You serious?"

I take a deep breath. "Yes. I took two tests this morning." I lay back on the headboard, dropping my head back, peering at him from the corner of my eye. "What do we do? I'm in school, I only work part time. I can't afford a baby. Can *we* even afford a baby?"

He brings me in for a hug. "It's okay, baby, we'll figure it out." He kisses me, then slightly grins. "So no more takeout?"

"Yeah, I'm totally not eating that."

Chuckling, he holds me close for the remainder of the night. Relief washes over me. I suddenly feel like everything's going to be alright.

"Oh, Skye, I was worried this would happen," my mother sighs. Breaking the news to my parents isn't going over so well.

"Mom, you do know I'm not a child, right?" I state, frustrated.

Sitting in the living room, my father just came in from work. He hasn't commented, but his rigid posture presents his feelings about the matter clearly.

"No, you're not, but being an adult means being responsible," Mom scolds.

"Listen," my dad finally speaks. "It's done already. But he better know he's pulling his weight."

I huff out a breath. "I know that, Dad."

My mom sucks her teeth and folds her arms. "Can't afford a *rass* pot to piss in but wants to make babies." Her accent is in full effect.

My dad's eyebrows knit together. "*You know that,* but does he? That he needs to be a man and put down the parties and friends? To now become a father, provider, protector, and care for his woman and child?"

My father may be disappointed, but in contrast to my mother, he always speaks from a place of reason.

"One good look at the *pissin' tail* boy, there's not one damn thing responsible about him!" Then there's my mother, the trigger finger.

"You have a promising future…" Dad begins, but I cut him off before he finishes.

"Dad, I can still have a promising future," I defend.

My mom stands. "That's not the issue here!"

Noticing the rising tension, my father ends the discussion. "Sylvia, calm down. It's late. Let's go to bed."

My parents climb the stairs; when I hear their room door shut, I sink into the couch, grab one of the pillows, and hug it tightly to my chest. Mortified, I bury my face in the pillow and sob.

After an abundance of tears, I think of Jason and his comfort, his optimism. They think Jason and I can't do this? Well, I'll show them that we can. We have no choice. I'll finish school, obtain my degree, and start my career. If he and I put our incomes together, surely we'll be able to afford everything we need. They have so little faith in Jason, but I don't. We love each other, and we'll get through this together.

CHAPTER 37

Skye

FIVE YEARS AGO

I withdrew from my classes this semester. Either I fail or finish with an undesirable passing grade.

I had been incredibly sick and had no idea why they called it morning sickness when my sickness lasted all damn day. I had to take unpaid personal leave from work for four months. Most of the time, it was hard for me to keep my energy up for an entire workday. I found myself apologizing to my boss more than I actually worked, and though she was patient, I felt terrible where coverage was concerned. When she offered me personal time, I took it without question.

In the middle of my second trimester, I finally began feeling better, but I didn't reapply for classes. Instead, I applied for full-time employment at the diner. Jason and I moved in together in a two-bedroom apartment downtown.

At seven months, with the help of my family, our apartment is nearly ready for our son's arrival. My parents had suggested that I don't move out of their house. They don't believe Jason will provide me with the support I need. But after the night I broke the news to them, I made my decision, and I've decided to stick by it.

Jason still frequently parties and spends most Friday evenings at his usual hangout spot, but I'm not against it. He works long hours, and things are going to change when the baby arrives, so I don't pester him about his free time.

"How many appointments has he come to?" Mom asks as we're seated in the waiting area of the doctor's office.

I roll my eyes. "Mom, he works."

She sighs. "If you say so." *Five... four... three... two...* "You know." Of *course it wasn't going to end there.* "Your dad never missed an appointment with you or your brother."

"Mom," I say, annoyed.

She raises her hands in surrender. "Okay, fine. Just take notice of everything."

My mom has taken days off to make every appointment. In the beginning, Jason came to all the appointments, but recently he's been pulling tons of overtime so he could stay home when the baby is born. He's missing moments now, so he can be there for better moments later.

My son's birth was the most painful, yet precious, moment in my life.

We named him Julias.

I went into labor at work. My boss brought me to the hospital, and it all happened so fast. Contractions had begun, but I had mistaken them for strong Braxton Hicks. My due date wasn't for another six days, and with four hours left of my shift, I wanted to finish.

When my water broke, the pain intensified instantly. By the time I arrived at the hospital, it was too late for an epidural. Jason didn't show up until after I'd given birth, whereas my boss stayed at my side until my mother arrived.

That's not at all how I had the entire moment planned out. I imagined my mother and Jason at my side during the whole thing. Nonetheless, I was incredibly grateful for my boss.

Following Julias's birth, Jason never took any days off. He said the checks I'd be receiving from disability wouldn't be enough to cover anything besides basic necessities like groceries or diapers.

I thought he had extra money from the ridiculous amount of overtime he had been working during the pregnancy, yet still he feared it wouldn't be enough.

I didn't question it. I let him do whatever he needed to ensure we wouldn't be without, and since we've moved in together, he hasn't defaulted on anything financially. But I've begun to long for the time we once spent together. We live together, but somehow, we're with one another less than when we lived apart. It has now been a year, and I'm beginning to grow suspicious.

His late-night hours are getting later, and the reason is always "working overtime." Some nights he knocks out on the couch, never coming to bed, and a few days ago, he reeked of alcohol. A few times, I'd ask him if he could stay home with Julias just so I could have a break, but he always tells me he can't, for God knows whatever reason, and I end up resorting to asking my mom, who is always happy to keep Julias.

I've let Jason off the hook more times than I should because he handles the bulk of the financial responsibility, but the time he spends with us is so little.

I truly dislike contention, but arguments between us have begun to transpire, and when he claims, *"I have to work hard to provide for us,"* I cease to respond.

This evening, I've decided to pick Julias up from daycare, but I'm not going home after. I drop him off with my parents and take a drive to Jason's job. To my surprise, he wasn't there when I arrived. *Are you surprised, though?*

Jason hasn't been my loving boyfriend in months. Sometimes, I feel as though we're not even together—we just live together. He goes through the motions at home, but I can't shake the feeling that he'd rather be somewhere else. Departing from the parking lot of his job, I head to his usual hangout spot—his friend Jonathan's home—where he claims he hasn't been since Julias was born.

My mind races and my stomach clenches as I grip the steering wheel, indignation at Jason's betrayal reaching me. Since when do we lie to each other? But I guess you don't know you're being lied to until the truth reveals itself. And I question why the hell I didn't investigate sooner.

As I turn down the street of the urban area, cars line either side of the narrow street, making it hard to dodge the oncoming potholes. I spot Jason's car. I park and slam the door behind me, then follow the loud music and echoing voices toward the back-yard. When I round the corner, it's not long before I spot Jason—and the sight makes me sick to my stomach.

He's leaning against the back of the house with a drink in hand. Some floozy is flushed to him. Still in place, unable to move, my hands become fists at my sides. I want to cause a scene, call him out, I want... to cry. *How could he do this to me?* It's when I witness him kiss the lanky, fire-red-haired bimbo—who clearly needs a touch-up—that I burn with fury. His tongue is down her damn throat.

I start to charge over, but I'm forced to stop when someone grabs my arm. Turning around, I'm faced with his friend, Jonathan.

"Not here, Skye," he says.

I stare daggers at him. "Not here? You knew he was cheating on me?"

"Look, I don't get involved. He's a grown-ass man," he says, aloof.

"Go get him, or I will blow up in your little party," I threaten.

Apathetic, he takes a sip of his beer. "And you'll be embarrassing no one but yourself."

I stare at him, processing. I hate that he's right. No one will see my side; I'll just look like a *crazy baby mama.* The mother of the child always gets a bad name when she's finally had enough and blows her top. They'll just record and plaster me on social media.

Anguish fills me to the brim and pours through my eyes. I shatter inside.

Jonathan, observing my state of distress, sighs. "Wait here."

He walks over to Jason and whispers something to him. Jason's head abruptly turns in my direction. He says something to the bimbo before approaching me.

"What the hell, Jason?" I force out my pent-up emotions.

He slides his tongue over his top row of teeth and sucks in his lips, thinking as he does all this movement with his mouth. He stands impassively, with not even an ounce of remorse, while I am here, crushed.

"Skye, I'm sorry." He finally speaks.

"You damn right, you are!" I snap. "All the overtime you've claimed to have been working, has that always been a lie? And what, you're cheating on me now?"

He looks at the floor, then back at me. "Look, the whole domestic life just isn't for me."

My eyebrows shoot up, and I cross my arms. "Really? And when were you going to tell me this?"

"I'm telling you now," he deadpans. *What a fucking jerk.* I could slap the taste out of his mouth right now.

"What about our son? What about me? Should we move out?"

He jerks his chin. "Skye, I can't do this right now," he says, then begins to walk away.

"Don't walk away from me, Jason!" I call to his retreating back.

"Go home, Skye. We'll talk about this later." He returns to the yard. I stand there to see if he's really going to go back to that turkey-leg, fire-haired bimbo, right in front of me. Instead, he walks past her, and she peers at me. I narrow my eyes, daring her to so much as return the daggers; she doesn't.

I hold my composure while leaving the property, but after I make it inside my vehicle, I don't drive off immediately. I rest my head on my steering wheel and cry inconsolably until there are no more tears. I've never been more humiliated in my entire life. I have nothing for myself.

To leave Jason, I'd struggle. I don't make enough money to live on my own. I'm exhausted as it is. I quit my education and dedicated my life to our little family, all to be betrayed.

My parents. They warned me, and I shunned them. How could I have been so stupid?

Finally, I start up my car and leave this wretched part of the city. When I arrive back at my parents' home, my brother's car is in the driveway. I didn't know he was coming, but then again, how would I?

King of surprises.

I'm usually puckered up to see Kumar, but I'm in no mood for laughs. I just want to curl up in my bed and hug my son.

At the first knock, Kumar answers. The wide grin across his face turns down at the first sight of me. I'm sure it's because I look like a pit of hopelessness right now, but he doesn't breathe a word. Instead, he brings me in for a hug, and I fall apart all over again.

My mother hears my muffled wails and approaches, placing a hand on my back, rubbing to soothe me. I lift my head, and tears of regret spill as I gaze into her empathetic eyes.

"I'm sorry, Mom," I manage through my tears.

With two palms on either side of my cheeks, she wipes my face with her thumbs as her eyes become glassy. "It's okay, baby," she pacifies. "Just come back home. This will always be your home."

Kumar releases me, and I hug my mom. "I just want to start over." I quiver through my sobs.

"You can always start over here, no matter what."

The teary spells simmer. We leave to the kitchen, where my father is leaning against the counter, arms crossed. His expression hardened, he asks, "So does this call for my shotgun?"

We laugh, but he's awaiting an answer. "I'm serious. Did he lay a finger on you?"

"No, Dad," I reply.

He nods with a stiff neck. "Good."

"We're going to need another roll of tape and a few more boxes. I'll be right back," Kumar says as he fishes through his pockets for his keys.

"Okay," I acknowledge, placing another dish inside bubble wrap.

I stayed the night at my parents' house, and now Kumar and I are at the apartment packing Julias's and my things. Jason isn't here, but I woke up to ten missed calls and a dozen text messages. All of his texts are apologies and blaming his claims from yesterday on alcohol consumption.

He fooled me once. I'd be a fool to allow him the opportunity to make one of me again.

After about thirty minutes of packing my kitchen items, the front door unlocks behind me. "I hope you only got medium boxes. We don't have much left," I say at the sound of the door opening.

"Where's your car?"

My movements pause at the sound of Jason's voice. It's early. He's *supposed* to be at work.

Continuing my work, I place the wrapped dish in the box beside me. "It's not here."

I hear him approach. "Who's helping you?"

"I took my name off the lease. I'm leaving," I say.

He wraps his fingers around my upper arm. I shrug him off. "So, you're just gonna take my son from me?"

I turn around. "Excuse me? You don't even spend time with him. I thought it was because of work, but no, that was a lie."

His features soften. "Skye, I'm sorry. Please, don't go. I'll be a better man, I promise."

I almost want to believe him. *Almost.* "If you want to spend time with Julias, call and leave me a voicemail or text me. I'm moving back in with my parents." I turn back around and remove another dish from the cabinet.

Jason knocks it out of my hand. It shatters on the kitchen floor. Shocked by his reaction, I face him, and what I witness is an expression I've never seen before. An irate, unpredictable Jason.

I back away until I'm against the fridge. With one stride, he's so close I can feel the anger radiating off of him. Apprehension crawling up my spine, I try to make a break for it, but he grabs my arms and pins me to the fridge.

His grip tightens. I shriek, "Jason, stop!"

"You think any man is gonna want you?" He scowls.

"Please, Jason. You're hurting me!"

"No matter how good your pussy is, no man is gonna want some single mom," he snarls. His grip grows even tighter. I squeal. He's unhinged.

I hear the front door open, but Jason doesn't. He's engulfed in rage, growling degrading insults at me.

"Get your fucking hands off her!" At Kumar's demand, Jason releases me. He begins walking forward, his attention no longer on me. An infuriated Kumar charges at him. One blow to the nose, and Jason stumbles backward, attempting to regain his balance. When my brother's fist connects with his jaw, he hits the floor.

Kumar begins kicking him. "Don't. You. Ever. In. Your. Fucking. Life." With every word, a kick follows until I grab his arm. "Kumar, stop. He's not getting up."

When his head cuts to me, his gaze is murderous. "Are you okay? Did he hurt you?"

I shake my head. "I'm okay."

He scrutinizes me, and his features soften. He reaches to touch my arm, and I wince. *Okay, so he did hurt me.*

He kicks Jason again. "Agh!" Jason growls.

I shake my head in pity at the useless trash lying on the floor. "Come on, let's get the rest of my stuff and go."

We're walking toward the living room when Jason yells, "I'm pressing charges!"

"Shut up, bitch." Kumar scowls. I smirk.

CHAPTER 38

Elias

"I moved back in with my parents and quit my job to focus on my last two semesters of college and care for my son," Skye explains. "My parents helped me through it all. It was never easy for them, but they did it *for me*. They weren't obligated. I was an adult who made my own choices, my own mistakes. I could never put them in a position like that again. Now, they're proud. I'm proud. I've lived and I've learned. I won't take risks that could jeopardize my future, especially after I received the easy way out."

She sighs. "Do you know how hard it was for my parents to do what they did for me? They hid it, but they provided for their adult daughter graciously. They'd never let me see the burden, but I noticed when my mother began working full time again. They didn't just care for my needs. They provided for my son until I got on my feet."

She pushes to her feet and earnestly continues. "So yes, regardless of how I feel, when anxiety rises, I push it down by reminding myself that I should be grateful for everything I've accomplished and the ones who helped me achieve it. I owe that to the people I love and who love me."

Listening to Skye, an unsettling feeling grows in me. I want to meet this Jason and rock his shit again. I don't care that she's over it or that her brother already did. The asshole had a diamond and took her for granted.

If I haven't learned anything else about Skye, I've learned that she's the epitome of selflessness. She'd rather live her life stifled for the sake of those she loves, and she's securing her future the only way she knows how.

But she's unaware that she's repaying that internal debt to those she loves by superficially flourishing, while internally, she's dying.

Love is her life force. It keeps her afloat. It's people like her who belong in this world. She deserves this place. Even in a fucked-up society like ours, she resonates more with the culture of this world than that of where we're from.

I stand with her because I want her to *hear me.* "Skye, how do you think your family would feel if they knew you've kept the desires of your soul caged?"

She slightly shakes her head. "They can never know. Everything will be alright as long as I remind myself when I begin to feel doubt that I have so much to be thankful for. That's what keeps me going when I want to give up, I remember what it took."

She thinks she'll be able to keep this up forever, but she can't. Her soul is starved, shackled, and it's become unbearable. She hangs her head and twiddles her thumbs.

"Look at me," I say, and she looks up. Taking both of her hands in mine, I gaze into her brown eyes. "Everything won't be okay. That's why you're here. You're afraid to make the same mistake, but you forget that you're not the same Skye from five years ago. You've grown, you've experienced, you've changed. Now tell me, what is it *you're* passionate about? Because I know it's not about that accounting career."

She plops back down on the couch. "See, that's just it, I don't know. I've never given any of this much thought."

I grin. "You ready for homework?"

She chuckles. "What is it now?"

"Tonight, think of something you'd pursue if there were no risks involved. If you were *here* permanently, along with your loved ones, what would you want? Be selfish with your list, it's only about you."

"Okay, I can do that." She takes a deep breath and glances at her watch before standing, picking up her bag, and tossing it over her shoulder. "Thank you, Elias, once again."

"Where are you going?"

"Back to Haven Downs, it's getting late."

I rise and stuff my hands in my pocket, square my shoulders, and rock back on my heels. "Didn't you bring that bag for an adventure?"

"Well, uh, yeah, but..."

I gesture to the stairs. "Upstairs to your left, you can use that bedroom. Get comfortable, I'm making dinner."

Her eyebrows knit together. "You've helped me more than enough, Elias. I'm not here to impose on your space. It's still early, I can..." She's rambling, but it's falling on deaf ears. I don't want to hear any of that right now.

"We set sail at first light," I interrupt.

Eyes widening, her lips upturn to a wide grin. A blanket of warmth wraps around my core as I witness her bright, sunshine smile. I won't push her away any longer. I'll witness every laugh, every smile, everything that makes her uniquely her, because this feeling with her trumps no feeling at all.

CHAPTER 39

Skye

I change into black sweatpants and a pink tank top, then take out my journal and place it on the nightstand. I'm uncertain of what Elias plans to cook for dinner, but I intend to help.

I walk into the kitchen, where he chops onions. Beside him are celery, garlic, and bell peppers.

"Where can I start?" I ask.

"With your list," he replies, still chopping.

Spotting potatoes on the counter behind him, I make my way to them. "I'll start with these."

The sound of the knife hitting the board ceases. "Skye, you don't have—"

"Are we mashing or roasting?" I interject.

A half-smile forms on his lips. "Mashing."

"Awesome."

"So, what are we having?" I peel the potatoes over the trash bin.

"Well, you're in the kitchen now, you tell me." He cuts a split in the salmon.

Looking around, I notice salmon, shrimp, asparagus, a tub of something—cream cheese, maybe? *Must be vegan, they don't milk cows here*—and ingredients for a salad. "How about I take over the shrimp and potatoes, and you deal with the salmon and whatever else?"

"Sounds good to me," he agrees.

Searching his cabinets, I find flour—*bingo*. Fried shrimp it is.

Dinner is ready. We place mashed potatoes, salad, sautéed asparagus, stuffed salmon, and fried shrimp at the table. For drinks, we have water, and Elias pulls out a bottle of wine with two glasses. *Is it me, or does this suddenly feel like a date?*

"Wow, I think we overdid it for dinner for two," I mention.

"Yeah, well, it'll be some time before we have a home-cooked meal, so enjoy," he says.

We take our seats, and I recall the mess we left in the kitchen. "We're totally cleaning that when we're done."

Concurring, we dig in. The food is absolutely delicious. While I'm enjoying the stuffed salmon, Elias has barely touched his. Instead, he continuously refills his plate with fried shrimp. *The shrimp I made.* I'm proud he's enjoying it.

"So, how do you like the shrimp?" I ask.

He takes a sip of his wine and shrugs. "Eh, it's alright."

He's baiting me, but I don't take it. I reciprocate. "Could say the same about the salmon."

"You could." He takes a bite of his asparagus. "But I didn't ask."

I narrow my eyes. He glances at me, aloof. *Ugh, I hate his stupid face.*

"More wine?" He offers nonchalantly as if he doesn't notice the wound he just inflicted on my pride.

"No, thank you."

After a few moments, he asks, "Is there anything else you'll need before we leave?"

I jerk my chin.

"Okay, we'll head for Land Kairos first. It's a twelve-day sail. We'll visit the surrounding waters before heading back."

I nod and simply voice, "Mhm."

"I'll gather up food for us, as well as whatever is left here."

No words. I simply nod again.

Come on, Skye, it was a joke. Get over it. Why am I like this?

"I'll get started on the dishes," I mention and gather our empty plates, presuming we're both satiated. I place the dishware and glasses in the sink and begin the process of soaping and rinsing.

I can feel it when Elias draws near. "By the way, the shrimp was delicious," he whispers in my ear, and it sends a shiver up my spine. *He really shouldn't do that.* Turning around, I'm faced with a smug smile. I reach behind me and let water from the faucet fill my hand before splashing that smirk right off his face. He flinches and turns his back to me.

"That's what you get for being an asshole!" I quip. I stand laughing, but in one swift movement, he turns, and I'm covered in the leftover flour I used to coat the shrimp. "Elias!" I squeal. I turn to face the sink and wipe flour from my eyes as he dies with laughter. *Oh, he thinks he's won.* I grab the extended hose on the sink as quickly as possible, then turn and spray his ass down. "You motherfucker!" I shout playfully as I drench him.

"Ah, shit!" he growls.

He makes his way toward me with his head down, preventing me from splashing his face. I step backward as far as the hose will allow, which is not very far at all. The hose bucks, and I abandon it. I make a break for it, but before I can take off, I'm being hauled up by my waist.

"Ah!" I shriek. "Ew! You're soaked!"

"Sorry, didn't notice," he grunts.

He tries to tackle me, but the floor is wet, and we both slip. With a loud thump, we hit the ground.

Elias fell backward, but he never let me go, so my back landed on top of him. Rolling off, I prop myself up with my elbows.

"Thanks for breaking my fall," I joke.

"No problem," he strains.

"You alright there?"

"A fall like that? Something's gotta be broken."

He peers at me from the corner of his eyes, and we burst into laughter as we lay there for a few minutes, joking about our infantile shenanigans just moments prior.

CHAPTER 40

Skye

After Elias and I finished cleaning the kitchen, I shower and change into gray shorts and a black tank top to sleep. I gather my dirty laundry and decide to check to see if Elias has a washer and dryer. I carry my dirty clothes folded in a towel downstairs and search for him. At the sound of grunts coming from the basement, I motion toward the open doorway leading downstairs.

Headphones in, he doesn't hear me, but at the sight of him, my lips part, and I stand, frozen in place. He's working out, shirtless, wearing just basketball shorts and sneakers, hanging upside down from a bar doing crunches.

The man is ripped, and my god, is he sinfully sexy. Masculine beauty at its finest. I've only seen him with a shirt on, and the sight is already stunning. Now he's bared, and I need—right now —anything to pull me out of this catatonic behavior.

Finally seeing me, he comes down from the bar, removing his headphones while moving toward me.

"What's up? I didn't hear you," he says. I'm still stuck in place... and he's getting closer... and closer. *Say something, idiot.* He stops before me and glimpses the towel balled up under my arm. "What's this?"

I stand in stunned silence with my lips slightly parted.

Hello, Earth to Skye. He's talking to you!

He tilts his head with a quizzical look on his face.

Now is the time to speak, dummy.

I jerk my head and pull myself back to reality, then shut my eyes for a moment to regain my train of thought. Looking down at the towel wrapped around my clothes, I bring it to my hands. "Um, washing machine," I begin, still facing down. "Do you..." I look up at him to finish my question but pause. No, I completely freaking freeze when I see the eyes I'm met with.

His emeralds grow dark, his brows furrowed. He's standing rigidly before me with a complete change in demeanor. It's intense, sending shockwaves through my entire body, catching me off guard.

Am I... turned on right now?

Elias

This is going to be a problem. I won't deny my attraction to her, but as of right now, I can virtually smell her pheromones.

We stand holding a stilled gaze until my eyes drop to her parted lips, and I resist every urge to collide my own with them. The scent of lavender is prominent around her freshly washed skin and dampened hair. Her lust-filled brown eyes dare me, her soft, parted lips provoke me, and her alluring aura beckons me.

But I won't goddamn budge.

Breaking the tension first, I turn and instruct, "This way," because if I stand there any longer, *she's mine.*

CHAPTER 41

Elias

After completing my workout, I packed food, clothing, and other miscellaneous items we'll need for the journey. Skye made two more trips to the basement during my session to put her clothes in the dryer, then to remove and fold them, and each time she passed by, she deliberately refused to make eye contact. I don't blame her. She even changed from those shorts and a thin shirt to flannel pajamas. *Clever.* And I lifted longer than usual to ease the tension.

It worked.

Focus regained.

After showering and preparing to call it a night, I decide to check on Skye, hoping she's comfortable.

Her door is cracked, but I knock anyway. "Skye?"

No answer.

I open the door and walk to the side where she's asleep and notice the book lying open flat on her chest, where it likely fell when she dozed off. I admire her for a moment—she looks angelic—and remove the book and slip her bookmark between the open pages before closing it and placing it on the nightstand.

She sleeps peacefully, but before walking away, I stand there and begin to wonder what things would be like if I had met her in the world we come from. If I had met her years ago, would I have discovered her tethered soul? Could I have helped her? Or would she have been able to hide it from me, like she's done to everyone else?

If I had met Skye five years ago, would I have chosen to remain here? Would I have been transported here at all? It would have taken one soul, one heart, equivalent to that of my mother's —*to Skye's*—to keep me back in our world. But at the time of my departure, I was leaving no one behind.

I pull myself out of my head as I recall similar questions landing me here—when I believed them true—*when I needed them to be true.* However, to question the possibility of time travel, there are some things that are indeed impossible.

I am placing my finger on the knob to cut the light from the lamp when I catch sight of her journal opened to her list.

Passion List
Write poetry
Write a book
Obtain a degree in English Literature
Go on a cruise from Canada to Australia
Write about the experience
Visit Paris, Dubai, Africa, and China
Write about those experiences
Write a mystery novel
Write a thriller
Writing career?
Fall in love
Get married
Have another baby

Her desires are centered around creativity, which doesn't surprise me. If she'd ever "selfishly" given thought to what she could be passionate about, she'd have realized there's not much risk involved. She just had to start somewhere.

Observing the last three things written on her list, I frown as a hollow feeling forms in my chest. I place her journal back on the wooden surface, cut the light, and move for the door. I glance back at her one more time before closing it. The last three things on her list linger in my brain.

Fall in love

Get married

Have another baby

The feeling in my chest remains, not because I want such things for her and me, but rather because even if I did—*or we did*—there's no chance of it happening. My mind travels further. I imagine it happening for her with someone else.

Skye is beautiful; her very essence is pure. She's beginning to set herself free. The probability of her fulfilling the last three wishes on her list is high, but the thought makes my chest pull tight. However, this is what she needs to free herself—for herself, her son, and her awaiting future. I'll help her while she's here, so that when she returns, *she'll dance.*

I lay in bed, but sleep won't find me. Something troubles me.

I sit up and lean on my headboard, twisting the knob of my side lamp until the bulb glows beneath the shade. I look around my room, but unsure of what I seek, I open the first drawer of the nightstand. Pulling out the black box I haven't opened since I firmly decided to put the world where I was born behind me, something about spending time with Skye has given rise to a feeling of longing. A familiarity to my old life.

I open the box. Its contents are the items that were in my pocket the evening I napped before waking on Livity. My wallet, my cell phone, and a ring box. Flipping open the ring box, I gaze at the fourteen-karat, oval-shaped diamond ring I purchased to propose to Jessica, then frown, thinking of how blind I must have been not to see her for who she truly was.

I have had ample time to revisit every moment with her, every argument, every dispute. I had been blinded by how I felt for her and distracted by my growing business. I didn't pay attention to the condescending reasoning she used to justify her absurd claims in every quarrel.

I power on my phone—no signal, of course—and go through old texts and photos, swiping past the ones of Jessica and myself and not paying them a second glance, but pausing at the pictures of me and my old crew.

Our Miami trip, New York City, Vegas, the cruise to the Bahamas, Mexico, and endless photos from our times at the lake house. I find an old video of myself with Neil, Tyler, Travis, and Bart cruising in Dynamite with the top dropped. They were tipsy as shit, hounding me to floor the pedal. I chuckle as I hear Tyler in the background. "Neil, get the fuck out, you sober bastard!" We were idiots, for sure. Tyler, the most boisterous of us all, is surprisingly the most reasonable.

As nostalgia sets in, I wonder how they're all doing, how their lives are turning out. Swiping again, it's a picture of my brother, Elijah. I wonder if he ever made it to the big leagues. Swiping again, there's a picture of my uncle Eric, the only person I'd ever regret leaving without saying goodbye. There was no option to bid him a forever farewell, but after Mom passed and even before, Uncle Eric was always in my corner. "Miss you, Uncle Eric," I whisper. "Hope you're doing alright."

Swiping again, I frown as I recall the night this photo was taken. It was the last *good* night I spent at the lake before returning. The very next time I visited was the night I ended every friendship I had.

CHAPTER 42

Elias

FIVE YEARS AGO

I haven't been to the lake in six weeks, ever since the shop started to become heavily trafficked. With business picking up at this rate, I've had to start looking into hiring another mechanic. But it's Friday evening, and tonight I plan to make an appearance. I reconciled with the guys after the argument months ago, and we've been alright since. I know they were only concerned, but that mentality as a whole is just all wrong. But I don't judge them.

They've never been placed in my predicament. We're bred from generations of wealth. "Being without," for them, is what I am. Granted, more than ninety percent of the population has even less. My current world may not resonate with theirs as it once did, but that's because they don't quite grasp the concept of starting from the bottom.

I swing by Jessica's place first; her vehicle isn't there, which means she's already at the lake. Good, because I have a huge surprise for her. I may not have seen the guys in weeks, but I've made it my prerogative to spend time with my girl every few days.

Everyone's vehicle, including Jessica's, is parked at the lake house. I kill the engine and pull the velvet ring box from my pocket, opening it to take a second look. Knowing Jessica, she's gonna love this shit. Proposal in front of everyone? The perfect scene and attention for a woman who loves to be in the spotlight.

I step onto the yard and hear laughter echoing from near the lake. I follow the sound to the gazebo and halt when it comes into view. Inside are Neil, Tyler, Bart, Mike, Miranda, Rachel, and... Jessica... and Travis. Jaw slack, I stand stuck, observing the scene before me. No one notices me—*yet*—but Jessica is sitting in Travis's lap, and his arm is around her waist.

If my heart beats any faster, it might erupt from my chest. Rage courses through my veins—blood boiling hot lava—and I bite down so hard my jaw incessantly twitches. I watch in silence. Travis pulls her even closer, whispers something in her ear, and she giggles. He then darts his fucking tongue out, licks her ear— and she likes the shit. I internally fucking explode.

I move into plain sight. Tyler notices me first and freezes, staring at me with gaping eyes. Rachel follows his line of sight and spots me next. Her hands fly to her mouth. Everyone faces me now, and the gazebo goes quiet. They stare me down like I'm some fucking ghost.

Jessica scuffles off Travis and scurries toward me. "Ellie, I... I know what it looks like..." Her voice is shaky, brimming with obvious trepidation.

Not saying a damn word, I glare at her. My infuriated expression isn't exactly helping her find her tongue, but I don't give a shit right now.

She hugs herself and hangs her head. "I'm so sorry... so sorry."

"Are you fucking him?" I ask, low and gruff.

She looks up with wide eyes. I move in closer. "Are you fucking him?"

She drops her head, covering it with her hands, and sobs. *There's my answer.*

Travis begins walking, and I know that piece of fuck isn't approaching me—especially not in this moment. He stands about three feet behind Jessica. "Jessica," he calls, and she looks back at him. "Come here, babe. You don't need this," he says, and she walks toward him.

Babe? And did she just listen to him? What the fuck?

"We were gonna tell you, El, sooner than later," he says impassively.

Did he just say that shit to me with a straight face?

"Tell me?" I smirk and address everyone else. "Oh, and let me guess, you piece of shits knew about this too?"

Tyler draws near. "El, bro..."

"Bro?" I cut him off. "Don't fucking 'bro' me."

"El, you've downgraded yourself and expect her to stick around?" Travis spits his crock of shit.

"Downgraded? That's funny, coming from a spoiled pussy that's never had to work for shit a day in his life!" I snarl.

I've lost control, and I personally don't give a fuck. The inept nut job shouldn't have said shit to me.

Neil speaks up. "Y'all should have let this man in on this a long time ago."

A long time?

"El, I've clued you in. More times than once." Tyler pleads.

"Tyler, you are in this with us. Shut up," Bart spits.

"I've been the most uncomfortable one with this shit the whole time! Look, I don't give a fuck. El, I don't deserve shit from you." Tyler turns to Travis and Jessica. "How many times have I threatened to tell El? Y'all begged and begged me not to breathe a word, assured me y'all would soon!"

Tyler is inflamed, but his anger is misplaced. He's upset with himself for not following his gut, and I admit, he did throw hints. I just never understood. Jessica cheating was the farthest thing from my mind, and cheating with my best friend was even farther. Regardless, I'm done with every last one of them.

I hear Travis nearing me as I'm turning to leave. I need to get out this instant before I lose my shit entirely.

"El, look..." He's getting closer, but I continue walking. He grabs my forearm, and whatever restraint I had left vanishes in an instant. When I turn, my left hook follows. A crack sounds as my fist connects with his nose. He hits the ground, squirming like the little bitch that he is, and I continue toward my vehicle. At his next words, my movements stall. "You're a fucking disgrace, Elias!"

Disgrace. I hate that fucking word.

He shoots back to his feet, and I charge at him. Since this motherfucker doesn't know when to shut his mouth, I'll shut it for him. He swings first, but I duck, grab his torso, and tackle him to the ground. I'm balancing myself on my knees, connecting my fist to his jaw, and retracting my arm to land another blow when a strong arm wraps around my neck, impeding my airflow.

"El, chill. He ain't worth it no more." It's Tyler. I struggle under his hold. He doesn't release his grip until I'm placated.

I gaze down at the sorry excuse of human flesh under me and decide Tyler is right. Jessica kneels by Travis and begins holding his head. "If you want to blame anyone, blame me. But please, don't hit him again."

I rise to my feet.

"Damn, this is all bad. Sorry, El. We weren't put in the best position," Neil says.

I look over at the ugly fucker. Remorse is written all over his features, but I don't give a shit that any of them feel culpable. I'm not giving them an ounce of amnesty. Let their guilt eat them alive.

"I don't want to see any of you fucks ever the hell again," I bark.

Travis, now sitting up, spits in the grass. Blood is trickling down his mouth. He says, "I'm sorry it had to be like this."

"Yeah, me too."

I reach into my pockets for my keys. They're empty. Tyler approaches me with my keys and wallet and hands them to me, then projects his voice for Jessica and Travis to hear him say, "Well deserved ass whopping." He pauses and reaches into his back pocket, pulls out the ring box, holds it up, and then turns his head toward Jessica. She gasps, and Tyler continues. "You dodged a nasty bullet. You can do better than her." Tears become visible in her eyes. Tyler hands me the box. "Good luck, El. I'm undeserving of your friendship." His shoulders tense at the weight of his conviction before he walks off in the direction of the parked vehicles. I glance down at the ring box and then to Jessica and stuff it in my back pocket before heading toward my car, never to return to this place, never to associate with any of them ever again.

CHAPTER 43

Skye

"Skye, wake up."

At the sound of Elias's velvety voice, I lethargically blink, but I prefer sleep even to the blurred sight of his handsome face. I turn over and ignore his wake-up call. He chuckles as I linger on the line of awake and slumber, but I choose the dream realm. Before I can drift back off, a hand touches my arm, and I groan in displeasure.

"Come on, sunshine. Time to take sail." His soothing baritone passes through my ears. I murmur something, I'm not sure what, but he responds with, "You can finish sleeping on the boat." I turn over again and look up to see a softened emerald gaze with a heavenly half-smile, and I slowly crawl out of bed. "I'll grab your bag. Just throw your shoes on," he says. "I'm sure you want this journal and book?"

"I'll take them," I murmur and rub the grogginess from my eyes.

We exit Elias's home, and the cool air touches my skin. Though I'm still half-dead, I follow closely behind him until we board his vessel, and I waste no time snuggling back under the covers in the bed of the cabin.

"Sleep well. We've got a long trip ahead," is the last thing I hear before I slip into slumber.

I awaken again at ten a.m., fully rejuvenated, to the gentle rock of the vessel. As I gaze out the bedside window, I'm elated at the view of the calming blue sea under a bright sun. I stretch, then hang my legs off the bed and head for the bathroom to freshen up.

I leave the cabin and walk up to the deck, where Elias is leaning with his forearms resting on the rail. Before approaching, I take him in for a moment. He looks to be admiring the purity of the current setting.

"Hey," I greet.

He turns. "Sleep well?"

Inhaling, I take a refreshing breath. "Is it weird that I suddenly feel more alive than normal right now?"

"No," he replies, facing forward again. "Why do you think I'm right here? This is my favorite part."

Standing beside him, I close my eyes for a few moments and become one with the breeze. "She's a beauty, isn't she?" I admire the sea.

"She is." He pauses. "But is she only a beauty right now because she's calm?"

"I don't get what you mean," I reply, in search of elaboration.

He quirks his lips and squints as if focused on his next words. "She's what you need her to be right now, so you can enjoy this very moment. But just as she is calm, she can become a raging beast when agitated, devastating all in her wake. Where is her beauty then?"

I turn and rest my back and elbows against the rail and look up at him. His gaze remains fixed ahead as his cropped hair blows in the wind. I don't give his question much thought and reply true to my heart. "Her reaction to her environment is only natural, she'd still be beautiful. Her beauty isn't on her surface, it's within her depths." He cranes his neck to look down at me. I continue. "She's ever-changing, just like people. There's never just one mode, there are multiple, depending on our environment, situations, and interactions. We adjust and change as we face challenges in life. But, unlike the ever-flowing sea, sometimes those trials cause people to harden at the surface to protect what's beneath, within our own depths."

His eyes move back and forth between mine, searching. He gazes back out at sea, and I tilt my head toward the morning sky.

"Hungry?" he asks.

"Please tell me you have a coffee maker."

He chuckles. "Come on."

I follow him to the small kitchen area. On the counter sits a small pot, warm with freshly brewed coffee. Now, the morning is officially perfect.

The sunset deepens the blue of the sea; the horizon is illuminated with scattering hues of orange and red. Elias and I sit in the front cockpit, covered in a thin blanket, as the disappearing sun chills the air. We have one night left at sea before arriving at Land Kairos. Our travels extended three days after docking at three other lands on our journey.

Catching an eyeful whenever we traveled inland to restock supplies and food, I've been sure to take plenty of photos and grab the lands' history books. After exploration, though the amiable environment remains similar among the cultures, it's clear no two lands are the same.

Land Arga is split into two halves by one very long, wide road. One-half is strictly residential. Homes are lined in rows and columns as one massive neighborhood, while the other half lays the markets, activities, schools, parks, centers, restaurants, and everything nonresidential. More people were there on bikes than on foot, but I suppose that's due to the land's layout.

In another land, Land Northellei, every market is connected

to a person's living space. In two-story establishments, their home might be on the upper level while a shop is on the ground floor. Others display merchandise and goods out in their yards.

"You know, I've become accustomed to the ways of the world, yet still, I wonder why people do these things when they're not obligated. I mean, I get the sense of purpose, but this is pretty farsighted, don't you think?" I ask Elias as we sit conversing about our recent visits.

"What else do they have to do? Sit at home and stare at their four walls every day? It's challenging for you to grasp at one hundred percent because, where we're from, how often do we contemplate what we actually want to do with our lives? We choose based on the options provided, and even then, the competition makes it difficult. Ultimately, we chase freedom and care for our needs. Well, what happens when you're born into a world where you're already free? Your needs are already met by the laws of the land. Freedom is as simple as a way of life; you don't have to fight for it. You don't have to work to live a stable life. So, what do you do then?" He pauses, allowing his elucidation to sink in. "You work to fulfill your own purpose, and in doing so, you serve others. Serving others in subservience to your own passion offers greater freedom than serving others because it is required to earn a living. No matter how much money you're paid, you'll always be a slave to the dollar unless your gains are earned through your passion. It's all still work, but which kind of work would you prefer?"

I take in what he says. "It didn't start this way. It's a ripple effect. It's only become this way after centuries of development. Just like our world, it began with trading and bartering. Now, look where we are. I'd have to spend the amount of time you've spent here to gain the full experience."

"It took some getting used to, but it became easier to accept after making the decision to stay. No longer questioning anything, I fully dive in, treating this world as a clean state. What became clear to me was that I now had *time*. Time to learn and time to decipher where I could fit into this society."

"So, you followed your passion here?"

He nods.

"And are you happy?"

He uses his left thumb to rub the right side of his jaw before he answers, "I am."

So he says, and he may be happy with his choice of work—he's following his passion. However, there's still something missing in his life. He's true to himself, but Elias is not true to his heart.

"Ready to visit your birthplace?" Elias jokes.

After fifteen days, we've finally anchored at the infamous Land Kairos, and I realize there's no actual port for docking. We move in on a beach.

"I know, right. I must see why this land vindicates me of all suspicion," I reply.

"Oh, you'll see."

Why does that make me nervous?

We walk further into the land but have yet to reach any sort of development. Overgrown weeds fill the area as we walk through a fortress of trees. After about twenty minutes without pavement, homes, or establishments in sight, I ask, "Do people even live here?"

"Yes. It isn't as populated as the surrounding lands. The roots of the people have lived here for centuries," he informs.

"What? So how do they continue to reproduce?" I stop in my tracks, suddenly disgusted. "Oh my god, please don't tell me..."

Elias shakes his head at my repulsive assumption. "Don't be ridiculous. It's not that. This place was populated by people of many different genealogies. Many different lineages still reside here. The difference is that people don't move to Kairos. They either move away, continue to reside, or come back. But those not native to the land do not stay, which is also why the population is not as vast as other lands."

"I wonder why that is."

"You'll see."

CHAPTER 44

Skye

The village is something you'd see in a movie when it's portraying a time before time itself began. The homes are made of unrefined wood, with roofs of sturdy logs covered with straw and leaves. And people are dressed in simple clothes. Absent of industrial developments, markets, stands, or neighborhoods, it's green, primitive living at its absolute finest.

An older woman is seated outside on a stool, knitting, and a young girl is sitting beside her playing with a doll. A group of women laugh and hang clothing on a line to dry while a man at the very top of a roof applies leafy material to enclose a gap.

As we travel through the village, a few people recognize Elias and wave, but no one acknowledges me except the small children I greet as we pass by. The feel of this place is far from inviting, and I wonder if they even like people here.

Apprehension trickles within me at the many frightening glares, so I move closer to Elias and take hold of his arm. I am no longer interested in exploring this land. It's quite obvious I'm not welcome. The palpable, uncongenial energy has me unsettled.

"Hey, you alright?" he asks.

I practically hug his arm. I'm grateful that he and I have gotten closer over the past few days. He's incredibly calm, in contrast to my obvious discomfort, and if I didn't trust him, I'd have taken off and gone back to the boat by now.

"Mhm," I sound.

"Look at me," he says.

I peer up at him, and his features soften as if he can see the fear written all over me. He wraps his arm around my shoulder and whispers, "You don't have anything to be afraid of. They won't hurt you."

"Okay, well... don't walk so far ahead of me."

He chuckles. "Right here next to you. We're almost to our destination."

"Which is?"

"Someone who helped me out some time ago when I arrived here. He's the leader the people look to."

"Okay, well, hopefully he's a bit more welcoming."

We approach a home similar to the others but slightly larger. Elias knocks on the log for a door, and shortly after, a tall, husky man answers.

"Bento," Elias greets. "Good to see you again."

"Back again so soon, son. You miss this place, eh?" The man, Bento, voices enthusiastically.

Elias laughs. "I'll never forget this place."

"Ah, no, you won't!" He's loud and joyous, starkly different from the vibe we got passing through.

"Bento, this is Skye," Elias introduces. "Skye, Bento. Unlike most of the other lands with a foundation of multiple leaders, Kairos has only one leader. Currently, that's Bento."

Bento adds, "Those lands need so many leaders because they demolish the habitat and build unnecessary things. Houses, machines, buildings, things they don't need. They destroy the environment. Many try to come and impose their ideas of change on our land. All this fancy talk about bigger houses and infrastructure. We turn them away. We have lived this way for many centuries. The animals, the trees, and the roots beneath our feet are all living. To sacrifice them for personal greed is despicable. This is their home too. Here at Land Kairos, we are one with the land. We only take what we need and allow the magic of nature to flourish."

"That's... beautiful," I comment truthfully.

Their principle belief that all things of the earth have a life worth living is remarkable. Now I understand the glares. Predisposed to new arrivals imposing a new way of life upon them, they're protective of the land.

He makes a gesture of appreciation with a head bow. "Good to meet you, Skye." He looks to Elias. "She is a dove, is she your wife?"

Elias does a quick flick of his nose with his index knuckle. "No, a friend. She doesn't get out much. I'm just showing her a land I'm fond of."

Bento raises his chin. "Ah, very good. Come in."

The interior of Bento's home is small, but it would be comfortable for people who live as they do. It's apparent no one here spends much time indoors; the homes are simply shelters to lay their heads and maintain privacy. Two tree trunks for tables, a small area to start a fire, and three wooden doors for a bathroom and bedrooms.

I'm introduced to Bento's wife, Dalma, and their two sons, Banchi and Darou. The warm welcome certainly helps take the edge off my nerves. While the two boys eat, Dalma offers Elias and me a bowl that we both politely refuse.

The energetic boys finish their meal and rush out of the home. Laughter is heard as they resume their play. As we chat, Bento informs me that they do not eat fish like those of the other lands. They only fill their bellies with what they can grow.

"When you plant seeds and care for them, they feed you. The food chain of the wild cannot apply to us because we do not need animal flesh to survive. While animals rely on instinct, we possess what they do not, something far greater—sense. We are aware they are not, and that makes all the difference."

I contemplate what he says for a moment. I've never thought

of it that way. Granted, when I return, I will be sinking my teeth into a fat, juicy steak, but the culture of these people sets them apart by their mere humanity, not just for people but for every single living thing.

A tanned brunette woman bursts through the door, pulling me from my thoughts. She pauses in the entrance, and her hands fly to her mouth at the first sight of Elias.

"Elias!" she cheerfully greets, running to him, then throwing her arms around his neck. "I didn't think you'd be back so soon!"

Her smile is bright. I wonder if I need to go vegan for a physique like hers: lithe and toned, her soft curves are perfectly proportioned. I go for two-hour runs every morning, and I still don't look like that.

Note to self: trade the apple pie for an actual apple next time.

Elias hugs her back and wraps an arm around her waist. "Kallia, how are you?"

"I'm doing well. Are you coming back?" she asks with hopeful eyes as they release each other.

Elias smiles but doesn't reassure her. "Kairos will always be a special place for me."

No longer holding a wide grin but still smiling, she says, "Well, glad to see you."

It's dawning on me how much the people here cherish him. He's never mentioned anything about having a relationship with those here, but it's as if they consider him one of them.

"Kallia, meet Skye. She's never traveled to Land Kairos," Elias introduces.

She faces me, and I can't deny how stunning she looks. With tailbone-length straight hair and a banging body, she's not dressed like the others. She wears a cotton crop top that exposes her navel and blue jean shorts. I also can't help but notice that she resembles something like *the perfect match for Elias.*

"Hi, it's nice to meet you, Kallia," I greet with a smile, approaching her. I extend my arm, gesturing for a handshake, but her smile turns down and her eyes travel down my body.

She mutters, "Hi," in the most unwelcome tone known to man. *Did she just mean-mug me?*

I retract my arm and chew the inside of my bottom lip before going back to where I originally stood. I notice Elias's jaw tensing. He shuts his eyes for a moment and takes a breath. Bento and his wife may have been pleasant, but Kallia's reaction doesn't differ from the residents we passed heading here.

"Kallia, is everything okay?" Dalma asks with concern.

"Yes, why?" she replies nonchalantly.

"That was ill-mannered. She isn't here to impose. Even if she was, we still do not treat *them* as such. We decline respectfully, just as they've come to encourage change, peacefully," Dalma admonishes.

I cut in. "No, please, it's fine. I'm sure after a while, new faces wanting to change what's already perfect as if something is wrong can make one grow partial to distrusting new guests. I haven't earned the trust of anyone here. I'm a stranger. I'm okay with proving that in no way is that my intention."

When I stop speaking, everyone is staring at me. I look over at Elias, whose lips are curved into a half-smile. He slightly nods in some sort of praise.

What the hell is going on right now?

"Elias, son." Bento, *someone,* finally speaks. "She is to be your wife."

Kallia rolls her eyes. They seem to be impressed with my small ramble. However, maybe she calls bullshit? I don't know. I wasn't bullshitting, but neither was I expecting a standing ovation.

Elias expresses that he'd like to give me a tour, and Dalma suggests we could all go. Bento leaves last, closing the door behind us, and we head east through the forest. Dalma and I walk in front, while Elias, Kallia, and Bento walk behind us. I keep my head held down, careful not to trip over any branches, but I'm itching to take in the surroundings. I give in and begin admiring the incredibly tall trees with branches extending long enough to intertwine with one another, blocking the view of the sky. Birds chirp from high-up nests. The earthy scent of fresh soil and damp moss pervades the air, and the unrefined purity ferments a feeling of comfort that makes it easier to truly empathize with the people's connection to the land. Nature is beautiful.

While I'm gazing away at my surroundings, my foot becomes trapped in something, and I lose balance. Jerking my body, wiggling my arms, I still can't catch myself.

It's over. Prepare for the fall.

My knees buckle. I'm going forward. I put my hands out in front to prevent face-planting when I'm grabbed around the waist, midfall.

"I got you. Pull your foot backward." *Elias.*

I do as he says and balance myself in his grasp, then look down to see what my foot caught.

"Knotted twigs. They'll win every time," Bento remarks.

"Watch where you're going. I could have tripped too!" Kallia snaps.

"Dial it back, Kallia. This is new territory for her, just as it was for me once," Elias defends.

She rolls her eyes and gives me a bitter expression.

"I'm sorry. I was caught in admiration," I admit.

This is their land, and I don't want to be the reason for any strife. Stepping over the twigs, she proceeds forward. I let them walk ahead while I continue behind. At the end of the forest stroll, we pause at an enormous open field—a large garden where they grow their food.

"This is the cornfield. Behind that are potatoes, onions, and other vegetation. Far west are the fruit trees," Dalma explains.

"East is a field of grain, and farther south is a cotton field," Elias adds.

"Can I see the fruit trees?" I ask.

Kallia turns to me. "That's my favorite place. I'll show you."

Her sudden change in temperament catches me by surprise, but it's welcome. "Okay."

"Elias," Kallia addresses. "Lance and the others are in the cornfield. Might you go hail them? They'll be pleased to see you."

"I'll hail them after," he says.

"No, go see your old peeps, *we* will be fine," I insist. I appreciate his protectiveness, but for right now, I'd like him to switch it off.

"I love the fruit trees." Dalma puckers up. "I'll go too."

I raise my eyebrows and smile. "And now there's three of us. Now go."

He moves in closer, searching my eyes for signs of doubt. "Are you sure?"

"Yes," I emphasize. "I want to do this. You did it, right?"

"Yeah, but—"

"Elias."

"Alright," he finally agrees.

CHAPTER 45

Skye

Dalma, Kallia, and I separate from Bento and Elias and proceed in the direction of the fruit trees.

"He's protective of you," Dalma observes.

"Yeah, well, I don't get out much."

She smiles. "I know that look. He cares for you very much."

Seriously, what is this look everyone but me keeps seeing?

"Well, we've become good friends, so I appreciate his concern, but I'd like to explore a little on my own as well," I admit.

"Wait," Kallia says. "You and Elias are just friends?"

I chuckle. "Uh, yeah," I reply in a stating-the-obvious tone. "What did you think we were?"

"It's just... well..."

"The way he looks at you, dear," Dalma interrupts. "It is fondness for more than friendship."

Yeah, well, nothing can ever come of it, so I won't allow my mind to go there.

"It's in your eyes, too, when you look at him," Dalma continues. "Love always starts small, then it blossoms into a beautiful flower."

Love?

The colorful sight of the fruit trees brings the greenery to life. Apples, mangoes, pears, and coconuts are in our current view, but there are many more trees spread throughout the area. I admire the view as the aroma of natural sweetness lingers in the air.

"Have you never seen apple trees before?" Kallia inquires.

"Actually, no. I haven't."

I'm not staring at the tree itself but rather at how succulent the apples look.

Moving further, I notice a shrub tree. *A lilac, or anima, shrub.*

"Who planted these?" I ask.

"Elias and I did," Kallia responds. "You like them?"

I grin slightly. "That doesn't surprise me. And yes, they're my favorite."

She smacks her lip. "Hm. I see."

Her tone changes slightly, but I ignore it. I'm in awe of this place.

"There are ripe mangoes further down. They're sweet. Want to pick one?" Dalma offers.

I'm distracted, drinking in the surroundings. "Sure," I accept.

"I don't see how you haven't turned into a mango yet. It's all you eat," Kallia jests to Dalma.

She points her finger at Kallia. "Mangoes are the best, hear?"

Kallia rolls her eyes and objects. "We'll meet you by the mangoes. She hasn't seen the bananas."

"Fine, boring bananas," Dalma grumbles. "I'm going to the mangoes."

Dalma parts from us, and I follow Kallia toward the banana trees.

"So, you like bananas?" I make conversation.

"Yes," she says insipidly.

"You know, Kallia. I really do admire the land here. In case you happen to think otherwise," I express. I honestly am enjoying the scenery, and exploring the culture firsthand is enlightening. I prefer to diminish any ill feelings.

"It's okay." She gives me a wry smile. "I can tell."

I'm not sure what to say after that. She isn't giving me much; I assume maybe she is trying to accept that my intention is genuine.

The bananas are all green and not quite ripe yet. Buckets hang off the branches attached to ropes.

"What are the buckets for?"

Her lips part to reply, but she presses them back together. She goes toward one of the buckets, and she gently tugs the rope as if testing it. She then pulls with more strength, and the empty bucket flips.

"The banana trees are high. We use a stick, place the nearly ripe ones in a bucket, and when it's full, we either bring it down or flip them," she explains.

She tests a few of the buckets without flipping them, then calls for me to flip one.

"I think this one is filled with bananas." She smiles. Her demeanor has changed, and she's seemingly in a better mood. I suppose she really loves bananas, or at least enjoys flipping the buckets.

I walk over and curl my fingers around the rope.

"Don't pull yet," she advises. "Stand right here and wrap this one around your leg to create tension. The bananas are heavy. The whole bucket will fall if you let go too quickly. Your leg prevents that."

I frown in confusion. "But they'll fall on my head."

"No, they won't. The bucket is set to flip opposite of the direction the rope is pulled. So, pull toward you with as much force as you can," she instructs. There's a look of mischief lingering in her smug smile as if this is some sort of prank.

Whatever. If she wants to get a kick out of bananas falling on my head, fine.

I pull the rope as she instructed as hard as I can, holding my head down so as not to get hit in the face, at least.

However, what lands on me are *not* bananas, and the sight leaves me in extreme terror.

Elias

I'm in the cornfield with Bento, catching up with Denti, Taka, and Lance, when a piercing scream echoes from the fruit trees.

Skye.

Trepidation pounces, and without a second thought, I break into a full sprint in the direction of the scream. I hear the guys hot on my heels, but I move with far greater purpose, swearing to God that Skye better not be hurt.

Kallia. No, Kallia wouldn't hurt her, would she?

I hear it again, a wail of agony. Regret seeps in for letting her go without me rather than following my gut. I'm running at full speed, but somehow it's not fast enough. When the apple trees come into view, the cries sound closer.

They're by the bananas.

The bananas. Wouldn't they tell her not to flip the buckets?

Dalma runs toward the apples from the direction of the mango trees. *She wasn't with them,* meaning that it was Kallia's idea to take Skye to the bananas. I fume. What the fuck did Kallia do?

In the distance, I see the banana trees, along with a satisfied smirk on Kallia's face. Cries of terror impale my ears, yet I don't see Skye—but *she's close.* Kallia abruptly turns when she hears my approach, and her smug expression disappears.

I sprint past her. At the sight of Skye, my heart bleeds. This is far from fucking funny. I want to rage but helping her is priority number one.

The rope from the bucket has her leg in a hold. She's on the ground, as far out as the rope will stretch, away from the snakes in a heap under the bucket. She's struggling to free herself from the rope, frightened at the close proximity of the creatures, and not paying attention to what she's doing.

I dash to her and kick away one snake slithering toward her before untangling the rope from her leg. She pushes to her feet immediately. Her first instinct is to jet, but before she takes off, I grab her. "Skye, look at me."

She's consumed with terror and not listening. Her face is soaked with tears, and she hysterically fights me to run off in her state of panic. "No! No! No!" she screams repeatedly, unhinged, unaware of anything around her, ready to take flight.

I place my hands on either side of her face and try to catch her gaze. I need her eyes to meet mine. "Skye, breathe. Breathe... in and out... you're okay. You're okay." With her eyes lasered on mine, she finally begins to breathe. Her movements slow, no longer fighting, and as her hysterics subside, she goes still. "Good, just breathe. You're okay."

Her bottom lip begins to quiver. I bring her in and cradle my arms around her. She fists my shirt and snivels into my chest. I bury my nose in her hair and allow her to release her cries.

I should have stayed with her.

I look over at the others. Dalma's hands cover her mouth, and tears stream down her face while Bento soothes her. Denti and Lance place the snakes back in the bucket. I glare at an impassive Kallia, needing to know why the fuck she did this.

"Sorry, I got your shirt all wet," Skye says moments after she's finished sobbing.

"My shirt is fine. Are you okay?"

She nods.

"Kallia, seriously?" Dalma expresses disappointment. "Pulling the buckets is dangerous."

"You shouldn't have allowed Skye to pull the ropes," Bento reprimands her.

Skye pushes herself out of my grasp.

"No, it's not her fault. She shook most of the buckets, and they were empty. That one was full, and we thought there were bananas in it."

I close my eyes and take a deep breath. Skye is too pure for any world.

"Wow. Didn't see that coming," Lance comments.

Skye looks to me with pleading eyes as she witnesses every-one's disappointment at Kallia. "Elias, it's not her fault."

While everyone tilts their heads down, Bento shakes his, and Kallia's eyes remain fixed on me. "Skye," I utter, still gazing at Kallia. My next words are going to humiliate her. As if wired to assume everyone possesses a heart akin to hers, she has an innate ability to see the good in everyone. I wish her pleas for Kallia were reasonable and true. I almost want to hide the truth from her. But I won't. She'll be mortified, but I won't lie to her. I break my stare-off with Kallia and look down at Skye's pleading eyes. "The buckets are snake traps."

I watch as humiliation grips her in an instant. Her eyes sink into their sockets, and she bites down on her bottom lip. She turns to Kallia. "What did I ever do to you?"

"Oh, come on. They were just gray-backs."

Kallia's response sends me over the edge I was treading. My anger takes hold of me. "It doesn't matter!"

Her jaw slacks and her eyes gape. My reaction shocked her. I've never been upset with Kallia for any reason. She's never witnessed me out of a controlled temperament. I've never had a reason.

But I've also never met this vindictive Kallia.

My eyes dart back to Skye. She's still. *Too still.* And that's never a good sign with her. I scrutinize her stance. Her hands are fists at her sides. She's tense as fury burns within her. A ticking bomb, moments from exploding.

"What the hell is wrong with you?" She charges after Kallia but gets nowhere. I quickly wrap my arms around her thin waist and hoist her back flush to my torso. "Let me go, Elias!" she snaps, angered—with every right to be—but I need to handle this. Kallia's actions aren't about Skye, they're about me. I must admit, this fire ablaze—I like it, but she has to calm down so I can deal with this.

"Skye, let me handle this. This isn't about you."

She settles down, and I let her go. "Then what is this about?"

"Yes, what is this about, Kallia?" Bento queries.

Kallia's nose scrunches; her eyes shimmer. "Because how could you love her and not me?" she shouts and takes off toward the cornfield.

Her admission weighs on me. I inhale deeply, shut my eyes, and let out a breath. Skye, no longer infuriated, stares into the distance, processing. Lifting her chin, she squints, searching my eyes. But she's *not* searching—she's already assumed. And uninvited fear creeps in at the possible assumption.

"Oh boy, well, today has been quite the day." Bento breaks the ice after the initial shock.

Dalma motions to Skye, and everyone goes their separate ways. "My deepest apologies. This is your first experience in our land. Had I known Kallia felt this way, I would not have voiced my opinions in her presence."

What opinions?

"Doesn't make this place any less comforting. Thank you for having me," Skye offers, and Dalma proceeds to the forest.

"Are you okay?" I ask Skye.

She frowns. "It's not me you should be worried about right now." She folds her arms. "You need to go talk to her. I'll wait right here."

I lift a brow. "Oh yeah? Under the banana trees?"

She looks up and uncrosses her arms, remembering where she is. "Okay, not right *here*."

Chuckling, I reach my arm to her shoulder, but she blocks it and gives me a look of disappointment before proceeding to the forest.

Damn, that stings more than it should.

CHAPTER 46

Elias

After bidding our goodbyes, Skye insisted on taking more pictures. She did—*plenty of them*—before we headed back to the boat. While she was amicable with everyone, she remains terse and aloof with me. Her cold shoulder is acknowledged. I haven't been forthcoming with her, but I will be. First, I need to take care of something.

"Hey," I call to her retreating back as she heads for the bathroom. She turns around. "I, uh…" I pause, clearing my throat.

"Go," she encourages. "Take care of your business."

Her words of understanding relieve my apprehension. A lingering question surfaces again. *What if I had met Skye five years ago? Would I have ended up here?*

Kallia answers the door after the first knock. It's obvious she's been crying. Guilt pricks at me for how she's feeling. We were once close. Although I was aware of her developing feelings, I was blind to their extent. I did her a favor by leaving—or so I thought.

Regardless, she and I both knew my time at Kairos was never permanent.

"May I come in?" I ask.

She nods and opens the door wider for my entrance. I come in and shut it behind me.

She hangs her head. "Could you tell Skye sorry for me?"

"Afraid you'll have to tell her that yourself."

"Are you going to marry her?" she asks dejectedly, fearing my answer. I won't lie to her. I'm not here to make anyone feel better by sugarcoating.

"I couldn't if I wanted to."

"Do you love her?"

"Kallia, I'm not here to talk about Skye. I'm here to talk about you."

She raises her head, finally looking at me with disheartened eyes. She's hurting. There's nothing I can do to fix that, but I can help her move on.

She faces down again and hugs herself. "Have you ever loved me?"

"Kallia, you are a dear friend to me. I care for you." I pause to allow that to sink in. She lifts her head again. "But I'm sorry. I do not love you the way you've hoped I would."

"You mean the way you love her."

I sigh. "Why are you so convinced I love Skye?"

"The way you look at her. The two years you were here, as close as we were, you've never looked at me that way. You're protective of her. Like..." She pauses, looking up. "Like a husband."

I take a breath and stuff my hands in my pockets. "Look, Skye, and I... it's not like that. We're—"

"Then you're lying to yourself," she interjects. "You know, even though I knew you were leaving Kairos, I had hoped you'd offer to take me with you. I would have jumped at the opportunity to go anywhere with you," she confesses. "But then you left. You *really* set sail. And when you left, you took my heart with you." She turns her back to me, as if whatever comes next is hard for her. "After the night... when I imposed on you... embarrassing myself—"

"I told you not to be," I interrupt. "I don't think of you any differently."

She turns on her heels and faces me. I can see a tear falling down her cheek. "That's what you said, but I felt your distance. You grew careful. Careful of everything you said and did around me. You did it to ensure I wouldn't take any of it the wrong way."

"I meant no harm," I say my truth.

"I know." She wipes her eyes and sniffles. "That's what makes it worse, because I know it was out of consideration for my feelings."

"Do you hate me for that?"

"Hate you?" She takes a deep breath. "Elias, I could never hate you."

"Kallia, you can leave Kairos; explore. It won't mean you regard Kairos any less. It's just you being you—the adventurous woman you are—strong and full of life. There is someone out there for you. That someone just cannot be me."

She assertively takes in my words and sheds another tear. "That means so much coming from you."

I wrap my arms around her shoulders and give her a hug— because that's what she needs. I don't hug the woman who's fallen in love with the wrong guy, I hug my friend because that's what she is to me—a dear friend. A weight lifted off my chest, this conversation was long overdue. "No more tears, tiger."

She smiles. "No more tears."

Skye

I'm towel-drying my hair when laughter approaches the boat. Stepping up to the shore are Elias and Kallia. And by the looks on their faces, everything has worked itself out. When they spot me by the rail, the laughter ceases, and Kallia looks down at the wooden bucket in her hands. Elias gives me an appreciative smile.

"Is everything okay?" I ask curiously when Elias climbs aboard.

"Yeah, I think she wants to talk to you," he replies.

"Well, okay then." I sigh, and I climb off the boat and greet her. "Hi."

"Hi," she replies timorously. "I just want to say I'm very sorry. How I treated you today was unjust. You never deserved that." Guilt-stricken, she darts her eyes to the basket in her arms. She's clearly nervous about my response.

"Apology accepted," I say.

Relieved at my pardon, a hint of a smile plays on her lips. "Here." She offers the basket of apples. "I saw you looking at the apples as if you really like apples, so I brought you some."

I take the basket with reluctance. "Thank you. Um, snakes weren't in this basket, were they?"

She giggles. "No. This is one of the baskets we use to pick fruits."

"Okay." I smile. "This land is truly a beauty."

"I hope to see you again."

My smile dissipates at that reminder that I won't be seeing anyone here ever again.

"You know, Dalma was right," she begins, "about the way Elias looks at you."

If I had a nickel for every time I've been told how Elias looks at me, I'd have quite the dollar by now. "No, you've got it all—"

"Two years," she interrupts. "And Elias has never looked at me the way he does you. If he did, I'd know because I was searching for it."

"Yeah, well, I'm not sure why. I've done nothing but annoy him to sail me across the world," I joke.

"And he's doing it," she utters. "I told Elias I wanted to explore, but I didn't get offered a trip around the world." She moves in closer and gazes at me with conviction in her words. "Listen, Elias isn't the kind of man you can annoy to do anything. He's doing it because he *wants* to. You've sparked something in him."

I lightly shake my head. "I'm not exactly sure what."

"You don't, but he does." She backs up and starts to walk away. "Take care, Skye. And again, I'm very sorry."

I wave goodbye, then turn toward the vessel to see Elias looking out at the horizon through the spyglass. He removes it from his eye and turns toward the shore, noticing me standing there—watching him—and his expression softens, his lips curving to a half-smile. A look I hadn't noticed before is suddenly prominent in his gaze.

Desire.

I feel it when my cheeks heat, and I smile back.

I've never acknowledged the brewing feelings I have for Elias, but I won't deny their existence. I push down the thought of anything with him and focus on the one thing that I undeniably do have with him. A true friendship. I can already feel that I'm going to miss him very much, and it's going to be painful.

As I make my way forward, I replay the events of this afternoon, and by the time I climb aboard, my smile fades.

"Everything alright?" His eyebrows pull together in concern.

"Yeah." I try to pucker up, distracting myself. "We've got apples." I hold up the basket and then bring it into the kitchen. Elias follows me.

"Skye," he says to my retreating back. "Look at me."

I want to say, no, everything is not alright. It bothers me that you won't share anything with me, yet everyone seems to think I'm special to you. In the beginning, I accepted that you weren't an open person. However, it's baffling that you still can't trust me as I've trusted you.

I want to help him overcome his own internal trials, as he's helped me overcome mine—but he won't let me in. He's seen the real me, and I've allowed myself to become close to him. And though that's my own fault, I care about him—and I want to know the *real* Elias. I want to say: *Let me in. Let me help. Let me see you.* Being so close to you and not knowing you is beginning to hurt. But instead, I turn around and smile when I say, "Nothing. I'm just a little tired. It's been a long day."

Elias

That fake smile again—I feel the pricking of a thousand needles when any smile of hers directed to me isn't her genuine sunshine. She smiles, but there's hurt in her eyes. And the pang in my chest delivers her justice. The events at Kairos were enough to leave anyone exhausted. Nevertheless, that isn't the issue.

She discovered much about my history with Kairos through everyone but me. I've refused to divulge any information about myself, past or present. And anytime she's inquired, I've shut it down. So now she won't even try. She's leaving it alone, just as I've wanted, but it's hurting her.

She's trusted me, let me in, allowed me to see her, and I've refused to respond in kind. To become close to someone, realizing you don't know them—*they don't want you to know them*—is not easy for a pure heart to take.

I've resided in this world for five years. Concealing myself has become second nature. However, this one time, I'll try, because the woman in front of me deserves it.

CHAPTER 47

Elias

"Can I talk to you?" I ask.

She nods, and I gesture with my head that we move toward the cockpit.

I won't talk about my life before this world, because that no longer matters, but I can begin with something from here. With all that she's been through today, she deserves to know the inexcusable "why."

"Remember when I told you that the guys I maintained ships for on Land Samoa offered to build a home for me, but I rain checked to voyage?"

She nods.

"It was two years before I finally reached out to them. I didn't travel around. I set out to Land Kairos, where I resided for those two years."

I start up the boat and head us out to sea before switching its controls to autopilot. "I met a guy, Lani, at shipwright school in Sandemia. He's from Land Samoa, and we voyaged for the equivalent of five months before he expressed that he was ready to return to his homeland. We traveled to every land near Kairos... but never Kairos."

"Was that purposely?" she asks.

"Yes," I reply. "It's rumored that the people of Land Kairos are barbaric and sheltered, but as you've witnessed, that's an exaggerated narrative. However, their objection to change causes them to be inhospitable to strangers."

"So, that's why you took up residence at Land Samoa? This Lani was a friend?" she questions.

"Guess you could say that."

"I mean shipwright school, five months of voyaging, a year as practically neighbors, working on ships, building a house... and *you guess* he's a friend?" she says disconcertingly.

I give her an apologetic look. She wants to know why, but that's not what I plan to talk about. "I decided I didn't care what the rumors about Kairos were, because what the people of this world consider barbaric probably pales in comparison to the world I'm from. When I arrived, I received the same glares you did, but I didn't care. No one approached me. Everyone had reentered their homes—except one woman."

"Hello, my name is Elias. Who is this land's leader?" I ask the woman standing before me.

She crosses her arms and narrows her eyes. "Why?"

"I think I may be from here. I have no family. I am twenty-eight years of age. I grew up in an orphanage, and my nearly disintegrated birth paper shows only my first name, day of birth, and a small area that reads 'Land Kai.' I can only assume that means I may be from here." I'm lying through my teeth using the knowledge I've gathered about the land to my advantage.

Her expression softens. "Follow me."

She leads me to her leader's home, where I'm joyously greeted by Bento. "Hello there! You've found your way back home, son. Don't you worry, you are welcome here."

The woman gestures for a handshake. "Hi, I'm Kallia. Do you plan to stay?"

I nod. "I would be honored."

"I was accepted instantly. When I became close with the people, I eventually asked Bento about the fire."

"It was a hot day. The warmest sun season we'd ever experienced. I was just a boy then, twelve years of age, and my father was this land's leader. The fire sparked in an area of the woods where no one resides. The adults tirelessly worked to extinguish the flames with large buckets of water, but the inexorable fire grew—destroying everything in its path. Our crops, trees, homes. Many fled, never to return, and many perished.

"The news of the fire spread across neighboring lands. Many leaders and others came to offer support, resources, and to help us rebuild. We offered them plentiful gratitude in favor of their kindness, but we stood strong in our culture. One with the land."

"I remained at Land Kairos because the people experienced grief, loss, and hardship. They may never know my story, but I could relate the closest to them. Despite their misgivings, they remained humble and grounded in their beliefs."

"Does Kallia remember the fire?" Skye asks.

"No, I learned she was in the womb. But her father died during the catastrophe. She was their only child."

"Damn, that's tough," she says sympathetically.

"Yeah," I agree. "Bento taught me how to build the homes they lived in and cut the trees. They only used dying trees or those with lifted roots, indicating they would fall soon. I spent most days with Kallia, who taught me everything else. From plowing the land, planting, growing crops, and harvesting to reading the posture of predatory animals, she's helped me in more ways than one. Of all people here, I consider her a friend."

I pause for a few beats. "Kallia did notice something unusual about me. She just couldn't put her finger on it. She was also under the impression that I found Kairos *again* because I was lonely."

"She's intuitive," Skye remarks.

"That she is," I agree.

"So, what happened?"

"I began noticing changes in her. Her appearance, for one. She began knitting clothing that complimented her sex appeal, far different than her usual. I still thought nothing of it. She's a woman. That's normal where we're from." Sighing, I continue. "She'd blush at mediocre things I'd do, and suddenly conversation starters were topics like marriage and children. Her energy around me changed in general."

"She was falling in love with you," Skye observes.

I nod.

"Although I felt the change, I ignored it. Until one night, I was asleep and felt hands caressing my back. I jumped up and turned on my lantern to see Kallia, naked in my cot, encouraging me to touch her."

"What did you do?" Skye asks.

"I denied her."

She looks down and whispers, "Oh my god, Elias."

"I wasn't rude about it. I apologized and truthfully expressed that I don't fancy her that way."

She shakes her head. "That's not it. She must have been so embarrassed."

"She was. She began to weep and apologize. I told her not to be embarrassed and that we'd act like it never happened. Easier said than done of course, but her friendship was important to me," I explain.

"Important to you?" Skye scoffs. She pushes to her feet and places her hands on her hips. "She became your friend, she saw something different in you than everyone else, and she fell in love with you. Not because you're fine as hell or had anything to offer. She loved you for you. And you couldn't love her back?!"

She begins pacing, and I'm in utter confusion as to how I just became the bad guy. I look at her, perplexed.

"Don't look at me with your ugly face!" she snaps.

My ugly face?

"I swear, men are so stupid," she mutters as she paces the floor.

"Okay, whoa, whoa, whoa," I repeat as I try to understand what the hell just happened. I lift from where I'm seated and halt

Skye's pacing, blocking her path. "Stupid? Really? Would you prefer I'd accepted her advances knowing I didn't share her feelings?"

"No, idiot, but—" She shuts her eyes and takes a deep breath to simmer down. "Since I've been here, you've considered no one else a friend, it seems, except her. When you speak of her, there's no question that you cherish your relationship with her."

"Okay." I attempt to grasp what she's getting at.

"Isn't part of that reason because she intuitively recognized that internally, you are in fact different *and alone.* She wasn't wrong. She became what you needed. A friend."

"Yes, I know that," I reply, still not understanding why I'm an idiot.

"And she fell in love with you, *for you,* Elias!" she exclaims. "*Not* the Elias at the surface. And you couldn't love her back?"

"She only thinks she loves me. But she doesn't love me," I say.

"She loves you, Elias!" she shouts in my face.

Something in me begins to bubble. "She can't love me!"

"And why not?" she asks. Destabilizing emotions brim, and I bite down until my jaw twitches. I turn to leave the cockpit. Skye is hot on my heels. "Don't walk away from me, Elias! Why can't she love you?!"

And that's it. The brimming emotions spill over. I swiftly turn to face her. "Because to love me is to know me. And no one here can ever truly know me!"

I study her nuance after my outburst. Her expression softens, akin to pity. The sight piques me, so I charge out of the cockpit. I don't need hers or anyone else's pity because, as always, I have never pitied myself.

Skye

And there it is. Elias's truth.

A part of him *does* regret his decision to remain in this world permanently, a world where no one can ever grasp his truth. No one to share his truth. In the beginning, he was content with being alone, only to discover just how *lonely* being alone can get.

A world full of good-natured people, but no one who could ever relate to him. His resentment may have sprouted from those who surrounded him in our world; it may have driven him to leave and reject companionship. However, deep down, he longs for the element that lead to such bitterness—but not with just anyone, but rather with people similar to those of his world. Our world. *Home.*

The people of Land Kairos were the closest thing to familiarity. Kallia noticed this longing, a need within him, but even she could never know the truth.

To live here is to hide forever.

Then that leaves me. I can wholeheartedly empathize with him, but growing too close to me is an internal death sentence.

My heart bleeds for him.

His heart is starved and yearns for love and togetherness—something he's felt once before, or he wouldn't be aching from the loss of it. He's stifling his heart from feeling, but to unlock the cage, he must let go. It's time to untether himself from our world and allow his core to unreservedly accept this one and the people in it.

After taking a breather, I decide it's time to find him. I go through the front deck and then around the side until the helm comes into view. When I see him, his back is turned to me. His shoulders are tense; he sits leaning forward and resting his elbows on his parted knees. I move in closer and place a hand on his shoulder. "Elias," I softly voice.

He removes the fists that were balled inside one another under his nose. "I don't need your pity, Skye," he rasps, low and defensive, but he doesn't pay me a glance.

"Elias, I don't pity you. Pity is for people who are weak. You are anything but weak."

His shoulders shift before relaxing under my palm. He takes a deep breath and lets his forearms fall between the opening of his legs. I take the opportunity to do something he may reject, but I no longer care what he chooses to reject, only what he needs. Unspoken feelings may linger between us, but as his friend first—as someone who cares for him—I choose the path he'll resist, for his own sake. I move between his knees, never removing my hand from his shoulder. He jerks back, lifting his chin, frowning at me.

"What are you doing?" he asks, off-putting. His eyes are bloodshot, but not a single tear was shed. He pushes down his agony, buries it in his depths, but all that does is strengthen the darkened veil that shields his golden heart.

With both my hands placed on either side of his shoulders, I gaze into his emeralds and softly say, "You don't *need* pity, but you *need* someone."

I slide my hands behind his neck, but he hasn't moved a muscle. "Let me be what you need, Elias."

I study his nuances. His features soften, and I move in closer, nudging him into my torso, and he doesn't resist. He buries his head into my stomach, and I bring my hands into his hair. He squeezes the back of my thighs as his emotions pour—and he weeps. And weeps. And weeps against me.

His pain jets through me as I wrap myself in all that is him. I carry his burden with me, help him shoulder his weight, and as I feel his pain, unrelenting tears flood my tear ducts until they spill over in abundance.

"For as long as I'm here, Elias Crawford, I'll be what you need," I whisper.

Elias

It has happened, somehow it has. The one thing I've been steering clear from *is* happening. She broke through the cage of my darkened core, and I've given in to her light, *her love*.

I *need* her.

I've needed her for years.

I believed that if I had only shared my experiences of this world, it wouldn't allow her into my heart, my soul; into everything that is me. But she's stronger than I imagined. She busted the chains that kept my heart shackled, enveloping my core with warmth, and I could no longer resist her.

The memory of weeping is far behind me, but as I hold her close, I release every pent-up emotion I've held over the previous years. Ripping my heart out of my chest, I hand it to her. When she leaves, my soul will hurt for her, my heart will suffocate for her, but for right now, I listen to her because *I trust her.*

I trust her when she says this is what I need.

After releasing the sorrows from my core, I gaze upon a tear-soaked face. She wasn't crying for me, she cried with me. *She felt me.* Sliding her palms to either side of my face, she wipes my tears with her thumbs.

"You did so good," she whispers in a cracked voice, filled with unwavering emotions. "So good. I'm so happy for you."

I stand and place my hands where she has hers on me, and I wipe her tears. Snaking my hands around her waist, she props herself up on her toes, wrapping her arms around my neck, and I pull her in flush. "Thank you, Skye," I whisper in her ear.

I inhale her lavender scent as I hold her close, engulfing myself in everything that she is. We stay this way for a few more seconds before I need a reason—this very instant—to break apart. "I'm going to shower."

We release each other. She smiles. "Okay, I'll make us something to eat."

I nod and walk away—I need to leave her presence before I fall victim to the compulsion to press my lips to hers. I want to kiss her deeply but refuse to go there. I keep drawing lines and then crossing them with her. Logical reasoning consistently takes a step aside in her presence. She weakens my willpower, and now I know why. Because where affairs of the heart are concerned, willpower be damned.

CHAPTER 48

Elias

Imarinate in the shower for longer than usual, soaking in the downpouring stream and pondering on the weight lifted off my chest—a sudden rejuvenation I failed to recognize I needed. Turning the water cold, I shock my weak flesh back to reality until the craving for more than a hug subsides. After finishing, I step out with a towel over my head, soaking up the moisture from my dampened hair. The scent of something delicious invades my senses, and I make my way to the kitchen to find Skye scooping broccoli next to salmon on two plates.

A smile stretches across her face. "I found wine. I had no idea you brought any onboard," she says. "Is it safe for the captain to have wine?"

I smirk. "A glass or two won't hurt."

She smacks her tongue and brings me a plate of salmon, steamed broccoli, and mashed potatoes. "Good! Because tonight calls for wine."

I chuckle. I'm going to miss the fuck out of her.

"So where are we going next?" she asks.

Satiated from our meal, we sit in the cockpit as the night sky blankets the sea. "Land Samoa, and then back to Sandemia," I reply.

"So, I have to ask," she begins, "why are you here?"

A disconcerted feeling rises within me from her question.

I don't like this.

I can't go there with her.

Unlike her, I'm well aware of the rationale for my being here, but that doesn't mean I care to talk about it.

"Skye," I say drearily.

At the sound of my unforthcoming tone, she sits up in her seat. "No, Elias," she says, unrelenting. "Don't hide from me."

I dart my eyes to her and decide to give in. After today, she's proven I need to talk about it, and I'd rather it be with her than anyone else—whether in this world or the next.

So, I tell her *everything*.

I pause and take her in. She's assertive but impassive. She's still; I'm unable to read her. When Skye goes still, she is usually on the verge of a violent outburst. My story is affecting her, so before I continue, I stretch my arm and gesture for her to sit next to me.

She slowly rises and comes toward me. When she takes her seat at my side, I wrap an arm around her as she rests her head in the crook of my neck.

"What happened before you arrived?" she asks softly.

I take a deep breath before I begin. My dreams became those of somewhere else when emptiness took hold of me. I took comfort in the void before I arrived, but that didn't send me here. Until recently, the isolation I felt after burning my bridges was no strain at all. However, having my soul's desires hindered by forces beyond my control was truly a dark place for me.

CHAPTER 49

Elias

"Your suspension is shot." I lower a customer's vehicle. "I'll do your shocks and struts for eight fifty."

"Damn, that much?" he asks in defeat. I'm reasonable by all means, but if I dropped any lower than I already do, I'd be selling myself short.

"That's a deal for this. Go shop around and let me know if you find a better offer." I hand him his keys.

He looks out in the distance, considering his options. I don't stand around waiting for him. I begin my pre-close routine.

"Put me down for Friday morning, payday and all," he finally speaks.

"You got it."

I'm locking up shop when a white Volvo belonging to the lot's property owner pulls in. "Elias, how you doing?" he greets me. Instead of exiting his vehicle, he rolls down the window to speak. Whatever he's here for, it's quick.

I pull at the garage door handle, ensuring it's locked, then approach him. "Not bad, Mr. Felix. What brings you over this way?"

He hands me a folded paper. "What's this?" I ask.

Removing his sunglasses, his expression looks apologetic.

"Look, I hate to be the bearer of bad news. I know you're becoming an established sole proprietor." He pauses and faces forward, looking through his windshield for a moment before turning to me again. "Your shop is getting popular around these parts, but I've already sold the property."

What the fuck? "What about our deal?"

"I considered that. Even declined the offer," he says before taking a deep breath. I'm unaware of the details or why he'd cross me, but his conscience is fucking with him right now. He steps out of his vehicle, closes the door, and leans against the side. "Elias, they doubled the offer. Cash up front," he admits.

Who would want this lot that damn bad? "Well, who is it? I'll pay them and save for their asking price."

"No. They want the space cleared in thirty days," he says in defeat.

"Thirty days! You've gotta be kidding me."

"My sincerest apologies. I've never done business with this company, but they're legit and interested in this place," he says. "That's no easy offer to pass up." He reopens his car door to enter.

"Curious, who bought it?" I ask.

"Crawford Investment," he replies.

My nostrils flare. Anger coils in my stomach. *That bastard.*

Mr. Felix's eyebrow quirks. "Ain't that your name? You know 'em?"

"Nah," I lie and walk away.

Felix pulls off. I jump in my car. Wasting no time, I floor the pedal of my Lancer all the way to Milton as rage courses through me. Why the fuck won't that bastard leave me be? He's attempting to sabotage me. My choices tickle the entitled shithead that bad? Yeah, well, we'll see.

As fury pumps through my veins, I beat on the front door of the home I once lived in as if the doorbell were nonexistent.

My brother answers. "Yo, El. What the fuck?"

I push past my father's little pet and stalk through the halls.

When I don't see him in his usual comfort zone, I turn back. "Where is he?" I bark at my brother.

"Who, Dad?"

Who else, dumbass?

"Why are you here, Elias?" I hear the devil in disguise behind me. The snake finally appears, holding a rock glass in his left hand with two fingers of whiskey, *his usual.* He hasn't been home long; his tie hangs loose with the first two buttons undone.

"Why?" I snap, approaching him, inflamed at his nonchalance.

A smug smile plays on his lips. "Why what?"

"Don't fucking play with me right now," I snap, my patience thinning. I want to knock all the teeth out of his mouth, but I instead clench and unclench my fists at my sides, leveling my head to the best of my ability.

"Or what?" He cocks an eyebrow. "You'll punch me like you did Travis? I'll have your ass in a cell tonight. Tread carefully, boy."

I don't ask how he knows about that. My kiss-ass brother probably told him. And how he knows? Probably from one of the pieces of shit I no longer consider a friend.

"Would it kill you to let me live?" I rhetorically ask. "I ask nothing of you. I've done this all on my own. Let me be, for God's sake," I plead in anger.

He narrows his gaze. "All on your own? Whose money do you think your mother spent to buy the condo and Camaro? You don't think I know about her paying your tuition fees? The money you received from her selling her gifts to you to open your little shit shop, whose do you think it was?"

I fume at the mention of my mother. He has no goddamn right to breathe a word regarding what she's done for me. "Mom was a lawyer, she had money!"

"Your mother quit law before you graduated high school, idiot boy."

"Then why did you let her do any of it if you were so against me?"

"What man wouldn't grant his dying wife's wish for her son? I ain't that cold, son."

I hate this sick son of a bitch. He speaks as if he did some noble deed. The news of how long Mom had really been sick burdens my chest, but I refuse to let it distract me. "Just let me keep my shop. I'll buy back the property from you. I had a contract with Felix. I was to have cash upfront in five more months to purchase it from him. I would've had it in three."

He takes a sip of his whiskey. "I saw that contract. Did you even have a lawyer review it?" he patronizes. "Any lawyer could have negotiated those terms. Did you even read the damn thing?" He smirks and pinches the bridge of his nose. "To put this in simpler terms, the contract states he'll sell it to you at x price by y time, but such terms can change without notice." He insults my intelligence with his arrogance.

Ignoring his condescension, I suck in my pride. "Just let me keep my shop."

A devilish grin stretches across his face. "How about this? Hire someone else to manage the shop, and you start a career at the firm."

He may be under the impression that he has me by the balls, but I'm not receptive to making a deal with the devil. "Hell will freeze over before I work for you."

"Then no deal," he utters.

"Why are you doing this?"

He takes another sip of the brown heat in his glass and rocks back on his heels, aloof and diabolic. "Welcome to the world of business."

Towering with rage, I charge out of the house in a huff. If I remain near his presence, I may do something I regret. Swinging open my car door, I pause before entering when my brother calls my name. "El!"

I suck in a breath. "What, Elijah?"

"Come on, just quit it. Stop making your life harder than it has to be." He attempts to reason. It's terrible, and he's the last person I'd take advice from. He chooses to be under our father like a little punk.

"My life isn't hard, Elijah."

He moves closer and places his hand on my door. "Why do you think he's so hellbent on your employment at the firm? He wants you to be the next CEO after his retirement. The board will undoubtedly vote you in. Wouldn't you want that?"

I look his pitiful ass in the face. "No. That's not my dream, it's his. If you dream of doing that, then you go for it. But it's not what I want."

"I would want that, but you don't think I know that Dad thinks I'm no smarter than a fucking doorknob?" he grumbles, the admission clawing at him.

Sympathy festers in the place of the resentment I have for my brother as my father's bitch. "Elijah, that's not true. Don't let—"

"Yes, it is," he interjects. "All I have is football, but you're smart as shit. You know how to do all that—whatever it is he does. I told him I'd learn everything, and he says he's willing to teach me, but I know he knows that I can't do it. He's hoping I get drafted. I'm barely passing business law as it is."

Gazing at my sorry-ass brother, guilt pricks at me. I should have taken him under my wing, but I was closer to Mom while he was closer to Dad. The tension between my father and I put a strain on our relationship. "If football doesn't work out, think of what you want to do next, not what you think he wants. Have you learned nothing from Mom?"

"Yeah, well, Dad is successful. That's inspiring," he says.

I'm done with this. "Elijah, I have to go."

"How much more do you need to lose, El?" he shouts.

I frown. "What?"

"Your friends, your girl, everything Mom gifted you—now the shop. How much more do you need taken from you before you see it won't work?"

I step toward my brother until we're mere inches apart. "Elijah, did you know about Jessica and Travis? And did you know Dad was buying the property my shop sits on?"

He lowers his head, and that was all the response I needed. Rage quickens in my blood once again. "Get away from me."

"El, look—"

"Now!" I snap. He jumps, startled by my reaction. I've never snapped at my brother, but as of this evening, he's as significant as a fly on the wall. He walks off, and I jump in my vehicle, skidding off.

I pour a drink in my closet-sized kitchen. The bitter taste hits my tongue, and as it passes through my throat, I welcome the sting. I suck in a breath through clenched teeth and down a shot before pouring another. I sit down at my computer and search the Internet for open lots. After finding none suited to be a mechanic shop, I shut my laptop and pour again. I recall my backstabbing brother's words—he's right. I am losing everything, but it's not my doing. I've been betrayed in every corner by those I held in endearment. One heartache after another in every direction. Why do I even need it? It's a reminder that the people a heart beats for can stick a knife in it at any moment. The only person who has ever truly loved me is gone. How cruel is life?

I begin to wonder where my mother could be and imagine her world to be a place of freedom and prosperity. And the imaginative thoughts comfort me until I drift into a state of sleep.

My last day of business rolls around, and I lock up shop for good. Another blow to the chest. A painful one.

My business was starting to flourish, and I'd foreseen a future of expansion. This was only my beginning, but everything had been falling into place. I could consider reopening in another town, but I've built rapport with the people here. My small shop had become a landmark.

Though I have more than enough money to hold me over until my next move, I still feel defeated. Money wasn't the most important factor when I opened this place; every waking day, I looked forward to starting my work on vehicles. This place filled me with a purpose, which was now replaced with an undeniable emptiness.

In my dismay, I've conjured a reality escape. Quite often, it has followed me to my dreams. But when sleep fades, I reenter hell, wishing to return to the place of my reverie.

Suddenly feeling a longing—I could use a Friday night at the lake—but fuck them all. Instead, when I enter my vehicle and turn over the ignition, I head somewhere that I shouldn't. But I need *her* comfort, at least just for a moment.

Since the incident at the lake five months ago, the guys have continued to call and text, but I've yet to respond. All but Tyler has reached out, the only one I'd ever consider giving the benefit of the doubt. The backlash affected him the most. He's accepted the termination of our friendship as his penance. I respect him for it, but I could never trust him—or any of them—ever again. I don't consider people I can't trust friends. I'd rather have no friends at all than laugh with those I fear may stab me. That's my code, and I live by it.

Her X7 sits outside. *She's home.*

I park out of sight, uncertain if I dare to go through with this. I begin to wonder, *have I gotten this desperate?* I'm sitting in the parking lot of my ex-girlfriend's condo because I need someone right now, and I don't know who to turn to who won't offer pity. Jessica's suggestions were never favorable, but pity was never her style.

I decide I'm going through with it but pause with my fingers on the car door when Travis's Porsche pulls in. He exits the vehicle, goes to the passenger side, and opens the door. Out comes Jessica. I watch her throw her arms around him while he grabs her ass. His tongue is down her throat before they part and make their way to the entrance of her home.

The sight fills me with indignation. I start up my vehicle and drive home. I find the ring meant to make Jessica my fiancé and stuff it in my pocket with plans of pawning it tomorrow. I turn on the TV, plop down on the couch, and throw my head back against the sofa while the show plays in the background.

Spartacus echoes through my apartment, the flicker of each scene the only light in the dark. I no longer am paying attention. Traveling to my escape, I feel the wind, hear the trees, and I exchange goods and services for nothing but gratitude. I imagine that's where my mother lives. No one can rip another thing from me because money holds no value for my purpose.

I fall asleep, submerged in my thoughts. When I wake again, I'm on a boat with white sails in the middle of the sea.

CHAPTER 50

Elias

Skye sniffles against me, and I rub her arm in consolation. She pushes to her feet faster than I thought she was capable of moving and doesn't say a word. She paces with fisted hands at her side.

"Skye?" I say her name in question, but I get no response.

She abruptly stops, and her expression hardens. "When I get back, I'm taking a trip to Georgia. I'm giving every last one of them a piece of my damn mind!"

She's sincerely upset and adorable. "Skye, no, you're not."

She stares daggers at me. "You saying I won't?"

My hands fly up in surrender. "No, ma'am."

"Don't call me ma'am!"

Snickering, I fight with myself to suppress a laugh. "Sorry."

She resumes her steps of anger. "And that Uncle Earl..."

"Eric."

"What?"

My hands fly up again. "It's my uncle Eric."

"Well, he could've done more."

I take a breath. "I didn't involve my uncle. Over the years, I've considered that. I should have reached out to him. If there's anyone at all I could talk to again from back home, it would be him."

I'm speaking, but it's falling on deaf ears.

"Oh, and your dad, and that friend fucker, Jessica and Travis that…"

"Skye!"

"What!"

She's going too far. It was hard enough to spill everything. I don't need it relitigated. Riled up, my story pinched the part of her that's reserved to protect and defend those she cares about. And though I'm doting on this fire within her—even when she's fired up at me—there is no burden I've experienced that I want her to bear as her own.

When she recognizes I'm adamant about getting her attention, her pacing ceases. I stand to my feet and place my hands on either side of her shoulders. "There's nothing you can do about it, and there's nothing I want you to do about it. It was years ago, and it's over."

"I'm sorry." She simmers down. "It's just that…" She bites down on her bottom lip in an attempt to keep her composure, but her inner eyebrows curve up as sadness creeps in. "They were so wrong, Elias. All of them."

Her level of empathy is immeasurable. It was someone like her I needed all those years ago. She was the friend I was searching for the night before I arrived. Instead, I weakened that night and expected the person partly responsible for my broken pieces to put them back together.

"I'm over that, Skye. I just wanted to share it with you."

She takes a deep breath. "No, you're not over it. You've harbored resentment. You let no one in. Your heart's emptiness misses love and friendship. You can try to deny it, but it's true."

I don't respond, I just gaze into her irises and process her words.

"Just as you told me I have to uncage my soul, you have to uncage your heart," she says.

Damn.

I move away from her, walk out to the deck, and take a seat.

She's not wrong. I'm aware that I block people out; it's purposeful. I may have befriended those at Kairos, but they don't truly *know* me. I took comfort in the relation to them, but even that was temporary. After a while, I felt the need to separate. Skye has been an exception to my rule of seclusion. *And the only exception I'm ever willing to make.*

She takes a seat next to me. "Elias." At the soft call of my name, I turn my head in her direction. "No one here can know what you've been through, but that doesn't mean they can't know you. It doesn't mean they can't love you. You are not what you've been through. You are who you choose to be now."

Standing, I walk to the rails and lean forward on my forearms. I look out to the blank sea under the gloomy sky. The setting epitomizes me. Dark, empty, and void of emotion—as I prefer. I take comfort in such an environment because it resembles the depths of my soul. However, it's Skye's light that reminds me that this isn't my depths, only my surface, the surface I've chosen to *protect* my depths.

Skye stands beside me and leans backward on the rail.

"You know," I begin, "I had begun to miss those bastards. Nostalgia hit a few times, and I would reminisce on the good times we shared. Somewhere, somehow, even good memories of me and my father were rekindled. Memories I lost sight of for years after our relationship turned sour." I shake my head. "Stupid."

"No, it's not stupid," she refutes. "Hey." She stands straight, pulling my arms for me to turn and face her. She places a hand on my chest. "It's the last time you allowed your heart to feel. It's telling you what it's longing for. Not necessarily the people, but the feeling. It's the *real Elias* underneath, begging to be *set free.* Your heart is reminding you of a time when you were happy. You *have* to set your heart free. It's time to make new loving memories in *this* world."

Make new loving memories. I place my palm over hers on my chest, gaze into her deep brown, beautiful eyes. I was under the impression that I needed to help her, but what I didn't realize was that I hid from her when her only intention was to do the same.

Make new loving memories. I've traveled with darkness over the last five years. It's my people repellent, and I'm content with it. I become close to no one so that I may walk away from anyone. My gloom was amplified by the isolation.

Make new loving memories. I've chosen the void, allowing its cold depths to comfort me. However, it was never comforting. It was protection for my heart at the price of my soul.

This woman before me shines her beaming light. And my demon, resentment, cowers before her presence. It's menaced by her forbidden ray of light. The darkness I take cover beneath can't withstand it. She eviscerates it, exposing me. I've fought her shining light, but she's refused to retract it.

However, now I realize that it's not her ray of light that my darkness cowers before—*it's her love.* To soften a cold, hardened heart is to be enveloped in warm love. *Warm love like hers.*

Make new loving memories in this world. I will, but I choose her to start the new memories with. I won't push her away any longer, even if the happiness she brings is only temporary. My heart makes the decision for me, and I cross yet another line when I lean in and kiss her.

Skye

When his lips meet mine, I accept it. Butterflies erupt in my stomach; I'm lifted onto clouds. My hand on his chest is still covered by his as he kisses me gently—tenderly—and it feels magical, soft, and inviting. I want more, but I don't act upon it. It will only go as far as he's willing. However, with this kiss, he slowly begins to open his heart.

If it begins with me, I'm okay with that because the journey to free my soul began with him.

When we part, I search his eyes for any sign of regret. There is none.

"I'm sorry," he says, ascertaining if I'm unsettled by his advance.

"Don't be," I say, softly. He removes his hand, and I drop mine to my side.

"You should get some rest," he advises.

"Okay."

I enter the cabin, close the door, and change into something comfortable before snuggling under the covers. What Elias doesn't know is that I've concealed my developing feelings for him. I would have traveled back and never divulged that I began to fall for him. But, as we cross the boundaries of friendship, the suppressed feelings surface, and I acknowledge them.

I focused on our friendship, knowing nothing could come of us, and now I'm afraid that *I want something to become of us.* Feeling like a young girl who's been kissed by her crush, I haven't come down off the high just yet. There's a smile on my face in the midst of my blush, recalling the soft touch of his lips and his mint scent. But it's only moments before the high settles down and the plight of our becoming sets in. What's to come will wound us both, and I shed a tear as the truth weighs in.

Elias

I wish she would have slapped me—slapped my weak ass back to reality.

After we parted, I searched for any sign of doubt and found none. Her soft, supple lips beckoned me for more, and it took all the temperance I had left not to pull her back to me and kiss her deeply.

My biggest fear is that she'd have let me, had I given in, but then what?

When I suggested that she get some rest because she needs it, that wasn't my sole reason. The moment she expressed that I shouldn't be sorry, I witnessed the barely visible flush tinting her caramel skin. I would have gone back in for another, and I wouldn't have stopped.

Defenseless against my desire in her presence, I know what she's doing to me—I've always known. And I took the risk of enrapture when I offered her this adventure with the conviction that my restraint was firm. However, now, even a domineering me *bends* to her will.

If only she knew the extent of the power she wields over me. But even among the purest of hearts and most compassionate of souls, she'd never take advantage. And that's why, for her, I'd *break*.

CHAPTER 51

Skye

In the five days Elias and I have been at sea since our departure from Land Kairos, we haven't shared another kiss. To my relief, there's been no awkwardness between us.

We spend most days playing a makeshift game of chess and going over my list. He suggests I start my first book based on my experience here, utilizing my journal entries for plot inspiration. But I've already thought of that. The night he tasked me with writing this list, introspectively, I discovered my passion for creativity.

If I had the choice to build a career that required me to explore the full extent of my imagination, I would undoubtedly do so. The problem was, I'd never given anything past my current career much thought. I began questioning my own internal solitude as I experienced the values of this society, but with Elias's guidance, I faced the solid reality of it all. Feeding the soul is important, and walking in your passion is how you do it; it is then you grasp your purpose.

We've dived into everything "me," and I withhold the sick feeling that rises when I think of him. His shop meant everything to him. His passion was ripped away because someone else had more than him. All his efforts were meaningless in the face of money. We live in a world where money is power, and the craving for such power has dehumanized many. Unfortunately, one of those individuals happened to be Elias's father, who chose to exploit his capabilities to cause his own son's misfortune.

"Why are you looking at me like that?" he asks.

"Nothing." I try to not ruin our cordial moment.

"Skye, what is it?" he presses.

I look out at the sea and gaze at the trees in the distance as the boat approaches the land we're to dock at next. "My parents, my father, my brother... we... they would have never..." I pause, refusing to dull the mood with my disheartening feelings. "It's nothing." I smile at him.

"I know. Your compassion is heartening, but don't pity me. I don't walk around with a chip on my shoulder. The actions others have done unto me have never been an excuse to impede my moving forward. I would have figured something out back in our world. I'm not the potato that softens in the boiling water."

I smile. His self-assurance is admirable. It makes him so much more handsome. "You're the egg that hardens."

His lips contour into a very sexy half-smile. "Damn right, girl."

And that hardened egg became damn near impenetrable.

We continue our conversation regarding my list, and I soak in the stories of his overseas travels with his family as a minor and with his old friends—*when they were his friends*. Intrigued, I am now looking forward to booking a cruise when I return. I can bet Chrissy would jump at the opportunity to travel with me. If not her, Kumar, for sure. I'm not loaded. I can't indulge in such extravagances frequently, but I've saved tremendously, and money can always be earned again. He doesn't make any comments about the last three things written, but I don't expect him to. To fall in love, become married, and have another child are affairs of the heart attainable through a mutual relationship. However, he's asked plenty about my son, Julias, admitting his admiration for the joy in my aura when I go on about him.

"So, he's a dinosaur that likes trains," Elias says. "Cool kid."

I giggle. "The best part is when he roars, and I actually play scared. He gets a kick out of it."

He grins. "He's a dinosaur, you better be scared. When he gets older, he won't be roaring at *you* anymore, so you better enjoy it."

I slap his arm. "Hey, shut your mouth, that's my baby! He always will be."

He smirks. "We won't even get into the trains."

"Elias!" He runs from me, and I chase after him. "You ass!"

There's a sparkle in his gaze when he listens to me talk about my son, and I begin to wonder if he's thought of starting a family of his own someday.

"Since arriving here, such thoughts never made the forefront of my mind," he says.

"Despite my naivety with Julias's biological father, I think you'd make a great father." I express my truthful opinion. "You've just begun opening your heart. You'll get there eventually. The sentiment of new life shouldn't be rushed. It should happen spontaneously as love grows and strengthens between two people."

"That kid's lucky to be born to an amazing mother. He'll realize that one day, just as I did," he says.

His commendation was unexpected, but it's appreciated to the highest degree. "That warms my heart. I try my best."

"That asshole never deserved a woman like you, Skye. I don't deserve your friendship as it is. I apologize for my ill-manner toward you in the beginning," he says sullenly.

"Elias, stop. I did nothing but bug you. All of what you're doing for me, I did nothing to deserve, but I..." My words are cut short when he shortens the distance between us in one stride and places a finger over my lips. His expression is serious; his energy dominating.

"You deserve everything, Skye," he utters low and deep.

My heart kicks up a notch as I gaze into his intense emeralds. A few strands of his hair fall over his forehead, and I bury the urge to rake it back. He removes his finger but doesn't move. There's something maddening happening inside me right now, and my eyes dart to his lips. The feelings I fight to suppress every day that I'm with him, brim, and I'm losing constraint.

He walks away, and I stand there at war with myself.

My mind and my heart battle. My heart screams "to hell with constraints," and my mind reckons I keep it together. *What is together?*

He rests his forearms over the rail. "We'll arrive at Land Samoa soon."

I don't respond, I *can't* respond. I'm glued to where I stand as I fight my heart's yearning for him. I rage against my physical being to be close to him; I hate my lips that crave him.

He turns around and responds to my silence with a quizzical look. "Skye, what's wrong?"

At his question, my mind wins. I take a deep breath and say, "Nothing."

I move away toward the cabin but stop when I hear Elias following me. "Look at me."

I can't turn around. I can't look at him. My constraints are holding on by a thread. "No."

"Why?"

"Elias, can I just be alone right now?"

"Did I do something? Whatever it is, I'm sorry."

Oh my god, can't he just shut up? I don't respond. I continue walking, and my heart twists with every step.

"Don't hide from me."

Asshole! That's my line. My brain is finding every reason to keep me moving forward, but my heart pleads to turn and face him. Every word that leaves his lips is a stab to my core. "You didn't do anything wrong. I just need to be alone."

"Look at me." And there's his famous line again.

I halt but refuse to turn, take a deep breath, and lift my chin. He continues forward until I can feel his presence directly behind me. If I turn around, my brain won't stand a chance, I'll melt like butter against the sun.

"Look at me," he whispers.

I turn on my heels, ready to push down my brimming emotions. It's Mission: Impossible when I'm faced with a pleading gaze.

"What happened?" he asks.

I don't answer. My heart wins.

I prop myself up on my toes, throw my arms around his neck, and crash my lips into his. He jerks, startled by my reaction, but he doesn't pull away. He gently slides his hands around my waist and pulls me closer.

Our lips lock and our tongues meet as he kisses me deeply. He places a palm to my neck, and his fingers spread at the base of my jaw. The touch of his skin ignites me. I'm in the clouds again, engulfed in his mint scent; his soft lips and the taste of his tongue send heat to my core.

Our kiss is tender, and I bind myself in this moment. Through our connecting mouths, I confess my feelings without words. The truth is, I'm falling in love with Elias, and I don't know how to stop.

Elias

She doesn't need to hide from me. I'm right there with her. My holding back was never for my sake, it was for hers.

I'll restrain if I must, or I'll let my desire for her run wild. If she's subduing in fear that I don't share her feelings, then I'll show her it's mutual. However, if it's prudence to prevent inflicting wounds with her departure, she need not worry.

I'll bear the loss of her when it transpires, but I won't allow such fear to hinder my time with her now.

For as long as she's here, I'll be whatever she needs.

When we part, I lament at the loss of her supple lips and the taste of her tongue against mine. Her eyes are glassy. "I'm sorry," she whispers.

"For what?" I ask, but it's rhetorical. She can kiss me whenever the hell she wants.

A closed smile stretches at her lips, and I run my thumb over the soft delicacy. "You think I'll ever deny these lips, woman?"

She bites down on her bottom lip as her cheeks heat. "I didn't know—"

"Well, now you know," I interrupt. I already knew that was the case.

CHAPTER 52

Skye

The most modern island in *this* world resembles a place found on twenty-first-century Earth, with brick-front homes, shops with modern glass doors, and concrete pavement. Horses with attached carriages traffic asphalt streets, cyclists ride on bike paths, and pedestrians stroll on the sidewalk.

"Well, Land Samoa certainly feels like home," I say.

"Samoa is one of the most popular lands and one of the oldest developed. Apparently, the leaders here have begun testing networking for radio broadcasting, but it's only in the research stages," Elias says. "Year after year, they discover and implement new systems and upgrades."

"Interesting. Why didn't you stay here?"

"Too many people."

I roll my eyes. "Of course."

We're walking through a quiet neighborhood heading to Lani's home—the *friend* Elias has yet to call a friend—when the incident at Kairos intrudes my brain. "Hey, you spent about a year here, right?"

"Yes," he replies.

"Do I need to be on the lookout for anyone trying to booby-trap me again?"

He chuckles. "No…"

I stop in my tracks. "That, *'no,'* wasn't confident enough for me."

He scratches his head. "I mean… I was never close to any women here, but… I've had a strange encounter or two."

"Define *strange*."

He stuffs his hands in his pocket. "One might define it as stalking."

"Seriously?" I dramatically throw my head back. "What are you? A female magnet?"

He cocks an eyebrow and stiffens his shoulders. "I don't see how. My face is ugly, *remember*?"

"Hideous," I deadpan. "Now indulge me."

He silently laughs. "Do I have to?"

"After Kairos?" My brows raise. "Absolutely."

"Skye." His tone changes. "I'm sorry about that. I didn't think Kallia would—"

"Kallia apologized for what *she* did. You don't need to," I interrupt.

"You didn't see what I saw when I found you. I never want to see that shit again. So yes, I'm apologizing because I should have followed my gut when I took notice of Kallia's hostility."

"It's still not your fault. I asked you not to come, although you insisted."

His face contorts into a look of humorous confusion. "Skye, are you arguing with me because you want me to take back my apology?"

Crossing my arms, I pout. "Yes, now take it back because I don't accept it."

He stifles back a snicker. "Fine. I take back the apology. Happy?"

Raising my chin, I straighten my posture boastfully. "Yes. Thank you."

"Aww, poor thing," I say, placing a hand on my chest. I am feeling a bit sympathetic when Elias tells me about the teenager who had a crush on him.

He laughs. "How do you find sympathy for everyone?"

"She was a baby. I know seventeen isn't technically a baby, but young and dumb is a real thing, you know. In ninth grade, I stalked this super-hot senior in the hallways. Never approached him, though. She's got cojones."

He bursts into laughter.

I smack his arm. "Don't laugh at me. See, young and dumb."

"I don't know what's funnier, that, or the fact that you said cojones instead of balls."

I chuckle. "Oh, shut up, so what happened next?"

He sharply inhales through his nose after his laugh calms. "Anyway, it was obvious she was young. Considering how innocently she approached, *and* her age, I wasn't too harsh. I told her she doesn't know me to *like* me and that she should like guys her own age."

"So, you never noticed her at the shipyard watching you?"

"Samoa is heavily populated. Spotting someone you're not looking for isn't easy. However, I kept a keen lookout of my surroundings after that."

I presume we've reached our destination when we turn down a narrow concrete path that leads to the blue wooden door of a home.

"Oh, and, by the way, I'm sorry," he says.

I give him a look of confusion. "For what?"

Knocking on the door, he gives me a mischievous grin and doesn't respond until someone begins unlocking the door. "Kairos."

When the door opens, I tuck in my bottom lip and bite down. *Ugh, I could smack that smirk off his face.*

"Hey, Elias. Long time!" a tall, dark-haired, cinnamon-skinned man greets.

They shake hands. "Lani, how have you been?" Elias replies.

"Been alright, yourself?"

"Good. Lani, this is a friend of mine, Skye," Elias introduces me.

His eyes dart to me with a pleasant smile. "Hello, Skye, nice to meet you. I take it you're here from Sandemia, too?"

"I am, I've heard a lot about you. It's good to meet you," I say.

"Skye here has never been to Samoa. I'm showing her around," Elias adds.

"You'll get an eyeful here, Ms. Skye," Lani says, and we commence a walking journey.

As the three of us stroll around the land, Lani and Elias catch up while I take in the surroundings. In a world like this one, I'm convinced this land is considered the concrete jungle. There isn't much greenery other than the trees and patches of open land near the residential neighborhoods. Elias was right about one thing: it is indeed populated. While looking at the infrastructure, I catch sight of a large amusement park in the distance. Lani and Elias are busy catching up when I tap Elias's forearm, and he turns his head at my distraction.

"I want to check that out." I point in the direction of the amusement park.

"Okay," he says, then turns back to Lani. "We're going over there."

"Yeah, you two go ahead," Lani says before he walks away. "Listen, meet at my place at six. It's a tenth, and I'm hosting."

"We'll be there," Elias assures.

Crossing the busy road, we begin walking in the direction of the amusement park. "What's a tenth?"

"Like a Friday. End of the week," he replies.

When we step onto the sidewalk, I stop and face him. "Elias, they *are* your friends."

Annoyance covers his features. "Okay, Skye, they are my friends. Happy?"

This cynical tone is not going to fly with me. "You became a part of this *'tenth,'* didn't you?"

"Yes," he says impassively.

"Then why did you imply that you just fixed ships for them, and they built your home as some indebted duty?"

"I never said that." He's terse. This isn't a conversation he wants to have, but I'm not brushing it off.

He walks past me. I catch up and stand in front of him, halting his movement. "You didn't call them friends, either."

His jaw tenses. "Damn it, Skye!"

"Don't hide from me."

His eyebrows furrow, and his eyes grow dark. He's withholding his truth again. He doesn't respond, but it finally clicks. I relax my posture and close the distance between us to place a hand on his chest. He's tense. Something is troubling him, something about those tenths became an issue for his heart. "You didn't just leave because you wanted to explore Kairos." My voice softens. He remains still and reaches for the dark veil to shield his core. "Those tenths were too close of a reminder of Friday nights at the lake. The nostalgia became unbearable." I put the pieces together. He shuts his eyes and inhales through his nose. He prefers to hold it in, reject the feelings. He loathes any reminder of people who've hurt him.

"You hated that you were missing your old friends. So, you left."

His eyelids part, and his expression grows even darker. He's resorting back to gloom, his void. "They didn't deserve my longing for them. I was repulsed by the idea that my core ever felt a need for them again."

I shake my head. "It's not them. Remember, it's your heart's way of telling you what it longs for through memories of when you felt love. These guys aren't your old friends. You may have moved on with your life, but you never let the anger go, so the tenths became painful. You have to forgive. Make new memories. It's okay."

He turns his head away, and I notice his features softening before he looks back to me with a hint of a smile formed on his lips. "You better cut it out before I kiss you."

I remove my hand and smile as my cheeks heat. I'd accept a kiss from him at any moment.

CHAPTER 53

Skye

The area is filled with laughter from children, adults, and teens. It's as crowded as any amusement park would be any place on Earth on a hot summer day.

"Elias, this is…"

"Just like our world?" he finishes.

"Yes. Oh my goodness," I express in amazement.

"The older the development, the more modern it is. Land Samoa has seventeen leaders keeping this place running," he informs.

I spot an ice cream stand and go toward the line. In front of us stands a woman and her son, who looks to be no older than five years.

"Mommy, I want *'nilla*," the little boy says.

"Okay, you'll get vanilla," she corrects him.

When we're next, Elias and I ask for a vanilla and chocolate mix. When we've been served, we thank the man before leaving the stand.

I catch sight of the little boy and his mother again and watch them for a moment.

He gobbled up his mini cone in mere minutes, making a complete mess of himself. His mother is attempting to thoroughly clean his mouth, but he won't keep still. He's edging to take off to the waterslide, barely containing his excitement.

"Mommy, can we go to the *waterswide, peeeze!*" he begs.

"Okay, Numi. Let's clean you up first." The woman brings the napkin to his hands, circling his little fingers.

"Yay!" He jumps up and down, making it so much more difficult to wipe him down. She finally gets him cleaned up, and without another word, he takes off.

"Numi wait!" she calls, running after him.

Smiling as I witness their interaction, he reminds me of my Julias—active and full of energy. When his mind is set on something, everything else is disregarded, including his safety.

My smile fades with a pang in my chest. I miss my little dinosaur so much. I long to squeeze him, hold him, and kiss his little cheeks.

"Skye?" Elias says my name, pulling me out of my daze.

"Huh?" I answer, noticeably startled.

"You'll see your son again soon. He'll be at his grandparents' home waiting for you to pick him up. Nothing's changed," Elias reminds me.

I smile again. "Yeah, you're right."

Returning to my sweet boy and my family is the easy part. Leaving Elias will be the most difficult.

Lani's wife, Liza, greets us at the door. Elias introduces us before gesturing toward the back door. We walk through their living room area, where canvas paintings of different sceneries hang on the walls, and then through their kitchen, separated from the dining room by a half wall. Past that, a few empty chairs and a wooden table filled with beverages and snacks sit on the concrete patio in the back yard.

Everyone joyously greets Elias—it's been a long time—and I'm introduced to Talia, Sebi, Armon, and Libby. I am greeted with a warm welcome from everyone except Libby, whose demeanor suggested my presence annoyed her. And I hope this isn't another woman who's in love with Elias and treats me like scum because of it.

For about an hour, they chatter in laughter and catch up.

"Elias, remember the young fangirl you had?" Lani mentions.

I watch as Elias shakes his head, clearly opposed to this being a topic of conversation.

"I just forgot to mention, she approached me almost a year ago now." Lani continues. "Saw her on Brooks with a boyfriend. She asked me to relay an apology to you when I see you again. Said, 'sorry for creeping you out.'"

"Aw. See? She was just young and dumb," I say.

He takes a sip of his beer and grins slightly.

"Or just dumb," Libby inputs with contempt.

"Come on. Don't judge, you've never been young and naive, stalking a cute guy?" I joke.

She narrows her eyes. "She was a child trying to be with a grown man."

Why the hell is she so tense? "Trying to be with him? That's dramatic. She only expressed that she liked him. She just had a crush is all. I can bet she looks back at that and is totally bummed out at her naivety," I say, relaxed.

"Well, seventeen isn't too young not to know better," she challenges.

She's got this passive aggression going on, and I wonder if she's always like this. "Still young enough to learn from it. Imagine someone in their late twenties or thirties doing that? Now that's a red flag."

Her nostrils flare. *Was it something I said?* She sinks back in her chair then looks over at Elias. Elias glances at her from the corner of his eye, expressionless, and brings the glass bottle to his lips. There's an obvious tension between them.

"So, you liking Sandemia?" Sebi gestures to Elias.

"I am," he replies.

He motions his fingers back and forth between me and Elias. "So friendship, or something more here?"

Elias does a quick flick of his nose with his index knuckle. "Nah, just friends."

Sebi grins and turns to me. "Well then, Ms. Pretty Lady, Skye. My name is Sebi Klein. I'm thirty-four and single." There's a twinkle in his eye as he attempts to flirt with me. I notice when Elias's jaw tenses. His expression hardens and twists in disgust as he stares daggers at Sebi. *Well, damn. Is that the look the girls claimed he gave Al?* I don't think Elias knows how to curtain his emotions. The man can speak without breathing a word. Does he even try to control his expressions?

"Congratulations," I say, patently sarcastic.

The guys laugh, and Sebi's ridiculous smile fades, replaced with embarrassment. Elias's features change into a satisfying smirk, and I shake my head.

I'm uncertain what sort of reaction Sebi expected from me, but to hit on me in front of everyone is tacky as hell. He played himself.

CHAPTER 54

Skye

As the sun sets in the sky, Elias and I call it an evening. We bid everyone a good night and make our way to the boat. The moment we board, Elias fires up the engine, and I head for the shower to begin my nightly routine. When I'm done, I throw on my pink pajamas and head to the kitchen to find an apple—freshly picked from the apple tree of Land Kairos. I take a bite and bask in the sweet taste.

"I'll be back, I'm going to shower," Elias says as he passes.

I nod, head to the bedroom, and find my journal to write about my experience and the setting of Land Samoa. I didn't take as many pictures as I had at the other lands. Land Samoa is fairly similar to many places in my world. I prefer to capture distinct differences.

Movement in the kitchen distracts me from my writing, so I leave the bedroom carrying the apple I've demolished to trash it— *and because I want to see a freshly-showered, damp-haired, mint-scented Elias.*

"Hey. I approach, tossing the apple in the trash. He's wearing a plain black t-shirt, a towel around his neck for his dampened hair, gray sweats, and black socks slipped in black slides. He's dressed as down and comfortable as ever, yet all I see is a handsomely carved man. *How is he always this fine?* I look like a wet mutt after washing my hair while he favors soaked perfection.

"Hey, did you like Samoa?" he asks.

"I actually did, but if I could ever live here, I'd stay in Sandemia."

He takes a bottle of water from the fridge and twists off the cap. "Sandemia just feels right, huh?"

I lean on the counter. "Can't explain it, but yeah."

He downs the entire bottle in seconds. "I can relate," he says after catching his breath.

"That woman, Libby, she was tense. Is she always like that?" I ask curiously.

He smirks. "You don't miss a beat, do you?"

"Nope." I pop the P in "nope."

He drops the bottle in the trash. "Remember my mentioning a weird encounter or two?"

"Oh dear." I catch a hint of where this is going.

He leans on the counter across from me. "She's a friend of Lani's wife. The guys don't know any of this, but she brought to my attention that she was interested in me and asked if we could spend time together outside of the tenths."

"And that was weird?"

"No. And you didn't let me finish, smart one." He reaches over and taps the tip of my nose. "I told her that I wasn't interested, but that didn't stop her from seeking out my whereabouts and popping up at the lodge every other day." He clears his throat. "Her consistent excuse was always 'she was in the area.' She'd ask to be invited in, and I declined every time. After her third or fourth visit, her showing up began rubbing me the wrong way, and I sternly told her to stop because I'm not interested in her. She snapped at me—told me I was missing out on a good thing. I didn't wanna hear all that shit, so I demanded she leave. End of story."

"Wow, you're like Sasuke." I note.

He chuckles. "Which one's your favorite?"

I suck in my lips with a grin.

His eyebrows raise. "Is Sasuke your favorite character?" I nod, and he bursts into laughter. "I bet it has nothing to do with his actual character."

"Oh, stop it. I was a girl then. Which girl didn't have the biggest crush on Sasuke?" I defend the twelve-year-old me that had every Sasuke poster. "Who was your favorite character?"

"Shikamaru. The analytical thinker."

"Shikamaru is a real one. But apparently, you're some female magnet like Sasuke," I joke. "Who do you think you are?"

"Nobody. I am nobody. I'm hideous."

I throw my head back and laugh. "Exactly. Not even all that."

Closing my eyes for a moment, I take a breath to calm my laughter. When I open them again, his dark emeralds burn through me. The blunt change in his aura catches me off guard. He studies my reaction, but I'm frozen in place. With one stride, he's so close. His mint scent fills my nostrils, and his intense energy encases me. I tilt my chin up at him. He's so quiet, his breathing still, making my pounding heart the loudest sound in the room.

My lips part. He snakes one arm around my waist and pulls me flush to him, then crashes his mouth to mine. He kisses me vigorously, far from gentle. It's possessive. And when he forces his tongue past my teeth, an unintentional moan escapes my throat. It does something to him, and he kisses me harder, ravishing me. My hands fly to his chest, and I grip his shirt in my fists. This intensity is fiercely taking hold of me. Our tongues are fighting, and I'm not winning—I can't catch a breath, he's dominating; whatever control I had has dwindled to a pulp. He tilts his head more, kissing me deeper, his tongue darting and tangling with mine. Another moan escapes my throat. *Oh my god, this man.*

My core is heated. His masculine energy envelops me, my femininity craves him, but I must contain myself. I feel the bulge behind his pants against me, and I try to ignore it, but my body deceives my mind when my leg lifts at his side. It's then he tears his mouth from mine, and I lower my leg before dropping my head to his solid sternum. My chest heaves while I catch my breath.

With a finger, he lifts my chin, and I gaze into his hooded eyes. "Now, what was that about an ugly face?"

His low, deep tone is velvety and smooth, traveling down my middle. I'm yearning for more. He removes his arm from around my waist, and I release his shirt. He walks away, and I waste no time heading for the bathroom—because right now, *I'm a mess.*

Elias

She started it.

CHAPTER 55

Skye

I'm having a hard time being normal. Still on a high from the kiss last night, I start coffee, but as I wait for it to brew, my mind replays what happened in this very spot just hours ago. I drift into a daze, and my fingers graze over my lips.

His soft lips against mine, the touch of his hand on my skin, his mint scent. Him devouring me with his tongue. I was ready to climb him like a tree. He stiffens against me, and it maddens me.

"... Coffee?"

I'm startled out of my daze by Elias's voice.

I turn on my heels, perturbed. "Huh?" *Shit, I didn't even hear him approach.*

"I said, are you going to drink coffee?" he asks.

Looking down at the coffee pot, I hadn't even realized it had finished brewing. "Oh, um... yes, sorry." *Get it together, Skye.*

I pour myself a cup and move onto the deck. I lean against the rail and gaze into the morning sky.

"We'll arrive back in Sandemia in a few more days." He stands in front of the cockpit. "Ever been rock climbing?"

"I haven't." I turn around to face him, leaning my back against the rails.

"There was an artificial one built in Sandemia not long ago. How about we take a day and check it out?" He offers.

"Yeah. Don't see why not. Sounds fun."

How is he so normal? It's like nothing happened for him, yet here I am, twelve hours later, still unsettled, trying to keep my feelings intact.

He stalks toward me, and I no longer have control over my body's reaction within close proximity of him.

No, no, no, no.

I'm already a ball of mush. Spare me today, please.

Or don't spare me, whatever.

See, I'm losing it.

He stops directly in front of me, and my heart immediately kicks up a notch. "Hey, you okay?" he asks, a look of concern in his expression.

No, I'm not okay! How are you okay? I tuck in my lips. "Mhm" is all I manage.

Eyes searching mine, his eyebrows draw together in a slight frown—his usual—before his gaze drops to my lips.

"Okay," is all he says before returning to the cockpit.

I turn back toward the sea and release the breath I was holding.

Get it together, Skye.

Elias

The hot cup of coffee in her hand wins.

CHAPTER 56

Skye

After a few hours, I finally came down off the high from our intense lip lock. It has been nine days, and Elias's affection toward me has grown—just as mine has for him. He smiles often now, and it's enough to warm my heart.

With every press of his lips to mine, I melt. Cuddles in the cockpit and random kisses to my forehead, I feel just how much he cares for me. We've talked, laughed, and shared ridiculous stories of past times in our lives. Most nights, I've fallen asleep in his arms in the main cockpit, but when the waves pick up and become rough, I cowardly make my way to the bedroom and snuggle in the sheets.

For the last thirty days, Elias and I have grown much closer. I had mentioned that when I return to our world, I plan to take a short cruise just to compare it to ours. He didn't respond. His lips became a straight line before he switched the subject.

And that's when I realized he's ignoring it.

He'd rather ignore my departure, but we must consider it. Every time I descend from the clouds, the reminder of my leaving dispirits me. The low hurts just as much as the high is bliss. I fall for him more and more with each passing day, and the higher we go, the harder we'll fall when the hourglass time reaches its end. So it has to end here.

We docked at Haven Docks near my residence. He planned to drop me off first before sailing around to dock at his home.

"So, did you enjoy our travels?" Elias asks.

I remove a bottle of water from the fridge and express my excitement. "Oh, I did. I can't believe we sailed for an entire thirty days! It was truly invigorating. Such an adventure. I've got so many ideas for a book..." I stop myself, noticing I'm on the road to rambling.

I turn in Elias's direction, and my heart warms at the deep affection contoured in his features. I sigh and smile as gratitude washes over me. "Thank you, Elias, so much. These last thirty days at sea, exploring different lands, have been liberating for me. Thank you so much for everything." I say. My words are infused with meaning.

He approaches me and brings my hands into his. "You don't have to thank me, Skye. I wanted to do it."

His admission resurfaces Kallia's words to me. *"Elias isn't the kind of man you can annoy to do anything. He's doing it because he wants to."* She really did pay close attention to him. *She knows him.*

I smile. "Not just for the trip. For teaching me all that you know. All that I needed to know. For helping me understand this society. For opening up to me, for becoming my friend." Tears well in my eyes. I pause before continuing. "For helping me discover my caged soul." My voice begins to quaver as a world of emotions evoke tears. "I have so much to thank you for, Elias."

His brows pull together as he recognizes what's happening. "Skye, what is this?"

The tears fall in abundance. We're not a couple, yet this feels like a breakup. I remove my hands from his and step backward, creating distance between us before turning away. I can't face him. "I don't want to spend any more time with you while I'm here." I barely get the words out, but as they leave my lips, the weight of the words crush me.

He closes the gap between us. "Skye, it doesn't have to be like that."

"Yes, Elias. It does."

"Look at me." *No, don't say that.*

Turning around, I gaze into pleading emeralds. The sight guts me. My heart begs me not to end our companionship, *not yet.* However, I have to do what's best for both of us.

"You don't have to do this, Skye."

"Yes, I do. *We* do."

I inhale deeply through my nose, exhale through my mouth. It's the best chance I have to keep my emotions intact. I storm out of the kitchen and into the living room. "Please go, Elias," I demand, my voice finally a bit steadier. "Don't make this any harder."

"Tell me why," he demands, his expression unreadable as he slowly walks toward me.

"What?" I whisper-shout, squinting in confusion. "It's what's best. You know it's what's best."

"Best for who?"

"Elias, please stop asking questions you already know the answers to."

"Tell me. He projects the bass in his voice. He's merely inches from me now.

"Elias, please stop. This is already so hard." I'm crumbling all over again; it's becoming unbearable. I'm fighting against my core to the best of my ability, and he isn't making it any easier.

"What's so hard?" He continues with the questions.

He's level, while I'm an emotional mess. What is he trying to accomplish here? I don't understand. I take a step back, and my bottom hits the back of the couch. "You know that I'm leaving!" I shout, losing control.

"We both know that. Now tell me why I shouldn't return." His frown deepens. *Is he serious right now?*

"Because it's what's best!"

"Best for who?!" He raises his voice.

"For both of us!" I yell, my voice full of pain as tears stream down my face.

"Tell me why!"

I shudder. I can't take this. "Because we're getting closer. Elias, please," I croak.

In one stride, he's in my bubble. "Not good enough, Skye."

"What better reason—"

"Tell me why!" he interjects. His voice pierces through me; my tears won't stop. My feelings brim, threatening to spill over. "Spit it out, Skye!"

From the depths of my heart, my truth leaks. "Because I'm falling in..." And before I can finish spilling my words, he eats them when he crashes his mouth to mine. He wraps his arms around my torso while I wrap my own around his neck. He kisses me deep and tender. He's pleading—begging me not to do this. Another tear falls from my eye because I know what he's asking for, but I can't. It already hurts. Imagine if we grow any closer?

Go love, Elias. You know how. You have friends. You've released your shackles. Now forget about me and go love.

Our lips slowly part. "I'm falling in love with you too," he says.

I gaze into his eyes and realize this was his goal, for me to admit my true feelings and to stop hiding from him.

"If parting now is what you believe is best, I will do as such for you. But don't assume it's what's best for me. I will only do what's best for you." His voice is low and filled with emotion. He curls his fingers under my jaw, then runs his thumb across my lips. "I'd rather spend every waking day with you and live with the memories forever." He presses a kiss to my forehead before withdrawing his hand. I'm faced with his retreating back as he proceeds to the door.

I lock the door behind him, lean back on it, plummet to the

floor, and I weep. My broken heart cries. It cries for him, for me, and for the love we have to let go.

CHAPTER 57

Skye

I spend the next two days indoors, writing in my journal and reading. I moved one of the small loveseats by the living room window to gaze out on the neighborhood.

One set of the coupled neighbors is outside with their young children again, and I clear my mind to focus on them. The small children, in their joy and laughter, remind me of my little dinosaur, Julias, whom I miss so much.

Residing in a quiet home for days at a time is unusual for me. I began to enjoy it, but all I've ever needed was temporary solitude, which I get when Julias spends a few days with his grandparents. To be in silence for long periods of time feels strange. I never want to be apart permanently. My heart could never bear it. It's the one aspect of my life that's nonnegotiable.

As I watch the little boy across the road bounce the ball with his miniature hands, I smile as the comfort of holding my Juji again washes over me. I'll shower him in kisses upon my return until he does his famous roar to scare me away.

My eyes drift to the couple outside watching their children, and I flip my journal to the page where I'd written my list to reread the last three items:

Fall in love

Get married
Have another baby
Elias appears in my mind. *Don't go there, Skye.*

We will never know if we could have made it that far. A question I've never asked before intrudes my thoughts.

What if I had met Elias five years sooner? Would he have chosen to remain here? Would he have ended up here at all? I was with Jason then, but could he have found a friend in me? Would that friendship have turned into intimacy eventually? And could he have helped me the same?

I pull myself out of my thoughts. There's no sense dwelling on impossibility. I decide to busy myself with something else and shuffle through the cabinets. I take out ingredients to make cupcakes. I suddenly miss Mauria. If she knew I had returned, she'd have shown up here by now.

"Skye! You're back!" Mauria joyously greets me with a huge grin.

"Surprise!" I smile, holding up the cupcakes.

"Ooh, mini-cakes, yum!"

So that's what they're called here. Noted.

She invites me inside. I greet Sam before following her to the dining area.

"So," she says after taking a bite out of one of the *mini-cakes*, "tell me all about the trip."

I take a breath. "Where do I even start? We visited Samoa, Arga, Northellei, Charri, and stopped at Kairos."

"Did you see why every other land is better than Kairos?" She shrugs. "Well, you're here, so obviously you know, but I mean, living that way is ridiculous."

"Well, it's not ridiculous. It's a choice." I've grown defensive of Land Kairos since learning their culture, and I consider their ideologies beautiful.

"Maybe, but why live like that if you don't have to? They make their own lives a struggle. And they're so out of touch with society. I think it's a good decision you made to venture out and live somewhere else. Look how sheltered you were."

This world may be different from my own, perhaps even better. However, Elias was right. It isn't perfect. Conflict and judgment of some form exist. Unless we all live as primitively as those of Land Kairos—and maybe even then—we'd still find some way to refuse equality. If everyone possessed the same things, we'd find another reason to consider someone beneath or above us.

Listening to Mauria, it's clear that she considers those of Land Kairos to be less than, yet she has no knowledge of who they are as a people. Is that their fault or her own? Why are they deemed the lesser of the masses because of their difference in opinion of how life should be lived?

"Have you ever gotten to know anyone from Kairos, Mauria? Well, besides me?" I ask.

"How can anyone? They're not welcoming."

"Maybe because they know everyone looks down on them. People that visit impose changes to their way of living without understanding their choice to live this way. You, just as the majority, claim they need to upgrade, but they don't consider modern living an upgrade. It's quite the opposite, and for that, you look down on them? How do you think that makes them feel? They are people, just like you and I."

"Others have only tried to help, Skye."

"They aren't lacking."

"They can live better. Comfortably."

"Better?" I raise my eyebrows. "That's where you're wrong, Mauria. See, you judge them but lack knowledge of their culture. 'Better' for them is being a part of the land. Their level of compassion goes beyond people and extends to nature itself. They see no good in eviscerating the land to build unnecessary structures."

She gives me a look of apology. "I'm sorry, Skye. I didn't know that, and I didn't mean to speak ill of your land."

I shake my head. "I'm not offended. Just thought I'd offer a different perspective."

She nods, grabbing another mini cake. "So, you and Elias were out at sea for what? Thirty or so days? I want all the details, now."

My cheeks heat at the recollection of my and Elias's time together. Rubbing my lips together, I clear my throat, suppressing my inner mush.

"Oh, look at you!" She raises her eyebrows, awaiting my spilling of the tea. "So did you guys—?"

"Oh, no, none of that." I deny the implication.

Her features go dumbfounded. "Tell me you guys at least kissed."

My tacit response is her answer, and her expression brightens. "So are you together now? Come on, tell me more!"

I snap out of the blush. "No, we're not getting together," I huff out as the reminder of reality sets in.

"And why not?" She frowns.

I grab a mini cake. The depressing reasoning calls for sugar. "Mauria, it's complicated."

She leans back in her chair and narrows her eyes. "You're hiding something. More than just a kiss happened. It's written all over your face."

Damn, she's good.

I roll my eyes. "I told him I didn't want to see him again."

"Um, why?"

"Complicated."

She leans forward and examines me. "Wait a minute."

I dip my chin. "What? Stop looking at me like that."

"You're in love with him!" she exclaims, and I nearly choke on my cake.

Are my feelings written on my head or something? How the

hell could she know that? Dropping back in her chair, she crosses her arms, waiting for me to deny it. If I do, she's sure it will be a bunch of baloney.

I open my mouth to do just that, but then shut it and drop my head. "Maybe," I say drearily. What does it matter if I deny it or not?

"Aw, Skye, well, what's the problem? Why did you tell him you didn't want to see him anymore?" she asks sympathetically.

"I don't want the feelings I have to grow any stronger."

"Wait. Does he not feel the same way you do?"

Her question lights a bulb—the perfect excuse for her to leave it alone. I nod.

She frowns. "Oh, what a jerk! What guy takes a girl out to sea for *that* long, kisses her, and doesn't expect her to fall for him? Let's go out on the town. No more talks of El-jerk."

Though I giggle at the nickname, I don't like that he's made out to be the bad guy. Still, no more talking about Elias is exactly what I need.

Elias

It's been five long days since Skye expressed she didn't want us seeing each other any longer, and I've fought every urge to show up at her place and tell her it's futile. But I'll take the blow if it means she'll suffer less if we part sooner.

There's something I'd like to give her before she departs. I've gathered supplies to work on the small project as a farewell gift when the time draws near. I find myself working out extensively and busying myself with menial work at the shipyard to keep my mind occupied. Any moment of free time and my brain does nothing but run to thoughts of her.

Truth is, I stopped caring about her leaving as long as I'd be able to spend every day with her until then. I'm well aware the knife through my core will hurt like a son of a bitch, but for her, I'm willing to bear it. Nevertheless, it isn't fair to ask her to bear the same wounds.

Make new loving memories. They've already begun with her. She's still here, yet farther away than ever before. I miss her like fucking hell.

I'm carving wood into two small cylinders when my doorbell rings. I'm not expecting anyone, but suddenly I'm hoping it's Skye.

I cover my project with a sheet and head for the door. Opening it, I'm met with a frowning Mauria with crossed arms. She's staring bullets at me.

"Mauria?"

"I don't like you." She's clearly displeased with me.

I raise my eyebrows in utter confusion. "Don't *like* me?"

"How could you do that to her?" she snaps.

I'm still confused, but I'm certain she's speaking of Skye. I sigh. "Mauria, what did Skye tell you?"

"None of your beeswax!"

Great.

"Okay, but I'd like to know what I did to her," I reason.

"You think you can just give her girlfriend treatment and think she won't fall for you?"

"Girlfriend treatment?"

"You kissed her! Took her around the world! And probably even more, but she won't say."

Okay, so she knows that much. "Mauria, Skye doesn't want to see me anymore."

"Of course not! She falls for you and thinks it's mutual, and it's not. I wouldn't want to see you again either! Why would you play with her feelings?"

So that's what Skye told her. But I'm sure she didn't expect Mauria to show up at my door. She just needed an excuse for Mauria not to ask any more questions. *Skye knows exactly how I feel.*

I take a breath. "Mauria, that's not it."

"Then what is it?" she demands.

"You really care about Skye, don't you?"

She dips her chin as if my question was preposterous. "Of course. She's my friend."

I don't think Skye realizes that she's making an impact on Mauria. She's concerned about me and her, but has she given her and Mauria's relationship thought? Mauria is growing to love her, and by the looks of it, Skye has grown fond of her.

"I introduce her to other really nice guys that are clearly interested in her, and she won't even give them the time. I know it's because she's still hung up on you."

Irritation pricks, and I frown. The fuck she mean she's been introducing Skye to other guys? I don't need to hear that shit.

At my change of expression, Mauria tilts her head. "Wait, you do feel the same as her."

"Look, it's complicated. It's best if you leave it alone."

She holds up her index finger. "Well, I don't want to see my friend sad. So uncomplicate it!" She begins to walk away, then stops and turns back. "And have a complicated day while you figure out how to uncomplicate it!"

If only she knew it's not that simple.

CHAPTER 58

Skye

"Yeah, so Elias is definitely crazy about you," Mauria says.

The casual mention as she steers the boat catches me off guard, and I nearly choke on my drink.

"I tell him that I'm introducing you to other guys, and he gives me the stare of death."

"Mauria, what?" I turn to her, appalled. She continues looking ahead, relaxed and unaffected by my reaction.

"I confronted him yesterday," she says, and finally glances at me. "Listen, if he told you he's not into you, he lied." She refocuses ahead, veering the boat left toward Land Zendovou's shore. Her expression hints at something akin to sympathy, but not for me.

"Mauria, what did Elias say?"

"It's complicated."

There's something she isn't telling me. She's terse and suddenly distant. I cross my arms and tilt my hips. "Spit it out."

Huffing out a breath, she faces me. "I don't know what's wrong with you two, but since the day we met Elias, the man has been tough. I've never met someone I thought was incapable of feeling. But yesterday, I saw something different. He's sad.

Broken. It's written all over his face." She turns forward. "At least now I know he's human."

I look out ahead. Just a few days ago, I was exploring these waters and soaking up everything that was Elias. My heart suffers and my mind no longer generates thoughts opposing us. Instead, I find myself fighting them both with my physical being. They've formed an alliance, and the only sword I wield is my *will*.

My will to do what's right for us.

My will to protect both our minds and hearts, as stubborn as they are. But I'm afraid the blade is wearing. I'm going through the motions with each passing day until time runs out. *Just a little while longer.* As the sand in the hourglass falls, the days are becoming anything but easier. *I miss him so much.*

I go into the front cockpit and gaze upon the sky above. It's clear; the waters are calm. But there's an impending storm tonight —similar to the storm, two people not of this world are fighting in their souls. And though it's a coincidence, I tell myself this one's for *us*.

We arrive at the spa by ten a.m. The storm isn't until tonight, but apparently rain showers could keep the town indoors for days.

After three hours of being pampered into utter bliss from massages, waxing, manis and pedis, we spend an hour in a steaming tub, soaking into relaxation as the water bubbles against our skin. *I have to find something like this back home.*

The subtle breeze in the air is refreshing after an hour in a steamy tub. The skies are still clear, and the day is bright. Mauria and I aren't quite ready to leave, so we browse shops, take pictures, and have lunch.

"Sam would have suggested I don't come out today, so I didn't tell him we were coming to Zendovou." Mauria squirts ketchup on her potato fries. "It unsettles me when he gives me the worried eye."

After inserting a fork full of lettuce in my mouth, I cover it with my hand to speak. "Why? Because of the storm?"

"Yes, that isn't until nightfall. It's because the boat isn't an open sea vessel. But if the waters are calm, it's fine." She bites down on two fries.

Searching the salad for more shrimp, I pout when I realize I ate them all. "He has reason to worry, Mauria."

She sighs. "I know, but I'm aware of sailing conditions. I've done this plenty of times." I shake my head. Mauria the risk-taker. "It's after five, we should probably head back."

"Aye, aye, captain." I rise from my seat and salute, then throw what's left of my salad away.

She squints in confusion. "What?"

I roll my eyes. "Nothing. Let's go."

"Mauria, when did you say the storm was supposed to touch down?" I notice the dimmed sky and shifting wind.

"Not in Sandemia until nightfall. I'm surprised by the sudden change, but it's coming in from the south," she informs me. Sandemia is north; the knowledge that we're sailing away from it brings me relief.

We're approaching the end of the pavement where the woods begin when I hear a soft cry of "Mama" in the distance. I glance in that direction and catch sight of a young girl, no older than six or seven years old, with tears in her eyes.

I nudge Mauria with my elbow. "Look. I think that child is lost."

Mauria follows my gaze. "Aww, poor girl. Her parents can't be far."

"Hey, are you lost?" I ask the child when we approach. She nods. I ask, "Where was the last place you saw your parents?"

She points to a nearby establishment. I take her small hand into mine, and we proceed to the eatery.

"What's your name, sweetie?" I ask.

She sniffles. "Shali."

"Well, Shali, my name is Skye." She looks up at me, and I smile. Her saddened features relax as her lips curve upward into a small smile. "Anytime you get lost, wait at the last place you were with your parents. They'll find you."

She nods. I'm filled with warmth remembering when the roles were reversed, and I repeated the words from a very sweet woman who was kind enough to wait with me until my mother found me.

Miss Elizabeth, Elias's mother. The recollection sparks gratitude that I am able to help another child by virtue of the way she helped me.

After no more than fifteen minutes of waiting, a woman spots us and jets in our direction shouting, "Shali!" It's clear it's the little girl's mother because she jumps for joy, running to her.

"Hi, I'm Skye, and this is Mauria," I introduce. "She was near the fountains looking for you."

"Thank you so much!" the woman expresses. "My name is Gradeshelle."

I offer her a warm welcome. "Stay close to your mom, Shali," I say before waving goodbye to them.

The moment I turn around, I'm faced with a Mauria I've never seen before. Something unsettling covers her features. "Skye, we have to go," she urges.

"Yeah, let's go. Hey, is everything okay?" I ask, concerned.

We pick up the pace as we walk toward the docks. "I think the storm is moving in sooner than expected. We have to head back to Sandemia," she warns. "We can still move ahead of it."

I nod. We're no longer power walking. We're jogging to the shoreline.

CHAPTER 59

Skye

Thick clouds in gray skies leak drizzling rain.

The calm sea at our arrival is now troubled at our departure. It doesn't appear detrimental, but I recall Mauria mentioned the vessel we're using is only safe for steady waters—which now worries me.

"Are we still okay to sail back?" I question and reluctantly board.

"Yes, but we have to go now," she urges, sensing my hesitance.

Apprehension weaves its way in at Mauria's harrowing. "Mauria, why don't we just stay here until the storm passes?"

"We'll be stuck here for days, no way!" Well, I guess we're on our way then.

Light drizzle has increased to heavy rain, and the current rocks the boat far more than I'm comfortable with. The sea that didn't seem so intimidating at departure is suddenly disturbing. And as trepidation creeps in, I wage war against it to remain composed.

"How far are we?!" I shout the question. The use of inside voices is impossible—the sound of the ocean and the kick of the wind demand to be heard.

"Forty minutes!" she replies. "The storm is moving in fast, but we'll make it!" Her optimism persists, but the perturbation in her voice speaks louder. I have no choice but to trust her—I don't know the slightest thing about sailing.

I constantly glance between my watch and Mauria's tight grip on the steer. It has been twenty minutes, and as time passes, the weather worsens. The pouring rain becomes a flood, and the massive winds paired with the raging ocean violently jerk the boat.

I don't know what the hell Mauria is doing, but she rides every wave and remains collected. I refuse to gaze toward the sea. Anxiety bares its fangs at me, and I'm holding on by a thread. I have to trust that Mauria will get us back. If I dare peek at the possible danger, I'm sure to lose all remnants of control.

I don't know how much time has passed. My eyes are glued to Mauria's hands. The vessel jerks harder, the roaring sea demands we leave, or she'll capture us. Her affiliates—wind and rain—torture us, adamant to grant her wish.

The boat jolts one last time before I hear a pop, and Mauria begins to heave. *Something is wrong.*

"Mauria?!" I call, but she doesn't respond. She removes her hand from the wheel and turns her head left. I follow her line of sight to the monstrous wave headed in our direction. A shockwave of terror spreads through my entire body.

Is this the end?

Elias

The storm wasn't supposed to hit until tonight, but showers have already begun. Tempest weather keeps everyone in for a few days, so I stock up on food, supplies, and small items to occupy my time.

I hope Mauria informs Skye of the usual procedure for a storm. I rethink the worry—they're neighbors. If she needs anything, I'm comforted knowing that someone is in her corner.

The scent of stuffed salmon cooking in my oven permeates the air in my kitchen. I gaze through the glass door of my back porch, finding solace in the gray skies. Nature reflects me for once in the last six days.

The waves crash against the rocks under the hill where my home stands. The thought that this will be a big one crosses my mind. The raging sea is akin to my raging heart that hasn't beat for anyone in years—*until her.*

On a sunny day, all I see is Skye and her sunshine smile. However, today, as the sunless overcast blankets the sky, I see me —and I wonder if she sees it too.

The oven timer beeps, pulling me out of my sullen thoughts, and I welcome the distraction. Placing asparagus beside my plated delight, a pounding at my front door halts my movements.

I grit my teeth as annoyance sweeps over me. I take pleasure in being the fuck alone; I don't want to see anyone's goddamn face. The pounding grows harder. Whoever is outside is beating with all their might.

Stalking through the living room toward the entrance, I wonder who the hell is out there in all this rain and why the fuck are they about to knock my door off its hinges.

I tear my door open and find a distressed, erratically breathing Sam. Mauria's husband. He's trying to say something, but he can't get the words out. I'm under the impression he ran all the way here.

"Pl... Please tell... Tell me." He's resting his hands on his knees, attempting to catch his breath. "Please tell me you have a vessel that can go out in this storm."

"Yes, but I wouldn't recommend it," I say. If he asks to use it, my answer is no, but I'll hear him out. "What's going on?"

He finally stands rigid after controlling his breathing. "Mauria and Skye are at sea... in my shoreline boat."

When the words leave his mouth, I hear the drum of my heart pound through my ears. Everything around me stills.

Skye is where?

CHAPTER 60

Elias

"Let's go." I close my door behind me, refusing to waste even a second locking it. It's unforeseeable if Mauria has some sort of plan, but Skye is terrified. I don't need to see her to know that she's losing her shit right now.

I crank the engine to my vessel and pray to every god possible that the tide hasn't eaten up their boat. As nerve-racking worry takes hold of me, I do something I've never done before—I ask a favor, hoping the heavens hear. "Mom, keep her safe. Just until I get there," I whisper.

"Where are they?" I ask Sam as I put distance between us and the shore.

"Southwest, in the direction of Zendovou," he replies.

The waters are rough, but it's only ill-fated for a shoreline vessel. The worst of the storm has yet to reach the waters surrounding Sandemia, but the farther south, the greater the chaos.

"Sam, what's wrong with your shoreline?"

He doesn't reply immediately. Something akin to guilt radiates from him, and he drops his head. "The steering cylinder. It needs replacement," he finally replies.

Anger wells in my chest. He's got to be fucking kidding me. I

325

want to ask him how he allows Mauria to take a boat knowing the steering could lock up at any given moment. That's careless. I push it down because, just like me, he's worried sick. That's his wife. He can deal with that shit later.

The farther south we sail, the more the current picks up. The rain deluges over the sea, and the wind whips unforgivably. The tide is high, but there's no storm surge. Nonetheless, a shoreline stands little chance.

"Mauria's waving!" Sam shouts. He spots their boat on the spyglass, but they haven't shown up on radar. As we veer closer, the radar pings. Looking out, their boat doesn't appear to be being steered—indicating the cylinder did lock up on Mauria midway. We gun it in their direction. A wave heads toward us, and I dive the nose until it passes. Mauria and Skye's boat hangs on by a thread. There's no control.

"Take this rope and tie it to the rail at the helm," I instruct Sam.

He grabs the rope. "Continue steering. I'll handle the rest."

I don't argue with him. One storm surge and that shoreline's a goner.

I look out and see Mauria. She's hanging onto the rail, but I don't see Skye. Where the fuck is Skye?

"Did you see Skye?" I ask him.

"No, but we have to get closer," he urges.

No shit, Sherlock.

I grab the spyglass from his hand and tell him to take the wheel. He hesitates but does it anyway. I need to catch sight of Skye.

I look through the glass, and my stomach clenches when I find her. She's on the floor in the cockpit, her face buried in her knees, her fingers intertwined over her head. She's in shock. *Shit.*

I take back the wheel and sail in as close as I can. Their boat isn't being controlled, so I tread carefully. An impact is sure to leave us stranded. At a safe distance to swing the ten-foot rope, I switch to a non-recommended autopilot. It's rather dangerous to do so in stormy weather, but given the circumstances, that's no concern of mine.

Sam's plan aligns with mine—toss the rope, and when they grab hold and jump, pull as they leap. However, what worries me is Skye's current state. The way she's curled into herself indicates she's having a panic attack.

"Mauria!" Sam calls. "We can't get any closer. I'm going to throw the rope."

Mauria acknowledges him, struggling with her balance while going into the cockpit for Skye. She places a palm on Skye's shoulder and says something. I watch as Skye slowly lifts her head. Mauria points in our direction, and Skye slowly stands, using the seating as leverage.

I finally catch a glimpse of her face, and my core weighs bricks at the sight.

She's petrified.

Her unstable movements and nearly lifeless expression hint that she isn't fully aware of what's happening. Overwhelming anxiety is paralyzing her psyche.

She keeps her head down—never turning it left or right— even as she stumbles from the vicious jerking of the boat. That's when it hits me—*she can't look at the sea*. If she glances at what she's facing, she may not make it.

Without a second thought, I jet to the steer and move my vessel closer. As risky as it is, I'm going to help her.

Sam throws the rope, and Mauria grabs hold of it. She says something to Skye. Skye nods and lifts her head. She keeps her gaze on Mauria even as Mauria is no longer looking at her. She needs something to focus on—anything, but she needs help. Both their hands grip the rope, but Skye hesitates while Mauria is prepared to jump.

"Skye!" I call. At the sound of my voice, her head cuts in my direction. "Just look at me. Don't take your eyes off mine."

Fear consumes her, but she's strong. She's fighting it with the thread of sanity she has left. They step back to get a running jump. Skye's eyes never leave mine. The waves have relaxed, and I'm well aware of the impending danger. Nonetheless, my gaze never falters. We still have time.

They begin running forward when Sam yells, "Hurry! Surge!"

It distracts Skye, and her eyes dart to him. He must be looking at the oncoming surge because her head abruptly whips in that direction. Just before the leap, she lets go of the rope—and only Mauria jumps.

"Fuck! Damn it, Sam!" I roar in frustration. He's pulling Mauria up as she horrifically screams Skye's name. But Skye stands frozen in place, staring at the receding sea as the wave builds.

"Skye!" I shout. "Skye!" I shout again, as loud as I can, but she's unresponsive. I have to cut the auto before that wave hits, so I don't wait for the rope. I wait for nothing. I retreat for a run and then jump overboard.

Landing on the boat, I steady myself before stepping into Skye's view and blocking the sight before her. I place two palms at the sides of her face. "Skye, look at me," I say. "Just focus on me."

She attempts to speak, but trembling fear grips her throat. Tormenting dread eats away at her senses.

"I'm going to hold you, but we have to run before we jump," I articulate clearly, ensuring she understands. When she nods, I continue. "Bury your face, don't look at anything."

I signal to Sam to toss the rope. He does. I grab it and encircle the rope around my forearm. We step back, run forward, and when we jump, I pull her flush to me, gripping her in my free arm. She buries her face into the crook of my neck and holds on to me for dear life. I waste no time when we make it back to my boat. "Off auto, now!" I command, and Sam immediately rushes to the wheel.

Skye remains clutched to me as tight as she can, and I don't let go. Holding her as close as she needs, I press a kiss in her hair, and we remain seated on the floor while Sam sails us back to Sandemia.

CHAPTER 61

Skye

Where am I?

I wonder as my vision clears. My head rests on a fluffy pillow encased in a silky red textile. I'm buried under a soft, bulky comforter. My eyes are open, but I haven't moved. I'm awake, yet still exhausted.

Sitting up in bed, I take in my surroundings. The room is large, but it's not mine, and it's filled with espresso furniture I've never seen before. To my left is a small open area—*a sunroom?* The sky is gray, and rapid droplets on the window are the only sounds that fill the space. A half-opened door leads to a bathroom.

Did I wake up in another world again?

Squinting, I try to recall my last memory. A sudden flash of waves appears in my mind, and I wince when a sharp pain accompanies it. I rub my temple to soothe the nerves.

I look down at my clothes. I'm wearing a white shirt that's larger than my size and black baggy shorts. Gazing around the room again, hoping to find some familiarity, I come up blank.

What happened?

A beige lamp sits atop a nightstand beside me. I open the first drawer, revealing a small black wooden box. Inside are a red wallet, a phone, and a ring box.

A phone?

Apprehension slowly rises at the thought that I've possibly returned to my world, but even there, this place is unknown to me. I open the wallet. Through the clear plastic is a Georgia driver's license. Taking a closer look, I realize it's Elias's.

This is Elias's bedroom.

But why am I here?

These must be the items he arrived with five years ago. Closing the wallet, I pick up the ring box. The large diamond rimmed with white gold, meant for proposing to his ex, glares at me in all its beauty. I feel a discomfort in my stomach. Why am I suddenly unsettled, as if I'm unaware of the history? I suppose gazing upon the elegant piece emphasizes the reality that he loved another woman so much that he wanted to marry her. Am I jealous? *Don't be ridiculous, Skye.*

I close the box and place it back inside the nightstand. The question of how I got to Elias's room is at the forefront of my mind. I hang my legs off the side of the bed and slowly stand. I go into the bathroom. Neatly folded on the counter are clothes that *I know* are mine with a toothbrush and washcloth.

I pick up the toothbrush, but when I touch my clothing, my hand flies to my temple, and the toothbrush hits the ground. A piercing sting pains my head, and a flash of raging seas tramples my brain.

What the hell is that? A memory? A dream?

I brush my teeth and splash cold water on my face to wash the drowsiness away. Surveying myself in the mirror for a moment, my hair is in a messy bun—but not the cute kind. My spiral curls are dry and frizzy, so I take it down. My hair falls to my hips, and the weight of my lengthy tresses limpens the frizz. I'm still not satisfied with its appearance.

I bring the collar of the white shirt to my nose, closing my eyes as Elias's mint scent fills my nostrils. As I bask in his scent, the recollection of his touch follows suit, and the taste of his soft lips against mine sends me to the clouds, just for a moment, until the sudden urge to empty my bladder pulls me from my thoughts. It's then I realize I'm not wearing any panties. *What the hell?*

I search my clothing and find them folded in my jean shorts. I sniff my own clothes and realize they've been freshly washed. *Did I wash them?* Then the thought of Elias washing them—*washing—seeing—touching my panties*—comes to mind. I'm not embarrassed, I'm just... I lift and spread them to see if they're at least one of my cute pairs. Well, they're pink. *Cute enough.*

I put them on and then pull his shorts back over them. Given the weather, I'm certain I won't be going anywhere soon. I exit the bedroom, and, nearing the stairs, I hear Mauria's and Sam's voices.

Why are they here? I descend the stairs. Their voices echo from the kitchen, so I go in that direction. When I come into view, all eyes shoot toward me. Deafening silence follows. I don't speak, but their reaction unnerves me.

Elias makes his way toward me, then pauses. I watch as his eyes travel down my entire body before he continues forward. It makes me self-conscious. I glance down at the clothes I'm wearing —*his clothes*—and I suddenly want out of them this instant.

"I... I'm sorry. I'll go change," I say, gutted, scurrying for the stairs. I'm so stupid. He put my clothes out so I could change, not waltz around in his like a girlfriend.

Before I can take another step, he's grabbed hold of my arm. "Skye, stop," he utters. I turn around and tilt my head to look up at him. "You think I care about you wearing my clothes?"

I search his eyes. There's not a care in the world for my attire, but there's deep concern in his irises that worries me. "I wasn't sure. It was just your pause... I mean... I really don't know." I stumble over my words, struggling with my thoughts.

"I just want you to be comfortable." He clears his throat. "But I do like you in mine."

A small smile plays on my lips. "They are comfortable."

"Are you okay?" he asks, concerned.

"Um, I'm not exactly sure." I squint, recalling that I can't remember the last twenty-four hours. "What happened?"

His features go blank. "Come on, there's coffee." He gestures toward the kitchen.

Mauria throws her arms around me. "Oh, Skye, I'm so sorry," she says, melancholy.

I hug her back, but I don't have a clue what she's apologizing for. She releases me, and my brows knit in confusion. "What are you talking about?"

Her expression drops, dumbfounded. "Wait, you don't remember?"

Bewildered, I shake my head.

"Okay, seriously, I need your superpower."

Elias comes around the island counter with a cup of coffee in hand. I take it, thank him, and then sit in one of the barstool-height chairs. "What superpower?"

Her expression implies it's obvious. "Um, hello? Your ability to forget traumatic experiences."

Something traumatic happened?

"The memory will come back. It's from extreme shock," Sam adds.

Shock?

"What about the boat?" Mauria openly asks. "Do you think it's still out there?"

Elias leans his back on the sink with his arms folded. "No telling."

"Yeah, if the current didn't rip it to shreds," Sam adds. "Good thing we made it back before the surge."

A shot of pain stings in my head. I wince, dropping my cup of coffee.

"Hurry! Surge!" Is that a tidal wave?

Another flash of treacherous waves enters my thoughts. I shut my eyes.

"Hey, Skye." I hear Elias's voice as if he's right next to me.

"Hey, look at me." I open my eyes. He's standing in front of me. *When did he round the counter?* "Are you okay? What happened?" He places a hand on my shoulder.

My eyes dart to the counter. "Oh my goodness, I'm sorry."

I regard the spill, but Mauria already has a cloth in hand, and Elias pays the splattered coffee no attention. His gaze lowers, and I watch his features contort into a frown. I follow his gaze to my trembling hand. I didn't even realize. He takes my hand in his and inspects it.

"Um." I squint as I recall the flashing scenes. "Sam yelled something about a surge. And then there was... a tidal wave?"

"Whoa, it wasn't that big. We weren't in a tsunami, girl," Mauria implies like I'm exaggerating.

"No, but that's what it looked like to her," Elias says broodingly, paying her a dark glance.

Mauria stiffens and storms out of the kitchen, charging up the stairs.

"She feels bad enough. Don't make her feel any worse," Sam defends his wife.

"I don't mean to offend her, but what happened shouldn't be taken lightly," Elias retorts.

Sam frowns and narrows his eyes at Elias. I'm flustered by what I may be in the middle of right now.

"You know, she was out there too. You don't have to be so damn insensitive," Sam argues aggressively.

Elias's nostrils flare, his jaw tensing. "Insensitive?" He glares at Sam. "And mocking post-traumatic stress isn't?"

Okay, whoa. Post-traumatic stress?

"She's not mocking, she's coping. This is how she does it."

"Yeah, well, too soon."

"You know." Sam crosses his arms. "You seem to *only* care about Skye, and we sympathize with her. But it was traumatizing for Mauria as well. I'm not asking you to be there for my wife. That's my job." Sam's voice begins to raise in anger. "But have some consideration for her feelings in all this."

I see the sudden change in Elias when his anger spikes, but he takes a deep breath and pushes down what he can. He releases my hand and faces Sam's direction, pinching the bridge of his nose with a sharp sniff. "Sam, one glimpse of Skye and you would have noticed her distressed state. I was next to you trying to prevent a seizure, and you screamed about a damn surge!" Elias snaps. I notice the pulsing in his clenched jaw. "Look." He lowers his tone. "I didn't go playing any blame game, but when you witnessed Mauria through the glass, you didn't even ensure Skye was with her. Your main priority, your distinct focus, was Mauria, Skye be damned."

Well damn.

I want to say something, but I don't know what. Whatever happened, was Elias the reason I made it out of the situation we were in? It sounds as though, no matter the fault, it was traumatic for all. And in that consideration, Elias pushed his personal disapproval aside. However, Sam's retorts awoke the sleeping dogs he chose to let lie.

Sam quirks his lips to speak, but Mauria does first. "He's right, babe," she says, defeated. *When did she get back down here?* "You've been telling me to stop taking the shoreline, and I haven't listened—"

"Mauria, don't—" Sam interrupts, but Mauria cuts in again.

"And yes, Skye had been hunched over on the floor of the cockpit since the first wave. She was in shock before you guys arrived."

I was? God, I'm such a wuss. Everyone else springs into whatever action necessary, and I become the baggage. *How about everyone just blame me? Wimpy ass Skye.*

"I... I didn't notice," Sam admits drearily.

"I saw what you were doing, Elias. To distract her. It was working," Mauria recalls. She comes further into the kitchen and stands next to Sam.

"I wasn't paying attention. I only focused on what you needed—" Sam says.

"Which was to the detriment of the situation," Mauria interrupts, "because I move with urgency under pressure, I know." She nods, a small smile forming on her lips. She gazes at her husband with love and sincerity. The sight makes me mushy. I suddenly want to experience that level of love and intimacy, the one I've treated as a disease since my last relationship.

He's in front of you. I hate my brain.

"Look, Elias," Sam begins. "I'm sorry."

"Don't apologize. We did what we had to do. It all worked out in the end," Elias replies.

Sam nods, and Mauria indicates that she wants some rest. She goes to the stairs, and Sam follows suit, but not before turning back and expressing his gratitude to Elias. "Hey, man. Thank you, really."

Elias nods and Sam continues following Mauria.

"Sooo, we were stranded at sea, or something?" I ask.

Elias smirks. "Or something."

I shake my head. "I get stranded at sea, something you only see in a movie, and I forget about it? How does one forget the cool stuff?"

He chuckles at my juvenile disappointment, and the accompanying grin warms my heart.

CHAPTER 62

Elias

The rain should subside by morning, and the guests occupying the only other furnished bedroom apart from mine shall be on their way. Skye, however, can stay as long as she pleases.

The other two rooms are empty because I don't get visitors. And if I did, it's no one who would be spending the night. That room is furnished because I grew tired of staring at three empty rooms. Skye is the first in five years to spend a night in a living space I occupy. She's been here less than one hundred days, made friends, and now I'm hosting sleepovers. How does that work?

If I wasn't so damn in love with the woman, I'd have docked them all at Haven Downs and made my way home, storm or not.

Last night, when we made it back to shore, Skye still had no sense of awareness. She clung to me as if we were still out at sea. When I asked if she wanted to shower, she couldn't reply, only staring at me with a blank expression. It was when I expressed that I'd stay right outside the door until she finished that she made her way to the bathroom, showered, and helped herself to her needs. Nonetheless, she was checked out. It was instinctive or muscle memory. She remained in a state of perturbation and wouldn't speak, gesture, or give utterance to a single thing.

I'm uneducated on matters of the human brain processing extreme stress, but my theory is that her conscious mind shut down to preserve her sanity. When I helped her get into bed and tucked her under the covers, before I could walk away, she grabbed my arm. She didn't speak a word, and fear overtook her expression again. In her state of dismay, she became dependent on my presence as an indication that she was indeed safe. I was okay with that, but I'm certain I broke a record—somewhere—of the fastest shower known to man after I placed a hand on her head and whispered, "I'll be right back."

I reentered the bedroom to see a panicking Skye sitting up, curled in herself, rocking back and forth. I rushed to her side and cradled her in my arms. "Hey," I whispered, "look at me." Her breathing slowed as her focus shifted to me. "You're safe." After that, she laid curled in my arms until she drifted to sleep.

Now Skye is no longer in shock, and she occupies my room. I'm in my basement working out until my muscles burn because I don't know what the hell to do with myself. I have garbage willpower in her presence, and now she's in my bed, safe, sound, and very well aware.

I glance at my finished project—my parting gift to her—and shift to the second one I had begun—contemplating, unsure if she'd accept it for what it is. I don't possess the special machine needed to craft it into the design of my liking, so, when the rain clears, I'll set out to find a maker to assist.

I'll never see her again, but she has to know that if things were different... I'd complete her goddamn list. The sudden thought pumps adrenaline back into me. And with my burning muscles, I increase the workout intensity to one that will leave me crippled tomorrow. But that burn pales compared to the scorching fire at my core.

I kill a bottle of water and glance at the clock, reading 11:10 p.m. Everyone is likely asleep, and I'm ready for a shower. I approach the door to my bedroom and lightly knock. When I don't hear a peep, I enter to see Skye peacefully in slumber. *Good.*

I slowly go to the bathroom, careful not to wake her, and commence a long shower.

Asleep, curled on her side, she doesn't budge when I pull the covers or when I lower myself in and the bed sinks. I shift to my side and wrap my arm around her waist, maneuvering closer as I get comfortable. I'm grateful she's sound asleep. The pink flannel pajama-wearing Skye I'm accustomed to isn't wearing shorts, and the knowledge wakes the man downstairs.

"Elias?" she murmurs in her sleepy state.

"Yes, right here," I whisper.

Shuffling, she places her arm over my grasp around her waist, then shifts close until her back is flush to my torso before drifting back to sleep.

Fuck.

I'm slowly awakened from dreamy spells to the sounds of soft whimpering. My eyelids part to see the darkness of my ceiling.

I'm on my back, is the first thought that comes to mind.

That's not how I fell asleep.

I frown, irritated that my nose isn't buried in her lavender-scented neck or that the curly strands of hair aren't brushed against my face, like they were when I'd fallen asleep.

The whimpering. I hear it again. My hooded eyes tear wide as awareness chases the stupor away. I become alert.

Skye is next to me. I reach over and click the light on my bedside lamp. The sudden brightness sears my eyes, and I squint. I turn over and witness a trembling Skye curled in the fetal position and whimpering beside me.

"Skye," I whisper before nudging her, but at my touch, her tremors progress and her soft whimpering becomes cries.

Shit.

I'm making it worse, but I have to wake her. I turn her on her back, and her breathing grows erratic. With each lift and drop of her chest, I know where she is. She struggles as the memory of facing death riptides back in, intruding her dreams, giving her no choice but to relive it.

"Skye," I voice louder. "Wake up, Skye." I shake her. Her bloodshot eyes tear open, but they're unfocused. She abruptly moves her head left and right, searching for reality. I'm hovering over her. "Look at me." She looks at me, and her eyes focus. "Breathe." I watch the movement of her chest slow as she calms. "You're not there anymore. It's over," I assure her. Her brown eyes grow glassy as the reality of what really happened finally sinks in.

I cradle her in my arms, and she curls into me, sobbing quietly into my chest. "Elias," she faintly voices through her tears. "She's still beautiful."

The moment the words leave her lips, I *know* what she's referring to. I gently rub her back, press a kiss to the top of her head, and whisper back. "Yes. Her beauty is within her depths."

CHAPTER 63

Skye

"Roses? That's so cliché," I joke, opening my front door to see Elias with a bouquet of pink roses in hand.

He smirks. "I know, but not in this case, because they're pink." I tilt my head and give him a quizzical look. He grins. "It doesn't take a genius to notice your favorite color is pink."

"Really?" I reply, curious if he's joking or if it's really that obvious.

He chuckles. "Do you even know your favorite color is pink, Skye?"

I roll my eyes. "Oh, shut up. Of course I know my favorite color, but it's not *that* obvious."

"No, not at all. Just everything you've added in this place and every accessory you possess is pink. But no, not obvious at all," he says sarcastically. Looking around, I realize the small items I picked up randomly are all pink, which is the sole reason I picked them. *Okay, so maybe it's a little obvious.*

He stalks closer with a daring expression. "However, I do have a question." His eyes glide down my body and then back to my eyes. "Are *all* your panties pink?"

My cheeks heat, but I alluringly sass, "Sounds like someone wants to find out."

He bites his lower lip. "Don't tempt me, girl."

The sound of his purring baritone in a state of desire sends heat to my core. I've craved more than his lips for some time, but we hold back. I don't think either of us knows why, but what's understood doesn't need to be explained.

"You ready?" he asks.

"That, I am," I reply as he hands me the flowers. "Thank you. They're beautiful."

He snakes an arm around my waist. "You're beautiful," he says and presses his lips to mine.

I love that our kisses happen without much thought anymore. They're spontaneous and done mindlessly; I could never tire of them. It has been twenty-two days since the catastrophic incident at sea, and I haven't been on a boat since. The morning after the night my memory surfaced, the gray clouds cleared, and the sunny weather returned.

Mauria and Sam had left for Haven Downs while I stayed with Elias another day. I grew conflicted between what my heart wants and what my will believes is right to protect us. But as I sat at the barstool-height chair in his kitchen, watching as he made us breakfast, the sword of my will shattered. The words he spoke the day I forced us to part resurfaced, and, with my mind, body, and soul, I shared the same feelings.

I went over to where he stood over the sink, wrapped my arms around his torso, and rested my head on his back, allowing his mint scent to envelope me. A tear fell from my eye.

"Hey, what's wrong?" He turned around and asked, concerned.

Lifting my head, I repeated his words as feelings of my own. "I'd rather spend every waking day with you and live with the memories forever."

I watched as his features softened and a smile appeared on his lips. He leaned down and pressed his lips to mine. Though we knew our forever would only last so many days, our memories will last a lifetime.

After that, neither he nor I held back again. We've spent every day together; nights, not so much, but we don't talk about the why behind that. What Elias and I have extends past fleshly desires. We spend more time enjoying outdoor activities than we do cooped up indoors. Nonetheless, while I've acted on my lustful yearning countless times, his discipline is commendable. I've never met a man as headstrong as he is, even when he's solid against me. But I suppose that's no surprise, as he was unbendable—even at sixteen—against his tyrannical father.

Mauria, Sam, Elias, and I decided to check out the new rock-climbing tower together, and it was a day of enjoyment for us all. Since then, the four of us have enjoyed various activities as double dates, I suppose, and as friends. I've taken an abundance of pictures.

I notice the difference in Elias's demeanor in the face of friendship. He and Sam have become closer. It brings me comfort to know that he won't allow the darkened veil to stifle his precious heart and whisk him back into isolation.

Our public displays of affection resemble an obvious couple —the intertwined fingers, random kisses, and an arm around one another at every moment. I feel like a teenager again. However, when I consider the feeling, it's not youth, it's *passion*. That's what I feel when I'm with Elias: passion, excitement, and love in all its bliss. Though we could never be a *real* couple, we don't address it. We *may* be ignoring what awaits us, but I no longer care. We'll deal with the aftermath when the time comes.

Enjoying the time we have left to spend, soaking in each other's presence has lifted a burden from my heart. I'm no longer fighting the urge to wrap myself into everything *him*.

Tonight, he's taking me somewhere he won't say, but he says it's special. So, I asked Mauria to help me find a date night dress, and she did not disappoint.

We decided on a red, close-fit, mid-thigh dress with thin straps and an open back. It complements my figure well, and with it, I wear a bracelet, a few rings, and black open-toe, three-inch heels. My hair is pinned to the top, my curls fall down by my shoulders, and just a few strands hang down the side of my ears.

Elias—as always—has yet to master the art of hidden expressions. His eyes are lust-filled as he licks that bottom lip of his, stripping me with his gaze. He's giving "man of the hour" vibes in his well-fitted black suit. The dark red, buttoned shirt under his black blazer reveals why he asked my apparel color earlier (but in lieu of "*what color are you wearing?*" it was "*are you wearing pink?*").

My burning heightens for the man standing before me. The neatly brushed-back man bun with a short strand that didn't get the memo hanging over his right eyebrow is what does it for me. *He's a total knockout.*

He places a hand on my back, and we walk through my front door. The night begins.

CHAPTER 64

Skye

Waiting at the edge of the road is a horse and carriage —and a face I haven't seen in some time, Destry, the guy who taught me how to horseback ride.

Elias gestures for me to loop my arm through his, and as we stride down the path toward the carriage, I hear the front door of Mauria's home swing open.

"Ah!" Mauria squeals, charging toward us. "You two look amazing! Skye, where's your camera?" Oh, that's right. I've been asking her to take so many pictures, she's become accustomed to my asking.

I take the camera from my clutch purse and hand it to her. She captures two photos where we stand and then another two with us on the carriage. She returns the camera before bidding us good night.

"Hi, Destry!" I joyously greet as we seat ourselves in the carriage.

"Hello, Skye. Good to see you again," he returns the greeting.

"Likewise, I'm coming back for horseback riding soon."

He nods. "I'll be there." He looks to Elias. "You two ready?"

We nod, and he signals for the two horses to take us away.

We have limited vision for the majority of the path—nothing but pure land and trees, not a home or establishment in sight. Elias informs me that this is the side of Sandemia that has yet to be developed.

We arrive at a large lake surrounded by trees in the far distance. A wooden bridge leads to the vessel that Elias sailed for our trip. *Also, the vessel used to rescue me from a storm at sea*, but most importantly, the vessel that witnessed our brewing love.

Then there's the sea.

She treasured our bond, felt it manifest at her surface, only to part after leaving her presence. *And so, she rampaged.* She rampaged at our parting, impelling us to be together from the cries of her depths.

"The waters are still tonight but are you okay?" he asks.

I smile. "Of course. I trust you. I always do." At my admission, his concern dissipates, replaced with a warm smile that meets the soft emerald gaze of his handsome features.

The cockpit is dim, but when Elias says, "Lights," warm-toned lighting brightens the boat, hanging off the sides and rounding each edge. The sight is beautiful, signaling a romantic evening on the lake. Taken by surprise, I gasp, "Oh my god, Elias. This is beautiful."

"You're beautiful," he says.

He holds my hand as we step onto the vessel. We approach a round table covered in white cloth at the very front. Atop it sits two folded cloth napkins with silverware tucked inside, two wine glasses, and a glass vase holding purple lilacs.

He slides the chair back, gesturing that I sit. "Elias," I say as my heart swells.

He bends to my ear and whispers, "Shush, I'm not done yet,"

and takes a seat in the chair across from me. "We're ready, Cap," he shouts, and the boat begins to move slowly across the lake.

"Who's the Cap?" I ask.

"Nobody important," he says nonchalantly.

"I heard that!" the voice yells. I giggle. It's Sam.

Elias chuckles inwardly. "Sam and Mauria helped me put this together."

A heartwarming smile extends on my lips. He's becoming friends with them.

Sam cuts the engine in the center of the lake, and I look up to see the mesmerizing glow of the full moon reflecting a path over the darkened waters toward us.

I move from my seat to the railing of the boat and gaze upon the moonlight in the night sky. "Elias, this is beautiful." Tender feelings of overwhelming bliss fill my heart.

He draws near and places his hands on my hips. "For a beautiful woman," he says and plants a kiss on my shoulder. We stand this way for a moment, soaking in the view, until a small bell dings, signaling dinner is ready.

Approaching the table, dressed in prestige chef attire, Sam has a tray with two covered white dishes. He places one before me and then Elias. "Wait, forgot something," he says, and Elias and I titter. He's not cut out for this, but he's trying his best to play his role as host. He comes back with the bottle of red wine in hand and pours a glass for each of us before placing a hand on the cover over the dish. "Now, it may seem strange at first, but this was Elias's recipe, and I tasted it. It's delicious," Sam warns.

I nod. Now I'm curious. I've known stuffed salmon to be Elias's signature dish.

Sam lifts the cover, and my eyes widen before shooting to Elias, who has an index finger curled over his lips, holding back laughter. He knows I have a million questions right now, the first one being: *why the hell do I have a Salisbury steak on my plate right now?* I'm glad he's amused, but I'm trying not to assume this man killed a cow for me.

"Listen, it looks weird, but really, it's good." I glance at Sam with an expression of pity, and the laugh Elias tried so hard to suppress huffs out.

Poor Sam. He's confused as to why Elias is laughing. "My reaction to the dish is entertainment for him, apparently."

"Well, you two enjoy. I'll be out with dessert in a bit." He dismisses himself.

"So, I found some ingredients to make something... impossible," Elias hints.

Squinting, I begin to ponder. He's obviously not coming straight out with it because of Sam.

He clears his throat. "Think vegan."

Looking down at the steak, I inspect it, my mouth hollowing as it clicks. A vegan burger. I laugh at myself for not thinking that first. The thought of him becoming some butcher just didn't fit.

I take a bite. It's incredibly tasty. I've never had a vegan burger, but if it's anything like this in our world, I'll have to get one. Shrimp, a baked potato, and broccoli sit on my plate—all delicious, but to save room for dessert, I take small bites from each group before pushing the plate aside.

Sam brings out a slice of vanilla cake with white icing, a scoop of ice cream, and a cherry on top. When we're nearly finished, I notice another boat heading toward us.

"Alright, lovebirds, my work here is done." Sam removes his chef's hat.

"Can we get some pictures before you go, Sam?" I ask. He nods, then I ask Elias to stand with me by the rail where the full moon glows above us.

Elias wraps one arm around my waist, and I place a hand on his chest. Sam takes two pictures, but before he places the camera down, Elias asks, "Mind taking one more?"

When Sam nods, Elias curls his fingers under my chin and swipes his thumb over my lips. It's then I realize he wants a photo of a kiss. Moving his fingers to the base of my neck, he leans in and presses his lips to mine. Sam snaps two photos before we part.

"I'm making a portrait out of that one. I'll hang it in my room where I can gaze upon it every morning when I rise," he says, low and filled with affection.

His words hit me deeply. It's beautiful, with a stab of pain. My heart twists at the thought of parting with him. How is it that I know the end is approaching, yet still, I cannot prepare? It feels impossible to prepare for. I find the love of my life, and he's in a world I can't be part of.

A tear falls from my eye. He wipes it away with his thumb and presses another kiss to my lips. It's then I choose to push down any feelings of a loss that has yet to come, deciding instead to enjoy each moment in all its beauty with the man who has my heart.

"Wait, right here," he says, after Sam sails off in the boat that came for him.

I nod, then Elias goes to the cockpit while I make my way to the table to take a few more sips of wine. When he comes back, there's a small green gift bag in his hand. "Open it," he says and hands it to me. I remove the tissue from the bag. Inside is a brown box. And inside the box is a toy train, carved from wood and painted green. A dinosaur is drawn on both sides.

"You made this... for my Juji," I whisper. My heart swells in gratitude for the thought about my son—my son he's never met but whom he knows I love more than anything.

"Not as advanced as the manufactured ones where we come from, but it'd be good for a collection," he says.

"No, it's perfect," I squeak, throwing my arms around him. "It has dinosaurs on it."

He chuckles, and I press a kiss to his lips.

"Dance with me," he requests.

A bit perplexed because I find it strange without music, I nod anyway.

He reaches into his pocket and removes a phone. *His phone.* "I have downloaded music, requiring no Internet for listening." He sets the phone on the table and touches the screen. "My mother loved this one."

I smile at the gesture, and he places his hands on my lower back to bring me close. I wrap my arms around his neck, and as the song begins to play, we sway. I recognize the melody. It's not on any playlist of mine, but it's a beautiful song. "I Hope You Dance" by Lee Ann Womack. I remember the song's message as the lyrics play, but suddenly a weighing feeling forms in my chest —but we continue to sway.

A reminder to remain humble. A promise to have faith in my hopes and dreams.

A tear falls from my eyes. But we sway.

As Lee Ann Womack's voice sings ever so graciously along the melody, I drop my head to Elias's shoulder. This hurts. Yet we continue to sway.

A reminder to stop settling for the path of least resistance. To allow my caged soul to remain free as I have in this world even if it means taking a chance. My soul is worth that chance.

I've caught on to what he's doing, and my poor heart cries. It breaks, shattering in my chest.

Even when the path is rocky, don't give up. Embrace the challenges, walk in my purpose. Through the melodic words, he promises not to return to bitterness. He's confessing that he's released the shackles of his heart.

Silently sobbing, I want to say something—anything, but the words are stuck in my throat. I want to tell him: No, *please, I'm not ready. Not yet.* But instead, I let him continue to hold me close —and we sway.

He's silent. But his silence is everything in the lyrics of this song. It's everything I've said, it's everything we've learned from each other. My hands slide from his neck down to his chest. I bury my face in his collar and weep for my breaking heart. For our love. *For us.*

He slides his palm to the middle of my back, holding me

closer—and we sway. He's aware that I know what this is now, *and it's painful.*

He's telling me to dance. And promising me that he will too.

He's letting me go. He knows that when I chose my heart, I chose to forget about our parting. He's telling me that it's time.

It's time to remember, time to let go—*time to say goodbye.*

The vegan steak, the comment about the portrait, the gift for my son. He was reminding me—preparing me to remember that it's time to untether. Let go of him, let go of Sandemia, let go of this world.

Unable to bear it, I break down where I stand in a downpour of tears. My swaying halts.

"Look at me, Skye."

I can't look at him. My chest—it hurts. My heart—it's breaking in the worst way. He never ignored my leaving. He knew the time would come when we'd have to address it. That time just hadn't come yet. But, at this moment, I'm still not ready, so I keep my head held down. And this time, I refuse the request of his famous words.

"Look at me, baby, please," he pleads.

Please spare me, just for tonight. I can't. Despite the thoughts echoing the hurt in my heart, I slowly lift my head, shaking it as I look into his emerald eyes.

"Elias, please. I can't," I plead through my tears. My voice quavers and my emotions are on full display as I break down in defeat before him.

"I love you," he rasps, sadness in his irises. "I love you so much."

"No." I shake my head. "Not yet. I'm not ready."

"It has to be now, Skye. Feel it now. Not when you get back." He places his hands on either side of my face. "And by the time you get back, you'll have already accepted it."

"Don't forget me, Elias." My voice cracks under the weight of sorrow.

"I could never forget you, Skye."

I knew this day was imminent, yet I still can't do it. It hurts as if it were unexpected. Holding me tight, he buries his face in the crook of my neck.

"Thank you, Skye," he whispers. "For everything."

CHAPTER 65

Skye

The song dies down. He brings his palms to my cheeks and wipes my tears with his thumbs. "I love you," he says.

"I love you too," I manage through my ever-falling tears.

Pressing his lips to mine, our kiss says everything that's hard to put into words. Unwilling to wait for him this time, I intrude with my tongue because I have much to say, but words are hard.

A groan escapes his throat, igniting a fire in me. I wrap my arms around his neck and take control with my tongue, attempting to pull another sound from him. I want him, all of him, with every fiber of my being.

He rips his mouth away. There's a feral look of hunger in his eyes. I frown at the loss, and at my nuance, he crashes his lips to mine.

He hoists me up. I wrap my legs around him, and he carries me toward the cabin. I hear when he kicks an inconsiderate chair out of his path. His lips never leaving mine, he lowers me until my back touches the soft, cushioned bed. Tearing his lips away again, he drops his head to my chest and groans.

"Skye," he growls, fighting with himself—his urge.

"Elias, no holding back."

He lifts his head and hovers over me, searching my eyes. He's looking for any sign of doubt, but there is none—*I want him.* I have for some time.

Bending, he presses his lips back to mine, kissing me tenderly and slowly, expressing his love. His kisses move to my neck, and I arch, sucking in breaths of pleasure. He darts out his tongue and licks from my neck, up my jaw, until he's back to my mouth.

He breaks away, standing rigid. His eyes never leave mine. I stand too and drop the shoulders of my dress until the satin material hits the floor and I'm bare before him. Our gaze remains locked while he removes his blazer, unbuttons his shirt, and loses the belt. "Turn around," he whispers, and I do.

Starting at my hips, he slides his hands up my curves. His touch probes my bare skin and strikes lightning within me. I throw my head back onto his shoulder. He reaches my breasts, cupping them, and caressing them—sending heat waves through my entire body. With one hand still cupping a breast, his other hand travels down over my belly and stops between my legs. Separating him from my sex is the thin material covering it. As he gently rubs the pulse between my legs, I exhale a soft moan. "Damn, baby," he whispers as I soak for him, and the sound of his voice combined with his touch heightens my need.

He removes my panties and when they fall, I step out of them. "Turn around," he whispers, and I do. Our lips meet again until we're planted on the bed, before he breaks away to remove my heels.

He takes a nipple into his mouth and sucks before releasing it with a pop. I inhale sharply, whispering, "Elias," as I exhale. He does the same to the other before moving lower and licking my inner thighs. The anticipation makes my breathing unsteady. I burn with need—need for him to touch me *there.* I squirm as my raging hormones grow impatient. I bite down on my bottom lip, attempting to keep it together.

He gazes at me with hunger in his eyes and darts his tongue out, sliding it between my folds. He laps at the bundle of nerves slowly, and the touch sends me into euphoria. I arch my back, and my hands fly to his hair. Circling with his tongue, he takes my swelling bud between his lips—and sucks.

Oh my god.

Throwing my head back, I let out a moan through staggered breaths as I climb to the edge. With every lap of his tongue, my moans grow louder, and when he sucks again, my hands become fists in his hair.

Moans coming to a halt, my body tenses, and with one last swipe of his tongue, my orgasm rips through me, and I cry out my release.

He licks all the way up my body until he reaches my lips and swipes his tongue over my bottom lip. He hovers over me. "You taste delicious," he whispers, and I bite my lip at the sight of intense desire in his emerald gaze. He bends to kiss me. We lock lips as I come down from my release.

He stands and backs away from the bed. I take notice of the bulge behind his pants. He stays there for a moment, his eyes traveling up and down my body. "Beautiful," he whispers before unbuttoning his pants. Losing the pants and boxers together, his stiff erection bobs out. *He's hard as a rock.* My eyebrows raise at his size, and he smirks at my expression.

Crawling between my legs, he positions himself at my opening. "I love you," he says.

"I love you too."

Our gazes remain locked as he slowly penetrates. I wince at the intrusion and shut my eyes.

"Look at me."

I do. I've never experienced this level of intimacy. This love is consuming, the kind only experienced once in a lifetime. The kind you can never let go of.

He sinks deeper, and I suck in a breath. My hands fly to his back, and I gently claw. He slowly moves out, then in again. "Fuck," he rasps. "You feel so good." Sliding back in deeply, he plants there, and we share a long kiss. "I love you so much, Skye."

A tear falls from my eye as I hear the emotion struggling in his throat. "I love you too." Before we let each other go, before we say goodbye, this aspect of intimacy that we've been denying ourselves, we finally share as our *last unforgettable memory.*

His jaw tenses as he fights his emotions, but I see it as his emeralds grow dark and his eyes redden. Running my fingers over his jaw, I shed another tear. "I'll never forget you."

We both share this pain. He struggles with the tears he bites back. His emotions brim, threatening to spill over. He can't hold back any longer. He pulls back his hips and slams into me. And I cry out, "Elias!"

Groaning, he pauses before slamming into me again.

And I scream.

He pistons his length in and out of me, a mix of pain and pleasure as his name pours from my lips, and I tense as my release builds.

"Eliasssss!"

I dig my nails into his arms, and he goes feral, driving into me deeper. I gasp on the brink of my climax. He sucks in a breath through clenched teeth. And my body stills; my moans cease. "Come for me, baby," he grunts out.

My second orgasm hits like a shockwave, my entire body convulsing beneath him. In the next moment, I feel his throb in my moist depths, and with one last thrust, he jerks, growling his release deep inside of me.

CHAPTER 66

Skye

I groan as I'm being nudged to wake. "Skye." I hear Elias's voice. "Skye, wake up."

Slowly awakening from my dream state after a night of bliss, I see a shirtless Elias, dressed in only his pants. "Take them off," I murmur, half asleep.

A half-smile forms on his beautiful face as he lightly chuckles. "Come on, you don't want to miss this."

Rubbing my eyes, the reality sets in that he's trying to get me up. I sit up in the bed and watch as he bends over to pick up his crimson shirt.

"Here." He hands it to me. "Meet me on the deck."

I throw on his shirt and button it until I'm covered. Still groggy, I splash water on my face before leaving the cabin. Walking up the three steps leading to the deck, I pause when I see Elias standing at the rail and gazing at the sky. He wanted me to witness the sunrise over the lake.

When he hears me draw close, he stretches an arm, gesturing for me to come beside him. He wraps his arm around my waist, and we stand there in silence, watching color slowly reappear in our surroundings with the rising morning sun.

On the surface of the water leading to the sea of our love, this level of connection is one I never thought I'd experience. A mix of emotions washes over me as I gaze upon the horizon. I'm calm; I feel joy, sadness, peace, and pain all at once. However, the most profound feeling of all is deep, everlasting love.

I may never get to see Elias again, but I will never forget what he's given me or how he made me feel. I've become passionate about much more than ever before. I've known love, but I've never known love like this. This isn't the love that blinds you—the love I feared. This love didn't begin at the surface. It began at the depths, then made its way to the surface. The love that blinds is the one utilized to forget, but Elias and I accepted ourselves before accepting each other. We released the shackles, opened the cages, and set ourselves free. We witnessed each other's pain through the unveiling—and held each other through the healing.

And through the passions of our souls, we created a love of a lifetime.

Elias sailed us to Haven Downs, and now he carries me in his arms to the residence I will be occupying for nine more days. I could have put my heels back on and walked, but when he saw that I really didn't want to, I jumped at the opportunity when he offered to carry me. Staring up at the beautiful contours of his features, I soak in this moment.

"What are you looking at?"

"You," I reply, smiling.

He smirks. "You're loving this, aren't you?"

"I am."

He smiles, and I lay my head on his collarbone. He's so perfect.

My perfect.

We haven't been inside for a full five minutes before there's a knock at the door. Elias answers, and it's Mauria. Barely acknowl-edging him, she squeezes past and runs toward me. She throws her arms around me and joyously squeals, "I'm so happy for you!"

I hug her back, but I'm confused. I look at Elias past her shoulder, and I mouth without sound, "What?"

Lifting his shoulders, he gestures that he has no clue.

She finally breaks the cheerful hug. "So where is it?"

I tilt my head. "Where's what?"

Her features drop. "You didn't say yes?"

"Say yes?" I ask, curiously.

She turns on her heels, facing Elias. "You didn't propose?"

He palms the back of his head. He's a bit uncomfortable at the spot he's being put on, and the sight is adorable. Mauria can be intimidating if you're not expecting an outburst.

"I was so sure the whole moonlight night on the lake was your plan to propose." She folds her arms in disappointment. "I was excited to see what kind of ring he had made for you." *So, that's how that works here?*

I bring a hand to my mouth to hide my chuckle. It was a beau-tiful night, but watching Elias's tongue tied for the first time ever tickles me. Something cool touches my lip, but it isn't from my middle finger, where a ring is already placed. My smile fades as I turn my hand around and hold it up in front of me. I realize there's another ring on my finger that hadn't been there before.

Gazing at the gold piece holding a diamond on my ring finger, tears well in my eyes. Elias must have placed this on me while I was asleep. He didn't propose because, realistically, he can't. However, the message behind the placement speaks volumes. If he could ask me to marry him, he would. If he could spend the rest of his life with me, he would. That's what this ring signifies. It's why it was placed on my finger rather than proposed to me. My heart melts before it explodes. If things were different, I'd say yes immediately and without hesitation.

Elias, noticing that I've recognized the ring in all its meaning, stuffs his hands in his pockets and clears his throat. Mauria's features soften when she sees me staring at my finger. She puts her head next to mine and stares at the ring with me.

"Aw, yours is a diamond," she admires. "I heard those are the hardest to make a ring from. They're virtually impenetrable." She looks over to Elias. "Good job, Elias!"

She suddenly becomes ecstatic. "I am so helping you plan the wedding!" she exclaims, excitement oozing from her. "Oh, and I am definitely your sister bride. I won't take no for an answer."

I bring a hand to my chest. Tears well in my eyes. Sadness cocoons me as I look at the woman who's been a dear friend to me since the day I arrived. She tilts her head in confusion when she notices my expression. "What's wrong? Why so sad?"

"I can't..." I begin to speak, but the words are stuck in my throat. I've grown to love Mauria and cherish our friendship. I'm going to miss her so much. What do I say to her? Where do I even begin?

Elias, noticing my struggle, strides over and places his palms on either side of my arms. I look up at him. "Hey, you can do this," he whispers. "Now is the time. I'll be outside, okay?"

I nod. He presses a kiss to my forehead before heading for the door.

"Mauria, can we sit?" I take a deep breath to simmer my emotions. As hard as this is, I have to do it.

She nods, and we move to the sofa. "Mauria." I shift on the couch to face her. "Elias placed the ring on my finger for me to find it because proposing to me would mean we *could* get married, but the truth is, we can't."

"Okay, but why?" She squints, assertively taking in my words.

"Because I can't stay here." As the words leave my lips, my emotions brew. I take another breath. "And he can't follow where I must return."

"Where? Land Kairos?" she asks, perplexed.

I don't know how to answer, but I want to tell her as much as possible. "Wait here," I instruct. In the bedroom, I pick up the hourglass. The sand in the top half is barely visible, and the bottom is almost filled. I head back to the living area, hourglass in hand, and show it to her. "I'm sorry, Mauria. I'm not from Land Kairos, and my time here is running out."

"Well, what happens when you turn it over?" she asks. I flip the hourglass to show her that it's fixed, that the sand from the bottom stops in the middle and never pours in the other direction. "I don't understand, is it magic?"

"I don't know. Maybe," I answer truthfully. "But I only have nine days left, and I'll have to return to *my* home, which is not of this world."

She's staring at me, waiting for me to divulge further, but I'm uncertain how. Taking a deep breath, I decide to spit out what I can as it comes to mind.

"I'm from somewhere very far, inaccessible to anyone here. It's not somewhere you'd consider some utopia or paradise, like this place seems to be."

"This is a paradise?" she asks, as if that sounds bizarre.

"To someone like me, yes. Where I'm from, life is very different."

"Is it the New York you mentioned when you first arrived?"

I did say that, didn't I? Big mouth. I pause before responding, and I hope I can explain this in a way she understands. "So, when I first arrived on Livity, I truly didn't know how I arrived or why. When you found the article, I was ecstatic because it meant someone here must know something. Well, that person turned out to be Elias. The passenger from five years ago was him. He arrived here from the same world I'm from."

She sighs. "Skye, I still don't understand. This place you're both from, why is he still here, and you have to go back when this thing, whatever it is, is up?"

"Because, like Elias, I will be given a choice. I have to go back."

She shifts on the sofa and bends her leg to rest on the couch, facing me. "Can I visit? Can you visit? I mean, there's nowhere a boat can't go. You arrived here on one, after all."

I give her a look of sympathy. My heart twists in my chest. I truly wish that were possible. "No, Mauria. It doesn't work like that. Elias made the choice, but his choice meant that he could never return. And when I make the choice to return, it will mean I can never come back." Tears well in my eyes as the reality of the words sinks in.

She shakes her head as questions still form in her brain. "Well, if this place is such a paradise, then why not stay?"

I drop my head before I tell her this. "Because I have people and family that I love and adore back home. People I can't truly be happy without if I make the decision to leave and live a life without them." I hiccup as I think of my parents, my brother— my entire family. Then I think of my most important reason, my Julias. "Mauria, I have a son. There's nothing—in any world—I would leave him for, even if it pains me."

Her eyes begin to shimmer with tears. "Is there no way to bring them here with you?"

I shake my head. "Transporting here is not so easy. Truth is, Mauria, I ended up here because the universe acknowledged my pleading soul when I stubbornly wouldn't." Bringing her hand into mine, the tears that threaten finally spill over. "I've learned so much from being here. You may not recognize this Mauria, but the pursuit of passions, catering to the soul, is a way of life here. In my world, it's not that simple. Life, where I'm from, can make that hard to grasp, especially for a particular group of people."

She grabs both of my hands, holding them in hers. "Did you find your passion here?"

"Maybe. I'm not sure. This is all new to me, but I know I've never been happier to start fresh, and I believe my new pursuit will align with my soul's desires. However, I've gained so much more than that from being here. I've learned just how precious time is, and I'll never get it back. So, there's a few changes I'll be making when I return."

She sniffles. "Are there more people like you and Elias?"

"If there were, Elias would have come across them by now. It isn't difficult for us to spot the familiarity in someone from our world." I wipe my tears as my emotions subside, and we begin to calm.

I'm afraid of what it may cause if people knew that others from different dimensions have traveled here. What it would mean for Elias if word spread that he was from a different world.

Where I'm from, people can be ruthless—harassing, without an ounce of consideration for the other party's feelings or privacy. It may differ here, but curiosity is all the same—and Elias isn't a man who would appreciate such attention. "Mauria, I won't ask you to hide anything from Sam, but at least for Elias's sake, could you keep this to yourselves?"

Her eyebrows raise. "Oh, no! Yes, of course. I hadn't planned on breathing a word. If either of you wanted this known, I'm sure you would have announced it." Her expression softens to a look of endearment. "I'm just happy that you trust me enough to tell me. I promise your secrets are safe with me."

Placing a hand on her chest, her eyes become saddened. "He has to go back with you."

Before I can respond, she pushes to her feet and jets to the door, swinging it open. "No! You have to go too," she cries to Elias.

Elias hurries inside and closes the door behind him. "It's not possible for me anymore," he says.

"But that's not fair!" Her empathy runs deep, she's absorbing our pain. Tears stream down her face. "You two are going to be so broken."

Elias moves to where I stand and wraps an arm around my shoulders. "I'd travel to any world to be with her, but I can't. So, I'll cherish the memories with her for as long as I live."

At Elias's words, Mauria becomes a ball of tears before us. I join her, crying once again, and Elias presses a kiss to the top of my head. I go to where Mauria stands and wrap my arms around her. "I'm going to miss you so much, Mauria. Why do you think I always took two pictures?"

"You planned to leave the other ones with me?" Her voice quavers.

"Yes," I whisper. "I never want to forget you. You would have been my sister bride. I don't know what that is, but it sounds like what we call bridesmaids in my world."

We both chuckle as we continue to cry. "I'm going to miss you, Skye." She sniffles, wiping her tears. "I also have something I wanted to tell you."

She places her hands on her stomach, and I look down with widened eyes. "Oh my god, are you pregnant?"

She nods, smiling. "Yes. Sam and I are having a baby."

I throw my arms around her again. "I'm so happy for you!"

Elias comes near and places a hand on my back. "Congratulations, Mauria," he offers. She thanks him, then he looks at me. "Why don't you spend the day with Mauria? I'll come back by the morning."

I nod and watch his retreating back until he leaves.

CHAPTER 67

Skye

I spent the entire day with Mauria. She's asked me a bazillion questions about what to expect with a newborn and even more about the world I'm from. I answer all her questions and give her as much advice as possible in reference to my experience with Julias.

We visited the art gallery and then strolled through Sheridan Park, taking more pictures before having them printed. Before we made our way back to Haven Downs, I paid Destry a visit for one last horseback ride.

"You were so afraid to go any faster on the horse. Now look at you, practically a pro," Mauria jokes as we sit on the bed, sorting through the photos.

I laugh. "Yes, I definitely was. Now, it's probably going to become a hobby of mine. I love it."

"You know, you should spend your remaining days with Elias," she advises. "Was your leaving the reason you chose not to see him again?"

I sigh. "Yeah. I was trying to prevent the pain from becoming any worse than it already would be if we'd gotten any closer."

She gathers her pile of pictures and shuffles them until they're neatly stacked. "I'll be honest. I knew he felt something for you, but he seemed like a man incapable of showing affection. I was afraid he would hurt you. But something changed. *You happened.* He's so much more relaxed now."

I place my photos in a bag, leaving only the double takes of Elias and me to sort through. "He wasn't always like that. Things happened in our world that made him grow a hardened heart. Having your heart stabbed as many times as he's had to bear can do something to a person, make them feel the need to protect it by not letting anyone in. I'm glad that he has you and Sam when I'm gone. I truly hope he finds love again."

She shrugs, her features contorting to something of displeasure. "Maybe he will, but it'll be a while before I could accept her. She'll have big shoes to fill as Elias's girlfriend, and I'll need proof that she's capable of filling them."

I laugh at her assertion, and she laughs with me. This is Mauria, she jokes through pain. That's her coping style. I pull her in for a hug, and our laughter turns to more crying. "I'm going to miss you so much, Skye. I've never met anyone like you in my life."

"I'm going to miss you too, Mauria," I express through my tears. Releasing her, I push her hair behind her ear. "But now you have something else to look forward to. A new journey. Motherhood."

CHAPTER 68

Skye

"I'm not going anywhere for the next eight days," Elias says with a bag over his shoulder.

I smile. "Good."

I open the door wider to let him in, and he suggests that we go down to the town registration and terminate the residency at day three-twenty-five.

"Okay," I agree, puzzled. "But that's six days after."

He drops his bag in the dining chair and glances toward the window. His eyes are downcast when he turns toward me. "Skye," he says, before pinching the bridge of his nose. "I may need a few days."

I give him a heartfelt gaze. He doesn't need to explain further. He'll need a few days to come to terms with my no longer residing here, and I wholeheartedly understand. "Okay," I say, barely above a whisper.

So today, that's what we do.

"Are you sure?" I ask Elias, whining, "I can be discreet. I'll just drop it in the mailbox and leave."

We sit on the bed, sorting through photos of us that I left aside. I try to convince him to let me deliver a letter to at least one loved one of his, but he's obliged to refuse, and his reasoning isn't enough for me. "No, Skye, it's too dangerous. I won't risk it."

I huff out a breath. "But I won't get caught. There has to be someone you'd like to give a message to. Come on."

"Maybe, but it's not worth the risk. That's final."

Fine.

"Did you take this?" I hold up a photo of myself looking through the spyglass aboard his ship. It's a striking shot. I'm wearing a yellow sundress that sways graciously with the wind. I remember this day because it was the only day I wore that dress.

"I did," he confirms, a satisfied grin on his face. He grabs a pen and turns the photo over to write something on the back. He took two photos and handed me the one he scribbled on. I turn it over to see he wrote, *"My Sunshine."* "This one will be my second portrait. I'll hang it in the living room across from my mother's."

My face contorts to a look of sympathy. My heart cries for the man sitting in front of me.

"No pity, Skye," he utters, observing my expression.

I want to wrap him in love, *my love*, forever, because he's been through so much. I've become that important to him. And it's another dreadful reminder in his living room, along with his beloved mother, of another love lost—another being that loved him solely for who he is.

I move the pictures aside and seat myself on top of him. My knees are bent at either side of him. I run my fingers through his hair and gaze into his deep emeralds. "I don't pity you. But can't I just love you? You're so strong." A tear threatens, and I don't fight it back. "Thank you for letting me in, for letting me love you."

He places his hands on the back of my neck, and I tilt my head until our lips meet. As we lip lock, he removes my shirt and I his before he lifts me up and turns, laying me flat on my back. Fitting himself between my legs, his kisses move down my body to my moist core. Closing my eyes, I throw my head back. Tonight, we make sweet, passionate love like never before.

Tonight is the last night. Elias and I lay in bed facing each other, awaiting Sylvester's presence. It's 11:16 p.m., and the hourglass passed its last grain of sand three hours ago.

"Will you see him when he comes?" I ask.

"I don't know."

"Will he knock?"

"No. He entered my room and asked about my decision. When I gave him my answer, he left the way he came, and the hourglass vanished."

"I love you."

"Not yet, Skye. Stay awake."

We hold each other close, our gazes never faltering, and we just talk. "You and my brother would have gotten along so well."

"I'd have raced him."

I chuckle. "Dynamite versus Thunder."

"That's some monster heat," he says.

"If it was at all possible to bring them here, I would. I prefer this world."

"I know."

I don't know how much time has passed as Elias and I chat, but we both hear when the front door opens. Sitting up against the headboard, we await Sylvester's presence. When he enters the bedroom, I take a quick glance at the clock—it's midnight.

"Can you see him?" I whisper to Elias.

"No. Is he here?"

I gaze at the old man standing in the doorway. "He's right in front of us."

I grab the small bag leaning against the nightstand and throw it over my shoulder as I come down off the bed. Elias stands along with me.

"Will you remain or return, Lady Skye?" Sylvester asks.

I don't respond right away. The pain of leaving festers, and tears begin to fall. Elias, intertwining his fingers with mine, whispers, "It's okay, baby. It's time now."

I lean my head on his arm and inhale his mint scent before answering Sylvester. "I will return."

"Please follow me," Sylvester instructs.

I nod, then glance at Elias. "He's telling me to follow him."

We exit the door of the home where I've spent the last one hundred twenty days. I look back, taking in the surroundings one last time. *It was comfortable here.* I close the door and hand Elias the keys. We follow Sylvester to Haven Docks. The boat with green and blue stripes, Livity, waits for me at the shore.

"Do you see the boat?" I ask Elias.

"Yes," he replies. "It looks the same as it did five years ago."

"Please board my transport, Lady Skye," Sylvester politely directs me.

"Okay," I reply in a shaky voice. I'm fighting a breakdown with every bone in my body. "Please, could I have a moment?"

Sylvester smiles. "Yes, you may."

Facing Elias, I stop fighting. I cry out the pain in my soul, the bloodshed in my heart. I sob into his chest. He squeezes me tight and buries his nose in my hair.

"Skye," he croaks and releases me, placing two palms on either side of my face. "Live. Follow the passions of your soul. Write a book, write two, and then write more. Travel, travel twice, then travel more. Don't confine yourself. Set your soul free. Walk for your purpose, Skye, *and dance.*" His eyes are reddened, emotions heavy in his throat, but he keeps it together for my sake.

Sniffling, I force my words through the lump of emotion lodged in my throat. I place my hands on his chest. "No longer close off your heart, Elias. Love; love hard. Make friends, love them. Let your heart love as you know love. You will love again. Cherish every moment as I've cherished with you."

He sucks in a breath through clenched teeth. His eyes shimmer as he fights back tears.

"No more shackling your heart," I say, my voice quavering.

He gazes at me with intense eyes and utters, "If you ever feel like giving up, if you ever feel down, think of me. I'll be whatever you need in that moment." His voice rasps as his emotions brim. "Just think of me, Skye."

"I promise," I manage to say through my tears. "Don't forget me, Elias."

"I'll never forget you, baby. I promise."

"I love you."

"I love you."

We share one last kiss.

One last hug.

One last inhale of his minty scent.

Elias: One last inhale of her lavender scent.

One last goodbye.

Elias: One last goodbye.

We release each other, and I commence boarding Livity. Elias touches the boat, but its existence defies matter. His fingers glide through it, touching air.

Sylvester moves off from the shore, and as the boat sails farther, my gaze remains locked with Elias. I sob as the distance between us grows; he stands there, never moving. I press a kiss to my fingers and then blow it toward him; he stretches his arm and catches it, then brings his fist to his heart.

The air becomes dense with fog, but I still see him. I watch as he stuffs his hands in his pockets, hangs his head, and walks away.

I call his name as loud as I can, "Elias!" But he doesn't stop.

I scream his name again, over and over, but he still walks away. That's when it finally dawns on me that he can no longer see or hear me.

Sobbing uncontrollably, I gaze in the distance until I see nothing.

Suddenly, extreme exhaustion drains me. My eyes strain to remain open. Laying on my side where I'm seated, my eyes finally droop, and everything goes blank as I drift into unconsciousness.

Elias

I watched as she faded into the distance until she vanished, and then I hung my head and made my way back to the residence she occupied just minutes before.

I enter the home, close the door behind me, and lean back on it. Every emotion crashes down at once. Every tear I held back wells in my eyes until they pour over. I break down where I stand. A tidal wave of pain crashes into my core, and there's no option of swimming out. A knife pierces through my heart, suffocation in my lungs. I want to tear this place apart like an inconsolable child because forces greater than us deny my being with her.

However, I don't, because I'd go through this shit again if it meant I got to be with her for another one hundred and twenty days. And suddenly my mind runs to the twenty-four days of stubbornness I went without her presence, and I hate myself for that shit.

When Mom died, I convinced myself that if I knew the day was coming, at least I could have prepared for the wound, but this time I knew, and it still made it no goddamned easier.

"Continue being the butterflies and sunshine you are, Skye. Follow your dreams and dance. Be happy," I whisper to no one as the tears fall in abundance from the depths of my soul.

A knock at the door pulls me from my sorrow. I take a breath and wipe my face. I gather myself and open the door to see Sam outside.

"You don't have to bear it alone, man," he says and extends his arm for a shake.

I grip his hand. He moves in for a hug, and I accept.

"Mauria told me everything. I just saw her go. You don't need to be alone," he consoles.

I fight back the tears, but they surface in defiance and spill over as they please. I remember this feeling. The memory of a previous loss and someone being there to tell me I'm not alone.

I remember this.

Travis and Tyler, when Mom passed. But this isn't Travis or Tyler.

This is Sam.

And I appreciate him for being my *friend*.

No more shackling my heart.

Skye

Beep! *Beep! Beep!*

My alarm sounds, tearing me away from a peaceful nap. *One Piece* plays on my mounted TV, and I look over to see my phone plugged into my charger.

Beep! Beep! Beep!

It pierces through my ears. I reach for it, hitting stop. The screen reads six p.m.—time to pick up Julias.

I gaze at my surroundings for a moment. I'm in my bedroom. *My bedroom.* A sudden, heavy feeling washes over me—a feeling of loss and sorrow. A beautiful dream that felt so real. I look over at the glass sitting on my nightstand. *I need to drink wine more often before naps.* I want to go back there.

"From the moment you arrive, until it is time for you to choose, time as you know it in the world you are from will remain frozen."

The words of that man I fell in love with in my dreams replay in my head. And as the grogginess dissipates, the words click in my brain. *That's right, I made a decision.*

Elias.

It *was* real. Where's the bag? Those were my memories. I pause before jumping out of bed as a subtle scent of mint grazes my nostrils. Looking down, I realize I'm wearing Elias's shirt. A glance at my finger, and there it is. The gold band holding the diamond sits on my ring finger.

It's the only sign I need before the tears spring.

It was all real, all of it.

I lay down and curl into the fetal position, hugging my pillow. Burying my face, I wail, releasing my pain into the pink satin covers of my pillow.

"If ever you feel down, think of me. I'll be whatever you need in that moment."

Elias's words replay in my head, and I cry. I miss the sound of his voice, the touch of his skin, and that handsome smile like a cool breeze on a blistering day. My broken heart weeps for our love.

"Cherish every moment, Elias. Unshackle your heart and love, my love. You'll love again," I whisper to no one. "Maybe in the next life, we'll meet again."

I take a deep breath and hang my legs off the bed. Lying on the floor is the bag of memories. I open it and remove the train Elias made for Julias, a white shirt that reads "Sandemia" in pink lettering, and the photographs.

I flip through the pictures. More tears fall as I long for the life I lived for just four months. What hurts most are the people I've grown to love that I can never see again. I get to the first photo Mauria and I snapped together, my first time horseback riding, and I smile through my tears, already missing her so much. She's going to be a great mother, and Sam a great father.

I look at the picture of Elias and me in front of the moonlight, bring it to my chest, and whisper, "I'll never forget you."

I shed one last tear and place all the photos in the top drawer of my nightstand. There's another face I've longed to see. Enough tears of loss have been shed; I need my joy. My little dinosaur.

"Is everything okay, Skye?" my mother asks, confused as to why I'm hugging her so tight.

I release her. "Yes, it's just been such a long day. Where's Julias?"

My mother opens her mouth to answer but shuts it when we hear Julias charging to the door. "Mommy!" The sound replaces all feelings of sorrow with pure happiness.

I bend down and cradle him in my arms, hugging him tight and pressing nonstop kisses to his little cheeks. "Hi, my Juji! Mommy misses you so much!"

"I miss you too, Mommy." He giggles. His small face scrunches to a frown. "Mommy, why you cry?"

I smile. "They're happy tears, because Mommy is so happy to see you!" I begin tickling him; his giggles fill me with joy.

I bring him to the car and strap him in his car seat. I hear my mother approaching behind me. "Skye, are you sure you're okay?"

I close the car door. "Yes, Mom. It's really just been a stressful week. I took a nap after work, so I feel rejuvenated."

She looks at me under scrutiny. "No, it's something else. I know you're your own woman, so I try not to show any worry. When I do, you grow distant from me. But I'm your mother, and I know when something is wrong. It's okay to just talk to me."

I bring her in for a hug. Of course, she noticed. How could she not? I was stupid to think I could hide my unhappiness from my mom. I hadn't realized she was afraid to pry, afraid I'd distance myself from her, but she's right, I have been. However, that was before Elias, before my journey. If I couldn't admit my unhappiness to myself, how could I have admitted it to anyone else? So I tell my mother, as I would want my child to tell me. I'm no longer a child, but I can never tell her that. She'll always see me as her girl.

"Honestly, Mom, you're right, and I'm sorry. The truth is, I hate my career. There was one point where I thought it was what I wanted to do forever. I have a good life and have achieved much through my career. I'm grateful for that. I'm thankful for how much you and Dad helped me. But now, I'm no longer happy with my choice. I've been settling for some time now. But I'm done with that. I want to start a new path."

Her features soften, relieved that I've admitted my truth to her in lieu of the same old, *"I'm okay, Mom."* "Well, what is it you want to do?" she asks.

"There are a few things, but I have one in mind that has me most excited. I'll fill you in on that later."

She smiles delightedly, and I give her another hug before telling her I love her and jumping in my car. Before taking off with my little dinosaur, I press play on the song I downloaded to my playlist before reversing out of the driveway. As I drive home, I sing the lyrics to *I Hope You Dance.*

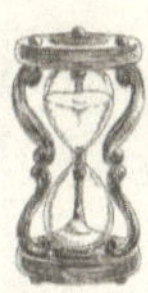

"Juji, come here, baby. I have a present for you!" I hide the small box behind my back until he runs out of the room where he's playing.

"A *pweasant?*" he asks, excited with anticipation.

Bringing the box around from my back into his vision, his eyes brighten, awaiting seeing what's inside. I hand him the box. The moment he lays eyes on the train, a cheerful smile stretches across his face.

"Choo choo *twain!*" he yells.

"Yes, turn it to the side," I suggest.

He does. "A *dinasouw!*"

I giggle. "Do you like it?"

"Yes! *Tank* you, Mommy!"

The joy on his face warms my heart. "It's from Mommy's special friend. He made it just for you!"

"What *him* name?"

"Elias."

"Okay, can I say *tank* you to *Eyeeus?*"

I chuckle at how he pronounces Elias's name. His inability to pronounce the letters R and L is so adorable. "I'll tell him for you, baby. Go play with your new toy."

As if he were waiting for me to dismiss him, he takes off.

I open my laptop and commence searching the Internet for Elias Crawford. Sure enough, a link to a missing person's article loads first. The headline reads:

Son of CEO David Crawford of Crawford Investment, Co., Elias Crawford, Reported Missing.

Another headline:

Twenty-Seven-Year-Old, Elias Crawford, Missing. Father, David Crawford, Offers Reward for Any Information of His Son's Whereabouts.

The most recent article was released five months ago:

Elias Crawford, Son of CEO David Crawford, Disappears. No Evidence to Determine Whether Dead or Alive.

I don't click any of those articles, especially because it will all be speculation. However, as I continue scrolling, one title catches my attention, and I click the link:

Elijah Crawford Speaks Out

It's a live video from four years ago from Elias's brother. I press play on the video and witness a defeated, broken Elijah:

"Big brother, if you're out there, if you see this, please reach out. At least let us know you're out there somewhere living man. Or just..." He begins to weep and his voice stammers. *"Please El, come home. I'm sorry. Dad's sorry. Jessica and Travis, your friends. We're all sorry. I'll do anything... Just, please, big brother, come home."*

I click off the video before it ends. It's heartbreaking, and I can't bear to watch anymore. I search social media and find Elias's page. There are comments under his posts asking him to reach out. The last post he made was announcing the closing of his shop and that he would update when he relocates.

He doesn't have much of anything posted besides pictures of him working on cars and photos of his shop's sign. Continuously scrolling, I find a picture of him, his mother, and his younger brother at the Lilac Festival. The caption reads, "Happy Heavenly Birthday, Mom."

Scrolling through the comments, I find the pages of a few of the friends he mentioned. I also found *the* ex-girlfriend, Jessica.

Well, she's pretty.

Last Elias told me, she was dating his ex-best friend, Travis. Doesn't look like it anymore. She's got a different guy on her arm. Her last picture from six days ago is of a diamond ring on her finger, captioned: *"I said, yes!"*

Someone commented, *"Sure you don't want his best friend?"*

I smirk. The Internet is unfiltered, that's for sure.

I browse through some of the other friends' pages. Everyone seems to be doing okay, but you can never tell with social media. No one deliberately airs dirty laundry for the world to see. However, the one thing that stands out among all their pages is that these guys are loaded. My income, which I consider to be pretty decent, is pennies compared to the people of Elias's world—*or rather, his old world*. Seriously, how do they live like this?

I click on Tyler's page. In contrast to everyone else, he hasn't posted anything in three years. His last update was a profile picture change from a selfie of himself to a photo of him and Elias. I recall Elias mentioning Tyler being the only ex-friend he would consider befriending again, but at the time—during his pain—even that he couldn't foresee.

Under the photo is a comment from Travis. *"He was my friend before any of you. You can ignore us all you want, but it doesn't absolve you more than any of us. We all wish he'd come back."*

It seems as though Tyler separated himself from them. I wish I could reach out to him. What if he's in despair? Elias warned me not to reach out to anyone, but sympathy rises for what this guy might be going through. My cursor hovers over the message icon, but I think the better of it, close my laptop and decide to check my phone that vibrated moments ago before I head for the shower.

Chrissy: We still on for tmrw?

The sight of Chrissy's text is a welcomed distraction. I miss her.

Me: Yes! I miss you!

Chrissy: You better. I've been taking new best friend applications since you abandoned me.

Me: They'll quit the first day on the job. Only I can tolerate you.

Chrissy: Lol. These things are true.

My mind runs to Mauria and just how much I enjoyed my time with her. My dear friend in Sandemia. I've spent more time with her in the last 120 days than I've spent with Chrissy in the last five years.

Butterflies and sunshine.

I inadvertently concealed the outgoing person I once was. And in another world, at the taste of liberation, I was truly *me*. The social butterfly at my core, and it felt *good*.

Me: Love you. Won't abandon you anymore, bestie.

As the water sprinkles over me, more tears fall. Though I've accepted the separation, my heart aches as I grieve. While I can't foresee the intimacy I shared with Elias with another man, there's one thing I can see: a change to my life. And it will begin Monday, when I step into Cathy's office, respectfully demote myself to assistant, and offer Amanda a promotion in my place.

No more caging my soul.

I stare at the wall. I'm unable to sleep. My heart still hurts. All my mind does is replay moments of Elias and me. But the thoughts aren't soothing me to sleep, they're keeping me up.

I turn on my lamp and open the drawer of my nightstand, removing my journal. I open to the first page and begin to read. The first few pages are everything I learned about the land and how it operates, and the next few pages are all I learned about Mauria and Sam.

After reading the summary I had written about Mauria, something gnaws at me. Something I never thought of before. I reread a particular line and wonder if it's accurate:

Mauria and Sam, voyagers, discovered Sandemia a year ago. After they married, they settled in Sandemia twenty days ago.

I recall the conversation I had with Mauria. I think long and hard.

"We were voyagers when we got married, and about a year ago we discovered Sandemia..."

Something doesn't seem right. If Mauria and Sam only discovered Sandemia a year ago...

"Sam and I have collected Daycomms from different lands for years. We have a pile of them..."

Elias arrived on Livity five years ago. Mauria and Sam hadn't discovered Sandemia until last year. So how would a five-year-old Daycomm, specifically about Livity, end up in their Daycomm stash?

Someone placed it there. Someone who knew we were looking for information. Someone who... saw the boat? Could it have been Sam?

No, Sam and Mauria grew up together on Land Tikita. It had to be someone who wanted to help but didn't want their identity revealed.

Someone from *our world.*

CHAPTER 70

Skye

FOUR MONTHS LATER

"*Make sure no one sees you. Drop it in the mailbox and leave,*" is what Elias instructed after I became a nuisance about allowing me to deliver a letter to a loved one. He declined the offer for my protection, but that wasn't good enough for me. So, I bothered him until he gave in.

Driving down the narrow street, the one-story home comes into sight.

"*If there's an old black Camaro in the driveway, that means he still lives there.*"

I see the old Camaro in the driveway, but there's another vehicle parked beside it, a much newer one. A silver Audi.

There's no one in sight as I drive up. It would have been ideal to come late at night, but the address Elias gave me is two hours away from my grandparents, and I'm not exactly comfortable driving through Georgia at night.

I park next to the mailbox and open my door, but I don't cut the engine. I plan to take off the moment I'm seated again. I walk around the hood of the rented vehicle and place the envelope inside the black mailbox, then quickly make my way back to the driver's side. I stop and turn back when I hear the front door of the home open.

Scurrying inside the rental, I shut the door and speed off. My heart pounds in my chest. That was so close. Relief surges through me as I drive away—but it only lasts a moment. Apprehension rises as I come upon the dead end. The rest of Elias's words come back to me.

"Drive past the house first, turn around at the dead end, then place the letter in the mailbox and leave the way you came."

I'm so stupid. That small detail—this is why it was important. I turn around at the dead end and drive back the way I came. There is no other house on this narrow street besides Elias's uncle. He knew that if anyone saw me coming, they'd know it would be for that one house.

Trepidation creeps up my spine as I'm forced to come to a stop. The Audi is no longer parked in the driveway; I'm staring at the side of it. It's parked in the middle of the narrow road, blocking me from passing. *No.*

Leaning on it is a man with dark shades covering his eyes. He's fair-skinned in contrast to Elias's easily-tanned olive, and he has silky black hair that brushes his shoulders that lacks Elias's waves. He's nearly as tall, and his athletic build is similar. He stalks toward my vehicle. With every step, the beating in my chest kicks up a notch. When he uses his knuckle to tap my window, I shake my head.

"I'm not going to hurt you," he says.

Still refusing to pull down my window, I plead. "Please, just let me leave."

His thin lips form a straight line, and he pulls my door open. A gasp leaves my lips. I had never locked it. I zoomed off without thinking.

"My guess is you didn't know there was a dead end down there," he observes.

"I... I please, I don't know anything," I manage, fear slowly bringing me under.

"Not according to what you left in my uncle's mailbox." He doesn't seem upset, but I get the feeling it's fake, sarcastic.

He removes his shades and bends until our eyes are lined. His aura shifts, as if the shades were a mask, and with their removal, his true intention surfaces. What was aloof and calm, now radiates darkness and vengeance. But it isn't Elias's darkness—this is unhinged, unpredictable, and terrifying.

Dark emeralds, under furrowed brows, stare at me. *I know those eyes.* However, I've seen Elias's hardened expression. Though it's intimidating, I've never feared for my life like I do right now.

This can be none other than Elias's younger brother, Elijah Crawford.

"Now tell me," he hisses. "Where is my brother?"

Elias

"It's a girl!" Mauria announces as I open my door.

I slightly grin. "Congratulations." I look behind her and see no one else. "Mauria, did you walk here?" I ask, frowning. Her swollen belly is quite large now. I can't imagine walking all the way here from Haven Downs was easy.

She nods.

"Come in," I offer.

She follows me inside and takes a seat on the sofa. I go to the kitchen to pour her a glass of water. "Does Sam know you're here?"

"No, I hadn't planned on coming, but I grew bored staying home." She gulps down the water in seconds. "Sam is helping someone build a patio on the other side of town."

"Okay, Mauria, but you know the stables were an option," I mention.

"Nope, they're booked today," she defends, as if that's a good excuse. "Can I put my feet up?"

I push the ottoman closer to her, and she props her foot. "Mauria, don't do that again. Write me a letter next time."

She hands me the empty glass. "I know, but you don't come out anymore. You know you can't isolate yourself. Sam and I are your friends."

"I haven't forgotten about you guys. I've been busy at the shipyard." I hold up the glass, gesturing to ask if she wants more water. She nods.

"Okay, well, I wanted to talk to you about the baby."

I stop and turn on my heels. "Is everything okay?"

"Yes. She's growing healthy."

Refilling her water, I return. "Then what's the matter?"

"Thank you, by the way," she says after a few more sips.

I nod.

"Well, I want to name her Skye," she says. "And when she gets older, I'll show her all the pictures of my time together with Skye and tell her where she got her name. It's the name of an awesome woman who became a dear friend to me."

I look up at Skye's portrait in my living room and grin. "She'd love that."

"I know, but what do *you* think?"

I give her a look of scrutiny. "Is that why you came here, Mauria? To seek my approval to name your daughter after Skye?"

She glances down at the glass nervously. "Yes. I... I mean... I know you two weren't *technically* married, but I also know that if things were different..."

"If things were different, she'd be my wife, and if I'd lost my wife, you would want my blessing before you named your child after her," I finish for her.

Looking up, she nods.

That's considerate of Mauria. However, she wouldn't be attempting to name her child after Skye if Skye were still here. "I appreciate that, but you don't need my blessing. Skye would have loved the idea of you naming your daughter after her in her absence."

She narrows her eyes. "Do I have your blessing or not?"

I chuckle. Leave it to Mauria to want what she wants. "You have my blessing, Mauria."

She smiles, thanking me. We chat for a few hours while she rests, and then I walk with her back to Haven Downs.

Mauria enters her home. Before I leave the neighborhood, I go toward the empty home where Skye resided before her departure. I take a moment and gaze at it, picturing her on the front porch, sipping her morning coffee, and reading the Daycomm. A hint of a smile plays on my lips as I recall those moments vividly.

"I miss you, my sunshine," I whisper before walking away.

"Young man." I hear a voice approaching and turn around. It's Mr. Alton.

"How are you doing, Mr. Alton?" I greet.

"Elias, correct?" he asks.

"Yes."

He glances over at Skye's residence and then back to me. "It seems Miss Skye is no longer residing here. May I ask why?"

"She traveled back to her homeland. Her visit to Sandemia was temporary."

"Ah, I see. Perhaps she'll be back to visit," he says.

I inhale sharply. "Unfortunately not, sir. She'll be unable to."

"Oh. Well, perhaps you can visit?"

Don't make this difficult, old man. I know you're just being polite but leave it alone.

I clear my throat. "Not so sure about that, sir."

"Well, why not?"

This is new. I'm getting a distinct vibe from him.

"It's difficult to explain." I flick my nose with my index knuckle. "Please excuse me, Mr. Alton, I must get going." I attempt to end the conversation.

He lifts his chin. "Sure, wouldn't want to hold you up."

I nod and begin pivoting to the exit.

"You know," he begins, but I continue walking. My jaw tenses. What the fuck is up with him? "The same energy that brought you here can bring you back."

Abruptly halting, I turn around. "What did you just say?" *Who is this guy?* I go back toward him.

"Do you want to be with her?" he asks.

"More than anything. Who are you?" I waste no time.

He stretches his hand for a shake. I accept, "Alton Windsor, Chicago, Illinois."

Astonishment stumps me. How the hell did I not notice? Which also means Skye's intuition was keen when she suggested something was strange about him. "You're from..."

He nods. "That's right. Been here fifty years."

That's why I haven't suspected him. He's resided here long enough to blend in with the masses. He's become one with the people. "What do you mean, I can go back? The hourglass... I made my decision."

He grins. "But you can still return."

I peer at him with scrutiny. "How do you know?"

"Because I have."

Acknowledgments

To the reader: Out of many books, you chose mine. Thank you for reading. You are why this is possible.

To my Beta and ARC readers: You are all amazing and vital in this entire process. I couldn't thank you all enough.

Thank you, Murphy Rae, for bringing life to my vision with this beautiful cover. Your skills are incredible.

Marissa and Andrew: Thank you for teaming up to help this new author out. I can never be more grateful for the effort put into my work.

To Ellie: Thank you for working with my steep timeline. You're my lifesaver!

To my brother, Rajan, my greatest listener. Thank you for your invaluable advice since the very first draft. I love you.

To my good friend Eileen, who pulled me out of self-doubt every time: Thank you for believing in me. I love you.

To my wonderful family, who aren't avid readers but will pick this one up for no other reason than because it's my work: Thank you for always supporting me. I love you.

To my dear friends Angel, Necee, and Quin, my hype team: I love you guys.

To my forever, Josh: Thank you for your unwavering support every step of the way. You ceased reminding me to eat but instead brought in the food when I was sucked into my writing, engulfed in my imagination, from dusk till dawn. I love you for everything that you are.

To my little girl: Mommy, followed her passion so you can follow yours.

About the Author

Rose Richards promotes her brand under the broad umbrella of fiction. She prefers not to crate herself under a sub-specific genre as she writes spontaneously from her ever-changing imagination. Today may be a romance, tomorrow a thriller, and next week metaphysics—or throw them all together and write a breathtaking story.
At the pause of the pen, she's either enjoying her family, tethered to a paperback, or glued to a show that defies all things reality.

Fiction? Maybe.

www.ingramcontent.com/pod-product-compliance
Lightning Source LLC
Chambersburg PA
CBHW021408310726
48971CB00005B/1253